KT-116-744

If the Shoe Fits

Jaye Carroll

POOLBEG

Published 2000
by Poolbeg Press Ltd
123 Baldoyle Industrial Estate
Dublin 13, Ireland
E-mail: poolbeg@iol.ie
www.poolbeg.com

© Jaye Carroll 2000

3 5 7 9 10 8 6 4

Copyright for typesetting, layout, design
© Poolbeg Press Ltd

The moral right of the author has been asserted.

A catalogue record for this book is available from the British Library.

ISBN 1 85371 957 9

All rights reserved. No part of this publication may be reproduced or transmitted in any form or by any means, electronic or mechanical, including photography, recording, or any information storage or retrieval system, without permission in writing from the publisher. The book is sold subject to the condition that it shall not, by way of trade or otherwise, be lent, resold or otherwise circulated without the publisher's prior consent in any form of binding or cover other than that in which it is published and without a similar condition, including this condition, being imposed on the subsequent purchaser.

Cover design by Vivid
Set by Pat Hope in Palatino 10/13.5
Printed and bound in Great Britain by
Cox & Wyman Ltd, Reading, Berkshire

2000
80p

If the
Shoe Fits
your the Woman
to wear it

Jimmy
& Arthur
XX

*All characters in this publication are fictitious
and any resemblance to real persons, living
or dead, is purely coincidental.*

About the Author

Jaye Carroll and her twin brother Peter were born on New Year's Day 1968 in Ontario, Canada.

Her family moved to England when she was five, where they lived for three years before moving to Ireland, which has become their permanent home.

At the age of eighteen, she went to Finland where she spent eighteen months working as a veterinarian's assistant and teaching English in her spare time.

She has also worked as a waitress, receptionist, office manager and dance instructor.

Jaye Carroll now writes full-time and is currently working on her second novel. She is also in the process of researching a major work about the treatment of women in Irish movies.

She lives in Dublin and is married with three children.

Acknowledgements

The characters in this book are entirely fictitious. Which is just as well: otherwise, they might hunt me down. The names of certain characters and locations may be similar to people and places in the real world, but I promise that it's just a coincidence.

This book could not have been written without the aid of several fine people . . .

The late Kate Cruise O'Brien, my first editor in Poolbeg, whose support and strength brought this book to life.

Val Shortland, who ably took over a difficult book and a more difficult author.

Everyone at Poolbeg: a great bunch of people who are all professional, cheerful and thankfully very patient.

A million thanks to my parents, who never stopped believing in me.

Thanks also to Doreen, Vampirella (not her real name, though it ought to be), Anita and Jim, Gary, Paul and Brad, Jo and Jack, Karen B, Mary-Jo, Fiona,

Catherine, Sarah, Maude, Ruth, Chris, Michelle and Grace (see? I said I'd remember!), Akil, Pearse, Helen and Chris, John McC, Marian, Bernhard, Ricky, Frank and KP, who have all uncomplainingly put up with mysterious silences and periods of absence while I worked on the book.

And as always, my beloved Lee. You are my world.

For Martina, Sheelagh and Janet
The best friends anyone could ever wish for

Chapter One

I'm not really into the club scene. I don't enjoy sitting around for the whole night while my friends are asked up to dance. And I really, *really* hate it when one of them thinks they're doing me a favour when they politely decline a dance and say to the guy, "Why don't you ask Susan?"

That's me. Susan Perry, always the last to be asked; and then only when it's too embarrassing for them *not* to ask.

Sometimes my best friends can be the biggest bitches in the world, even when they don't mean to be. In fact, *especially* when they don't mean to be.

So I don't bother nightclubbing much. Except that sometimes I don't have much of a choice. This time, it was Laura's birthday. She was twenty-two, and she wanted to go to Frodo's on Leeson Street, because that was the very first nightclub she ever went to. That was when we went out for Sharon's first engagement party. Sharon was Laura's cousin, four years older than her.

Laura was only sixteen at the time, and God, I don't know how the bouncers couldn't tell . . .

On that night six years ago, Laura was giddy as hell, but trying to be cool and sophisticated at the same time. She sat with the rest of us at the tiny, cramped table, her glass of white wine in her hand, trying to give bedroom eyes to a guy on the far side of the dance floor. Hah! *Bedroom eyes!* In those days, Laura couldn't even manage *behind-the-bicycle-sheds* eyes. But somehow she was still able to get this guy interested in her.

He wandered up to the bar, and stood leaning on it, pretending not to look at her. Laura knocked back her drink in one go, and said to me, "I think I'll get another drink."

I nodded. "Sure. Pernod and black for me."

"Well, I won't be back straight away . . ."

"Laura, that guy's old enough to be your father. He's in his thirties at least."

She sighed and tutted like a good teenager. "Susan, I'm just going to talk to him. He looks OK."

I smiled, and said, "I admit he doesn't look bad. Just don't forget who you are."

"What?"

"Remember who you are, not who you're pretending to be. Not who he wants you to be."

She still didn't understand.

I expressed my thoughts in simpler terms: "Don't turn into a bloody gobshite over him."

She got up. "Well, thanks for the advice, Mother Teresa."

And then she turned her back to me, and slinked her way up to the Mysterious and Handsome Stranger. I must admit, I was impressed. She must have practiced slinking. Maybe her parents had bought her a slinky when she was a kid. I was kind of jealous of her, of course, the way she was so full of confidence. And she's learned a lot since then. Now, Laura can slink sexily, giggle delightedly and squirm in anticipation in ways that most men just can't resist.

She ended up on the dance floor with this guy, snogging her heart out. Something to tell her friends the next day in school.

A sixteen-year-old girl masquerading as a woman in her twenties . . . Even now, when I think about it, I still get the creeps. But that's the story of my life: My friends get all the really good-looking men, I end up with the creeps.

Anyway, I digress. So there we were, having "a great time" in Frodo's. Laura's twenty-second birthday. The place hadn't changed much in six years, despite having gone through about eight changes of owner, name and dress code. It ended up back as Frodo's for some reason. Probably the new owner thought it was cool or clever, or something. Or maybe he had a good memory and no imagination.

There were five of us there that night: Me, Laura, Sharon, Jackie and Wendy. I only got to know Jackie and Wendy because they were Sharon's friends from work, and she'd been *my* friend since school. Laura, as I said earlier, was Sharon's cousin. I think Sharon minded her when they were kids, or something like that. They were certainly closer friends than any other cousins I'd ever met. I'd invited my friend Barbara from work, but she'd just looked at me with one eyebrow raised. "Frodo's? It's a kip." She was right. Frodo's is the sort of place where you can't wear open-toed sandals in case you catch something from the carpet.

It was a Wednesday, so that meant "Ladies in free before eleven" night. Which in turn meant that we were just about the only unattached women in the place. Most of the rest of the clientele were male twenty-somethings from one of the banks (and you know that the collective term for people who work in the bank is "a wunch"). They drank a lot and guffawed quite a bit. They made it clear that they had money, and they were there on the pull.

I'm generally not the target of these "pulls." Being over six feet tall is a boon when you're a seven-stone supermodel with no hips and tiny breasts, or when you're a buxom Valkyrie with luscious platinum hair and a flying horse, but it's shag-all use when you're barely able to squeeze into a size sixteen and your hair always looks as though you've been driving with the window open.

All right, so I'm not being fair to myself. I'm not that bad-looking, but I certainly don't have one of those slender, sexy, cat-like figures. Not unless you find Garfield sexy.

The DJ that night in Frodo's was one of those thirty-five-year-old men who look like they live in a penthouse apartment with white leather and chrome and fake-ebony ornaments of naked women everywhere; or "pornaments" as my friend Anthony calls them. The sort of men who have a huge record collection, but no CDs . . . it's all albums, because they insist they can tell the difference: "CDs have a plasticy sound, man. You know. It's all digital." Their favourite bands are Supertramp and The Eagles and Yes, and they still can't believe that Roger Waters is no longer with Pink Floyd.

This guy was wearing white jeans, a wonderful Hawaiian shirt – of the type favoured by actors playing the part of movie producers in *Beverly Hills 90210* – thinning hair tied back, dazzling teeth, little round shades, single earring, hairy arms . . . You know the sort. A stereotype he may have been, but at least he had Dolby.

While I was watching the others being successful on the dance floor, I started to imagine that the DJ was glancing over in my direction.

I say "imagine" because I've made a fool of myself often enough, imagining that someone was interested in me. It's not that I haven't had any boyfriends, it's just that the sort of men who were interested in me were usually the loser friends of better-looking guys. The old "I don't fancy yours much" sort of thing. I'd be with Sharon or Barbara somewhere, and these two guys would start chatting us up. Or rather, the good-looking one would start chatting up Laura, and his skinny pal with the thick glasses and the three-sizes-too-big collar

5

would grin shyly at me, thinking that if he got lucky I might help him misplace his virginity.

Those nights generally ended up with the good-looking guy going off with whatever friend I was with, while I'd be stuck with the gobshite. I always wondered if they saw *us* the same way . . . "Listen, Keith," – the loser's name would always be Keith or Owen or something in Irish with too many silent Ds – "What about those two? I think the huge big fat one's giving you the eye." Nudge, nudge. "After all, you don't look at the mantelpiece when you're poking the fire, right?"

So I ignored the DJ, but I kept watching him just in case he *was* looking in my direction. And it turned out that I was right. He glanced over from time to time, and even winked at me once.

Desperate I might be, but I wasn't the sort of lonely woman who fell for the first show of affection that someone gave her. They had to be rich as well.

Things got bad after about fifteen minutes, when my bladder started demanding attention.

Contrary to male popular belief, women *can* go to the toilet on their own. Maybe we can't pee standing up, but the process isn't so complicated that it takes more than one pair of hands to accomplish it. Good thing, too. Imagine if it *did* take two people . . .

Visiting the Ladies – or the "Babes" as it was called in Frodo's: the Gents was wittily called "Dudes" – meant walking right past the DJ's box. That wasn't really a problem, because I could just dart past when he was flicking through his wooden crates of seven-inch singles trying to find another Eighties Madonna song. What was a problem was that Laura, Sharon, Wendy and Jackie were all up on the dance floor. As I was clearly the designated bag-minder, I couldn't just leave the table without having a back-up operative.

I tried to catch Laura's eye, but it seemed to me that she was deliberately having a better time than I was. Sharon was nowhere to be seen, and Wendy was letting one of the bankers read her body language as though it was Braille. Jackie was the nearest – now only a few feet away from me – but she wasn't looking my way.

I called out to her. "Jackie!"

She didn't notice. She was paying a lot of attention to the geeky lad who had invisible strings connecting his eyeballs to her nipples.

I was about to get up and tap her on the shoulder when I noticed a group of standing-up people greedily eyeing our table. I knew that if I left the table for a second, they'd swoop like vultures.

Jackie still hadn't turned around. I briefly considered throwing a pint glass at the back of her head but I decided it wasn't lady-like. So I called her again, only louder. Still nothing. So the third time I roared out her name, microseconds after the music stopped.

Everyone, of course, looked in my direction.

I hate that. I'm not by nature a clumsy person, but when I do draw unwanted attention to myself, my appearance tends to make matters worse.

The DJ muttered a few words about the next song, and set it spinning. The nightclubbers were soon once more "gettin' on down" and "shakin' their funky thangs" as though nothing had happened. And Jackie finally excused herself, turned around and marched over to me.

All is well, I reassured myself. Minor embarrassment, not many dead.

Jackie was scarlet, and I knew what was coming next. She dropped into the seat beside mine and tried to make herself invisible. "Jesus Christ! What brought *that* on?"

I gave her what Paddington the Bear used to call "a very hard stare indeed," and said, "I've been trying to attract your attention for *ages!* I need to go to the bog, and I couldn't just get up and leave our stuff – *and* the table – to the mercy of that bunch of scavengers."

And now she was guilty as well as embarrassed. "Well, you should have said."

"That's what I was trying to do." And then I said, "It's all very well for you lot to go off and leave me here sitting on my own, but the least you could do is come back from time to time and make sure I'm all right. *While I'm at it, I know for a fact that the only reason you brought me here is that you know no one will ask me to dance and that I'll mind your bloody bags for you.*"

Actually, I didn't say that last bit, but I was thinking it, and she knew that I was thinking it. And I knew that she knew and so on. It was one of those things that we just never discussed. I mean, I didn't know Jackie *that* well.

"Well, go on, then," she said testily. "I'll wait here until you get back."

I stood up, something that takes longer for me than for most women because I've got further to go. "Right. I'll be as quick as I can."

As I walked past the DJ's box, I noticed for the first time that he wasn't alone. There was a younger DJ next to him, who I assumed had probably been apprenticed to the older DJ in some bizarre Freemason-style ritual. I joined the short queue for the "Babes," and glanced back over at DJ jr. He looked at me shyly, and looked away. His Master said something to him, and he shrugged.

My naturally overactive imagination worked out a scenario: The older DJ was called Curtis, and his young pal was his nephew, who was just starting out in the trade. The nephew's name was Darren, and he was twenty-one, the age of initiation into the Guild of Disc Jockeys. Darren knew that on his first night he had to seduce a tall woman to gain full membership and the acceptance of his peers. The taller the woman, the better. Maybe they had charts or something. Darren, unknown to all, was actually destined to become the next Chief High Grand Master of the International Guild of Disc Jockeys and Television Presenters. He had a birthmark on his right thigh in the shape of a 1976 Technics Music Centre.

That was about as far as I got when I reached the door. It didn't take long to complete the business, but I spent more than a fair amount of time messing around with my hair in the mirror afterwards. It wasn't easy, because the mirror wasn't set high enough in the wall, and I had to sort of crouch down to see myself. I could have taken off my shoes, but the floor wasn't the sort you could eat your dinner off. In fact, it was clear from the stains here and there that a few people had used the floor for quite the opposite purpose.

I was just about to leave when Sharon arrived. She didn't bother with the cubicles, she just squeezed in beside me and stared at herself in the mirror.

"I hate this fucking place," Sharon said. "Whose stupid idea was it to come here?"

"Laura's," I said. "You should have objected a bit harder."

"Was that you I heard earlier?"

"Yeah. I was trying to catch Jackie's attention."

"I noticed."

"Well, I had to have a piss." I turned and looked at her. "It wouldn't hurt for one of you to check on me from time to time."

Sharon nodded. She knew this argument well. "I know. But you don't have to sit on your own. You could come up on the dance floor with us."

"And who'll mind the bags and drinks then? I'm just saying it's not fair. I had to refuse *several* dances because I couldn't find anyone to take over on bag-guarding duty."

"Really?"

"Well, no. Not really. But it *might* have happened."

Sharon was a good friend. She knew how I felt about being a wallflower. She also knew that I always got a bit morose when I'd had a few drinks.

"This is why you prefer pubs to clubs," she said.

"Yeah. Well, it's more why I prefer sitting at home watching a video to going out."

"You'll never meet Mr Right sitting at home."

"I don't know about that . . . I get a lot of pizzas delivered. And there's always the chance of another General Election. All those fit young politician's dogsbodies calling to the door with their leaflets, explaining manifestos and party policies."

"You want to go home?" Sharon asked.

I could tell from her expression that she was enjoying herself – or at least she had been until she started talking to me – so I shook my head. "No, I'm fine. I don't want to stay too late though. Promise that you'll check on me every half an hour?"

She promised, made a quick trip to the loo and we wandered back out.

I had completely forgotten about Darren, the apprentice DJ, until he stepped right in front of me and smiled. "Hi. Would you like to dance?"

Chapter Two

Sharon looked back at me and grinned like mad, then waggled her eyebrows and mouthed, "Go for it!" I sent her a telepathic e-mail that read, "Help! Man attack! Moral support required! Don't know what to do!" She ignored it, the cow, and darted away across the dance floor.

I turned my attention to my potential suitor. He was my height, but I was wearing heels, so that put him at about six foot two. Short brown hair, reasonable build, nice-looking. I said, "Sure. What's your name?" I didn't want to keep thinking of him as Darren, because that might cause complications if I shouted out "Darren! Yes! Oh yes!" in the middle of a sordid sex scene. Well, I like to plan ahead.

"Sam," he said. "Yours?"

"Susan."

So we stepped onto the dance floor at the very second that Sam's pal put George Michael's *Careless Whisper* on the turntable.

I didn't know whether Sam had asked Jackie or one

of the others what my favourite slow song was, but that was it.

He held me close, but loosely, if you see what I mean. We were face to face, rather than chin over shoulder in the more common method. I got the feeling that he was interested in more than just a quick dance. I don't speak from much personal experience, just the second-hand experience of years of watching couples on the dance floor, but because he was looking right at me I knew that he wanted to talk. That meant he wasn't just looking for a one-night shag.

"So, Susan. Where are you from?" He asked.

"Cabra. What about you?"

"Dun Laoghaire. I've got a flat in Clarinda Park. Do you know Dun Laoghaire?"

I shrugged. "Not really. I've been through there a few times. I went to a wedding in the Royal Marine Hotel a few years ago." Well done, Susan, I said to myself. Babbling like a fool already.

"Ah, yes . . . The hotel with the ferries at the bottom of the garden, as my mate Paul from Nottingham calls it. That's just down the road from where I live. Well, down a few roads. Isn't it a small world?"

"It used to be a medium world," I said, "but with all this rain we've been having . . ."

He generously laughed at my terrible joke. "So, what do you do for a living?"

"I'm a lumberjack," I said. "I do a lot of work overseas. You know the Sahara Forest?"

"You mean the Sahara Desert?"

"Yeah, well that's what they're calling it *now*."

He laughed again, though I couldn't believe he hadn't heard that one before. Or maybe he had, and that's why he fed me the straight line. It didn't matter either way, though. I liked his laugh.

"What about you?" I asked. "Are you a DJ, or are you just helping out?"

"It's a nixer. Dave's just a friend. I'm ashamed to say that I work in a video shop. I prefer to tell everyone that I'm between unemployment benefits at the moment."

"Well, there's nothing wrong with working in a video shop," I said, because it's something I'd always wanted to do myself . . . I'm a complete movie addict; I have more videos than the government has scandals. "Are you a film buff?"

"Sort of . . ."

I smiled. "Sort of? Let me guess. Your hesitation is because you're embarrassed to say that you couldn't care less about *Casablanca* and *It's a Wonderful Life*, and your favourite movies generally have big explosions, aliens, and people calling each other 'Asshole' while they run away from bad guys with machine guns that are loaded with special bullets that can only hit railings."

"That's not a bad guess, except that it's *The Piano* and *Babette's Feast* that I'm embarrassed to say I couldn't care less about."

"Ah, you're a proponent of the nouveau-braindead style of motion picture."

"Yeah. I've heard that Barry Norman has hired a hitman to sort me out."

"Then given a choice between *Die Hard* and *The Sound of Music*, you'd go for the former?"

Sam smiled. "Well, let's just say that Bruce Willis in bare feet and a dirty vest has got a slight edge over Julie Andrews making clothes out of curtains and jumping up and down steps. But then, it all depends."

"On what?"

"On the company."

I'd seen enough movies, soap operas and mini-series to know what he was up to. He'd arrange to meet me on Friday evening, then when he saw me waiting outside Eason's on O'Connell Street, he'd realise that the woman he took a fancy to in the darkened nightclub was a lot less attractive in daylight.

"Your line," he said suddenly.

"What?"

"You're supposed to ask what sort of company I'd prefer to be with when I'm watching movies."

"Am I?" I frowned. "That's funny. There must have been a misprint in *The Girls' Bumper Book of Chat-Up Lines.*"

"You've read it too, then? So why don't we skip all the nonsense and get to the end of the book?"

I swallowed. He really *was* going to ask me out. "What, you mean the index, or the ten empty pages with the word 'Notes' written at the top?"

He laughed again. "Are you busy on Friday night?"

"Are you asking me out, or just doing a survey?"

"I'm asking."

"Well," I said, "I don't have any *specific* plans . . ."

Chapter Three

The slow set ended, and Sam had to go back to the DJ box. He made me promise to talk to him before we left, so that we could arrange when and where to meet on Friday night.

I wandered back to our table in a sort of haze. I had that familiar "this isn't really happening to me" feeling, the kind I always get when I have a dream in which someone asks me out. Of course, in my dreams he usually then turns into a cauliflower or something.

Jackie was gone, and Sharon was standing watch at the table when I got back. She could barely contain herself. "Well? Tell me!"

I sipped nonchalantly at my now warm and quite disgusting drink. "Tell you what?"

"What happened? What's his name? Did he ask you out?"

"Hmm? Oh, you mean *Sam*? Oh, he's just an old friend."

She rolled her eyes. "Sure he is. He's not bad-looking, actually."

I didn't know whether to be delighted about what had happened, or pissed off that Sharon seemed surprised that a good-looking man had asked me to dance. I decided to be delighted, because – as my mother was always telling us – it takes fifty-eight muscles to frown, but only twenty-three muscles to smile. I remember one time when my brother was in a really foul mood because his girlfriend had dumped him, and Mam tried to cheer him up with this little platitude. He just stared at her, and said, "Well, how many muscles does it take to *sod off and leave me alone?*" My mother is not the type to take offence at something like that. She just said, "Probably a lot more than it would take for you to storm off to your room and slam the door, like you usually do."

Everyone always told me that I got my sense of humour from my mother. My brother was more like Dad: not exactly humourless – there were things that the two of them could find absolutely hilarious, though I have to point out that these were not often the same things, because they barely talked to each other – but Mam and me, we were slightly more laid-back about everything.

Whether or not I got my sense of humour from her, I know that's where I got my height. Or partly, at least. Dad was pretty tall as well. My mother had a different build from me, though. She was a lot slimmer, not big-boned and awkward like me.

Sharon wanted to know everything about Sam. I actually spent about twice as much time telling her about him than I had spent *with* him, and I guess that probably meant something. I was smitten.

There's something about a person showing interest in you that makes them all the more attractive. That's particularly true with people like me, because we're not so used to attention. I'd always been afraid that I'd end up marrying the first person to propose to me, because I'd be so starved for love that I'd convince myself that I loved him.

I was determined that this wouldn't happen with Sam. I mentioned this to Sharon, and she just frowned in that way she does, giving her fifty-eight facial muscles a good workout, and told me that I was jumping the gun a bit.

She was right. I changed the subject, and asked her where she'd disappeared to earlier in the evening.

"I was talking to some fella. He's a bit of a creep, though. I went to the bog to get away from him."

I nodded. "Not another recently-hatched duckling?"

"Yep. Anyway, he kept asking me what my favourite Bruce Springsteen song is, and don't I think that Michael Jackson looks like some woman from *Star Trek*, and stupid stuff like that."

"Which woman from *Star Trek*?" I asked. "Not Doctor Crusher?" I spend a lot of time in front of the telly.

She shrugged. "I dunno. She has leopard-skin marks on her face, he said."

"Ah. Jadzia Dax, from *Deep Space Nine*," I said knowledgeably. I thought about it for a few seconds. "Actually, he's right about that."

18

"Oh God! Not you as well! Maybe I should introduce you to him!"

I grinned. "Sorry, but I'm spoken for." Even though that wasn't strictly true, it felt wonderful to be able to say it.

And at that moment, Sharon glanced around, froze for a second, then quickly turned back to me. "Shit. Here he comes."

He was a baby duck, all right. He had that sort of shy, youthful grin which says, "I know that I've just met you, and I realise that we barely know each other, but I'm going to follow you around for the rest of your life and even when you're sixty I'll be phoning you in the middle of the night and hanging up when you answer."

"What's his name?" I asked quickly.

"Jimmy," Sharon said, paying close attention to her drink.

Jimmy reached our table, and sat down beside Sharon, putting his hand on her thigh. He nodded at me. "How's it going?"

"You must be Shane," I said. Then, without giving him time to correct me, I continued, "You know, if you don't mind me saying, you're not as big as Sharon said. I mean, that doesn't bother me, because I don't really like men with too many muscles." I said all of this in my "wheee! I'm half-drunk and I don't know what I'm saying" voice.

Jimmy paused, his pint half-way to his lips. "What?"

"Can I have a go in your car?" I asked him. "Sharon says you have a deadly car. What is it again? A Sirocco?"

"No, it's . . . You must be thinking of . . ."

I cut across him. "You're earlier than we thought you were going to be." I glanced at my watch. "Well, not *that* much earlier."

Jimmy didn't stay much longer. He made some excuses about his friends calling him over, and departed.

Sharon waited until he was gone, then grinned. "That wasn't bad at all."

"It's what I get paid for," I said. "And I thought it might work better that the usual plan."

The "usual plan" – which we'd only used twice, but it was successful because both of the men had been fairly drunk at the time – began with me burying my face in my hands and trying to look upset. Sharon would then put her arm around me.

When the Sharon-fixated young man reached our table, Sharon would look up at him. "Oh, Susan. I'll just be a minute."

"OK," I'd say with a sob. "I'm sorry."

Sharon would stand up, and explain to her pursuer that I was upset because today was the anniversary of the day my boyfriend had run off with my ex-best friend. It was a nice, simple plan, and it allowed Sharon to use portions of her legendary "Aren't all men just a bunch of complete bastards?" routine. That was enough to put almost anyone off.

Sharon and I had been friends since we started in secondary school, so we were usually pretty good at knowing what each other was planning. If the situation demanded it, we could come up with the finest bullshit imaginable, and we usually got away with it. Once – and I stress that it was only once – we had to pretend to be lesbians to get away from a couple of guys who wouldn't leave us alone. It didn't work, though. We were a lot younger then, and we weren't really aware that some men find the idea of lesbians absolutely fascinating. In the end, we had to ask the barman to get them to leave us alone. Then the barman gave us a funny look and said, "So . . . Em . . . You girls are, uh . . ." We never went back *there* again.

"God, what a prick," Sharon said. "I don't know why I even bothered to talk to him in the first place."

"How are you to know? They don't have the word 'Prick' tattooed on their foreheads. They come to places like this disguised as normal people."

She smiled. "As disguises go, it wasn't a bad one."

"Well, as I'm always telling you, if you go to nightclubs the only people you're going to meet are people who go to nightclubs."

"Yeah? Well, what about your Sam, then?"

"*My* Sam? He's *my* Sam now, is he?" I rubbed my hands together and cackled. "One up for me, eh?"

"And for him," Sharon said, wearing her serious face.

I knew where *this* was leading. Sharon and I had had this conversation many times, and it began along the lines of "There's nothing wrong with you that a bit of self-confidence wouldn't fix." Then it drifted into "And there's nothing wrong with being tall. I'd *love* to be as tall as you are. Men like tall women." Occasionally, when she was feeling really depressed, Sharon would say quietly, "Eric always fancied you, you know."

I hated it when she talked about him. Eric was Sharon's first fiancé. They got engaged when Sharon was twenty. They announced their engagement, and said that they hadn't set a date yet for the wedding. It might be a few years away, they said.

I knew from the start that it was a mistake. I was the first one she told about the engagement, and I practically begged her not to tell anyone else. "Wait until you're sure," I told her. "The last thing you need is everyone watching you for the slightest argument, and using that so they can say 'I knew it would never last.'" Sharon didn't want to know. She loved Eric, he loved her. They were committed to each other, and getting engaged was a way of solidifying that commitment. And more to the point, she wanted me to be her bridesmaid.

We argued about it a lot, and it almost ruined our friendship, because at one point she blurted out, "You just don't want it to happen because you'll be embarrassed to walk down the aisle when you're taller than everyone else!"

Ouch! That really hurt, and not just because it was true. It hurt because I knew she'd intended it to hurt.

Anyway, the whole thing fell apart after five months, and I was there to help her pick up the pieces of her life.

So, I didn't want that particular conversation to raise its ugly head once more. Especially now that things were looking up for a change. It's all very well to get self-indulgent when things are bad, but it's tempting fate to start analysing things when they're going well.

It's like that thing about diaries . . . I'd been keeping diaries since I was ten, and a few years ago I read through them all. The first thing I noticed was that I'd really only written about the bad things that had happened. When things were going well, I was usually too busy or too excited to write much.

The second thing that surprised me about my diaries was the hundreds of boys I'd had a mad crush on and then forgotten about within a couple of weeks. Most of them were just boys in the estate or in school, but I also had this major thing for Harrison Ford after I saw him in *Raiders of the Lost Ark*.

I still sort of feel embarrassed about my crush on Harrison Ford, and it usually takes me a few minutes to get comfortable watching one of his movies. That's not really because I had the crush on him, but because when I was twelve my mother caught me in my brother's bedroom kissing his Indiana Jones poster. She laughed a little, then said, "Well, the least he could do is take his hat off."

When we'd all had enough and decided that it was time to start heading home, I took a deep breath and walked over to Sam in the DJ box.

He smiled when he saw me. "Are you heading off now, then?"

"Yeah."

"Are you all right for a lift home? We're packing up soon and we've got the van."

"What, you're going to go miles out of your way just to drop me off?"

He looked embarrassed. "Dave lives near you, don't you, Dave?"

Dave saw that Sam was talking to him, and pulled off his headphones. "What?"

"You live near Cabra, right?"

"No," Dave said. "Dolphin's Barn." He put his headphones back on and went on cueing the records.

Now Sam looked even more embarrassed. To save him, I said, "Thanks anyway, but Sharon has her car. She'll drop me home."

He nodded. "Right. So . . ."

"So . . ?" I waited. This was the really, really awkward bit. Had he changed his mind? I wondered. No, I told myself, not likely. Not if he's just offered me a lift home. I felt the urge to say something clever, and decided against it, because (a) I couldn't think of anything, and (b) it might put him off. His train of thought appeared to have run into a fallen tree, or something, because he wasn't getting anywhere. I had no choice but to bring up the subject of Friday's date. "What about Friday, then?"

"Sure," he said, with visible relief. "Where and when?"

Well, bugger that! I said to myself. I debated whether I should say "Whatever you think," and decided that would be very much the wrong thing. Take charge for once, a little voice inside me said. "Under the clock at Eason's, at eight?"

Sam said, "Great. But what about making it earlier? I'm on a half-day on Friday, and I get off at two."

"Well, I wouldn't be able to make it before seven. Have to get home and scrape off the sawdust, you know."

He laughed at that. "Seven it is, then."

And then it hit me: he didn't remember my name! I could understand that; I'm usually pretty terrible at names, and have been known to forget someone's name immediately after they've introduced themselves.

I spent the next few seconds trying to think of a way to remind him without making it too awkward for either of us. My mind had gone blank. Luckily, we were saved by Dave, who nudged Sam in the side and pointedly said, "Better say goodbye, then."

Sam got the hint. He left the DJ box and came around to me. We stood looking at each other. It wasn't wasted time, though. I gave him a good once-or-twice-over and decided that he wasn't bad-looking at all. Then I finally thought of a way to solve the name problem. I turned to Dave, and said, "Well, thanks. You played a great set."

Dave shrugged. "No problem."

"I'm Susan, by the way. Sam was telling me that you're his uncle . . ?"

They both exchanged puzzled glances, and then I remembered that, no, Dave was Sam's friend. *Shit!* The uncle bit came from the story I'd made up about them earlier. And I couldn't even worm my way out of it by saying, "I must have misheard you, with all this loud music," so I was forced to say, "or did I dream it?" It was pretty lame, but it was my only option.

"Dave's a friend, not an uncle!" Sam said. "I don't know where you got that from!"

I did my best to smile, then I gestured towards Sharon and the others who were waiting near the door. "Well, I've got to go. So, Friday at seven, outside Eason's?"

"See you then."

I nodded.

Neither of us moved, either closer or away. As awkward moments go, this one didn't want to go anywhere.

And then Dave's voice boomed out of the microphone: "Ah, just kiss her, you fuckin' eejit!"

Chapter Four

The girls laughed all the way home. Oh, it was absolutely hilarious! Not just that Dave had made a holy show of us in front of my friends and everyone else in Frodo's, but also because Sam *did* kiss me – which I admit took a lot of courage after Dave's little trick – and also because everyone had stopped to watch us, and they clapped and cheered when it was over.

I had never been so embarrassed in my life, and I've had quite a few embarrassing moments. Only a few days before I'd accidentally called my boss "Mammy" in front of some of our most important clients.

Wendy and Laura were sitting in the back of the car with me, and they just couldn't shut up about it. I was going to be the talk of the town, it seemed, until Sharon saved me. She turned around and said, "It's all very well for you two to laugh, but Susan's the only one of us who's got a date for Friday night." That shut them up for a few minutes.

Then Laura said, "So what's he like? Is he a good kisser?"

Jackie joined in. "I thought he was really cute. What's his name?"

"Sam," I said, glad to be on safer territory. "What about the guy you were with?"

"Don't know his name," she said. "He works as a stockbroker. Said he has a BMW."

The rest of us went "Oooh!" very loudly. Jackie has a thing about men with big cars.

So Jackie proceeded to tell us all about the guy she met. She was planning to go back to Frodo's the following week, and see if he was there. Naturally, she wanted us to go with her.

"Not me," Sharon said. "I'm knackered as it is. It's two in the morning. I'll be lucky if I can stay awake for the rest of the week. I'm never going clubbing in the middle of the week again."

Wendy scoffed at her. "Yeah? Well at least you're not going to have a hangover. Mine is coming on already. I knew I should have had another drink before we left."

"Yeah, but you have no money left," Laura reminded her.

"*You* have. You could have bought me one."

"You didn't ask."

"I shouldn't have to. You saw me sitting there with an empty glass."

There was more like that, and once again I was glad that I didn't go clubbing with them more often. Then again, I reminded myself, if I hadn't gone tonight I wouldn't have met Sam.

My thoughts must have shown on my face, because Laura suddenly said, "Hey, you bloody cow! You changed the subject on us!"

In her half-drunk state, Laura was pretty easy to fool. I just argued that I had *not* changed the subject.

"Yes you did! You always do," Wendy said. "Remember that time when your brother had his twenty-first and you said that you were thinking of not going because Fintan wouldn't ask his mate Anthony 'cause they had a fight over something and you said that you wouldn't go without Anthony and *we* said that you must fancy him or something?" She paused to take a breath. "Well, you changed the subject then. You got me talking about what I thought of Anthony."

"And you said that you didn't fancy him," I reminded her. "As if we'd believe that."

"Yeah? Well, what's to fancy about him? He's boring."

"He has a good job, *and* a new car," Sharon said. "And I heard he's great in bed."

We all turned to stare at her.

She grinned. "He goes straight to sleep, and he doesn't hog the duvet or anything."

I laughed. "Does he say his prayers?"

"Yeah, but instead of saying, 'God bless Mammy and Daddy and Uncle John' and all that, he gives their RSI numbers. Just in case God blesses the wrong person."

"He *is* good-looking, though. Nice bum," Jackie said. "I wouldn't mind him myself."

Sharon and I went "Oooh!" and sniggered a lot. Childish, I know, but we were in that sort of mood.

Jackie nudged me in the shoulder. "Check him out, Sue. Find out if he's interested."

"Sure, but don't get your hopes up."

"You went out with him only a few weeks ago," Wendy said.

"That wasn't a date," I said. "I'd arranged to meet him, and this thing came up in work, so I brought him along. One of our clients was having a launch for their new software, and Anthony knows a bit about computers, so he was happy. He spent most of the evening talking to their new salesman."

"So . . . *nothing happened,* right? We believe you." Wendy said evilly. "We all know you're just getting him to teach you to drive so that you can sit next to him."

This eventually lead into a deep and dirty discussion about the various men that we knew. That kept us going until Sharon dropped me off at my house.

I was up – though not really awake – at seven the next day. It was a bit later than usual, and I knew that I'd be late for work, but I didn't care. I'd hardly slept for thinking about Sam during the night.

Naturally, my overactive imagination got the better of me. I almost managed to persuade myself that there was no point in turning up for the date because Sam wouldn't be there. He hadn't meant any of it; it was all just some sort of stupid game. Or worse, he'd been so embarrassed by Dave's trick that he wouldn't be able to face me. I began to wish I'd given him my phone number so that he could call and cancel. It would be more honourable than just standing me up.

The bus from Cabra to Rathmines is a real bastard in the mornings, and because it was a later bus it was worse than usual. It crawled through Phibsboro, took eight years to get through the city centre, then sort of slowly kangarooed the rest of the way, stopping at every stop and every set of lights, carefully manoeuvring to hit every pothole. The gear stick had obviously broken off or been stolen, because the bus never managed to get out of first gear. To call it "the bus from Cabra to Rathmines" is an exaggeration: it left me on the South Circular Road and I had to walk the rest of the way.

I stopped in the newsagents for my breakfast: a Mars bar and a pint of *super-fabbo-drink-this-and-you'll-be-a-slim-petit-gymnast-for-the-rest-of-your-life* milk. I was aware that the Mars bar would counteract the delicate nutrient balance of the milk, but what the hell, I'd just walked over a mile, so that had to count for something.

Work was the usual. Boredom punctuated by rare moments of great hilarity. The company I worked for was called Complete Office Solutions. We did management consultancy and customer relations stuff for a whole bunch of other companies. In other words, we told the other companies how to do their job. One of the first things we told them about was the importance of paying their bills on time. That was always a hint to let them know they should pay *us* on time, a sort of veiled threat that if they didn't, the spell would wear off our wonderful advice and they'd be doomed to failure.

At times, the whole thing amazed me: I knew practically nothing about management consultancy and customer relations. I only got the job because I went for an interview as an office administrator and the boss was impressed with my "common sense." I sometimes got the impression that she thought only a very few people were born with the "stating the bloody obvious" gene.

Whenever I had to "consult" on a particularly awkward problem, I employed that wonderful method known as Occam's Razor – the simplest solution was generally the right one – and I think that the boss had suspicions that I had some sort of insider knowledge.

The other reason this industry amazed me was because an employee like me could spend weeks on a project without doing the slightest bit of actual work, and still produce Progress Reports that were impressive enough to make everyone else think I was the backbone of the company.

My colleague Barbara was in the kitchen when I arrived. I caught her attempting to sneak away with the last cup of coffee without putting more on.

"I'll do it after the Project Meeting," she argued feebly as she darted away, no doubt hoping that some other poor sod – me – would go to the trouble of making a fresh pot.

I responded with a knowing "Hmmm," and put my milk in the fridge, but not before writing "Susan's Milk" all over it with a pink highlighter. Amongst my co-workers there was someone who was guilty of multiple counts of Grand Theft Milk. I strongly suspected that it was the same person who regularly left used teabags on the edge of the sink and put a wet teaspoon into the sugar bowl.

However, the worst person to work with in an office, far worse than the person who never goes to the shops for anyone else – the boss, in other words – was the person who didn't drink coffee unless someone else has just made it. We had one in our office: His name was Kevin, and for the most part he was fairly tolerable. But he sat at his desk at around eleven, making his now-cold coffee last as long as possible, watching for people coming back from the kitchen with a steaming cup. He wasn't easily fooled, either: A couple of times I came back with tea, and he didn't budge. He had the psychic ability to tell tea from coffee at thirty metres. Then he'd jump to his feet and charge into the kitchen. And as if that wasn't bad enough, he had his own mug – with "Kevin's Mug" written on the side in indelible marker, just above the Spider-Man logo – and it was a lot bigger than any of ours.

I put on a fresh pot of coffee and wandered back to my desk, passing my colleagues who – dog-eared notebooks and well-chewed pencils in hand – were heading towards the small meeting room. On Thursday mornings we had the weekly Project Meeting. This lasted a couple of hours, during which we explained to the boss why we hadn't managed to get anything done during the previous week. I was always very eager to speak first at those meetings, because otherwise one of the others would steal my best excuses.

The boss was a little late for the meeting. She did this occasionally, to make us think that she had to take time out of her busy schedule to run the meetings.

As I sat down, Kevin looked up from his doodling and said, "You know, I think that there's something really sinister about a boss like ours who insists on capitalising the words Project Meeting."

"Do you really?" Asked Barbara coldly. She didn't like Kevin much.

He nodded. "It's as though she secretly knows the whole thing is bullshit, and by using capital letters she can make it all seem important. That's why she's always using words like 'proactive' and 'status' every chance she gets, and 'Implementation Phases' and 'Control Documents.'"

Kevin finished his monologue and sat back, awaiting praise, or at least a reaction of some form. None was forthcoming, because we'd heard that little speech before.

After a few minutes the boss arrived. "We'll have to make this quick," she said. "I've got about a million things to do today." One by one, she went around the table requesting our Current Project Status.

I was last, and I knew while Danny and Barbara were always fairly concise with their reports, Kevin would take ages: he still hadn't learned that those who are making good progress tend to have the least to say. I'd figured that one out ages ago, so I knew that even if I had accomplished nothing since the last meeting, I shouldn't bombard the boss with lots of elaborate excuses.

I was daydreaming about the night before with Sam when the boss suddenly asked, "What do you have to add to this, Susan?"

I was aware that Danny had been talking, but about what I had absolutely no idea. "Well, that depends, doesn't it?" I grinned at my colleagues, to give the boss the impression that she'd missed something only highly-skilled and intelligent office workers would notice.

"What do you mean?" She frowned, and began to rub the fingers of her left hand, a weird habit she'd picked up lately. I suspected Repetitive Strain Injury. My boss's name was Victoria O'Toole; her boyfriend and her son called her Vicky to her face but the rest of us were too scared. Most of the time, we didn't even call her by her given name – that is, the name she was given at birth: we'd given her a few other names from time to time – we generally just referred to her as "the boss."

"Well . . ." I sipped my coffee and tried to remember

something about the conversation. Or, failing that, some way to distract her. I decided to keep my backup plan – to spill the coffee all over the table – for a real emergency. As luck would have it, I was sitting directly across from Danny, who was incredible fastidious and had been neatly ticking items off the agenda. My own agenda was now covered with little doodles and was close to illegible. The next item on Danny's list was the revision of the Parker Technology contract, on which I was allegedly working. Saved! "I'm still waiting for their staff hierarchy," I said. "They shuffled their people around after we placed Neil Forsythe with them." It was even true.

"How's he getting on?"

"Great," I said. "Apparently he already has orders worth over a hundred thousand."

"Good . . . And once you have their hierarchy, then how long?"

"A couple of weeks, at the most." This was a relatively safe estimate, even more so this time, because I knew she was going on holidays – I mean, visiting potential clients in the States – on Monday week.

Vicky-poos raised her eyebrows in mild surprise. She wrote something down on her notebook. "Two weeks, that's quicker than I would have thought."

Bugger, I said to myself. Now what have I got myself into? "Maybe three weeks," I said. "But two should be enough."

Danny looked up at me. "For a complete rewrite of all their documentation? You're kidding."

A complex string of swearwords built up inside me. "It won't have to be a *complete* rewrite, just the *Core Plan*." I knew I could get away with that, because no one but me knew what the *Core Plan* was. Especially since I'd just made that phrase up.

After what seemed like hours, the meeting was finally wrapped up. I wandered back to my desk, and made a mental note to talk to Danny later, because I knew he'd have a "to do" list prepared. Danny was fairly quiet, but he was usually willing to break off work for a chat. I could find out exactly what I'd agreed "to do." Two weeks should be enough time to come up with a good reason that would explain why I hadn't done anything.

Barbara came over to my desk, and sat on the edge. She was our personnel manager, and she was holding a holiday application form, which was her usual excuse for a chat. If the boss ever appeared and saw us deep in conversation, we could easily turn it into a discussion about how many days I'd already taken.

Barbara was the one I was closest to at work, but I wasn't really sure why. We were completely different people. She was a real out-going type, she was short, pretty and full of giggles. She was also very promiscuous: she'd slept with most of the male staff, including all our freelancers. Each of them thought that they were the only one, but Barbara confided in me about everything.

For example, she told me that Danny was as neat and

fastidious in bed as he was in work. He folded his clothes neatly before he got into bed. He even remembered to turn off his mobile phone and his pager. When he made love, she said, he carefully divided his attention between each of her breasts, making sure that neither of them felt left out. And he kept asking, "Is this all right? Am I hurting you?" Afterwards, Barbara said, he spent about fifteen minutes apologising for leaning on her hair, or for having taken so long getting the condom on. "But is he any good?" was all I wanted to know when she first told me.

She just shrugged. "He's considerate."

Barbara had even slept with our boss's son, Stephen, and he was only sixteen at the time. It happened during one of the Christmas parties in the office. They locked themselves in a cubicle in the men's toilet, and went for it right there on the bog. Apparently, five people came in to use the loo while they were at it, and one of them was Kevin, who was in the next cubicle for at least ten minutes. Barbara said that either he had the worst bout of constipation ever, or he was busy making the beast with one back.

But though I knew a fair bit about Barbara's personal life, I wasn't willing to tell her that I'd met someone. At least, not until Friday had come and gone. So when she asked, "How did it go last night?" I just shrugged.

"Not bad. It was better than I'd expected."

"Meet anyone?"

"You know me. I ended up minding the bags. I only went because Laura wanted to go."

"Well, it *was* her birthday. You couldn't really say no."

"Yeah," I said, "but when I made a suggestion on my last birthday she was too busy."

"I remember that," Barbara said. "We went to the pictures. Not exactly Laura's style."

"This is true. Laura's only interest is in the pleasures of the flesh. She has double-jointed hips and knees, and from what I've heard she'd have no trouble getting a job in a circus as a sword-swallower. That girl has consumed more semen than all the sharks in all the *Jaws* movies put together." I realised who I was talking to, and added, "The lucky cow."

Barbara wasn't fooled, but she didn't comment. "So. No luck on the man front last night, then?"

To take the edge off the insult, I decided to tell her about Sam. I even told her about Dave's nasty trick. She laughed at that, and slagged me a bit, so I knew that I was forgiven.

At exactly three minutes to lunchtime, Barbara and I went over to the Deli counter in Centra, and had them make up rolls. I've always believed that what we have for lunch is a direct reflection of our personalities. For example, I had the same thing every day: a ham and coleslaw roll, a can of coke, and a Twix. On paydays, I splashed out on a king-size Twix. On the other hand, Barbara was forever trying out new stuff from the deli counter, even those really weird salads that seem to be made up of salad cream, cold pasta shells, Rancheros and Windolene.

Danny generally brought in sandwiches from home. They were always perfectly triangular . . . I had this image of his sparklingly clean bin, in which he'd carefully stowed away all of the reject slices of bread: The ones he didn't cut straight, or those maddening rogue slices that have big holes in them. If he was feeling really wild and reckless, Danny bought a large sliced pan, three medium tomatoes and a pack of twenty cheese slices. It was quite disturbing to see him wearing his most serious expression while he was sizing up the tomatoes at the Fruit and Veg counter.

Kevin bought all the kids' stuff, like Hula Hoops and Chomp bars, and a box of Frosties or Honey Nut Loops if there was a good free toy. There was nothing more disconcerting than watching Kevin spend the afternoon dipping into his box of Frosties and typing with one hand. Kevin had a line of Kellogg's special edition "Monsters in my Pocket" lined up on the edge of his desk. When I was really pissed off at him for something I'd go over to his desk, when he was off stealing someone else's coffee, and I'd rearrange the little bastards.

My own desk wasn't one to write home about. It was covered in piles of paper that one day I intended to sort through. I didn't subscribe to the old saying – "a tidy desk is a sign of a tidy mind." The partition between my desk and Danny's was covered with little notes and *Dilbert* cartoons on my side, and with a single tiny year planner on Danny's side. Actually, that year planner said a lot about the kind of person he was; he spent a whole day trying to get it to fit on one page, and every Monday he updated it and printed out a new version. He had a folder in his drawer containing the old planners. No crumpling something into a ball and firing it across the room at an unsuspecting person for *him*; everything was neatly stored away.

Barbara and I ate our lunch at her desk, because there was a lot more room. Also, she was situated in a much quieter part of the office, so no one bothered us much. It gave us a chance to talk about Sam.

I expressed my fear that he might not turn up on Friday, but Barbara shook her head. "He will, trust me. What are you planning to do?"

"I'm not sure."

"Well, from what you say he doesn't sound like the decisive type. *You'll* have to make the decisions." She paused. "That's not really a good thing. I mean, you're not exactly the bossy type yourself. If he's content to let you make all the moves I don't foresee a happy relationship."

"Oh, thanks a bunch for the ego boost! You really know how to make someone happy."

She shrugged. "I'm serious. But maybe he was just shy last night. See how it goes tomorrow before you decide to dump him."

I thought about this. "I've never dumped a boyfriend. They always dump me first."

Jaye Carroll

"The trick is to be able to predict when they're going to dump you, then you do it first," Barbara said. "Watch out for things like 'We need to talk,' or 'Why don't you go out with your friends, and I'll go out with mine?' The strongest sign of all is when they keep talking about changing their job, or sharing a flat with one of their friends. It's a sure sign they're thinking about breaking it off."

I shrugged. It didn't really apply to me. "I've always wondered what happens when both sides of a couple are too scared to break it off."

"They get married."

I laughed a bit, and then stared at her. "How do *you* do it, Barbara? How do you attract men? I know I'm not *that* bad-looking, but somehow I only ever get the geeks." This was something we'd never really discussed, and her reaction told me that it wasn't a topic she was comfortable with. Normally, I'd have backed down, made some daft comment and changed the subject, but I really wanted to know. "What's the secret?"

She hesitated, and then said one of the deepest things I've ever heard her say. "It's not what I do, it's what they see."

"Which is?"

"Everyone says that men are led by their dicks, and when everyone says something like that, it's easy to laugh it off and think that it's nothing more than just something people say. But for a lot of men it's true. They see me, they like what they see, and that's all. But you . . ." She stopped, and stared at me.

"Go on," I said. "I won't be offended." Actually, I was pretty sure that I *would* be offended, but I wanted to hear it anyway, even though I had a strong feeling that I knew what she was going to say.

"You scare them. The sort of men that are attracted to me don't like their women as tall as them, or cleverer than they are. You're both. A dangerous combination."

Yeah, that was it. I'd heard it before, from my mother, from Sharon, even from myself. Should I pretend to be short and dumb, so that I'd have men flocking to me? Yeah, sure. Then I'd be landed with a bunch of men who were *worse* than geeks, they'd be "lads." You could always tell their sort. They had cars with lots of lights on the front, and they steered with one hand. They were always the first off when the lights turned green. They drank a lot and talked tough. Real men.

And I knew about people like that, because that's exactly what my brother Fintan was like. Jacket with "Nike" written across the back. Called women "birds" and had very strong opinions on which was his favourite Spice Girl. Followed Liverpool with a passion, and knew what "offside" meant. Thought that Eric Cantona and Liam Gallagher were good role models. Had met Barbara once and kept asking about her.

"What sort of man *do* you want?" Barbara asked suddenly.

"I don't know. Yet. Someone who'll be good to me."

She nodded. "You know that Danny fancies you like mad, don't you?"

This was news to me. I glanced over at his desk, but he wasn't there. Probably in the kitchen with his set square, making sandwiches. "You're kidding," I said. "He looks at me like I'm dirt. Say it ain't so, Joe," I added, remembering a line from an old Murray Head song.

Barbara shook her head. "He has these illusions about you, that you're some sort of goddess. And when he hears you shouting "Bollocks!" when something isn't working out, you're destroying his illusion. For a while. Then you'll say something clever and he'll start looking at you like you're an angel again. You'll have noticed that he's always the one who laughs longest at your jokes."

"I always thought that was because he doesn't get to hear many jokes. But it does explain why he's always so eager to help me."

She grinned. "So . . . I know you're not mad about him, but would you go out with him? Would you overcome your objections for the sake of love?"

I took a deep breath. "Why didn't you mention this before? Why didn't you say it yesterday, before I met Sam?"

"Because you brought up the subject now. Sort of." She finished the last of her sandwich. "Anyway, don't let it get to you. He'll wait." She turned her attention to her computer. "Now, get lost. I've got a deadline for this afternoon."

I wandered back to my own desk, and sat staring at the screen for the rest of the afternoon. I wasn't able to work. It seemed that every time I glanced up at Danny, he was looking back at me. The truth was, much as I slagged him, I did kind of fancy him a bit, and I'd been incredibly jealous when Barbara told me they'd slept together.

And that began to bother me even more now. I couldn't help thinking that Barbara had always known that Danny was interested in me, and she'd slept with him anyway.

Chapter Five

I wasn't in the best of moods when I got home, which was unusual for a Thursday. Friday in work didn't really count, it was just a doss day, so on Thursday evenings I was usually raring to go, getting all fired up for the weekend.

Not that I ever did much at the weekends. Fintan was always out, and my parents generally went down to Blackwater to the caravan on Friday evenings, so I had the whole house to myself. I spent Saturdays wandering around town and Sundays I lay in until about four, then stayed in my dressing gown for the rest of the day. I was the only person in the house who had complete mastery of the video, and I was the only member of the local video shop who got all the new releases put aside for her. In fact, when I went to the video shop they usually pounced on me: "What about *The Last Boy Scout*? Any good?" "What was the name of the Goldi Hawn movie that Spielberg directed?"

I remember one time I wandered into the shop, and Mark, the middle-aged guy who owned the place, put down the phone and called me over to the counter. "Miss Perry," – he always called me by my last name – "what's the name of the guy who was in that movie with Chris O'Donnell? The one where they're in a sort of boarding college together."

"What do I get if I win?"

He laughed. "This isn't a competition. I have a bet on with Sean." Sean was Mark's brother, and he owned a small video store in Donabate. "The first one to get his name is to ring the other back. But if you know the answer, you can have two free rentals."

"New releases?"

"Recent."

"Recent and Recommended," I bargained.

He considered this. "OK."

"Brendan Fraser. *School Ties*."

Mark grabbed the phone and punched out his brother's number. "Brendan Fraser," he said as soon as it was answered. "And the movie he was in with Chris O'Donnell was *School Ties*." He paused. "No, I just remembered it." He looked at me. "No, she hasn't been here for days."

After a few minutes, Mark put down the phone again. "Right. Now he's bet me that I can't tell him the name of the first guy who played James Bond. I know it can't be Connery, because that's too obvious."

"Barry Nelson," I said. "He made an hour-long

television show of *Casino Royale* back in the fifties or something."

I had this vague plan that If I ever got found out and fired from work, I was going to get a job in a video store. I knew that the money wouldn't be as good as I was used to, but since I spent half a fortune every week renting videos – and another half a fortune buying them – it'd probably work out at about the same.

Thinking about videos made me think of Sam. Not that he was far from my mind to begin with. This weekend would be different. A date on Friday night.

As I slowly munched my way through my cheese on toast in front of the telly, I realised that I actually had abdominal butterflies in anticipation of the following night. What was worse was that I'd have to meet him straight from work, because there wouldn't be enough time to get home and change. And that meant bringing everything into the office: my good jacket, my good shoes, make-up, decent hairbrush . . . I wondered whether I'd be able to wash my hair in the ladies at work. I wouldn't need to bring the hairdryer – not even my little travel one – because I could use the warm air hand drier, the one with the instructions that had wittily been modified to read, "1. *Push butt to tart.* 2. *Rub hands under arm air.* 3 *Stop auto.*"

Bringing everything into the office would be a clear signal to everyone that I was going out, and they'd want to know the whole story. But if I get in early, before everyone else, I told myself, then I can hide the bag under the desk, and go out to McDonald's for breakfast. Then I'll come back at my usual time, and if anyone comments on my clothes – I usually wore jeans and a sweatshirt to work – I'll just tell them that I didn't have anything else that was clean.

The end of the day would be easy enough, because everyone disappeared early on Fridays, especially the boss, who left work so early on Friday afternoons she had to take the morning off to make up for it. So I planned to just hang around until everyone was gone, then change. It would only take me half an hour to walk to O'Connell Street, so I'd have plenty of time to get ready.

And then, my mind being the strange and treacherous beast that it was, I started to wonder what Danny would think if he found out I was meeting another man. No, I told myself, forget about that. That's dangerous ground. Start thinking about that, and next thing you know you'll be flirting with him.

I was suddenly angry at Barbara for telling me that Danny was interested in me. She couldn't have picked a worse time if she'd tried. Maybe she did try, I thought. Maybe *she* wants him.

I was saved from this line of thought by the doorbell. It was Anthony, my friend from three doors up, calling to give me my free weekly driving lesson. I'd known Anthony for as long as I could remember; he used to push me over into puddles when I was seven and he was four.

He was one of the few male friends I had who wasn't someone in work or the boyfriend or brother of one of my female friends. Anthony had bought his car a few months before and had been giving me driving lessons every week since.

He dangled the car keys in front of me. "Ready?"

"No. But let's give it a go anyway."

He handed me the keys and I climbed into the driver's seat, while he spent about five minutes putting on the L plates, stopping whenever he noticed a dirty mark on the windscreen or bonnet. At last, we were ready. He got into the passenger seat, put on his seat belt, and said, "Let's go."

I'm not too bad now, but I'm the first to admit that for a long time I was a really, really crap driver. Whenever we got above thirty miles an hour I was hanging onto the steering wheel so tightly my knuckles turned white; I forgot which was left and which was right; I never remembered to use the mirrors. And Anthony used to sit there politely correcting me as I tried to move from fourth gear to reverse while I was going around a corner, saying things like, "you should be moving into third now. No, that's first again. Third is the other way. Now mind that car in front. Yes, I know it's miles away, but it's stopped and we're doing forty-five. The limit is thirty on this road, by the way. You can tell by the signs. Watch – that was a pedestrian crossing. You're supposed to stop if there's anyone waiting to cross."

At the end of each session, I always felt absolutely

great, and Anthony was a complete wreck. But he still came back for more, the sucker.

This time, I was determined to do well. I did the mirror-signal-manoeuvre thing I'd heard so much about, put the car in gear, took off the handbrake, gently nudged the accelerator, put the handbrake back on, took the car out of gear, canceled the indicator, then took a deep breath.

"OK," Anthony said. "Now, you know what you did wrong?"

"Yeah, yeah, yeah," I said. I turned the key in the ignition. "That better?"

"Much."

I went through the procedure again, and within minutes we were pottering along at five miles an hour. "I must be doing well," I said, nodding towards the mirror. "Look! We're in front of all those other cars!"

"Very funny. You can speed up a bit. Take her up to thirty."

I did as he said. "Take *her* up to thirty. How do you know this car's a girl? It's blue. Wouldn't a girl car be pink? Wouldn't it have long luscious eyelashes on the headlights?"

"And lace trim around the bumpers and a bow on top," he said. "Susan, when I said go to thirty, I sort of meant you could move up a few gears as well."

"I'm planning to." I was sweating like mad, hunched over the wheel with my tongue sticking out.

"Well, put that plan into action before you burn out the engine and I'm forced to kill you."

I was at that awkward stage in learning to drive where I still had to look at the little map on the gear stick to remember which gear was which. I swore that the only car I'd ever buy would be an automatic. A male one.

Pretty soon we were driving along the Navan road, heading towards the Blanchardstown Centre. I'd successfully navigated the three awkward roundabouts, and Anthony was in a better mood. He only occasionally made comments along the lines of, "Susan, I know you're special, but even *you* are only allowed to drive in one lane at a time," and, "I must have forgot to tell you about the *secret* pedal. It's the one between the accelerator and the clutch. We call it 'the brake' and it's designed to slow the car down."

After an hour or so we arrived back at my house. I was pumped high on adrenaline, and I knew I'd done well because Anthony found it easier than usual to stand when he got out.

"That was brilliant!" I said. "I love driving! I'm *definitely* getting a car!"

"I'd wait a while, if I were you. The novelty of driving wears off when you've spent a few Friday evenings stuck in traffic on the Naas dual carriageway."

I invited him in for a cup of tea, which he gratefully accepted. We met Fintan as he was coming out of the kitchen. Fintan mumbled "Hiya" and went up to his room.

Anthony and Fintan don't get on at all. They used to

be great pals – Anthony was three years younger than me, same as Fintan, and they went to school together. But over the years they'd fallen out and gone their separate ways. I remained friends with Anthony, partly because I knew it annoyed Fintan, partly because I genuinely liked him.

We went into the kitchen. Anthony politely waited by the door until my mother had gone through the usual "The weather's very changeable, isn't it?" and "Are you sure you wouldn't have coffee instead?"

Anthony informed my parents that, yes, the weather was changeable, yes, it was a disgrace about the latest government scandal, no, he'd had no luck finding a better job, and, finally, it was indeed very warm yesterday. For this time of year.

We escaped into the sitting-room. Some people have a living-room, others a lounge, others a TV room. I always felt awkward in someone else's house if I used the word "sitting-room" when they were more used to "the front room." Of course, it got worse when I called their couch a sofa, or a settee, or "that big lumpy brown thing covered in biscuit crumbs and dog hair."

The television was on in the corner, broadcasting world news every fifteen minutes to an otherwise empty room. I grabbed the remote and changed the channel, just in time to hear the Sky One announcer tell us exactly what was about to happen in this week's episode of *Melrose Place*, to save us the trouble of watching it.

I didn't watch many soap operas, only *Coronation*

Street and *Brookside,* but Anthony watched them all, even – God help him – *Glenroe.* I had this theory that Anthony only watched these "chick programmes" – as Fintan called them – so that he'd have an excuse to chat to the girls in work.

"So, how did it go last night?" Anthony asked. "Who was there?"

"Laura, Jackie, Wendy and Sharon. We were in Frodo's, on Leeson Street."

"What's it like?"

"A bit of a kip. Expensive drink, loud music, lots of flash little twerps from the banks. The usual."

He raised an inquisitive eyebrow. "Meet anyone?"

So I told him all about Sam, including the upcoming date. Anthony was a little more tactful than I'd expected: instead of immediately trying to find something wrong with my date, he seemed to be genuinely impressed.

"He sounds OK," Anthony said.

"But . . ."

"But what?"

"You were going to say, 'He sounds OK, but . . .' something. You always do."

"Not this time. It's about time you found someone who wasn't a complete gobshite."

"You're telling me. No, Sam could be OK. At least he's not shorter than I am. No offence," I added. Anthony is about two inches shorter than me. He's not self-conscious about his height – well, he wouldn't be, because he's about five-ten – but hanging around me couldn't be too cheering for him.

"So what are you going to do if it does work out?"

"How do you mean?"

"I mean, if it does work out, are you looking for a full-time relationship, or what? The video shop would go bankrupt if you were on dates all the time."

"Hah! What about *you*? When was the last time you went out with someone?"

He shrugged. "I'm not really into the dating scene."

"But you would be if you could find anyone mad enough to go out with you," I said. Then I remembered what Jackie had said last night on the way home in the car. "That reminds me, you know Jackie?"

"Big hair, huge muscles, green skin and torn trousers?"

"No, that's the Incredible Hulk you're thinking of."

"Remind me again."

"She's about five-eight, red-head. Big hips and no breasts."

He shook his head. "Can't place her."

I thought for a few seconds. "Lives just off Fassaugh Road.

Her dad's a taxi driver."

He looked at me blankly.

"She danced with you for two solid hours at Fintan's twenty-first? She was all over you."

"Yeah . . . Hang on . . ." He frowned in thought, then tapped the floor in front of him with his foot. "Drinks

Carlsberg and puked right on that spot there when you had that video party at Christmas?"

"That's her."

"You're not going to tell me that she fancies me?"

"Well, she *said* she did, but she might be lying. What do you think?"

"I think that at this stage I'm a bit past being set up with your friends." He shook his head. "Nah, I'm not really interested. But don't say anything yet. I might as well keep my options open." He picked up the previous night's paper from the floor, and began flicking through it. "Look, the personal ads. See? I don't need Jackie. I can find true love in the Evening Herald."

"Yeah, but only if you love fish and chips."

"I do, as it happens. Here's one: 'Lonely housewife seeks male companion for mid-afternoon fun.' That sounds interesting."

"For all we know, that could be my mother. Or *your* mother."

"Well, it would save on petrol. How about this: 'Gorgeous SWF, 38-26-38, mid-twenties, looking for someone to treat her like a lady.' Now, that *does* sound good!"

"Don't you think that perhaps she might be lying? I mean, if she's so wonderful, why does she need to advertise?"

"Maybe she's shy."

"Shy enough that she can't find someone, but not too shy to put an ad in the paper? Yeah, I believe that all right."

"That's not really fair. I'm sure there are lots of good reasons someone would have to place a personal ad." He paused. "Though I can't think of any at the moment."

I nodded. "I can understand someone putting in an ad if they were looking for something a little different, but for an ordinary relationship it doesn't make much sense."

"Not for me, then . . ." He continued reading. "Some of these are great . . . 'Middle-aged man, tired of the same old love interests, seeks younger woman for tedium and hate. All serious letters answered. No cranks.' He should have said, 'No *other* cranks.'"

"Now, you see, that's the sort of ad *I'd* put in," I said. "Something different. Maybe you should put an ad in yourself. Something like, 'Lonely young man, early twenties, seeks Kate Moss or equivalent. Must be rich sexual athlete with own pub or hotel. Please include photo and a stamped, undressed envelope.'"

"I'm not *that* desperate for someone. I hope." He looked at his watch. "Well, I'd better go. Same time next week?"

I nodded. "Yeah. Thanks again."

When he heard me closing the front door after Anthony, my dad peered out into the hall. "You busy?"

"No. What's up?"

He closed the kitchen door and went into the sitting-room. I followed him in.

"You didn't touch your tea," he said.

"I'm wasn't in the mood for it."

"Ah. Man trouble," he said knowledgeably.

I scoffed at this. "As if."

Dad sat down on the sofa opposite me. It was strange seeing him sitting there: I was in *his* chair, and he didn't look at me as though he was expecting me to get up, as he usually would. Like most families, we all have our own places in the kitchen and sitting-room. Luckily, as there were only the four of us – and Fintan never stayed in the same room as my Dad – we didn't tend to have many "I was sitting there" arguments.

"Your Mam's been talking about moving again," Dad said. "It's just in the idea stage at the moment, but . . ."

"Yeah," I said. "I know what she's like. Soon it'll be little brochures and stuff left casually lying around. And then it'll be talk of mortgages."

He nodded. "She's got the idea that we'd be better off out of the city, maybe out in Meath somewhere, in a smaller house. If we sold up here, we'd get enough to pay off the rest of the mortgage and have a hefty down-payment on a new place."

"This sounds like it's well into the *planning* stage, Dad, it's not just a casual idea."

"She's been thinking about it for a while."

"And what do *you* think?"

"Well, with the job it doesn't matter much where I live. In fact, being out of the city would probably make things easier. The trip to Cork or Galway would be a lot quicker if I wasn't always up against rush-hour traffic."

That made sense, I decided. Then a thought occurred to me. "When you say a smaller house, how small exactly do you mean?"

"Well, Fintan's been talking about moving out for a while now." He meant, of course, that they'd been fighting a lot, and Fintan had been *threatening* to move out. "And you're twenty-five," he added. "It can't be much fun for you stuck here with us."

So after Dad left the room – "giving me time to think things over" he called it; "running away from a potential argument" is a lot closer to the truth. I sat in a daze through *Murder, She Wrote*. I didn't even pay attention when my favourite shampoo ad came on, the one where the two good-looking guys are in a changing room, and one spots the other's shampoo. "Head and Shoulders? I didn't know you had dandruff!" Then the other guy looks at him and says, "What kind of talk is that for a grown man, you stupid bastard?"

OK, so I was in a bad mood. I should have guessed that Dad wouldn't help. It's a well-known fact that parents are injected with a special mind-altering chemical that enables them to make any bad situation worse. Not that the situation with Sam was bad, far from it, but it had the potential for going bad, and that was what I was bothered about.

Relationships were not easy for people like me. I'd been fairly guarded ever since I was in secondary school and

I first overheard one of the teachers referring to me as, "the really tall one."

I met my first boyfriend when I was fourteen. Adam was sixteen, and I thought he was a god. He was so cool. Everyone in school thought he was great. Good-looking, well-built, taller than me – for a while – and really laid-back about everything. And he had a really relaxed home life: his parents let him smoke in the house, which to us was a sure sign that he was grown up and sophisticated.

During the whole two months we went out, I don't think that Adam ever really noticed me. Girls were something he picked up like a kleptomaniac in a pound shop. Oh, he was always kind, and generous, and willing to listen, but I could have been anyone, as long as I looked good and followed him around.

It all broke up quite suddenly. He phoned me and said, "I think we should break up, OK?" I was so shocked that all I could do was say, "if you're sure that's what you want." He said that it was. "No hard feelings, OK?"

I was devastated, and spent months on a complete downer. It was as if he'd just ripped my heart out, sniffed at it a bit, then tossed it aside with great indifference. "Oh, another girl's heart. I wonder what's for tea?"

By the time I finally got over him, he'd gone through about five other girlfriends. None of us meant anything to him. I couldn't even hate him for the way he'd treated me: as I said, I don't think he ever even noticed me. I still believe that if he'd realised how hurt any of us had been, he'd have changed his ways.

That was pretty much the start of what Pink Floyd would call "The Wall." With every comment of "it must be hard to get things in your size," or "your Dad's not keen on this jumper, Susan, it might fit you," or "How's the weather up there? Ha ha, just kidding. I bet you get that all the time," with every one of those comments, I metaphorically placed another brick in the wall. And pretty soon I was so good at building that wall that I was able to lay bricks on it without anyone else having to make a comment.

Once I left school and was officially no longer a stomping-up-the-stairs-and-slamming-the-door teenager, I relaxed a bit. College was easier: Everyone in Kevin Street was weird anyway, so it was easier to fit in. It was also easier to hide away and not be noticed. After a time I became less worried about most of the comments about my height. To some degree, the wall was still there, but at least I could see over it.

I don't want to dwell on being tall too much, but how about this for one last moan: It's almost impossible to get decent shoes in a size seven and a half. OK, call it eight.

Eventually, I went to bed, wrote some depressing stuff in my diary, and lay down to sleep.

A few minutes later I was up again, and gathering my things for the date with Sam. This was complicated by not being able to find a bag that was big enough to carry everything. I had hoped that I'd be able to wear my normal scruffy clothes to work, and bring my "going-out" clothes with me. In the end, I decided to wear my dating outfit to work.

I knew exactly what everyone was going to think when I walked into the office in the morning . . .

Chapter Six

I arrived early, as I'd planned, but I hadn't expected to find Kevin sliding up the shutters. He looked me up and down. "Did you get it?"

I sighed. "Kevin, I wasn't going for an interview."

"Did someone die?"

I pushed past him. "Get lost."

"Is it your Annual Performance Appraisal, then?" he asked, stressing the three words.

I marched up the stairs, with him following rather closer than I'd have liked. "If you must know," I said, "I'm breaking these clothes in for a friend."

He whistled. "Is she single?"

"No. She's married to a Mafia hitman."

"Is he bigger than me?"

"Who isn't?"

He stopped. "Hey, that's not fair. I'd never comment on *your* height."

Then I stopped, and looked back at him. He was right. "Sorry," I said. "I'm just a bit edgy today."

Kevin nodded, and went on climbing the stairs. I waited until he caught up with me and we walked up the rest of the way together. It felt strange, as though we'd suddenly crossed a barrier between us.

"So I take it you have a big date tonight?"

I nodded. "Something like that."

"Anyone I know?"

"How can I tell? I mean, who do you know?"

"Lots of people," he said. "I'm so popular I don't bother with an address book. I just carry the phone book around and cross out the people I don't know."

"Tell me something," I said. "You live in a flat, don't you?"

"Yeah. In Rathgar."

"I've been thinking about moving out of home. What sort of rent does a person pay around here?"

He shrugged. "Anything upwards of sixty a week, depending on what you're looking for."

"What about a ground floor flat with a separate bedroom and bathroom, that sort of thing?"

"I don't know," Kevin said as he moved around the office turning on the lights, printers and photocopier. "Maybe a hundred, hundred and twenty. But only if you want actual windows. I knew a guy who lived in a basement on Oakley Road in Ranelagh. I mean, a real basement. OK, it was painted and all that, but there were no windows. And the ceiling was about six foot from the floor. Not exactly suitable for most people to live in. But this guy didn't mind. All he used it for was sleeping in. Mad bastard altogether. Great crack."

"Kevin, you describe all your friends as mad bastards who are great crack. Don't you know any boring people?"

"Sure. Why do you think I work here?"

"The social status, obviously. The same reason I do."

He dropped into his chair and turned on his computer. "Seriously, though. Don't you think that most of the people here are boring as hell?"

"Like who?"

"Danny, for a start. Oh, he's clever all right, but there's more excitement in a bottle of prune juice. And Barbara."

I knew he wasn't Danny's number one fan, but his attitude to Barbara surprised me. "I thought you liked her."

"She's sexy as hell, but have you ever noticed that all her stories are set in a pub? Either that, or she tells us stories about other people, that she heard in the pub. For me, a woman has to have more than a good capacity for alcohol."

"What about Bernadette, then?" Bernadette was Kevin's last girlfriend. Very much a pub-dweller.

"Why do you think I dropped her?"

"Because she said you were the most self-centred, self-righteous bastard she'd ever met, and she hoped you'd die," I answered, quoting from the farewell fax she'd sent to him at the office, and which arrived when he had a day off. He saw it the next day, pinned up on the noticeboard.

"Yeah, but that was because she asked me what I really thought of her. So I told her."

I wandered over to my own desk, dropped my bag and coat, and grabbed my coffee mug. "Remind me never to ask you what you think about me."

"I'm sure it wouldn't be anything bad."

"Oh yeah. I *believe* you."

Kevin handed me his Spider-man mug. "Wench, get me coffee."

"Sure. And I promise to try not to spit in it."

"So *that's* why your cappuccino always tastes funny."

I nodded. "And that's why Belgian chocolates are weird."

He laughed, but I knew he didn't get it, which made me happy. It wasn't actually a joke or a clever one-liner or anything like that, but I couldn't think of anything so I just ad-libbed in the hope that Kevin would *think* it was a joke. He couldn't stand anyone being cleverer than he was, so that sort of thing usually worked.

As the morning dragged on, the office began to fill up at its usual pace for a Friday: Everyone knew that Vicky the Boss Lady wouldn't be in until around noon, so they took their time. And everyone – without exception – asked me how the interview went. I made sure that they were all aware I was *not* looking for another job: If the boss got the idea that I wanted out, she probably wouldn't hesitate in finding a replacement, and the last thing I needed now was to find myself dividing my time between flat hunting and job hunting.

By the time the boss finally arrived – after phoning from the car saying that the "meeting" had dragged on longer than she'd expected – we were hard at pretending to work. Kevin was hidden behind his computer reading a comic. Barbara was playing *Tetris*. I was pretending to type furiously but was actually trying to get my nails to dry. Danny was working, the traitor.

I glanced at the phone. Line five was active, which meant that Vicky was on the phone: she always used line five: we'd all agreed never to use it, so we'd know when it was safe to talk. I peeped up over the partition and said, "Hey, Danny."

He looked up from his work. "What's up?"

"What are you working on?"

"The T&J plan."

"Busy?"

He pushed himself away from the desk. "Not really. What's the problem?"

"No problem. You live in a flat, don't you? I'm thinking of moving out of home. Know any good, clean places that are incredibly cheap?"

He shook his head. "If I did, I'd move there. What sort of place are you looking for?"

"Well, a good, clean place that's incredibly cheap. Other than that I'm not bothered."

"Yeah, but there's lots of alternatives. You could share a house with a bunch of people, or just share a flat, or get a bedsit by yourself. And the price depends a lot on where you want to live, how secure you want it to be, and the sort of amenities."

"Amenities?"

Without getting up, he pulled himself and his swivel

chair around to my side of the partition. "Washing-machine, phone, your own bathroom, cable TV, electricity included in the price, that sort of thing."

"Well, I haven't given it that much thought. It'd have to be somewhere big, because I've got a lot of stuff."

"You couldn't leave most of it in your parent's place?"

"Not really. They're thinking about moving."

He mulled it over for a few seconds. "Then you could get a mortgage and buy their place. Then you wouldn't have to move at all. And you could get other people in as lodgers. If you had two lodgers paying you, say, two-fifty a month each, that'd cover most of the mortgage."

"Now, *that* is not a bad idea," I said. It was certainly worth considering. I had no idea how much a mortgage would cost, though. And I also didn't know how much my parents would want for the house. I had the vague idea that there was something about having to pay something like ten per cent of the mortgage up front. "I don't know if I'm ready to buy a house," I said. "I mean, that's a very serious commitment."

"Yeah, but like I said, if you had lodgers they'd be paying most of it. You'd have to get people you trust, though. I mean, I'm paying three-twenty-five a month for what is basically one room and a shared bathroom. I don't have a washing-machine, no cable, and the place is damp."

Kevin called out, "Phone down!" and we all scurried back to work.

The boss appeared a few minutes later, and called me to her office.

Uh oh, I said to myself. This is it, she's letting me go. Of course, I always thought that, just in case, but I had the sudden fear that she'd just discovered I hadn't done any work for the past year.

"Close the door behind you, Susan," she said, sitting down behind her expensive desk. "Have a seat."

I sat. And waited as she fiddled around with something on her computer. While I waited, all sorts of things went through my mind, ranging from "It was all Kevin's fault" to "my, what big teeth you have, Grandma."

Vicky didn't actually have big teeth. She was mid-fortyish, quite slim, with shoulder-length, dyed strawberry-blonde hair that she got retouched at least once every month. She wasn't exactly stunning – she was more what old people might call, "a handsome woman" – but she carried herself well. Plus, she dressed in expensive clothes that were a good ten years too young for her.

Finally, after deciding that she'd let me stew long enough, Vicky turned to me. "Right . . . I know it's not time for your Annual Performance Evaluation, but I thought it would be nice to have a little chat." She tapped at the computer a bit more, then laced her fingers together and leaned forward, resting on her elbows. "How are things?"

Then I remembered that her latest boyfriend was one of those "time and motion" and "treating the workers at the same level" fanatics. I pictured the two of them fumbling about on her sofa during News at Ten, with him saying "naturally, Vicky, you have to – grunt – respect each of the – grunt – staff members – as much as you respect – pant – the clients." Then I corrected the idea, because I knew he'd never use the term "staff members." He'd say "production operatives," or "valued employees."

"Things are OK," I said. "I've been putting a lot of work into the Boseman contract, and I think that there won't be any real problems."

She waved her hands dismissively. "No, no, I mean you. Yourself."

I shrugged. "I'm fine." I realised that this wasn't enough, so I added, "My parents are planning to move, so I'm thinking of getting a flat." I paused, and realised that she still wanted more. "Or maybe I'll just buy a car."

"And any luck on the boyfriend scene?"

Now, *that* hit me out of the blue. What was she up to? What difference did it make to her whether I had a boyfriend? It certainly wouldn't make any difference to my work – or lack of it. "Oh, the usual."

There was more like this, and slowly it dawned on me that she was desperately trying to make conversation. As though we were friends. I knew she didn't have many friends of her own, or at least if she did they had strict instructions never to call her at work.

Well, she hired me because, she said, I was good at figuring things out. As soon as I realised that, I was able to figure out what she was getting at. "You're getting married," I blurted out.

She stared at me. "So much for secrets." She sat back,

and lit a cigarette. Our office has a no-smoking policy, but hey, it's her company. "How do you know? Did someone tell you?"

"You're going away on Monday week," I replied. "You said it was for a series of business meetings, but you still haven't said who they're with. Things like that." I didn't add that she'd been out of the office a lot, and making a lot more phone calls than usual, or that I'd suddenly remembered how she'd been fiddling with her fingers a lot lately, as though she was getting used to wearing a ring: I'd learned long ago never to tell anyone everything I'd noticed about them, because then they'd become too self-conscious.

"You're very perceptive," Vicky said. She seemed to be impressed.

Yes, I said to myself. Perceptive enough to know that you're going to ask me to look after all the clients while you're away.

Vicky told me at length about the wedding, the honeymoon, and what her teenage son thought about getting a new daddy. She also told me a fair bit about Nick, her fiancé who – despite his taste in women – actually sounded OK. It was going to be an expensive wedding and honeymoon, though: they'd figured on it costing about twenty grand. She giggled in an unconvincing schoolgirlish way when she mentioned this, and said that her father had told her he was thanking God he didn't have to pay for *this* one. When she mentioned that, I had a sudden vision of my own father after receiving the same sort of news: In my vision, Dad didn't say much, he just gibbered and frothed a bit.

I was surprised, though – she hadn't asked me to look after the clients. I guessed that would come later. Vicky banished me from her office with strict instructions not to mention anything about the wedding to anyone, particularly not to any of the clients. Which surprised me because lots of them were rich and they would have bought her great wedding presents.

Oh, what a dilemma . . . When I went back into the slave pit Barbara looked up at me, clearly wondering what was going on. I gave her my best "I don't know what all *that* was about" look, and returned to my desk. It was almost lunchtime, and I could see Barbara getting ready to saunter over and casually ask me about my unscheduled meeting, so I phoned Sharon in the hope that it would put Barbara off long enough for me to think up a good story.

Sharon answered after the second ring – her company has a policy of "don't let the phone ring more than twice, because that gives the customers a bad impression." It was a pretty stupid policy, but I couldn't complain publicly about it because my company taught it to them.

"Mobile Services, Sharon speaking, how may I help you?"

I put on my whiny American voice. "This is Radio One-Twenty FM. I'm sorry, but if you'd answered with 'Radio One-Twenty plays all the hits' you would have won a thousand pounds."

"Yeah, sure. FM radios don't go up to a hundred and twenty, Susan."

"In that case, this is the police. Your car has been impounded."

"What's up? Worried about tonight?"

"To be honest, I'd forgotten all about that," I lied. "It's been pretty busy all morning." Another lie. How easily we lie to our friends, especially about things that don't matter.

"Lucky you. I've been watching the clock. After the great struggle for the hour hand to get all the way up to twelve you'd think it'd swing back down to six in no time. This place is deader than a Christmas afternoon when there's only a James Bond movie on."

"Which one?"

"The one with Grace Jones in it."

"*A View to a Kill,*" I said, as show-offy as ever. "Theme music by Duran Duran."

"I remember that. And I remember you wetting yourself that day when you saw Simon Le Bon in Arnotts. At least, you *said* it was him."

"It was. I'll never forget the way he didn't pay any attention to me. Only a truly great superstar could ignore someone in that way." I sighed. "Not like these so-called rock stars these days. In our day, you got a much better class of famous person. Remember when we saw Nik Kershaw in the airport?"

"Anyway . . ." Sharon said, reminding me that it was getting close to one o'clock. It was a sort of rule between us that we didn't phone each other during lunch. Only on company time.

"Anyway, two things. First, I was wondering where

you were going to be tonight? Just in case Sam doesn't turn up."

"Don't think like that. He'll be there."

"You're going to feel guilty as hell when I'm crying to you on the phone in the morning."

"Well, look, where and when are you meeting him?"

"Seven, at Eason's."

She went "hmm" and then said, "OK. I don't know if we'll be in town but if we are, I'll try and walk past Eason's at about half-seven, OK? And If you're there, I'll make a big show about being late so that all the other stood-up people won't think you're one of them."

"Great. Thanks."

"So what was the other thing?"

"I forget," I said, and racked my brains for a few seconds. "Wait, here's something. It wasn't the thing I was thinking of, though. Remember what Jackie said about Anthony? Well, he's not interested."

"Good for him. I knew he had taste. I wouldn't mind him myself."

"Oh God, don't *you* start. I'll have to set myself up as his agent."

"Yeah, but would you want ten per cent of whatever he gets? You'd have to start living a whole different lifestyle."

I laughed. "At least it would *be* a lifestyle. I remember what it was I was going to say now . . . My folks are thinking of moving. I'm going to get a flat. Or share a house, or something."

"Knowing your mother, they could be gone in a

couple of weeks. They might even have moved by the time you get home."

Barbara threw a crude paper airplane onto my desk. The word "Lunch!" was scrawled on it in big letters. It was immediately followed by another with the word "Now!" I wrapped up the call to Sharon. "Listen, I'd better go. Let me know if you hear of any flats or anything, OK?"

Sharon said she'd keep her eyes open, and hung up.

"Right," Barbara said. "Let's go." She grabbed her bag and made for the door. On the way out, we passed Kevin, who was incredibly cheerful because he'd just opened his bag of Barbecue Beef Hula Hoops and found the last cardboard dinosaur he needed to complete his collection.

Chapter Seven

It was pretty tough waiting for the afternoon to end. I even thought about doing some work to kill the time, but I knew that none of the others would ever speak to me again.

As usual, High Commander Vicky disappeared just before three. Another one of those important Friday afternoon meetings that only ever seem to happen in a place where her mobile phone doesn't work. Not that we ever needed to ring her.

Once, though, when Kevin was really pissed off about something, he phoned her mobile every two minutes, and hung up when she answered. He said it made him feel better. His plan almost backfired, though, because she checked the phone logs and saw that someone in the office had made over forty calls to her mobile number. Kevin made the excuse that his phone had been acting up, and that he'd called her once, and then the phone had somehow been using the redial feature all by itself. He added that when he'd realised what was going on, he dialed a non-existent number, so the now-automatic redial was calling that number instead. Then he told her that one of his mates knew a lot about phones, and he'd told Kevin how to reset the system. Kevin apologised that he hadn't been able to do any work for the afternoon and said it was because he'd had to reprogram all the speed-dial numbers.

We were all stunned to hear him come out with such a transparent lie, but she believed it. And to make matters worse, she commended him on getting the problem sorted out without having to call in an expensive engineer.

But back to that afternoon . . . Three o'clock, and I was swinging back in my chair, staring at the ceiling, wondering how much all the ceiling tiles would weigh if you put them together. Half-three, and the whole bunch of us were gathered around the window, watching some poor guy's illegally-parked car getting towed away. Then we counted a hundred passing cars, calling out to Danny the make and colour, and whether the driver was wearing a seatbelt. Danny put them all on the computer and made a chart.

At four o'clock, Barbara and Kevin were playing a game over the network, Danny was counting the change in his jar – stacking the coins into little piles of ten – and I was debating whether I should get something to eat now, which would mean I might be a bit hungry again when I met Sam, or if I should just wait, which would not be a good thing for me if Sam had already eaten.

I elected to get a can of Lilt and a bag of crisps. I

bought salt 'n' vinegar flavour because I know from bitter experience that there's nothing worse in the world than kissing someone who's recently eaten cheese 'n' onion crisps . . . I've always believed that the family planning clinics should hand out cheese 'n' onion crisps instead of condoms. I mean, the Pope wouldn't have a problem with that form of contraception.

At about a quarter to five, Kevin came back from the toilet and said, "Did you ever notice that if you have Sugar Puffs for breakfast you can still get the smell when you have a piss?"

No one bothered to answer. We were all getting our stuff ready to go home.

And then I remembered that I wasn't going home, and that I'd planned to stay in the office until about half six, and then walk into town to meet Sam by seven.

It was tough watching the others leave. Barbara wished me luck, and that reminded Kevin about my big date, so he told me that if I got stood up, he'd get his mate Gerry to beat the shit out of Sam. And that was when Danny found out I was going on a date.

He stood by the door like a little boy who'd been playing in a toy shop and who'd just looked up to discover that his mother was nowhere in sight.

"I, eh, hope it goes well," he lied.

"I'm sure it will. Thanks."

"OK then. I'll be off. See you on Monday?" He said that as though he wanted me to assure him that I was actually going to come back on Monday, that I wasn't running off forever with someone else.

"Sure. Have a good weekend."

He nodded. "Thanks. Bye."

And just like that, he left without wishing me a good weekend, and that was something he always did.

I realised that I was feeling guilty. And then I realised that until Barbara had mentioned yesterday that Danny was interested in me, I'd never really given him a second thought, so there was no reason I should feel guilty now. Then it occurred to me that he probably had absolutely *nothing* to do for the whole weekend. And I felt guilty all over again.

And *then* I told myself to get a grip. I should be worrying about Sam instead.

The office was really, really quiet. After I'd brushed my hair a million times and put on a modest amount of make-up, I had nothing to do but wait.

And as luck would have it, the phone rang just before six o'clock. It was the boss.

"Ah, Susan, you're still there."

"Oh, I hadn't realised what time it was. I'm just finishing up."

"I was just checking that everything's OK."

Yeah, sure, I said to myself. You mean you're just checking up on us. You know we're never here this late on a Friday. So, I wondered to myself, why *is* she ringing? "Everything's fine here," I said. "How did the meeting go?"

She tutted. "This is just a coffee break. It looks like I'm going to be here for *hours* yet."

Oh, really? I said to myself. Then it occurred to me

that maybe she really *was* in a meeting, and she was trying to give a good impression to her clients by phoning the office at six o'clock on a Friday.

"And they might have to continue on Monday morning," she said. "So I'll probably be in late. You'll have to hold the fort until I get in. Is that OK?"

"Sure." This was the start of it, I knew. Check that the office can run smoothly with me in charge, and pretty soon she'll be able to bugger off to the States on her honeymoon without a care in the world.

She said her goodbyes, hung up, and before too long it was twenty past six.

Time for me to go.

I arrived at Eason's at five to seven. There were already a couple of dozen people there waiting for their dates.

It's an awkward situation, waiting in public for someone. Many times I'd walked down O'Connell Street and passed the anxious faces, each young man peering at me and thinking, "Is that her? No, too tall. I wasn't *that* drunk." And when they noticed me looking at them, I could see them thinking, "Of course, I was deaf and blind the next day, so maybe . . . No, it's all right, she's walking past."

I don't care what anyone says about first dates, it's worse for a girl. The average man will shave and put on a clean shirt, and consider himself "all dressed up" but girls go to a hell of a lot more trouble. Not counting the panic, and all the phone calls to our friends, we have to worry about things like whether we should wear make-up, and whether we should dress the same as we did when we met them in the disco, because everyone knows that men don't remember things the way we do, and they might not recognise us. And then we worry about things like, "what if he's ugly?" and, "what if he doesn't turn up? Everyone will know I've been stood up and they'll think I'm an idiot."

So we stand there, watching the passers-by, occasionally glancing at our watch and trying to give the impression that, "no, he's not late. I actually arrived early, but that doesn't mean I'm desperate."

Then half an hour passes, and we start telling ourselves that maybe he meant *last* night, or maybe he said eight, instead of seven. Maybe he said *Bewley's*, not *Eason's*.

You know you're really getting paranoid when you start thinking, "hey, Eason's is on a *corner*! Maybe he's just around the corner and he's been there for ages!"

And eventually, you have to make that long walk – in front of all the others waiting for their dates – in the direction of your bus stop. And you have to do it without crying or swearing out loud that all men are complete bastards.

Believe me, I know all about being stood up: it's happened to me many times. Once, I know for a fact that my date did turn up, but changed his mind when he saw me in daylight.

As I say, I've been stood up many times.

Luckily, this wasn't one of them.

Chapter Eight

He arrived at two minutes past seven, and – get this – he apologised for making me wait.

So we got our first good look at each other in daylight. I was actually pretty pleased: he wasn't a monster. In fact, he was quite good-looking. Dark hair, cropped fairly short, reasonable build, good straight teeth. Not bad at all, I decided. And he'd put a bit of effort into his clothing: good clean denim jacket and jeans, immaculate white shirt that I strongly suspected had been bought in Dunnes that afternoon, clean boots.

"So, what would you like to do?"

My first reaction was to say "What do *you* want to do?" but I caught myself in time. Instead, I said, "first of all, I need your Access or Visa card number and three forms of identification."

He grinned. "I have a note from my mother, will that do?"

"It will as long as it's not signed 'Sam's Mother,'" I said. "Are you hungry?"

"That depends. Are you?"

I sighed. "Uh oh . . . I had a feeling you'd say that." I pointed in the direction of O'Connell bridge. "Let's just start walking, and see where we end up."

He rubbed his hands together enthusiastically. "Gosh, that's an absolutely brilliant idea!"

We began to walk in that direction. "So, waiting long?" he asked.

"A few minutes. What did you do for the afternoon, then?"

"I went back to the flat, tidied it up a bit, had a shower, and then just sat around and worried for three hours."

"Worried?"

"Well, I wasn't sure if you'd turn up. I was afraid you might have had a better offer. And to be honest, I'm not in the habit of asking strange women out on dates."

"I did notice that you seemed a little uncomfortable the other night," I said.

"Frodo's isn't my sort of place," he said. "I have this thing about nightclubs . . . I'm always afraid that the women I meet there will turn out to be the sort of people who just like going to nightclubs."

"Well, I was only there because it was my friend Laura's birthday. I offered to arrange a party in McDonald's, but she said that was childish. I happen to know that she's just scared of Ronald McDonald. So, why *were* you there? Do you do the DJ thing a lot?"

Sam shook his head. "Nah, I was only in Frodo's because Dave wanted someone to give him a hand. Well, actually he didn't really need anyone to help out while he was working, just to carry stuff in and out of the van." He clenched his fist and flexed his muscles. "Feel that!"

I put my hand on his biceps. "Ooh! Nice! Is that *real* denim?"

"Yes," he said. "It used to belong to Denholm Elliott."

"Gee, you're a pretty funny guy," I said in a squeaky American accent.

Sam stopped walking and turned to me. "What do you mean by that?" It was a damned good Joe Pesci impersonation.

"I'm just saying, you're a funny guy, is all."

"What, you're saying I'm funny-looking, is that it? Is that what you're saying? You think I'm funny-looking?"

"Yes."

He grinned again, and we walked on. "So what's your favourite movie, then?" he asked.

"I don't know. I know what my *least* favourite is, though. *Four Weddings and a Funeral*."

He looked disappointed. "I enjoyed that."

"I did too, until everyone in the universe wouldn't shut up about it. My mother bought it for me for my birthday, because she wanted to see it but she'd never splash out on anything like that for herself. Now any time I complain that I have nothing to watch she says, 'Why don't you watch *Four Weddings and a Funeral*?' And every time someone visits *they* want to see it. And that bloody Wet Wet Wet song was everywhere. Couldn't get away from the thing. What's *your* favourite movie? Not counting *Die Hard*, of course."

"Hmm . . . That's a tough one. It would have to be . . . *Die Hard 2*, I think. No, I don't know. I like lots of films for different reasons. Like, last year, my mate's girlfriend was raving about *Strictly Ballroom*. I thought, yeah, sure, it's a girl's movie about dancers. *Australian* dancers, at that. I thought it would be like *Home and Away – The Musical* or something. But it turned out to be one of the best films I've ever seen."

I nodded. Yes, I decided, I like him. He has a good sense of humour, and he knows his movies. What more could I want from a man? Apart from untold wealth, of course.

By now we had reached College Green. Sam glanced over at the gate to Trinity College, and said, "ah, my old hangout."

"What did you study?"

"I didn't study anything," Sam said. "I used to hang out there when I was waiting for the bus to Dun Laoghaire and it was raining. What about you? Third level education?"

"Not really. I studied psychology for a while, but it was driving me mad so I quit. I did all sorts of word-processing courses and a bit of secretarial stuff, but in the end there was no escape, and I had to get an actual job."

"So what do you do? Aside from being a lumberjack."

"I'm a management consultant's senior dogsbody. We do training courses for companies who want to be better able to manage their staff. Actually, the truth is that we visit lots of companies, watch how they do things, write down their good ideas, and tell them the good ideas we've picked up from other companies."

"So you're a Concept Redistribution Engineer?"

"Yeah, I like that. I'll remember that next time the boss is sending me out to buy the milk."

"How about a pizza?" Sam asked. "The Gotham Café place thingy is just around the corner. They serve mighty damned fine pizzas."

"They do indeed," I said. "But this is Friday night, and I'll bet we have to wait an hour."

"Do you want to try anyway?"

"Sure."

I was right. The nice young chap at the door in The Gotham explained that they were full. Sam told him that was OK, because we'd had nothing to eat so *we* weren't full. This clever trick didn't work, though.

"We won't have a table for about an hour," the door person said. "I can take your name, if you like. You can wait next door in the pub and I'll call you when your table is ready."

"Can we give you our order now?" I asked. "That way, we won't have as long to wait when you do call us."

The door person just smiled, and asked, "Name?"

"The Great Arthur Cranberry," Sam replied.

"And his lovely assistant Janice," I added with a curtsey.

The door bloke was clearly not in the mood. "Cranberry," he muttered as he wrote. He glanced at his watch. "About eight."

Sam slipped him a pound coin, winked knowingly,

and said, "If someone chokes to death, you be sure to give us their table, OK? There might be another pound in it for you."

So we retired to the pub next door, which seemed to be packed with pizza-starved people. "What'll you have?" Sam asked.

"A pizza," I said. "But failing that, a Seven-Up."

I found a couple of empty barstools against the wall, and propped myself up on one. I watched Sam getting the drinks, and it was as if I'd known him for years. I felt so comfortable with everything he said and everything he did, it was hard to believe that we weren't already a couple. And it seemed to me that he sensed it too. He was relaxed, much more so than he'd been on Wednesday night.

Thinking about it, I realised I was more relaxed too, and I guessed that was because he was comfortable with me. Could be a vicious circle, I thought. Both of us relaxed because the other was relaxed, or something. I found myself wondering what my mother would think of him, and I put a stop to that line of thought rather quickly. My mother had never met any of my boyfriends, apart from Adam, and she hated him.

Sam came back with the drinks. "I've just realised I don't know your last name," he said.

"Yeah? Well, the other night you didn't remember my *first* name."

The tips of his ears turned bright red. "I have a lousy memory for names," he said, then carefully and deliberately added, "Susan Something."

"Susan Perry," I said. "So how come you remembered my first name this time?"

"After you left I wrote it down on the back of my hand. But first I had to ask Dave what it was again. And yesterday morning my mother called into the video shop and the first thing she said was, 'Who's Susan?' I couldn't figure out who had told her, until I copped that it was still written on my hand. Which reminds me, Ms Perry," he added, after a long swig at his Coke, "Do you prefer to be called Sue, Susan, Susie or what?"

"Susan," I said. "I have a cousin called Sue, and she's older than me, so I've always been Susan. What about you? Is it Sam, Sammy, Samuel or Samsonite?"

"None of the above," he said. "It's Samwich."

"Is this because you're a ham, and your jokes are cheesy?"

"Lettuce hope it's nothing like that."

I groaned. "Your jokes are *much* worse than mine. What's your surname?"

"O'Neill. Of the South American O'Neills, of course. Not the Indonesian O'Neills who've been in the papers so much lately."

We chatted for ages, exchanging family histories and dumb stories, and by the time Gotham's finest arrived to tell us the table was ready, we were both in stitches.

The conversation was pretty much the same during the pizza. Sam, I was surprised to discover, didn't drink. I brought this up at one point, and Sam said, "I haven't had a drink in about seven years."

"Why did you give it up?" I asked.

"I'm an alcoholic."

"Oh." I felt like a complete fool. For the first time that evening, I couldn't think of anything appropriate to say, so I said, "Really?"

And Sam – the sneaky bastard – grinned and said, "No, not really."

I could have choked him there and then. "You bloody sod! You really had me going there."

"Sorry. Couldn't help it. It's the first straight line you've fed me all evening." He munched away at the last slice of his pizza, then – through his mouthfuls – said, "You haven't really said much about yourself."

"There's not much to tell," I said. "I was born approximately twenty-five years ago and I've lived all my life with my family in Cabra. Though I'm about to change that. My parents are thinking about moving, so it's time for me to get my own place and leave the nest."

"What about your brother? You said he was still at home as well."

"Yeah, well, Fintan will have to find somewhere himself. I don't care as long as it's nowhere near me. We're not the closest. He has a real chip on his shoulder about everything. I think he's still annoyed at me because I had the nerve to be born first. I keep telling him that it wasn't my fault, I was too young to know better, but that doesn't make a difference to him. He thinks that I got everything and he got nothing. Which is not true. He never does *anything* around the house, and I'm still paying more than him. OK, so I've got the bigger room, but I offered to swap with him a few years ago. He didn't want to because he thought that his friends would laugh at him if he moved into a girl's bedroom."

Sam laughed. "As though that would make him a sort of room-transvestite?"

"Yeah. When I was twelve, and he was about ten, his bike had a puncture and he wanted to go cycling with his friends, so I offered to lend him my bike. He wouldn't even consider the idea. He sulked for ages, until I fixed the puncture for him. Then he made me swear that I'd never tell anyone."

"Your brother has some real problems," Sam said. "I'm lucky like that. I have no siblings."

"What! You mean you've no one to lend your money to and never see it again? How hard it must be for you. Fintan used to practically beg me to set him up with my friends, and then he'd treat them like dirt and I'd have to spend hours consoling them. My best friend Sharon won't come into the house if she thinks that Fintan is there or is likely to come home soon. She won't even come to the door when she's collecting me, she just waits outside in the car until I come to her."

"What happened between them?" Sam asked.

"Nothing really. Fintan only cares about being seen with good-looking girls. He doesn't give a damn about them otherwise."

Sam leaned back in his chair. "Well, I don't want you to be offended, but it sounds to me like your brother is a class-A prick of the first order."

"Oh, he sure is. Though my mother's convinced that he'll settle down one day."

"Hah! I had a lot of friends like him in my drinking days, and that's the reason I stopped. I was afraid of turning out like that. I shared a flat with one of my mates for a while, and he got drunk every night. It got so bad that my other friends stopped calling around." Sam shook his head. "He was dirty, too. Let me tell you this, Susan . . . If you're getting a flat, make damn sure you know who you'll be sharing with. Martin never washed anything, including himself or his clothes. He never closed the fridge door when he took something out of it. He didn't *once* take out the bins. If I hadn't been around to clean the frying pan and wash the dishes he would have poisoned himself."

When he finished speaking, Sam's face had a rather nasty expression I hadn't seen on him before.

"You're still really annoyed about that guy, aren't you?"

"Who wouldn't be?" he said, rather abruptly. "He was a prick."

I had a feeling I knew what Sam's real problem was. "So what did everyone else think of him? His other friends, I mean?"

"Oh, they all loved him. 'Martin's a great laugh, he's great crack. The life and soul of the party.' I don't know . . . Most of his friends were just the same, anyway. A bunch of drunken morons."

"What about girls?" I asked. "Did he have much luck with them?"

Sam gave a short, harsh laugh. "Oh yeah. More than I did, anyway. Martin and whatever girl he was with that week would come back pissed from the pub when I was watching a movie or something, and they'd just sit there and talk and fart and belch all the way through the movie, as if it was absolutely hilarious or something. And if I asked them to shut up, they'd get worse. It got so bad at one stage that I ended up moving the telly and video into my room – they were my telly and video anyway – and one night I came in late and found them in my bed watching *Basic Instinct* and her giving him a hand job."

"Jesus! What did you do?"

"I threw them out. It *was* my flat. Still is, I mean. That's where I'm still living."

By now I knew exactly what Sam's problem with Martin was: plain and simple, he was jealous that Martin enjoyed himself much more and got on better with life than he did. "How long ago was all this?" I asked.

"Three years, just about."

I nodded, and said nothing.

He looked at me. "Why?"

"Have you seen him since?"

"Yeah, a few times. He can't remember what he was really like. And he still thinks we're best friends. He keeps saying we should get together some time, go for a few drinks."

"Well, maybe you should. Talk to him, and get it all out in the open."

He sighed. "Susan, I really don't need advice about this. I don't have a problem with him any more."

"That's not what it sounds like," I said.

"Yeah, well, you weren't there."

"A few minutes ago I said that it sounds like you're still annoyed with him, and you said, 'Who wouldn't be?' Maybe I wasn't there, but I've been listening to what you've been saying. You'll have to either make peace with him, or let it go. It's not healthy to keep all that bottled up inside you. You're going to end up extremely bitter about it, and it won't be *his* fault, it'll be yours." And as soon as I said that, I realised that I should have kept my big mouth shut. Earlier in the evening it might have felt as if we'd know each other for years, but the fact is I really knew almost nothing about him. Certainly not enough to try and psychoanalyse his problems.

Sam was silent for a few minutes, then he pushed away his empty plate. "Well, it's getting late. I suppose we should be going."

"It's not even half-nine," I said. "Do you want to go down to Bewley's, and get a coffee or something?" It was a desperate attempt to save a lost situation, but I had to try.

Sam picked up the bill. "Nah. I'm not in the mood. Back in a minute." He got up and went to pay the bill.

Oh, well *done*, Susan, I said to myself. You've managed to piss him off, and now you'll never see him again. He'll make some excuse about having to open the shop early tomorrow, then he'll walk you to your bus stop and leave you there. He won't wait for the bus, and he won't kiss you goodnight.

I was one hundred per cent absolutely right. Sam left me at the thirty-nine bus stop, said that he'd call, and went on his way. He didn't look back.

How can he call? I wondered. He doesn't have my number. He probably can't even remember my surname.

I felt like shit. I was incredibly angry with myself, and at the same time I felt more sorry for myself than I ever had in the past. I felt guilty, and embarrassed. I had the whole bunch of negative emotions charging around my system, each one forcing its way to the top every couple of seconds to try and grab my attention.

All that preparation, all that worry, and I'd ruined everything. I kept saying to myself, "Think how *he* must feel. There we were, having a great time, and I spoiled it. Made him feel like dirt."

A young couple were cuddling in the bus shelter, and that made me feel even worse.

The bus trundled up fifteen long minutes after Sam had abandoned me at the bus stop. I noticed that my hands were shaking as I fished out the exact fare.

And instead of whisking me away home, where I could lock myself in my bedroom and have a good cry, the bus waited, and waited, letting on loads more people. Cheerful, happy people who were too inconsiderate to notice that I was wretched and miserable.

By the time the bus finally began to move, my mind had gone through all sorts of crazy things, like, "I could phone Frodo's and try to track down Sam's friend Dave, then I could ask him how to contact Sam," and, "Why didn't I just follow him when he walked away? I could have apologised."

The bus driver swore at some drunk who was trying to get in when the bus was moving. That snapped me out of my self-pity a bit, and suddenly it was like every other date I'd had in the past few years.

I was going home alone.

Chapter Nine

At times like that, all you want to do is go straight home and into bed, and stay there until the pain begins to fade. But the universe isn't like that. The universe is like fucking *Sesame Street*. Just when you least want human contact, the universe pops up with a cheery smile and a silly hat and says, "Hey, don't be sad! Things are never as bad as they might seem! Come on, we're going to sing a little smiley song to chase away the blues!"

Goddamn *Sesame Street*! I'd always hated those stupid muppets. The always-smiling Ernie and his suspect pal Bert. Oscar the Grouch, the homeless muppet, exiled from ordinary society because of his physical deformity – one single eyebrow – and forced to live in a bin. And Big Bird. I especially hated Big Bird, who always reminded me of Vera Duckworth from *Coronation Street*.

There is nothing – and I mean *nothing* – that can make you feel worse about yourself than someone telling you, "Cheer up, it's not all that bad!"

Well, as far as I was concerned it *was* all that bad.

It was just after ten when I got home. My parents heard me coming in, and my mother called out, "You're home early."

I was not in the mood. "Better not get used to saying that," I called back. "I'm not going to be coming back here for much longer."

My dad opened the sitting-room door and looked out. "What happened?"

"What do you mean, 'what happened?' The usual happened. Nothing. Like my whole life."

"You didn't get stood up, did you?"

"No. No, I didn't. But I might have been better off if I had. At least then I wouldn't . . ." I cut myself off. I really didn't want to talk about it.

My mother, who is occasionally wiser than she lets on, came out into the hall, and led me into the kitchen. She sat me down and poured me a cup of tea. My dad hung around the door, not really knowing what to do or say, until my mother ordered him back to the sitting-room.

When he was gone, she sat down opposite me and said, "Do you want to talk about it?"

"No."

"Ah," she said, knowledgeably.

I didn't like her tone. "What do you mean by that?"

"At a guess, I'd say everything was going fine, until you said the wrong thing. Am I close?"

I couldn't help myself. I did something that I hadn't done in years. I broke down in tears. Through my sobs, I explained what had happened.

And my dear mother just patted me on the arm, and said, "Susan, it's not all that bad."

So I snapped. "Yes it is. It's that bad, and worse. But it's not just Sam, it's *everything*. Look at me! I'm twenty-five years old, and I'm going nowhere. I can't get any man to take me seriously, because they're all intimidated by my height. And any boyfriend I *do* get I manage to irritate the hell out of them, because I have to prove I'm better than they are. I have to be cleverer than they are, and sort out their problems for them. All my friends are doing great. People treat them with respect, but everyone thinks I'm some sort of freak. What's the first thing people say when they're telling someone else about me? They don't say that I'm good-looking, or intelligent, or nice, or anything like that. They say, 'She's really, really tall.' I wouldn't be where I am in work if my boss wasn't a woman. People treat me as though I'm a freak."

My mother just looked at me, and said something I never expected. "I know."

"What?"

"When I was in school there was a girl in my class who was five feet nothing, and she must have weighed about sixteen stone. Half of the girls in the class made fun of her, and the other half avoided her because they could never think of anything to say. Every time they looked at her all they could see was fat. I think that hurt her more than any name anyone ever called her."

"Well, I'm sorry for her, but what's the point of this story?"

She smiled. "Susan, if you can't tell me the point, then you're not half as intelligent as you think you are."

"I see," I said. I tried to think about it, but my mind had gone blank. "Did you miss anything out?"

"No."

"Then all I can think of is that people are a bunch of hypocrites who are too wrapped up in themselves to realise how much the things they say and do can affect other people."

"Absolutely correct," she said. "No one's like that all the time, but everyone is at one stage or another."

"So all the people who treat me like a freak, I should just say to hell with them?"

"No." She stood up, and brought her cup to the sink. "You don't understand at all," she said. "When you do, then you'll have learned something."

She went back to the sitting-room, and I sat there alone for a while, trying to figure out what my mother had meant. But I wasn't making any progress. All I could think of was Sam, and how he looked as he walked away from me at the bus stop.

After another cup of tea and a few biscuits, it hit me. I had thought that she was asking me to compare myself to the fat girl in her story, but she'd actually been comparing the fat girl to Sam, and comparing me to all the people who didn't know how to treat the girl. I'd been so busy being clever that I hadn't seen that he didn't want advice. Even when he *said* that he didn't want advice, I just kept piling it on.

As I said, occasionally my mother can be very wise.

Chapter Ten

So it *was* all my fault after all.

I wasn't able to contact Sam, so there was no way I could make amends. I had to let it go. There was no point in my beating myself to death about something I couldn't change. I started giving myself the sort of advice I'd given to Sam, for pretty much the same reasons: You can never go back, only forward.

I mentioned before that my mother is not the sort of person to let the grass grow under her, but now I was beginning to realise that was because she was decisive, not indecisive. She moved on in life precisely because she knew what she wanted, and how to get it.

She wanted to move house, and I had no doubt that it would happen. It would change all of our lives, but she knew that, and it might well have been one of her reasons.

I picked up the paper and began hunting for a flat.

That cheered me up a bit, because I've always loved the small ads in the paper. I've even been tempted to put in a few myself, something along the lines of, "Female cleaner wanted. Must have experience of cleaning females," or perhaps, "Mature woman required to mind own children in own home."

I didn't find any suitable flats, but I did find one of the ads which Anthony had read out the previous night: "Middle-aged man, tired of the same old love interests, seeks younger woman for tedium and hate. All serious letters answered. No cranks."

It intrigued me. I mean, what sort of nut would place an ad like that? Someone looking for a bit of fun, I guessed. Or someone who wanted to find a woman who had a bit of personality. Or maybe he was quite simply stark raving mad.

How could I resist it? I found a pen and paper, and I wrote him a letter . . .

Dear Box Number thirty-three,

I read with curiosity your ad in the Personal column of the Evening Herald. I am a twenty-five-year-old woman, also tired of the pressures of society to fall into a "normal" relationship. I am interested in writing to you, as I am sure it will be boring, and – who knows? – perhaps a spiteful and embittered relationship will soon develop.

Regards,

Susan Perry.

I put the letter in an envelope, addressed it, and went up to bed. Then I "snuck" down a few minutes later and brought the letter back up with me. I really didn't want Fintan to find it and start asking awkward questions.

I couldn't sleep, of course. For a start, my bed was too short: my feet stuck out over the end. They'd been doing that for years, but it really bothered me that night.

When I was thirteen and still growing at an incredible rate, I read about some girl in America who was six-foot ten, and she'd had an operation to reduce her height. They did this by removing one of her vertebrae, then basically removing big chunks out of her leg bones. If I remember correctly, they managed to get her height down to about six-three. Of course, she had to learn to walk all over again, and I'm sure that none of her clothes fit her anymore, and no doubt everyone stopped referring to her as 'the really tall girl' and started calling her 'the girl who had that operation.'

Still, I thought that this was the most wonderful thing I'd ever heard of, and I was convinced that by the time I was an adult height-reduction surgery would be all the rage. I thought that all I'd have to do was save up enough money and book myself into one of the many clinics that would have sprung up all over the world. I managed to save about twenty pounds, and then went mad one day and spent it all on Billy Joel albums. I liked Billy Joel because at that time he was with Christie Brinkly, and she was taller than he was.

The other reason I couldn't sleep that night was because I kept going over the evening in my head, and trying to think of ways to make things better again.

I started to fantasise that Sam was half-way home when he realised I was right, then he'd probably spend ages trying to track me down . . . I'd told him about my local video shop, and how everyone there knew me, so maybe he'd end up phoning every video shop in Cabra until he tracked me down. And then, after a couple of weeks, I'd wander into the video shop and Mark would tell me, "Susan, there was a guy in here looking for you. I didn't give him your address, but I said you might be in tonight. He said he'll call back later." And then I'd hear the door opening, and I'd turn around, and Sam would be there.

Or . . . He'd go back to Frodo's every night until I turned up again, and if I never went back, he'd still be there in the year 2050, sitting in the corner, while the grandchildren of Frodo's current clientele would nudge each other and ask, "Who's the old guy in the corner?" Then the robot barman would say, "he's been coming here for over fifty years, waiting for the woman he once let slip away." The kids would just shrug, turn away and forget about him, then ask the android DJ to play the latest Cliff Richard record.

Or . . . Some day I'd be dragging my four screaming kids through town, and I'd spot a familiar guy standing outside Eason's. He'd have that look in his eye that says he'd been waiting for someone, and he wasn't ever going to give up. My kids would spot him, and giggle at his unfashionable clothes. Brad, my eldest, would ask, "Who's that, Mammy?" Then Harrison, ever the joker, would say, "He was put under a spell by an evil witch." The twins, River and Keanu, would giggle even louder at this, but I'd tell them that Harrison was right. "And I know," I'd say, "because I *was* that witch."

Enough is enough! I said to myself. Get some sleep!

It didn't work. My clock radio showed that it was still Friday, just about. It occurred to me that I hadn't been to bed that early on a Friday in ages. In an ideal world I'd be going to bed that early, only not alone.

That made it worse . . . I checked the date, and counted backwards. I hadn't had sex in seven and a half months.

I wasn't sex mad by any means, but I was only human. A twenty-five-year-old woman cannot live on Val Kilmer movies alone.

I lost my virginity when I was twenty. It was a one-night-stand sort of thing. I met this guy at a party. I can't remember much about him now apart from the fact that he had a *great* body. He must have really worked out. I remember that we were both incredibly drunk, and that everyone else at the party was pairing off. Without a word, we went out into the back garden, stripped each other off in about half a second flat, and another half second later it was over, and we were lying naked on the grass, side by side, staring up at the stars.

After a few minutes, I noticed that his interest was starting to rise again. So we made love a bit more slowly, paying more attention to each other, and it was a lot better. I actually felt something that time.

Afterwards, we got up, got dressed, and he went home. I had to wait for Sharon to come out of the bathroom to give me a lift.

I'd had sex eleven times since, with three different men – thankfully, I even had a relationship with each of them. I didn't know if that made me promiscuous, or a slut, or whatever. And I didn't care. Sex is a natural thing and no one should be ashamed of it.

Nor should anyone be ashamed of *not* having sex . . . Seven and a half months wasn't the longest time I'd gone without, but it was long enough.

I did think about sex quite a lot, but I rarely talked about it, even with Sharon or Barbara. There's a Hollywood myth that whenever a bunch of women get together all they do is talk about men's bums. In my experience that's not true. When a bunch of women get together they talk about school. Wendy and Sharon are forever going on about which teacher had it in for them, which subjects they hated the most, who made the biggest mess in Domestic Science, who used to go out with who, and who didn't go out with who but fancied them like mad.

"Oh for God's sake," I muttered to myself. I turned over in bed, but I wasn't any more comfortable on that side. So I tried to sleep on my back, but that never works because I end up with my hands behind my head and they get all numb and useless. Once, a couple of years ago, I fell asleep like that, and I woke up the next morning to the blaring sound of the Strawberry Alarm Clock on FM104. My arms were completely dead, and I couldn't control them enough to get them to shut off the damn radio. My mother came in to see what all the fuss was about, and found me stark naked, standing over the clockradio with my arms flailing all over the place as I was trying to hit the "off" switch with my nose. That was *not* an easy one to explain.

I still couldn't sleep. I thumped my pillow to remove some of the imaginary lumps, but it didn't work. So I thumped it again. I ended up kneeling on the bed beating the shit out of my pillow. If there had been a gun in the house I'd have been arrested for pillowcide. I threw the pillow onto the floor and tried to sleep without it.

Then, as always happens when I can't sleep, I started imagining bits of my life as though they were movie trailers . . .

"She was a cheerful, good-natured girl," said the impossibly deep American voice-over expert. "All she wanted was a good night's sleep." A quick clip of me tearing the pillow apart. I'm played by a younger and taller version of Kathleen Turner.

Then a shot of the courtroom. The judge – played by Peter Cushion – slams his gavel down. "Susan Perry, you stand accused of the heinous crime of pillowcide. How do you plead?"

A close-up of my tear-stained faced. "Not quilty, your honour."

My lawyer, played by Mattress Dillon: "You honour, the evidence in this so-called 'pillow-case' is purely circumstantial."

I sat up suddenly in bed. "Jesus Christ," I muttered. "I have got to get some sleep!"

A video, I decided. Watch a film and fall asleep downstairs on the couch. I got out of bed and searched through my piles of movies. *Sleepless in Seattle*. Yeah, right. *The Long Kiss Goodnight*. Not a chance. *Coronation Street: the First Twenty-five Years*. That'll do.

I snuck quietly downstairs so as not to wake my parents, then discovered that they were still up and watching the rap videos on MTV.

"Oh for crying out loud!" I said. "What are you two still doing up?"

My father laughed. "Just another five minutes? Please?"

"Can't sleep, love?" my mother asked.

"No. My brain is driving me mad. I'm too hot. My pillow is a bastard."

Dad raised his left eyebrow at my mention of the B word. "You really are in a bad way. I haven't heard you say anything like that since you were about four." He winked at my mother. "Remember that?"

She grinned, and said to me. "We collected you from your first day at school, and you said, 'I learned a new word.' We asked you what it was, and you said, 'Bastard!'"

"Yeah, absolutely hilarious," I said. "If you want, I can let out a whole string of words that'll have you lying on the floor clutching your sides."

Dad sighed and shook his head. "Susan."

"What?"

"Sit down, and listen to me for a minute, OK?"

I sat. "Right. Fire away."

"I will. Listen carefully. There is nothing wrong with you."

It was my turn to sigh. "Look, Dad . . ."

"I mean it. All of these things you think are wrong, they're all in your head. And before you use *that* as an excuse, remember that everybody's a little bit paranoid. That's how we protect ourselves."

I nodded. There were four empty Heineken cans on the ground beside my Dad's chair. He always got philosophical when he was half-way drunk. "You're absolutely right, Dad." I had to agree with him quickly, before he really got going. He'd been known to talk for hours using the same sentence over and over.

When my Dad was drunk, he could spend the whole night describing something incredibly trivial which happened that morning. When he was at his worst, he started putting small ornaments on the coffee table. "This is you, OK? And this is him. And this magazine is the car. Well, no. Not *this* magazine." Then he'd turn to my mother. "Where's that magazine Fintan had yesterday? The car magazine. The one with the Porsche on the cover."

I'd find myself going, "yeah, Dad, I know. Yeah. You told me. Stop telling me." And at the same time he'd be saying, "No, you don't understand. Look. *This* is you, OK? The ducks are Fintan, but the little bell is you. Are you with me? Do you follow so far?"

And if my Mother was drunk as well, it was even worse. "That wasn't a Porsche on the cover of Fintan's magazine. It was a Ferrari. And it wasn't yesterday he had it, because he wasn't here all day yesterday. It was Wednesday, and I remember now because you said that you'd cut the grass but then you didn't because it was raining and you took the washing in. Which reminds me . . . Susan, do you want your white blouse washed for tomorrow? Because if you do, then you're out of luck because I don't have the time. I did wash your other white blouse, though. Not the one with the buttons. The one that you wore when you and Sharon went out the other night. Remember? She was wearing a T-shirt that I thought was too small for her . . ."

Eventually, they went to bed. I put in the video, turned off the light, curled up on the sofa and fell asleep thinking that when *Coronation Street* began all those years ago and Ken Barlow was younger he looked a hell of a lot like Mulder from *The X Files*.

Chapter Eleven

Saturday morning arrived. I watched some of the kids' shows, but they weren't as good as the shows that used to be on when I was a kid. I used to watch them in my dressing-gown and slippers, curled up on the sofa with a bowl of Frosties on my lap. OK, so at twenty-five I was still doing the same thing, but I wasn't enjoying it as much.

My parents had been up early, and had departed for to the caravan in Blackwater. They'd inherited the caravan from my Grandmother when she passed away a couple of years earlier, and pretty much every weekend they drove down. My Dad usually had business down in Wexford on Mondays anyway, so that saved him having to drive down in the rush hour traffic.

That left me in the house with nothing to do. Sharon worked most Saturday mornings, so I didn't want to bother her. And anyway, I wasn't in the mood for explaining that I'd completely screwed up my date with Sam.

The video shop opened at eleven, so I wandered down there, and dropped my letter off on the way. I didn't expect to get a response, but I figured that it couldn't hurt.

Mark was just sliding up the shutters when I arrived. "Morning, Miss Perry," he said. "How was your date, then?"

"How did *you* know about that?"

"Well, you didn't call here last night, and I told you last week that we'd be getting that Three Stooges tape in, so I just guessed."

"I forgot about the Stooges," I said. "And you're right, I did have a date. And it didn't go tremendously well."

He opened up the shop. "Come on in, and tell me about it."

Mark was about ten years older than me, but he wasn't like most middle-aged people I knew. He was very relaxed, for a start, and he wasn't the sort of person who wouldn't watch a movie just because there was someone in it he didn't like. My mother did that: she absolutely refused to watch anything with Sean Connery in it, because she'd read a few years before that he said that he wouldn't have any objection to hitting a woman "if she deserved it." I wasn't impressed when I heard this myself, but I still thought that Sean Connery was far and away one of the sexiest men who ever lived.

Mark was very well-built, and fit for someone his age. He cycled everywhere, and looked like he was a good few years younger. He was also about six-foot three, which was one of the reasons I liked him.

So Mark sat on his side of the counter, I leaned against the other side, and I told him more or less everything that happened. At the end, he just shrugged and said, "Well, I wouldn't worry too much about having lost him forever."

"This is the old 'plenty more fish in the sea' argument, isn't it?"

"No, this is the brand new 'let's have a look in the phone book and find the video shop where he works' argument."

I slapped my hand down on the counter. "That's a fucking great idea!"

He took out the Golden Pages from underneath the counter.

I said, "But . . ."

"You're worried that he might still be annoyed with you?"

"Yeah."

"Well, I'll phone the shop and tell them that I've had a customer looking for a particular movie, then I'll find out if your Sam is working there, and we'll just play it by ear. OK?"

"OK."

"So what's the name of his shop? And what's his surname?"

"I don't know the name of the shop," I said, "but I presume it's not Xtra-Vision or Chartbusters, because he would have said. His surname is O'Neill."

We were lucky: on the first call, Mark said, "Yeah, hi, this is Mark Shanahan in Home Videos in Cabra. Listen, a customer has asked me to track down a movie, and I've been ringing around to see if anyone has it. It's . . ." He took a quick glance at the pile of returned videos waiting to be reshelved. "It's a sort of cheapo sci-fi horror movie, called *Mutant on the Bounty*." He paused. "No, I'm not kidding. No, he doesn't know the director. He certainly doesn't know the label. Well, yeah, maybe he *was* having me on. No? Well, thanks anyway. What's your name, by the way?" He paused, then looked up at me and smiled. "Sam O'Neill. Right, thanks again, Sam."

Mark put down the phone. "There you go, Miss Perry. Who says we don't provide a service?"

I didn't know what to do. I had the address and phone number of the shop where Sam worked . . .

"Are you going to phone him?" Mark asked. "Or are you going to go to Dun Laoghaire and casually walk by the shop a hundred times until he spots you?"

"Or am I going to forget about it?"

"If you do that, you'll spend the rest of your life wondering about what might have happened. I say go for it. You have nothing to lose but your self-esteem."

"Of which there's not much left," I said. "OK. I'll do it."

"Excellent! And you'll let me know how you get on?"

I nodded. "Yeah. Thanks, Mark. I owe you one."

I went home, had a quick shower, and tried to get my thoughts in focus. It was Saturday, and by the time I got into town it would be after twelve. Then it could take up to another hour to get to Dun Laoghaire.

And what if he wasn't pleased to see me? What if he freaked out, or refused to talk to me? How was I going to feel then?

But if I didn't go, if I didn't at least try to sort things out, I'd feel worse. I began to think that if I hadn't said anything to Mark then I wouldn't have this to worry about. Things would be a lot simpler.

Decisions, decisions . . . I took a deep breath, and tried to clear my head. Go or stay? Take the chance or take it easy? Risk making an even bigger fool of myself or risk losing a potential boyfriend?

All right, Susan, I told myself. Do it. Take the chance.

Chapter Twelve

I made it to Dun Laoghaire without loss of life or limb. And I found myself across the street from Sam's shop, wondering what to do.

I couldn't see if he was there, because of all the posters and stickers in the window, but the shop was definitely open: people were coming and going all the time.

Which meant the shop was busy. I really didn't want to have to talk to him in front of the customers.

I thought about waiting. He was bound to come out for lunch at some stage. Yeah, I told myself, but if the shop opened at, say, eleven, he might not get lunch until about three or four. I looked at my watch. It was ten past one.

I crossed the road, pushed open the shop door, and went in.

There were about eight customers there, and Sam behind the counter, staring at me.

I walked up to the counter. "Hi."

"Hi."

I said the first thing that came to mind: "You left your hat behind last night."

"I don't have a hat."

I heaved a sigh of relief. "Oh, thank God! I thought I'd lost it!"

Sam suddenly laughed. "I didn't expect to see you here. I never expected to see you again."

"Yeah, well . . . Look, I'm sorry about last night. Sometimes I say the wrong thing."

"No, don't apologise. I'm sorry for the way I acted. I don't know what got into me. I was waiting at my bus stop when I realised I had no way to contact you. I ended up chasing after your bus."

My mouth dropped open. "There was a guy last night trying to get on the bus after it started moving! I forgot about that. Was that *you*?"

He shook his head. "No, that was just some old drunk. I saw him, and I thought the driver would slow down to let him on. I was going to jump into a taxi and say, 'follow that bus!' but there weren't any taxis around. Friday night in the city, and everything."

"So . . ." I said.

"So . . . Do you want to try again? Tonight?"

"Maybe," I said. "But I can't wait around Dun Laoghaire all day until you get off. What time is that, anyway?"

"Eight," he said. "Sorry."

I considered this. "I don't fancy going back home. I'd only have a couple of hours there before I had to come back."

"You could wait here, but the boss might come in. He'd freak. No, I know. There's a place up the road that lets out rented accommodation. You could check it out, see if there's anywhere you're interested in. At the very least, it'll give you an idea about prices and stuff."

"I just might do that," I said. "And I suppose I could look around the shops. What time do you get off for lunch?"

"Hah! The boss is supposed to come in at four and cover for me, but he's usually late."

"Well, are you allowed to eat behind the counter? Because I could bring lunch back."

"Great!"

We looked at each other. "Right," I said. "I'll be back."

"OK. See you then."

I nodded.

And then I remembered what had happened on Wednesday night in Frodo's, as we were saying our good-byes. We didn't have Sam's friend Dave to tell us what to do this time, so I took the initiative. I leaned forward and kissed him.

Chapter Thirteen

I checked out the rented accommodation place but there wasn't anything there that really suited me. I was sort of thinking of somewhere big and cheap, with good security and deaf neighbours. Still, I did learn a few things. I learned that anywhere big enough was either too expensive or too far away, often both, and anything that I could afford was the sort of place that squatters move out of.

There wasn't anything in the shops that I couldn't get in town – apart from little Dun Laoghaire souvenirs, and I wasn't too keen on buying sticks of rock – so I wandered down to the People's Park and sat on a bench watching the kids play.

We used to go there sometimes when I was a kid. In fact, on my mother's bedside table there was a photo of me and Fintan and Dad sitting on a blanket in the park, squinting into the camera. It wasn't a particularly good photo, but she liked it. Fintan was about a year old when it was taken, and he had the beginnings of the same surly expression he grew up with. Dad had lots of hair in the photo, and sideburns. This was the mid-seventies, after all. You couldn't see them clearly in the photo, but no doubt his jeans were flared as well.

In the corner of the photo you could see my mother's shadow. When I was about seven I used to be fascinated with that shadow. It was my mother when she wasn't more than a young woman, caught unexpectedly in a photo she was taking.

Sometimes I wondered what it would be like if I could go back in time to meet them when they were young, like in *Back to the Future*. What were they like? I barely know them now, and sometimes it's hard to imagine that they were young once. I mean, they were already married before Elvis Presley died. They heard the Beatles' songs when they were new. Their first television set had only three channels, and it was black and white – this was before the word "monochrome" was invented to boost the sales of black and white sets – and they'd never heard of a video recorder, a personal computer, a Sony Walkman, a microwave oven, or any of the other millions of things that my generation takes for granted.

And I'll bet they never expected my generation to think of them like that, like they were old.

At about a quarter to four I went into a newsagents and bought lunch. I had no idea what Sam liked, so I bought things that Fintan and Kevin and Danny liked: sandwiches and sweets. I also bought crisps, two apples, two bananas, two bottles of Snapple, and a couple of Cornettos for afters.

When Sam saw me carrying the stuff into the shop, he practically jumped up and down in delight. "This is great! Oh, hey, Cornettos! I haven't had one of them in years!"

So we stuffed ourselves. Sam put *Sommersby* on the video and we managed to watch most of that before his boss arrived. Sam quickly cleared away the debris of our lunch, and said, "Right, we'll be off, then."

His boss looked me up and down – mainly up – and nodded. "Back in an hour, OK?"

We went across the road to a busy café, ordered lukewarm coffee the colour of mud and flavoured with just the lightest hint of Fairy Liquid – well, we didn't order that, but that's what we got – and I started the apologies again.

"Forget it," Sam said. "You just, well, you said the things that I've been avoiding admitting to myself." He sipped at his coffee, grimaced, and took another sip anyway. "I'm not usually that moody. I don't know, maybe I was just too worked up over meeting you. Anyway, I was out of order. It's me who should be apologising."

"I'm relieved that you're not pissed off at me," I said. "I'd have felt an even worse fool after coming all the way out here."

"Well, *I'm* relieved that you made the effort. I didn't even know where to begin looking for you. I was thinking of ringing all the management consultant places in Ranelagh until I found you."

"You wouldn't have had much luck, then, because I work in Rathmines."

Sam laughed. "God, I'm useless! How is it I can remember the title, director and stars of every damn film I've ever seen, but I can't remember important stuff." He sighed, still grinning. "I'm glad you came looking for me."

"Me too."

He got up out of his chair and came around to sit on my side of the table. "I had a great time last night, until I buggered everything up."

"*You* didn't . . ." I started, but he silenced me with a kiss.

The evening dragged until Sam was relieved at eight. We got a bus straight into town, but there wasn't anywhere to eat that you didn't have to book last week for, and all the pubs were packed with sixteen-year-olds trying to look older. So we ended up just walking around, holding hands.

Occasionally, Sam asked me about some building or other – he seemed to be under the impression that I knew the city better than he did – so if I couldn't tell him, I just made it up . . .

"That's the famous memorial to the legendary architect-turned-movie-maker, Isombard Kingdom of the Spiders. He pioneered the use of pebble-dashing semi-detached caravans in the year eighteen seventy-two. Over there is the GPO, which – it is said – is haunted by the ghost of a rebel who was killed in the Easter Rising."

"Really?"

"No, but let's start telling people that, and see how

long it takes before the story gets back to us." We walked on. "Straight ahead, at the top of O'Connell Street, is the Ambassador Cinema. Legend has it that in nineteen eighty-three Susan Perry went to see *Return of the Jedi* in that very cinema."

Sam said, "Hey, I went to see *Return of the Jedi* there as well!"

"Oh really? Well prove it! What was I wearing?"

"You had on a Zorro mask and bright pink flip-flops. I remember it well. And Luke turned out to be Leia's brother."

"And the Ewoks were so *cute!*" I squealed.

"What, not those damned teddybears? God, I hated them."

And that was how the evening went, we just walked around, chatting about nonsense until it was time for the last bus. Sam walked me to the bus stop, and this time he waited. We kissed for a while – and it really felt good to have other people look on in envy for a change – until I realised that Sam could well miss *his* last bus.

"You'd better go," I said. "Will you phone me?"

He nodded. "What's your number?"

We exchanged numbers, and then, after a final kiss, he was gone.

When I got home, Fintan was in – for a change – sitting in front of the telly. He grunted a greeting. There was a tape in the video, and I could have sworn he'd just put down the remote control when I walked in. Pornography, no doubt, I said to myself. Probably something along the lines of *Hot Chicks Get Steamy*, or *Luscious Licky Lesbians*.

"What are you watching?" I asked.

He shrugged. "Some film."

I watched for a few seconds. "Ah. Donald Sutherland and Julie Christie. *Don't Look Now*, it's called."

"Yeah. It's crap."

"No it's not. It's a classic."

I dumped my coat and bag, made myself a cup of tea, scavenged some biscuits from the press, and returned to the sitting room. The tape was now out of the video and hidden away somewhere.

"You could have made tea for me," Fintan said.

"You've probably been sitting there all night. You could have made it yourself."

"I was watching this."

"Right," I said. "So, what did you do last night?"

"Went to the pub with Fintan and Sarah."

Fintan had two friends also called Fintan. There was Fintan Dunbar, who was about seven feet tall, had really long hair and a thick beard, and always looked angry – he reminded me of a caveman who'd been woken from hibernation a few months too early – but he was actually a really nice guy. Sort of like a Heavy Metal Buddhist. I'd never been able to understand why he hung around with my brother.

The other one was Fintan O'Shaughnessy, an annoying little twat who thought he was a real charmer. He was the one who was going out with Sarah. And believe me, they suited each other. The best way to describe them was "wind-swept and uninteresting."

"So, what do you think about the move?" I asked.

He shrugged again – well, when you're good at something . . . "I'm moving out anyway, so I don't care. I'm going to buy one of those flats in town, one of the ones on the quays."

Normally, I would have been rolling on the floor laughing at this grand scheme, but I was in a good mood and I didn't want to have an argument with him. I just said, "Those places can be pretty expensive."

"I know, but I have a mate who can arrange a mortgage for me."

Bad news, I said to myself. Fintan had lots of "mates" who could arrange things. Whatever you wanted, he claimed to know someone who could get it. Need anyone beaten up? Fintan knew someone who knew someone who was thrown out of the French Foreign Legion for being too tough. If your company van needed an expensive service to pass the DOE test . . . Not a problem. Fintan's friend Lar's cousin was a mechanic, he'd sort it for a hundred quid, no questions. Interested in salvaged gold from the Titanic? Piece of piss. My brother knew people who knew people who were well in with a team of divers . . .

"So how does your mate do that, then?" I asked.

There was nothing Fintan liked more than bragging about the wonderful people he knew, so he sat up and actually turned towards me. "You know how you have to be able to prove you have a regular income? And you have to have, whatever, ten per cent of the price already in the bank, right? My mate Richo knows people who can arrange that. You tell them the cost of the place, then they put ten per cent of that into your bank account, and for the next six months they put a regular amount in, like it's your wages. Then, when you get the place, you pay them back – plus their costs – and you're in the clear."

"Yeah, but you have to pay the ten per cent to whoever owns the apartment in the first place. Then the mortgage people pay the rest, and you pay them for the next thirty years."

But he had an answer for this: "I know that. So what you do is, if the place costs fifty grand, you get a mortgage for fifty-five – you tell them that it's for furniture, or a new bathroom – and that covers you."

"Fifty thousand isn't nearly enough, you know. You should be thinking about twice that at least . . . You're not really considering doing this, are you?"

He gave me his surly expression. Not his very best surly expression, just his everyday one. "What's wrong with it?"

"There's a special technical term for the people your mate knows," I said. "They're called loan sharks. They have several payment plans, many of them involving lengths of steel pipe and your knees."

He shrugged again. "Yeah, well I might ask Dad to lend me the ten per cent."

"And you know what he'll say."

"He might say yes."

"Oh yeah, he *might*. But then again, he might just laugh in your face. And now that I think about it, I can figure out which of the two is more likely."

Fintan was completely unfazed by this as well. He stared at the TV for a while, then said, "What are *you* going to do?"

"Get a flat. Rent one, I mean. Probably somewhere near work." Or maybe Dun Laoghaire, I added silently. "I've been talking to some of the guys in work about it. They have some pretty good advice. I'll probably just get somewhere small and cheap, and save up for my own place."

"You probably have a fortune saved anyway," Fintan said, with a large dollop of bitterness in his voice. "It won't take long."

I ignored that. "I was looking at a few places today, but they were all too dear or too disgusting. I'm going to go looking again tomorrow."

"Are you going to get a place to share, or on your own? Only, you could buy one of the apartments on the quays. If you got a two-bedroomed place, you could get the other person to pay rent."

This was similar to Danny's idea, but I didn't even want to consider it because I knew exactly what Fintan was getting at. "I don't want to do that, not yet, anyway." And I sure as hell don't want *you* as a lodger.

We didn't say much more for the rest of the movie, then I went to bed. That was the last real conversation I had with Fintan while I was living in that house.

Chapter Fourteen

Sunday . . .

Sam phoned at about one in the afternoon, but said that he was working the late shift in the video shop and wouldn't be able to meet me. We agreed to meet during the week. We talked for almost an hour, and – taking the plunge – I said that I missed him. He said that he missed me too.

Then I phoned Sharon, and I started to tell her about Friday night. After a few minutes, she stopped me, and said she'd call around, if Fintan wasn't there. He was, so we decided to go for a drive.

"Tell me *everything*!" Sharon demanded even before I'd closed the car door. "What happened? I assume he turned up, yeah? And where were you yesterday? I was trying to phone you for ages."

So I told her the whole thing, more or less. I made myself sound a little more callous when I was describing the bit about Sam going into a mood, so that she wouldn't get the wrong end of the stick and tell me to dump him.

It worked, because Sharon agreed in the end that I'd landed quite a catch. "You seem to be suited," she said. "Both of you are movie mad and you're both full of stupid jokes. I just hope I never get stuck in a lift with the two of you."

After a few minutes, she said, "Anyway, the reason I spent all bloody day yesterday trying to get hold of you . . ."

"You weren't just on a gossip hunt, then?"

"Never. No, you were saying about getting a flat, right? Well, I was talking to Jenny on Friday night, and you know she's getting married, right?"

I nodded. Jenny was Sharon's cousin, on the other side of the family from Laura. Jenny and Sharon were just about the same age, and were fairly close friends.

"Well, Jenny lives in a place in Ranelagh, a sort of big bedsit."

"I remember. You spent the night there that time when you couldn't get a taxi home from town."

"Yeah. And she's moving out next week, because they've just got the keys to the house. She phoned me to ask would I give her a hand moving."

"Aha! You reckon I could move in there, then?"

"Yeah. We could go and see her now, if you like. She said she'll be spending the whole weekend packing. If you're lucky, the landlady will be there as well. I've met her a couple of times. She's all right, but she's very selective about the tenants she takes. If you make a good impression, you could be in."

I thought about it for a few minutes. Yeah, I said to myself, why not? It can't hurt to check the place out.

Chapter Fifteen

So that was how I found myself somewhere to live. I moved the following Thursday night. I had to cancel a date with Sam, though, but it was the only night that Sharon had free. God, she must have had a tough week . . . First, she helped Jenny move her stuff out, then she had to help me move my stuff in. I swore that if I ever got myself a car I wouldn't tell anyone about it.

It was a mid-terrace house of the style I always called Georgian, though whether or not it actually *was* Georgian I didn't know. There were six flats in the building. Mary-Anne, the landlady, lived downstairs, which was handy because she was just about the only other sane person there. I don't know where Sharon got the idea that she was very particular about her tenants, because as far as I could tell the others were all complete nutters.

There were two flats on the first floor: Mine and Sandra and Brendan's. They were about my age, and they'd been living together for a couple of years. They were also the noisiest people I'd ever met, always fighting.

Upstairs, there were three more flats. I know that sounds as if the building was upside-down, but it was just because the flats got smaller as you went up. Andrea, Roger and Mrs Brannigan were the tenants upstairs.

Andrea was thirty and completely neurotic and absolutely useless. From the way she latched on to me I got the impression that she didn't have a friend in the world. Roger was a teacher, in his fifties. Mary-Anne told me that he'd left his wife for another woman, and then the other woman left him, so now he just sat in his room and drank, which is nice work if you can get it. Mrs Brannigan was older than the house, and that's saying something. She complained about everything, so we all avoided her as much as possible.

Anyway, all that was *after* I moved. Before that, there was most of a week of work to get through . . .

I got into the office fairly early on Monday morning, and Kevin was already there. He didn't mention my date – he wasn't the sort of person to remember something like that – so there was no way I was going to bring it up. Instead, he told me about his weekend, and the various mad bastards who were great crack that he went to parties with. He had a pretty full life, if you ignore the fact that he never had a girlfriend for more than a few weeks at a time.

Barbara, naturally, wanted to know everything. I

gave her the Reader's Digest condensed version, in which nothing bad happened on Friday night and my trip to Dun Laoghaire on Saturday wasn't born of desperation. She was happy for me, she said, and told me that I'd have to bring Sam along next time there was an office do.

At about eleven, I remembered that Darth Vicky had said she wouldn't be in and I was in charge. It made absolutely no difference to the way we worked, because none of us did anything anyway. Except for Danny, who was busy in a meeting with one of our clients. When he emerged from the meeting, he spent the rest of the morning typing up his notes and writing a Meeting Report. The boss loved those.

The only remarkable event of the morning was that Kevin went out to buy milk without having to be bribed. Barbara and I speculated that he might be sick, but we didn't inquire, as he'd no doubt have told us. Kevin was always ready and willing to discuss his eating habits and bowel movements in great detail. We did our best not to pay attention, but one time I'd mentioned that people like him who were obsessed with their excrement clearly had too much time on their hands, and next thing we knew he was going on about the Saint Patrick's Day milkshakes that they serve in McDonald's, and how your shit turned green if you had about five of them in one day.

Sam phoned after lunch, and Barbara immediately found work to do right beside my desk.

"How's it going?" Sam asked. "Busy?"

"Not really," I said as quietly as I could. "Are you in work?"

"Nah. I have to go in later, though. Listen, are you busy tomorrow night? A friend of mine has got me two tickets to the preview of the new Coen brothers movie. It's supposed to be great."

"Better than, say, *Fargo*?" I asked.

"Oh yeah. Better than *Raising Arizona*, I've heard."

"This I have to see," I said. "Where and what time?"

"Outside the Savoy at eight. The movie starts at nine, but we can get something to eat first. That OK?"

"Sure, thanks. Hey, you'll never guess what happened yesterday afternoon."

"Elvis played in Lansdowne Road?"

"Yep," I said. "He lost three-nil, though. No, since you can't guess, I'll tell you: I found a flat. My friend's cousin has a place in Ranelagh, and she's moving out sometime during the week. We called to see her yesterday, and I spoke to the landperson, and she said it's OK for me to take over the place. It saves her having to find someone. So, I'll be moving in when Jenny moves out. It's a pretty big place. It's really only one room, but it has its own bathroom and a little sort of kitchenette area."

"That's great! I'm telling you, you won't know yourself. For a start, you'll save a couple of hours a day travelling. If you want a hand moving your stuff, I might be able to persuade Dave to let me borrow the van. I won't be able to do that until Saturday morning, though." He paused. "No, wait, I'm probably working on Saturday again. It'll have to be Sunday."

"It's OK, Sharon said she wouldn't mind. I've already started packing my books and videos. Thanks anyway."

"Well, I'd better go. I have to get something to eat before I go to work. So, I'll see you tomorrow night, then?"

"Definitely," I said, and wondered if that made me sound like I was lovesick or something.

"OK then. Maybe I'll phone you tonight, if it's not too busy, OK?"

"Yeah. Or maybe I'll ring you. I'll only be packing tonight. It shouldn't take long."

It took us about five minutes to say goodbye and hang up. There was a lot of "see you" and "I had a great time on Saturday" and "I'm really looking forward to the movie" and things of that nature.

When I finally did hang up, Barbara smiled sweetly at me and asked, "Who was that, Susan?"

I sneered at her. "It was the vet. She said you'll have to be put down."

Barbara's grin grew wider. "Was it lover-boy, then? Did Sam the Stud phone to make sure you were staying in line?"

I wished she hadn't said that. From the other side of the partition, I heard Danny's frenzied typing suddenly stop. It took a few seconds for Barbara to realise what she'd done, and then she cringed and mouthed "Sorry!" For all the good that did.

Danny wasn't in the best of moods for the rest of the day. I mean, he'd known I was going out with someone, because he heard about it on Friday, but maybe he'd been trying to forget about it. He certainly wasn't happy at being reminded.

But there was nothing I could do about it. He'd never said or done anything that indicated to me that he was interested, and though I'd always been vaguely interested in him, there wasn't a chance that I'd do anything about it, not when I'd found someone with an actual personality. I'd only found out the previous week that Danny fancied me anyway, and I'd never have found out if Barbara hadn't told me. No, there was no way I was going to drop Sam for him.

It was strange, though, to suddenly go from a position of no boyfriend to this. I kind of liked the feeling. I was beginning to get an idea of what Barbara had to go through.

Chapter Seventeen

I met Sam on Tuesday night, and before the movie, when we were getting something to eat in Eddie Rocket's, I told him more about the flat. I have to say he was pretty surprised that I'd already found a place to live. "It usually takes *ages*," he said. "You'll end up paying for this in your next incarnation."

"Yeah? I must have been a monster in my last one, then."

"Don't tell me your life is so bad."

I leaned across the table. "Well, it could be worse. I mean, I'm pretty happy with the way things are starting to work out . . ." I said this in what I hoped was a seductive manner, and then for good measure I pursed my lips and blew him a gentle kiss.

"Don't *do* that! I don't want to be in an embarrassing position if I have to stand up in a hurry!"

I waggled my eyebrows Groucho Marx-style. "So, what position *are* you in?"

"I'm in the 'Please God make everyone else in this

place vanish suddenly' position. Combined with the 'I wonder just how much pressure the buttons on my jeans can take' position."

Well, we went to see the movie, cuddled a bit during the scary parts, and that was all. We had to run for our buses, but I promised to meet him later during the week.

As I said, I wasn't able to meet him on Thursday because that was the night of the big move, so I had to phone him on Thursday afternoon to cancel. He was a little disappointed, but he cheered up when I hinted that we'd meet up on Saturday night and I'd give him a tour of the flat.

On Thursday evening I was in my bedroom, packing the last of my clothes into a couple of boxes, when Fintan knocked on the door and peered in.

"So, you're really doing it, then?"

I nodded.

"OK." He stood looking at me for a few seconds, then turned away. "See you."

"Yeah, bye." I said; I couldn't think of anything else to say to him. I had the feeling that *he* was going to say something else . . . I wasn't expecting him to break down and cry and ask me not to go, or anything like that, but he did seem to have something on his mind. I didn't dwell on it, though, because I was too busy wondering what had happened to my good shoes.

Sharon arrived just before eight. It took us about half an hour to load up her car, and I was thanking God that Dad wasn't around, because he'd no doubt have spent ages working out a "system" to get the most amount of stuff into the least amount of space. I had a system of my own, naturally, which involved cramming everything I could into the boot and back seat, and leaving behind the stuff that wouldn't fit.

Fintan came out and offered his services just as Sharon and I had finished packing the last box. Sharon didn't look at him, and he didn't look at her, and the tension was almost unbelievable; you could have cut the air with a chainsaw.

I told Fintan that, no, we were fine, but thanks for offering. "If you like," I added, "you can bring the stuff that won't fit back upstairs."

"OK," Fintan said. "Well, I'll see you."

"Tell Mam and Dad that I said goodbye, will you?"

"Sure." He said goodbye again and wandered back into the house.

Sharon got into the driver's seat, and started up the car. "Ready?" she asked.

"Yeah." I picked up my remaining box of books, climbed into the passenger seat and rested the box on my lap. "Yeah, let's go."

Sharon put the car into gear and pulled away. I didn't bother looking back.

On Friday evening – it really was weird just walking home from work and getting in before half-five – I grabbed something to eat, had a quick shower, then got the bus home to see how my folks were getting on without me. I was a bit disappointed to discover that they hadn't really noticed the difference. I mean, it had been nearly a whole day.

My mother handed me an envelope and said, "This arrived for you this morning."

I didn't recognise the handwriting. It was absolutely impeccable. Even the stamp was positioned with remarkable accuracy. I almost had a panic attack when it suddenly occurred to me that it might be a love letter from Danny. Or worse, a suicide memo.

I ripped the envelope open, and it was only then that I recalled my response to the ad in the paper.

Dear Ms Perry,

May I call you Susan? Many thanks for your letter. It really was most awful and cruel of you to send it. However, as you are quite possibly only writing as a joke, I won't give you my real address and details just yet. Perhaps you could write to the Box number again, and – If I feel bothered – I'll write back.

Rot in Hell,

J.

Christ, I said to myself. This guy is either a psycho or he has a lot of time on his hands.

But there was something about it that I really liked. Maybe it was the handwriting, which was so neat it could almost have been done on a computer, or maybe it was that 'J' clearly wasn't looking for someone to tell him he was great all the time. I got the impression he wanted someone he could really communicate with.

My mother butted in on my thoughts. "Anthony called around for you last night. He was fairly annoyed that you hadn't told him you were moving."

"Shit. I never even thought of telling him. Did he say he'd be home tonight?"

"Don't ask me," she replied. "Call up and see if he's there."

I felt a bit – well, a lot – awkward about doing that. I hadn't told him about what had happened with Sam yet. And thinking about that, I realised I still hadn't got in touch with Mark in the video shop to thank him.

In the end, I phoned Mark, and promised him a more detailed explanation soon, and then I called around to Anthony. He was getting ready to go out, but he didn't seem *too* annoyed with me. He wanted to know all about Sam, though, so I gave him my new address and he said he'd call around some evening next week.

I spent the rest of the evening with my parents, and at about half-past ten I delighted in saying, "Well, I'd better be off home." Dad offered to drive me, but he'd had a few drinks – just enough to think he was still sober and anyway he'd always been a careful driver – so I caught the bus instead.

On the way, I read through J's letter again. I decided I liked him, and that I'd write back.

Chapter Seventeen

By some miracle, Sam's boss let him off work early on Saturday. I was sitting cross-legged on the bed in my dressing gown, watching the telly and picking my toenails at the same time, when he phoned.

The phone was right outside my door: I'd learned over the past couple of days that I had inherited the title of Custodian of the Phone, because no one else ever bothered to answer it.

Sam told me that he was off for the rest of the day, and that Dave had just called into the shop and was about to head into town. "Dave says he can drop me off in Ranelagh. That's if you don't mind an unexpected visitor."

I didn't know what to say. Sure, I was planning on showing him around the flat, but that was supposed to have been later on, when I'd psyched myself up enough, and tidied the place a bit. I wasn't even nearly ready.

Sam took my hesitation to mean that I didn't want him to come. "We could still meet in town," he said. "If you want."

"No, listen. You can come here. I was just surprised, that's all."

"OK. I'll be there in about half an hour."

I hung up and charged around the place like a maniac, trying to get the flat into some sort of order and get dressed at the same time. After a few minutes I began to slow down, and allowed myself a little think. OK, I informed myself, there's absolutely no food in the place. There isn't even any milk for tea. Not that there's any tea either.

The small table was piled high with books, CDs, videos and clothes, as were both of the chairs and the single armchair. That meant the only place to sit – apart from my old beanbag – was the bed. I found myself checking the bed to make sure the sheets were clean . . . No way. Not a chance. I wasn't going to let that happen, not yet. All right, Susan, just move the stuff from the table and chairs and dump them on the bed. That'll put a stop to any romantic ideas. And dress scruffily. Yeah, let him see me at my worst: dirty jeans, the thick baggy jumper with the holes in the elbows. No makeup. Hair all over the place. Yellow Marigold gloves smelling of Domestos. And for the guaranteed unsexy finishing touch, the old Garfield slippers.

But I decided that wouldn't work: Sam was a man, he'd find me sexy if *he* was in the mood, no matter what I looked like. So in the end I concentrated on clearing off the table and chairs, and making the place look as neat as possible.

That only left my appearance. I checked my watch,

and guessed I had about ten minutes to spare. I dressed casually: jeans – my good pair – my staggeringly expensive £11.99 blouse from the House of Dunnes, and ordinary, boring flat-heeled shoes. And then I sat down and waited.

And waited.

Men and women have vastly different concepts of time. Sam said "half an hour," which meant half an hour once he and Dave actually got into the van and started the journey. But first, they had to do those men things that mean they're always late. They had to talk about football, argue about whether Kim Bassinger was better looking than Meg Ryan, quote an entire Monty Python sketch to each other, call over to the local pub just in case there was a match on the telly, and so on.

Sam arrived about two hours after he'd phoned. Which was just about the time we'd planned to meet in town anyway. "Sorry I'm late," he said when I opened the front door. "Dave met someone he knew and we just couldn't get away."

I leaned closer and sniffed the air. "I can't smell drink off you. Have you been in the pub?"

He grinned. "Would you ever get off my back, woman. We only dropped in for none."

"OK," I said. "You're forgiven for making me wait for hours and hours and hours. I won't ever bring it up again for a while."

"Can I come in?"

"Only if you promise not to be good," I said, and instantly regretted it. I'd already hinted to him on Tuesday night that he might be getting more than a firm handshake and a peck on the cheek. I added, "Just kidding. Come on in."

Sam followed me into the flat. "This is the flat," I said. "Quick tour, wasn't it?"

He looked around. "High ceiling. It won't be too easy to heat this place in the winter. But other than that, it's not bad. Is that the bathroom? Can I have a go of your toilet?"

I gasped. "*You* go to the toilet! This has shattered all my illusions about your godhood."

"I knew you were going to take the piss out of me," he said. "So, can I?"

"Yeah, but make sure you leave the toilet seat up when you're finished."

He went into my little bathroomlet and closed the door. I called in, "By the way, there's absolutely nothing to eat here, so we can go out if you want. There's a pizza restaurant around the corner. Well, it's up the road and around a couple of corners. It's a good place. I went there a couple of times with the gang from work."

"Susan?"

"Yes?"

"I can't go if you're talking to me."

For some reason, I thought this was absolutely hilarious. I was still giggling when he came out, holding his hands up like a surgeon about to go into the OR. "You don't have a towel in there," he said.

"Oh yeah. Sorry, I dumped it in the laundry basket when I was tidying up." I rummaged around and found a fresh towel. "So do you want to go out for something to eat?"

"Sure. What do you want to do after?"

I shrugged. "We could watch a video." I pointed to the boxes of tapes. "Have a look and see if there's anything you're interested in."

From a getting-food point of view, *that* was a mistake. We spent hours going through the videos. Sam had seen almost all of them, and had opinions about them. He was also able to quote scenes from most of the better-known movies. And then he found my copy of *Patriot Games*, and started to do the most amazing impressions of Harrison Ford.

"If you're still hungry, we could just phone Dominos and order a pizza," I suggested. "If you don't mind staying in . . ."

Chapter Eighteen

So . . .

That was how it started. We ordered a couple of pizzas and two cokes. Sam didn't find any videos among my collection that he particularly wanted to watch, so he started to rummage through my record and CD collections. I discovered then that not only had we very similar tastes in movies, we had almost identical musical interests. I say *almost* identical: Sam admitted to having more than a passing interest in classical music, and he sure as hell didn't want to listen to my *Kids From Fame* or *Now That's What Sam Doesn't Call Music 17* records. Apart from that, though, we were both avid fans of David Bowie and Suede.

When the pizzas arrived, we ignored the table and chairs, and just sat cross-legged on the floor, talking and listening to Peter Gabriel-era Genesis. When it began to grow dark, I put on my bedside lamp. I really wished I'd bought some candles.

Occasionally, when you ignore the important

political heartfelt songs that make you feel guilty for enjoying them, Peter Gabriel can be damned romantic. Sam and I began to get really cosy, both of us propped up against the bean bag, arms around each other.

The only annoying thing was having to get up every twenty-five minutes or so to turn over the record . . . And then I stopped bothering, and just put the radio on and snuggled back down beside Sam. He was really, really warm. He'd taken off his shirt and was wearing a skin-tight white T-shirt. He wasn't exactly muscular, but he did have a nice body.

I noticed that he had a few chest hairs sticking out through his T-shirt, and I grabbed one and pulled it gently.

"Ow! That bloody hurts!"

"Sorry, I thought it was a cat hair, or something," I lied. "Here, let me smooth them out for you." I moved on top of him, sitting across his thighs, and began to rub his chest, paying particular attention to his pecs. He reacted in the way I expected: he shifted further down on the bean bag and put his hands on my hips.

I leaned forward, and began to massage his chest more vigorously. I pulled the band from my hair and let it hang free, cascading over his face and neck. Sam tilted his head up, and kissed me deeply.

The tiny part of my brain that was still thinking rationally reminded me that earlier I'd been absolutely positive that I wouldn't let anything like this happen. The rest of my brain told the rational part to shut up and let me get on with things.

I slid my left arm around his neck, and pulled him as close as I could, and let my right hand slide down his chest, across his stomach, heading for his belt buckle.

That was as far as I got. Sam started to tense up and jerk a bit, and tried to pull away from me. The first thing I thought of was that he was choking to death. Almost immediately after that thought came another: that he had much more self-control than I did. And then it occurred to me that perhaps he didn't have *any* self-control at all, and he'd just prematurely soiled his underwear.

I didn't expect him to be silently laughing his head off.

I began to giggle. "You're ticklish!" I reached out for his stomach again, and he rolled off the bean bag away from me, still laughing, but this time out loud.

"No, no! Don't!" he screeched, clutching his stomach and sides. "Get away! Get away!"

I made a lunge for him, and ended up face down in the bean bag. When I looked up Sam was sitting as far away from me as he could crawl, still giggling. There were tears running down his cheeks. "God, I'm sorry," he said. "I should have warned you!"

I made a few more half-hearted attempts to tickle him, and each time he barely managed to push me away.

I think it was then, watching him sitting against the wall, laughing his head off like a giddy six-year-old, that I first realised I loved him.

We didn't make love that night. Instead, we just talked, and laughed, and I had just about the best time I'd ever had with someone.

At about one in the morning we got incredibly hungry, so we went out to the twenty-four hour Spar in Ranelagh, and spent a small fortune on chocolate, ice cream, biscuits, crisps, Coke and other junk. On the way back to the flat we each carried a bag, so that we could hold hands.

When we got in, Sam started rooting through my press looking for spoons for the ice cream. He found a very mangled knife that I'd used as a makeshift screwdriver when changing the fuse in my hairdryer. "What's this?" He asked, holding the knife up. "Have you been seeing Uri Geller behind my back?"

"I use that for cutting potatoes when I want to make crinkly chips," I said.

"I thought you might have bent it with the power of your mind." He put the knife away and came back with the spoons.

"Do you believe in that stuff?"

"The paranormal. The supernatural. The occult. Ghosts, goblins and psychic powers. UFOs, Atlantis, the Bermuda Triangle, moving statues, God, aliens, astrology, reincarnation and aromatherapy . . . Nope. I'm a complete skeptic."

"And you're an atheist?" I asked.

He nodded. "Swear to God. Yeah. I hope that doesn't bother you."

"Not really. Everyone has to find their own path," I said. "But everyone has to have *something* to believe in."

"Not me. I think that when we die, it's all over. I think that science has explained everything that people consider to be supernatural, or if not then it's just because we don't have all the information."

"So you've never had a paranormal experience? You've never been thinking that you haven't seen someone in ages, and next thing you know they arrive at the door?"

Sam shrugged. "I once knew a girl who could knock over cups of tea using only her feet. I swear to God, I'm not making it up. She'd put a cup on the floor, and within seconds she'd forget about it and manage to kick it over. What about you? What do you believe in?"

"Well, I'm not totally convinced about aliens and ghosts and things, but there has to be more to this life than we know. I mean, my dad says that when he was growing up people had heard about acupuncture and everyone thought that it was just a stupid Oriental superstition. But now it's a recognised medical practice."

"So?"

"So people once thought that the idea of a round earth was heresy. And they once thought that this planet was the centre of the universe. But that was just because they didn't know any better."

Sam smiled. "But that's *my* argument. Anything that was once thought to be supernatural, and has since been proved, has a rational, scientific basis. The end."

I latched on to this immediately. "Aha! So you're saying that if something can be explained by scientific methods, then it's no longer supernatural!"

"Yeah. Because the word 'supernatural' implies that

it's beyond the natural. But as time goes on, the definition of 'natural' automatically changes to include the things we know to be true."

"This sounds like one of those arguments that could go on for hours."

Sam checked his watch. "I should be going. I've got to be in work at twelve. It's way too late for the last bus now . . . Is there a taxi rank in Ranelagh?"

"There is. But you can stay, if you promise that you won't try anything." That wasn't what I wanted, of course. What I wanted was good, old-fashioned, rampant, ripping our clothes off and roaring at the top of our voices sex. But, what I didn't want was a relationship that was based purely on sex, as some of my other relationships had been. That sort of thing only leads to problems when one half of the couple stops fancying the other and discovers that they have nothing in common other than the fact that their naughty bits fit together rather nicely. No, I wanted us to be in love first. Sex could come later. "So, what do you think?"

"OK. Thanks. I promise to behave. What are the arrangements? Me on the floor?"

"You wouldn't be comfortable. If you keep your undies on, and you don't mind me wearing my pyjamas, we can share the bed."

"You sure do drive a hard bargain, Miss Perry."

I didn't get much sleep, but that was because it was only a single bed and every time Sam moved I woke up. He was true to his word, though: he didn't try anything. In fact, he just curled up to me, and was asleep in minutes.

I woke him at ten, and ordered him into the shower while I went out to get something for breakfast. When I got back, he was washed, dressed, and had actually cleaned up the stuff from the night before.

After breakfast, I walked with him to the bus stop. We told each other what a great time we'd had the night before, kissed good-bye as the bus pulled up, and I headed back to the flat with absolutely no idea what I was going to do for the rest of the day.

As I was unpacking a few of the boxes, I found the letter from J. I decided I might as well write back.

Dear J.

No, you may not call me Susan. That's a name I reserve only for my friends, one of whom you most certainly are not. Your letter – which I read when I found myself with nothing else to read – was dull and unimaginative. Your handwriting is so pathetic it's absolutely hilarious; didn't you ever learn how to write? Perhaps you should invest in a typewriter, if you're not too mean. Do not write to me again.

Definitely not yours,

Ms Perry.

PS Just in case you do decide to write to me again, and I sincerely hope that you will not, you should take note that my address has changed. I have left home, for fear of your letters contaminating my family. I felt that it was my duty to move, as I was the one who brought the plague of 'J' upon them.

Writing the letter killed a few minutes, but I still had no idea what else I was going to do for the day. I turned on the telly, but the only things on were Grand Prix racing

– oh joy, seventy-five identical laps on *three* channels – a programme about farming in Scotland, a very old period drama, and omnibus editions of the week's soap operas, most of which I'd already seen.

I tried to remember what I used to do at home on Sundays, but that didn't help. When I was at home, I was always so glad to have the place to myself that even ironing seemed like a rare pleasure.

I glanced over at the laundry basket. I suppose I could do the washing, I told myself. There wasn't a washing machine in the house, but I was vaguely aware that there were a couple of laundromats – or whatever they're called – in Ranelagh. That might waste another couple of hours. But when I started to go through the piles of clothes and sort them into colours and whites, I decided it was too much effort, so I gave up.

Sunday dragged. It got so bad at one stage that I even considered going in to work. But then I snapped out of it and told myself not to be so stupid.

It was a very long day, and more than anything else I wanted to be with Sam.

Chapter Nineteen

Monday crawled around, and things weren't too bad in work, because old Vicky-Vaporub was off on her honeymoon. I had to be careful not to mention that in front of the others, though, because they didn't know.

Anyway, I had been left in charge. There wasn't much to do: a couple of training sessions, a few reports to write up, and one or two preliminary meetings with potential clients. Nothing we couldn't handle.

When Barbara came to me on Monday afternoon and asked if it would be OK if she took the rest of the day off, my first impulse was to turn her down, because I didn't want to be seen by the others to be an easy touch. But then I decided that there wasn't anything for her to do, so she might as well. "Go ahead," I said. "But just this once, OK? You'll find I'm quite the tyrant if you cross me." I tried to say this as though I was only messing around, but I knew what she could be like, and I really didn't want her to think she could take advantage of me.

So Barbara went on her merry way, leaving the three

of us to cope with whatever situations might arise. None did, though, and the day ended quite peacefully.

Danny still wasn't really talking to me. He answered me whenever I spoke to him, but he wasn't voluntarily making conversation. I kept telling myself that, hey, it's not my fault, but that really didn't make me feel any better.

I considered the idea of taking him aside, and – in my new and unfortunately temporary capacity as his boss – ask him what was bothering him. But I knew that wouldn't work. He'd end up even more depressed and I'd feel bloody stupid about it. Maybe that was why Vicky never really joined in with any of the conversations. It was hard to manage a group of people and be friends with them at the same time.

Anyway, Sam phoned just as I was about to lock up the office. Everyone else had already gone, so I sat there on my own, chatting to him while I played Solitaire on the computer, for a good hour. Every now and then he had to put me on hold while he dealt with a customer, and when he came back to the phone he acted as if I'd been gone for years.

Eventually, we arranged to meet on Wednesday night, and said good-bye. I played with the computer for another half an hour, not really paying attention to it. I was thinking about Sam. I liked him a lot, in fact, I liked him more than anyone else I'd ever met. We were definitely suited to each other, there was no doubt about that, and what's more we also found each other attractive.

I had a feeling that my friends would approve of

him, and as soon as I thought that, I realised that it was getting close to the time for at least some of them to meet him. Though whether or not Anthony would like him, I wasn't sure. Though he was a few years younger than me, Anthony sort of thought of himself as my older brother – maybe that was one of the reasons he and Fintan didn't get on.

I decided to phone Anthony and invite him round to the flat. After all, I had nothing else to do that night. And he could be good fun, if he wasn't in one of those "I'll never get a girlfriend and everybody hates me" moods that he tended to slip into from time to time.

His mother answered the phone on the second ring.

"Hi, Mrs Harrington. It's Susan. Is Anthony there?"

"Hold on a minute, love. I'll get him. How are you? Anthony was telling me you moved into a flat."

"Yeah, I moved in last week."

"It must be a big change for you, having to cook and clean and everything like that."

"Oh, it's not too bad," I said, though the truth was I'd yet to do any of that. "I'm more or less used to it at home, anyway."

"And how *is* everyone at home? I haven't seen them in ages. No, I tell a lie. I saw Fintan the other day coming back from the shops. He's got very quiet these days, hasn't he? He hardly said hello to me."

"He's just moody, Mrs Harrington."

Next, she wanted to know about the weather over the weekend in Ranelagh, and then I had to tell her all about the flat, then about work. What I really wanted to do was cut across her and say, "Listen, just get Anthony for me, for crying out loud!" but I was too much of a coward to do that, so I had to suffer. Eventually, after what seemed like hours, she remembered why I'd called, and toddled off to find her son for me.

"How's it going?" he asked. "Only I can't stay long, I'm just off out."

"Well, don't ask me about my job, the flat, the weather or the price of bread in Spar, because I've just had your mother filling out a detailed report."

Normally, Anthony would have gone along with this, and filled me in on some of the daft things his mother had done lately. She's dead nice, but occasionally she's a bit scatterbrained.

But, this time Anthony was clearly not in the mood for someone making jokes – however good-natured – about his mother. "So you phoned me just to tell me stupid things, yeah?"

"Well, no. I phoned to see if you wanted to call around tonight and see the flat. But if you're going out, it's not a problem."

"Yeah. Sorry. I'll phone you in a few days, OK?"

"OK," I said, wondering exactly what it was I'd done to upset him. All right, I knew that I hadn't told him about the move, but there wasn't any time. It had all happened fairly quickly. And besides, it's not as if I had to tell him *everything*.

So that was it. I went back to the flat and plonked myself in front of the telly and had a good sulk.

At about eight, there was a knock on my door. It was

old Mrs Brannigan from upstairs. "Hello, Susan, I was just wondering how you were settling in," she said, her head darting back and forth as she tried to look past me and see what sort of a mess I'd made of the flat.

"I'm fine, thank you. I'm still sort of unpacking, though . . ."

Somehow, with all the manoeuvring skill of Mikhail Baryshnikov covered in butter – now *there's* a thought – she managed to squeeze in past me. "Mary-Anne tells me that the girl who lived here before was your cousin."

"My friend's cousin," I said. "I don't really know her."

She sniffed. "Cold girl. Not very friendly. And a bit loud at times. Never went to Mass." She picked up a book and peered short-sightedly at the cover. By sheer luck it happened to be a romance novel, and not *The Antipope* by Robert Rankin, which was right next to it. "You have a lot of books, dear."

"I do read a lot," I said, for want of anything better to say, like "Sod off out of my flat, you nosey old bitch."

She continued to poke around. "And music. And films."

I knew that I wasn't going to get rid of her easily. "Would you like a cup of tea, or something? I was just about to make a pot," I lied.

Mrs Brannigan carefully lowered her ancient frame into the good chair. "Oh, that'd be lovely, dear. You're very kind. So few young people are, these days."

That was when I discovered that I didn't have a teapot. So I had to make the tea in the teabag-in-cup method so beloved of people in flats.

While I made the tea, she wittered on about how things used to be in her day: nineteen shillings and thruppence ha'penny for eight hundredweight of coddle that would feed her family for a month, going to school over the hills to avoid the Black and Tans, being sent out to work in a bakery for thirteen hours a day when she was nine, that sort of thing. All done without shoes.

I made and served the tea without a word: there was no real need for me to do anything but nod occasionally, or shake my head and go "dear oh dear" when it seemed necessary.

I was thinking about Sam, and all the things we'd hopefully soon be getting up to in my bed, when I realised that she was waiting for me to answer. What had she been asking me? Oh yeah, what I did for a living.

"I'm . . ." I couldn't think how to describe my job, so I said, "I'm the office manager in a place in Rathmines."

My participation wasn't really necessary, I discovered. "That sounds nice. When I was young, women weren't allowed to be managers. Even in places like Woolworths – they're all gone now, I'm sorry to say – all the managers had to be men. And when you got married, you were expected to give up your job and live off your husband's wages. And in those days . . ."

Why is it, I wondered, that I can barely remember last year, but old people can remember their entire lives as clearly as if they've been memorising their diaries? Maybe they have been, I answered myself. After all, what else had they got to do?

Next, it was recipes and cooking tips for Christmas Pudding. "I still make a pud every year, even though there's no one but me to eat it. Still, that's the good thing about a pudding, they last. We didn't have Tupperware when I was a girl. We didn't even have a fridge. We used to have a pantry, and we'd wrap everything in newspaper to stop it from going off." She suddenly laughed. "And these days people talk about recycling as though it was just invented! After the war, *everything* was recycled! You couldn't afford to throw anything out. My brother was in charge of collecting paper and string on our street."

I found it very hard not to snigger at that, it sounded so stupid. But then, *my* brother couldn't collect his thoughts. "Paper and string?" I asked, sadly aware that I was prolonging the torture.

"Oh yes. There used to be a rag and bone man who came around on Tuesdays. Lovely man. Strange eyes, mind. And he'd pay a penny for a big bag of string. A penny was a lot of money in those days."

I suddenly got this bizarre image of a filthy young boy racing barefoot along a cobbled street after the rag and bone man, clutching two plastic Centra bags filled with tiny scraps of string and old newspaper.

Luckily, I was saved from another trip down memory lane – in those days, of course, it was a thriving community known as Memory Avenue, and a trip down there cost a farthing, but it was a ha'penny if you wanted to sit next to the driver – by the noisy arrival of Sandra and Brendan, who lived in the flat next to mine. As usual, they were arguing.

I glanced at my watch. "They're home early," I said. "The pubs don't close for another hour yet."

Mrs Brannigan nodded. "Very nice couple," she said, then leaned forward and whispered. "I'll tell you something, if you don't let on . . . They're married. They eloped just before they moved here. Her parents don't approve of him."

I grinned. "Married?" Is that what they told you?

"Oh yes. Nice couple. They're a bit on the noisy side, but that's because they don't have any money. But when you're young and in love, you don't need money. Young Sandra told me that her parents hardly speak to her any more because they think she's living in sin. And she can't tell them that she's married, because then they'd cut her off altogether."

"I see." Obviously, Sandra and Brendan knew what sort of nosey old biddy Mrs Brannigan was, and they didn't want *her* to know they were living in sin. They should have just told her to mind her own business.

At last, she put her untouched tea down and forced herself to her feet. "Well, I'd better be off. It was lovely to have this chat with you, Susan. We'll have to do this again. So few young people are willing to talk to the likes of me."

"Not at all, I've enjoyed it," I lied. Then I found myself saying, "Call down any time you feel like it." The rational part of my brain jumped in five seconds too late and told me to shut the hell up. I meekly informed the rational part of my brain what had just transpired, and it said, "Well, bugger that, then."

As Mrs Brannigan got to the door, she had one last thing to add. "If you ever find yourself a nice young man like Brendan, take my advice. Don't get married. Live with him for a couple of years."

That caught me out. "What?"

She smiled and patted my arm. "Don't be too shocked, dear. I know that living in sin is, well, a sin, but it's a worse sin to marry someone and then leave them. Best to get to know them first, eh?" And with that, she opened the door and left.

"That is one weird old lady," I said to myself. My "flabber" had been well and truly "gasted".

I found it a lot easier to adjust to the changes in my life than I'd ever imagined I would: I mean, within a couple of weeks I had a new home and a steady boyfriend. And on top of that, new responsibilities – albeit temporary – in work.

And I'd made a new friend, strange though he was. The mysterious 'J' wrote back . . .

Dear Susan,

I must admit, so far you are the only person to reply to my ad in the Herald with any seriousness. You are clearly a sad and lonely person, and deservedly so. I would guess that you are extremely overweight and rather ugly, probably a virgin and likely to remain so (unless of course you have the luck to meet a blind drunkard). I read your letter whilst wearing a pair of rubber gloves, in case your diseases can be transmitted by mail.

I can recommend a good course in psychology if you really

feel the urge to help yourself, though perhaps the world would be better off without you.

Please die, J.

PS If you do write again (and I'd rather you didn't), then sprinkle the letter with perfume, or – better still – with a strong disinfectant, to mask the smell.

This was a challenge I could not resist. It took me a couple of days to compose a letter of sufficient nastiness to send to him, but that wasn't enough. I decided I needed to make a serious statement. Then on Thursday afternoon I spotted something in the pound shop down the road from the office . . .

Work was fairly busy, but not so busy that I couldn't sneak into the boss's office and spend a few minutes wrapping my gift to J and writing the accompanying note:

Dear J.

I resent your accusations about my figure. I am not overweight, nor do I have acne or any other skin diseases. Only a sicko would suggest such a thing.

And how dare you suggest that I'm a sad and lonely person! You're the one putting the ads in the paper. Only a complete scumbag would even think of such a thing. You are clearly an experienced shit-eater.

And you still haven't invested in a typewriter, as I suggested in my last letter. What's the matter with you? Are you really that stupid?

I am sending you this fluffy toy cat, which cost a lot more money than you are worth. As soon as I saw it in the shop window I thought of you. You know where you can stick it.

Susan.

It wasn't an expensive cat – it only cost a pound, which was not entirely surprising as I bought it in a pound shop – but it was the thought that counted. I wrapped the cat and the note in some very old bubble-wrap that had all the bubbles burst, stuffed them in an envelope, and stuck it in my bag to bring home. When Sam arrived at the flat at about seven, he naturally wanted to know what it was.

"It's a toy, for a friend," I said.

"Anyone I know?" He turned the package over and examined the address. "Who's 'J'? And why a box number?"

"Oh no!" I gasped. "You've stumbled on to my secret life! Yes, I'm one of those girls who sends her used and unwashed panties to complete strangers! Will you ever forgive me?"

"I will if you give *me* a pair of your panties," he said with a particularly lecherous twinkle in his eyes.

"Why don't I just buy you a pair? That way you could have some in your own size."

He grinned, and put the package down. "So, what is it, really?"

"OK. I saw this personal ad in the paper the other week. This guy wanted someone to write to that he could fall in hate with. So I wrote to him, and he wrote back a very nasty letter. So I wrote one back to him, and so on. That's a toy cat that I'm sending him."

Sam raised an eyebrow in disbelief. "I preferred the story about the panties."

"Hmm . . . Now that I think about it, so do I."

"You know," he said thoughtfully, "We've been going out for – what? – eight hundred years now, and I still haven't seen your panties."

Uh oh, I said to myself, I know what he's getting at. It wasn't going to be easy to change the subject this time, but I gave it my best shot. "Yeah? So? I haven't really seen *your* undies. You jumped in bed too quick the other night. What do you normally wear, anyway? Boxers or Y-fronts?"

"Neither, now that you ask."

"What do you mean, neither? Don't tell me you're naked underneath your clothes."

"Naked? God, no," Sam said. "I have the entire lyrics of Wet Wet Wet's first album tattooed on my back. How could I ever be naked with that? No, actually, I wear jockey shorts. Y-fronts are too, well, unsexy, and boxer shorts are as uncomfortable as hell. The only reason any man wears boxer shorts is because women tell them that they're sexy." He sighed. "I don't know, the things we do for you."

"Oh really? What about low-cut dresses, high heels, short skirts and tons of make-up? You think that they're comfortable? Sure, women wear stuff like that because it's so much easier than throwing on a pair of jeans and a T-shirt."

"Point taken," Sam said. "I apologise on behalf of my gender . . . No, wait. I take that apology back. All those things you lot wear is the price you pay to have boxes lifted and jars opened for you. That's only fair."

I tutted and shook my head. "It sounds to me like you're just trying to get me into an argument."

"Hah! It's just like a woman to think that."

I held up my hand. "Wait, wait, before we go off on this particular tangent, are you hungry? I'm starving, and I thought we might eat out tonight."

Sam nodded. "Sure. Whereabouts?"

So we booked a table at a little restaurant in Donnybrook – it would be handy enough for Sam to get the bus home from there – then went for a quick drink first. I'd been pleased with myself at having managed to divert the topic of conversation from my panties, but it didn't help much. Pretty much everything Sam said while we were in the pub was angled towards the subject of sex, and why we weren't having it. I was able to deflect most of this, but when we were in the restaurant, just after the food arrived, Sam completely changed tack and caught me out:

"So, the thing is, and I don't want to sound like I'm forcing the issue, but we've been going out for few weeks, and we're both adults . . ."

I stopped with my fork half-way to my mouth. "Yes?"

"And I was wondering where we are going with this relationship, exactly."

I put my fork down, and stared at him. "Meaning?"

"Are we likely, sometime in the foreseeable future, to actually have sex at some point?" He looked away from me, and continued eating.

All right, I said to myself, time to face the subject. I did – definitely – want to sleep with him, but my previous experiences had shown me that relationships change quite drastically once sex is brought into the equation. "Sam, I don't know what to say to that. I mean, yes, I do fancy you, and – eventually – I'm sure we'll get to that stage. But not yet. We barely know each other."

"But you told me before that you've already had boyfriends who you were sexually active with. And I'm guessing that the first night in your flat we'd have done it if I hadn't been ticklish and broke the mood. I'm just wondering if it's me."

"It *is* you, that's the point. I want you for who you are, not for your sexual prowess. Look, with my previous boyfriends it was sex first, 'what's your name again?' later. And I don't want that this time. Each of them got what they wanted from my body and decided they didn't want to know my mind. I'm not going to let that happen again. I swore that I was going to take control of my life, and I mean it. I don't ever want to be used. Each of those bastards has probably had a dozen other women since me. The next time I have sex with someone it'll be something that strengthens the relationship, not something that defines it."

Sam looked at me, and simply nodded.

"Do you see what I'm getting at?" I asked.

"Yes."

"Well?"

"I love you too."

Chapter Twenty

There it was, the 'L' word, out in the open, charging around us like a frisky dog let off his leash in the park.

For the first second, I was thrilled. Yes, I loved him. I'd known from our first night in the flat that I could love him, and now here he was admitting that he loved me too. And then I was actually annoyed at him, for presuming that I loved him when I'd never said anything directly to that effect. After that, I was annoyed at myself for being so transparent. That feeling was followed quickly by one of embarrassment: what if he hadn't loved me, but had still been able to see past my oh-so-clever charades and word-games? Then, for another few seconds, I was annoyed at *him* again, because I thought that he was just saying that because he knew I wanted to hear it.

Then I told myself to get a grip and stop trying to analyse everything. And then I was thrilled again, because – despite all my other feelings on the subject – Sam loved me and I loved him and we both knew it.

There's a certain golden feeling you get when you're in love, a gentle glow that sort of blocks out all the bad things for a while . . . It's not that common a feeling, but when it hits you, you know all about it. And I had it then.

Sam watched me in silence for a while, then said, "You know, you've been awfully quiet since I told you the name of my favourite rock group."

"You can be an absolute bastard, you know that, Sam?"

He looked suddenly serious. "Well, like you, when I can't think of something to say I just try to make a joke of things." He reached across the table and took my hand. "I meant it, though. I never thought I'd hear myself say this to anyone, but I love you. And – before you tell me that I can't love you because we haven't known each other long enough – believe me, I can, and I do. I mean, look at us. We're perfect for each other. We have the same sense of humour, the same tastes in music and films, we're attracted to each other – at least, I hope we are – and we're the same age, more or less. How much more perfect can it get?"

I still didn't know what to say, but I sure as hell did my best to resist making any jokes.

"Or am I wrong?" Sam asked. "Have I just made a complete fool of myself? Did I completely misinterpret the signs?"

"No," I said. "No, you didn't."

"So . . ."

"I do love you," I said. "I can't think of anyone else I'd rather spend the rest of my life with. But weird as this might sound, I want to know you as a friend first, before we become lovers."

"Hey, no, wait. I'm on a completely different subject here. I'm not still talking about sex. I'm talking about commitment." He paused. "Actually, that sounds an awful lot like I'm about to propose, or something. Believe me, I'm not. But I think that one day, maybe I will. If you see what I mean."

Our waiter took this exact moment to suddenly appear and ask if our food was all right. It's a well-known fact that waiters carry around a little device that beeps when the diners have their mouths full or are talking about something important.

"Everything's fine, thanks," Sam said.

The waiter looked a little miffed that we weren't about to complain, and stalked away.

"Let's finish up and get out of here," I suggested. "We'll go for a nice long walk and talk about things."

We ate as quickly as we could, drank our drinks, paid and left.

Once we were out in the cold night air, things seemed a little different. I didn't know how to bring up the subject, and Sam wasn't talking either. After a few minutes of this awkwardness, I decided to bring up a different subject, just to break the ice.

"Sam, tell me something. What do you want from life? I mean, what do you want to do with yourself?"

"Get a great job, make a fortune, retire when I'm thirty, get married, have kids and live happily ever after. What about you?"

"Never mind about me for now. Seriously, OK, if you found out that you had only twenty-four hours to live, what would you do? Assuming that you could do anything you want. Money and reality are not an obstacle."

"OK. I'd do all those things I've never been able to do. I'd drive a train. Wanted to do that since I was a kid. And I'd go bungee jumping, and hang-gliding, and skydiving. And I'd drive a formula one car around Silverstone. I'd go and see the pyramids, and Alaska. Always wanted to go there. I'd star in an action movie. I'd make love to what's-her-name from Ally McBeal. I'd play centre forward for Crystal Palace at the FA Cup final – well, you did say that reality was not a problem. Oh yeah, and I'd play lead guitar for Pink Floyd. How's that?"

"That's a pretty full day," I said. "Pick *one*."

"Centre forward for Crystal Palace at the FA Cup final. No doubt about it. Why?"

"Just curious," I said. "It's one of those things I think about."

"What would *you* do?"

"I don't know."

"Hah!" Sam said. "*You* don't know what you'd do, but I'm supposed to? I thought you said it's one of those things you think about?"

"It is, but I never reach any real conclusions. One day it'll be one thing, next day it'll be another."

"Well, give me a few examples."

I shrugged. "You know, the usual stuff that people

think about. Rescuing puppies. Climbing Mount Everest wearing nothing but a kilt and flip-flops. Beating the living shit out of some smug ultra-thin supermodel. Going to Japan. Astonishing everyone in the universe by suddenly discovering that I can understand all languages including Irish. All that sort of thing."

He laughed. "You think that's the usual stuff people think about? Jesus, I'd hate to be a psychologist trying to find my way around *your* mind! I'd need more than a map and a compass: I'd need a team of bloodhounds with X-ray vision and a time machine. But what's your point?" Sam asked. "I mean, why did you bring it up?"

"You can tell a lot about someone from their answers," I said. "Though it helps to know the person to begin with."

"So what can you tell about me, then?"

"Not much," I lied. "I don't really know you well enough to interpret your answers." I was feeling incredibly morose all of a sudden – one of my patented mood swings – and I really just wanted to go home.

Maybe it's that little paranoid person inside me that says things like, "You look fat in those jeans" and "She's not really your friend: she's using you so that she'll look better in comparison." This little paranoid person generally appears at important times and manages to spoil the mood . . . I've got a reincarnated waitress living in my head, and she's taking ego-shattering lessons from my mother.

This time, Little Miss Paranoid was telling me that if Sam loved me then there must be something wrong with him. I had the sudden recollection of the American superhero comics that Fintan used to buy a few years ago. I used to read them when there was no one in the house. Anyway, it's one of those superhero rules that if the hero ever falls in love with a woman, and she finds out his secret identity, she has to die by the end of the story. Generally, she's killed when the supervillain of the piece blows up a building in an attempt to kill the hero, and the girl – who's usually an investigative reporter – is "covering the case" and just happens to be in the wrong place at the wrong time. This gives our hero the opportunity to go all angst-ridden and self-blamey for a few issues. Either that, or the girl gets trapped under a piece of fallen masonry, and the hero has to let the villain escape while he saves her. This leads her to realise that being the lover of a superhero is not all it's cracked up to be – despite the tights, the muscles and the stretching powers – and she goes off to live in a monastery.

I had that "this can't last" feeling. This was accompanied by a thought which went along these lines: "Sam's too anxious to fall in love." Following closely behind was the thought, "and so am I."

I'd seen a lot of my friends go down that road, and – particularly when I was a teenager – I was afraid that it would happen to me. Being left on the shelf is not a nice thing, and it's a fear that men and women both have: Shelfophobia.

It hit my cousin Sue when she was twenty-nine. She'd had a few broken relationships (some of them were not so much broken as crushed into sand and kicked in her face) and when she finally met the man she was to marry, I believe that she only did so because she thought she'd never get another chance. He loved her, he was very good to her, and I think she managed to convince herself that she loved him too.

That said, they're both very happy. Or they believe they are . . . Which might be the same thing, I wouldn't know.

Then Sam nudged me and said, "You're doing it again."

"What?"

"You've got that faraway look that you get when you're bothered about something."

"Hmm . . . You know me that well, then?"

"Oh yes."

I gave him a sly grin. "But how do you know it wasn't a calculated 'faraway look' to make you *think* that I'm thinking about something, when really I'm thinking about an entirely different thing?"

Sam returned the grin with one of his own. "And how do *you* know that I wasn't just pretending to not have seen through your calculated far-away look, for my own devious purposes?"

"And perhaps I have good reasons for actually mentioning my far-away look . . . Maybe I'm trying to trick you into revealing something about yourself. Some dark secret that you'd prefer to keep hidden."

"Ah, but what you fail to understand, Mrs Peel, is that my manipulative skills have steered this conversation specifically in this direction, for those very same devious purposes of which I believe I spoke earlier."

We went on like this for a good ten minutes, and at the end of it we really had no idea what we were talking about.

Little Miss Paranoid felt very put out at being upstaged, and she went away into the darkest corners of my mind, where she sat muttering sly and nasty comments to herself and eating her curds and whey. Or was that Little Miss Muffet?

"What's whey?" I suddenly asked Sam.

"What's *what*?"

"Whey. As in Little Miss Muffet."

"Whey do you want to know?"

"I was just thinking about Little Miss Muffet."

He nodded. "So, you were thinking about Little Miss Muffet for no apparent reason, the whey one does."

"I can see wheyre *this* conversation is going," I said.

"I heard a true story about a couple who spent all their married life arguing whether the third little piggy had roast beef or bread and butter. They couldn't ever agree, and they ended up getting separated."

"God. If only someone had taken the time to tell them about roast beef sandwiches, their marriage could have been saved. Anyway, I don't believe those sort of stories. The gang in work are forever telling them. They're just urban legends. Like the one about the cup holder."

"I don't know that one," Sam said.

"Well, according to the story, there's this guy working in a computer company, and he gets a phone call from one of the customers complaining that the cup holder on her PC is broken. The woman – for some reason, it's *always* a woman complaining – says that the cup holder was fine for a few months, but now it's broken. The guy can't understand why she has a cup holder on her computer. He asks her if it was a sort of promotional give-away, or something, but she insists that all PCs have one. Eventually, he figures out that she's talking about the CD-ROM drive, and she's been using it to put her coffee on."

Sam nodded. "Well, that'd probably be a lot more funny if I knew what you were talking about."

"Yeah. Well, the point is that last year that story was doing the rounds in work. We all got e-mails and faxes about it, and everyone who told the story claimed that it had happened to them, or that they personally knew the guy who took the phone call. I asked everyone who sent me the message to name this friend of theirs, but they couldn't, because it was really a friend of a friend."

"But they still insisted that the story was true . . ." Sam said. "I know what you mean now. Remember Martin, the guy I used to share a flat with?"

How could I *not* remember him? Inwardly, I cringed. Inside my head, Little Miss Paranoid jumped to her feet and shouted "Don't screw it up this time!"

Sam continued. "He was forever telling these supposedly-true stories about things that happened to friends of his. His favourite was the one about the food-poisoning that his friend got in a foreign restaurant in town. Sometimes it was a Chinese restaurant, sometimes it was Indian. It depended on which nationality he hated at the time."

"Don't tell me," I said. "This is the one where the friend's stomach is pumped and it turns out that the food contains five different types of sperm, right?"

"Yep. And we all know that hospitals have very sophisticated sperm-identification machines."

"And that they always examine stomach contents for sperm," I said. "Yeah, I've heard that one a few times. Speaking of hospitals reminds me of the one about the guy who wakes up in a hotel after a night on the town, only to find that he's in the bath, and it's packed with ice."

"No, I know this! Dave told me this one only the other week! The guy had met some absolutely gorgeous woman, and she got him incredibly drunk. And when he woke up, he felt really, really sick. Much worse than just a hangover. So he went to a hospital, and they discovered that while he'd been unconscious someone had stolen his left kidney." Sam laughed. "Jesus, I *believed* that!"

"Dave probably did too," I said. "I believed it when I first heard it. It was even on the radio a couple of years ago, reported as a true story."

Sam looked at his watch, and decided that it was time to start heading towards the bus stop. As we walked, he mentioned that one of the reasons he liked me was because I was smarter than him.

Now, that was *not* something I'd ever expected a man to say, but I set it aside to worry about later. As it

was, there was only a few minutes before the bus was
due to arrive so Sam and I indulged in some much-
needed rampant cuddling, the way you do.

It makes me wonder why people bother with
hanging up mistletoe at Christmas. For real romance, all
you need to do is equip your living room with a bus
shelter.

Chapter Twenty-one

I'd arranged to meet Sam the next night. He was going to meet me in the office after work. I was a little worried about it, because it would be the first time he'd met any of my friends, and I was concerned about what Barbara would make of him. And vice versa. I was also kind of worried that Barbara would test out her patent vamping techniques and steal him away. But I decided that wasn't too likely, because I was a lot bigger than she was and I knew how to fight dirty.

As I lay in bed that night, I thought over what Sam had said about liking me because I was smarter than him. It was just too weird to take in.

Even though I'd told him I loved him, I wasn't now entirely sure that I did. I liked him a lot, that was certain, and I wanted him in a purely physical way; in fact, I wanted him in a purely physical way *right now*, I concluded, after a brief analysis of feelings I had lost touch with some time ago. Maybe tomorrow night, I thought. Maybe that'll be the time . . . I deliberately pushed those thoughts aside: they could wait another day.

I'd never believed that men are somehow genetically smarter than women, or vice verse, but it was certainly sometimes true that while men *pretended* they liked women to be their intellectual equals, only a few of them could ever truly respect someone who didn't understand the offside rule and couldn't be bothered to find out.

My thoughts began to drift . . . What *is* it about men and football? I wondered. Or men and cars, for that matter? Men worship the four elements: Drink, women, cars and football. Though not in that order, of course. Football comes first. And cars. They come first as well. And as is well known, women never come first . . .

Sometimes I think that men are still primitive hunters. They have to have the best of everything. They have to have the best car, the best-looking girlfriend, their favourite football team has to be the best. They have to be able to drink more than their friends. That last one is weird. I mean, picture the scene: A group of male friends are talking. This will most likely be in a pub.

First man: I had so much to drink last night I almost couldn't see this morning.

Second man: Oh yeah? Well, *I* got so pissed that I was still drunk at lunchtime today.

Third man: That's nothing. I had eighteen pints last night, and when I got back to the flat I found a bottle of wine we had left over from Christmas, so I drank that, and you know when you drink so much that you drink your way right through a hangover so that you don't even notice it? Well, that's what happened to me.

Fourth man: I had one pint last night and I was so sick on the way home that I nearly felt a bit weak.

Long, awkward pause.

First man: Let's kill him.

Maybe I'm being a bit mean. I know that not all men are like that. Though sometimes it really does seem like they are. They're the same with cars (if this was a movie, there'd be one of those wobbly-dissolve things that are used to indicate an imaginary scene . . . But this isn't a movie, so you'll just have to imagine it):

First man: I was doing a hundred and twenty on the motorway last night. This guy in a souped-up Ferrari was trying to race me, but he didn't stand a chance.

Second man: Yeah? Well, the other day I overtook a cop who was chasing someone for speeding.

Third man: That's nothing! I was trying to park in town, and there was one space left, and this bastard came up in some flash car and he was trying to squeeze into the space before me, even though I was there first! So I sped up real fast, until I was level with the space – and he was heading right towards me – then I did a handbrake turn and spun the car right into the parking space. You should have seen it!

Fourth man: Yesterday morning I drove around to the shops for my mother and I almost didn't stop in time for someone trying to use the pedestrian crossing. God, it gave me such a fright!

Long, awkward pause.

First man (to third man): He's *your* mate, isn't he?

I was just about nodding off when that fucking couple from the flat next door arrived home and started doing things like rooting around in the wardrobe with the acoustically-perfect hangers, flushing the toilet a hundred times, and playing the first ten seconds of every song on every CD they owned, until they finally settled on playing Elvis Presley's "Crying in the Chapel" over and over. They were laughing, giggling and singing for ages, and when I was finally just about asleep I was woken by an almighty crash, which I took to be Brendan leaping off the wardrobe onto the bed. Wearing his Batman costume, no doubt.

I was too tired to complain, and definitely too tired to get up and join them.

Chapter Twenty-two

I arrived in work the next morning in a much better mood. That was partly because it was Friday, and partly because it was payday.

It turned out to be one of the worst work days I'd ever had.

Things started well enough. Danny said "Good morning" to me when he arrived, and the others seemed fairly cheerful. There was a bit of work to be done, but nothing that we couldn't either rush through in a couple of hours or put off altogether until Monday.

But at about half nine, we got a call from one of our clients, who was not in a good mood.

I've mentioned before that we did management consultancy, which in theory was basically us telling other companies how to better control their staff. The way it worked – again, in theory – was that we had a team of five people who went out to these other companies and spent a few days with them, seeing how they did things. To keep our costs down, our people were freelancers. They generally only worked a couple of days a week – two of them were lecturers in their other jobs, one worked part-time in her local Credit Union, and the remaining two flogged Amway stuff to their friends to supplement their incomes.

So, our people wrote up detailed reports and gave them to me, Danny and Kevin. It was our job to analyse their findings, and make all sorts of recommendations. Most of these recommendations were along the lines of "stop employing all those unqualified and lazy relatives" and "pay people what they're worth." Occasionally we had to schedule things like staff training sessions and stuff like that, which meant booking guest speakers, arranging hotel rooms and organising caterers and so on.

Some of the smaller companies used us to do their general hiring and firing: sometimes a client would need a new manager, and we'd be asked to place an ad in the papers, conduct the interviews, select the most appropriate candidate, and make them an offer. Or they might have needed to get rid of someone, so they'd get us to do their dirty work.

This is what this client had phoned to complain about. A couple of months earlier, we'd been asked to find a new Sales Director for a computer software company that was branching out into a new market. The company was Parker Technology, and they'd decided that they wanted to snare the Irish and UK home education markets: their idea was to create a suite of programs that would pretty much tell secondary school kids everything they were already learning in school, only with cool graphics and music. They wanted to call their software suite "DeskWare," until Kevin pointed out that it sounded too much like "The Square". So they called it "EduSoft" instead, which is a pretty poxy name in my opinion.

Anyway, the guy we found for them was Neil Forsythe, a forty-three year-old ex-teacher, who was a bit of a computer buff and had also been a salesman in the past. Actually, it was me who found him, and I think that was one of the reasons that our boss began to see "great things in my future."

Neil Forsythe was a quiet, short, round man who looked like he couldn't punch his way out of a wet paper bag, but he was very, very good at his job. He took to it like a duck to orange sauce: in a couple of weeks he'd managed to get orders worth just over a hundred thousand pounds.

But the powers that be in Parker Technology were not happy with him . . . Mr Parker himself told me so over the phone:

"I'm sorry, Miss Perry, but I'm afraid you'll have to find someone else."

"I see. But . . ."

He interrupted me. "You'll have to find someone else. As soon as possible. And *don't* think that you're going to receive your commission."

"Mr Parker, if you could just explain what the problem is . . ."

"Do you want me to come around there? Is that it?

You want me to come around and explain the problem?"

"I'm not sure that's necessary," I said, because I couldn't think of anything else to say. "You seemed to be happy enough with Mr Forsythe a couple of weeks ago."

There was a long pause, after which Parker said, "Miss Perry, I would like to schedule a meeting with you this morning. In your offices."

I knew that Parker was expecting me to say that I wouldn't be able to meet him until next week, so I rustled some papers and tapped loudly on my keyboard. "I believe I can reschedule my ten o'clock appointment, if that suits." You arrogant bastard, I added silently.

Parker said that it did suit him, and he hung up.

I checked my watch. Parker was bound to arrive early for the meeting, so that meant we had about twenty minutes to prepare.

First things first, I told myself: Let everyone know what's going on. So I gathered them together and told Kevin to comb his hair and Danny to sit at my desk where he'd be more visible. Then I sent Kevin out to buy good coffee and expensive biscuits. Kevin then offered to contact one of his friends, who for only twenty-five quid would come into the office in a suit and sit at a desk pretending to work for the whole morning. With things beginning to move, I ran into the boss's office and gave it a damn good tidying. For good measure I randomly took out a folder and opened it on the desk. It was my plan that when Parker arrived, I'd look up, see him, then close the folder and put it away.

Barbara came through for me brilliantly. She said that she'd phone her friends and get them to phone her every few minutes, so it would seem as if the office was incredibly busy. She came up with the idea of piling up stacks of paper on the little table next to the photocopier, and running one of our consultancy reports through the copier a couple of hundred times. She even suggested that she watch me through the glass in the boss's office door, and if I needed help I was to scratch my right earlobe, and she'd interrupt the meeting with an extremely important phone call that I'd been waiting for.

When Parker arrived at five to ten – with two of Kevin's besuited mates charging around the office looking busy, the smell of expensive coffee brewing in the kitchen, and the phone ringing off the hook – he had calmed down a bit, and seemed reasonably human.

Barbara showed him into "my" office, I did the folder thing, and I shook his hand. "Mr Parker. Now, what can I do to help?"

He sat down opposite me. Bernard Parker was one of those fairly wealthy English fifty-somethings who still think of Ireland as one of the colonies. Not in a bad way, though. Parker was the sort of foreign national who went out of his way to "embrace the Irish spirit" in a big way. You know the sort I mean: they go to the Rose of Tralee and the Horse Show every year, they go on their holidays in West Cork and they play golf in Portmarnock. They drink only Guinness and Jameson and they talk about "the crack" all the time.

When he spoke, it was clear that he wasn't expecting

a fight. "As I said on the phone, I want you to find a replacement for Neil Forsythe."

"May I ask why?"

"Mr Forsythe is just not right for the company," Parker said. "Any more than that I'd rather not say."

"I see," I said, even though I didn't. "But if you look at this from our point of view, Mr Parker . . . You were very pleased with Mr Forsythe when we first placed him with your company, and I believe that Parker Technology stands to sell a great deal because of his efforts."

He nodded. "That is true. But we have problems with Mr Forsythe that far exceed the advantage of his presence. The terms of our contract state that we have three months to evaluate any staff members you place with the company."

"That contract also states that your company must provide us with a written report on your reasons for dissatisfaction." I knew that because it was part of our standard contract and I'd written it myself. "You must also understand that Complete Office Solutions has a contract with Mr Forsythe to provide him with a satisfactory position. Any other company with whom we hope to place him will wish to see his references," – this wasn't strictly true, but he wasn't going to know that – "so again I must ask you for some valid reason."

"I'd rather not do that, Miss Perry. Perhaps when Victoria returns I'll meet with her, but I certainly won't discuss this matter with *you*."

I didn't like the way the bastard put the emphasis on "you", but I knew better than to take it further. I really didn't know what else I was supposed to do at this point, so I took a chance. A quick search through my vast memory of bad movies gave a me a bit of a hint: "If Mr Forsythe has been involved in any activities of a criminal nature we will naturally have to take this matter to the authorities."

Parker said nothing, so I continued:

"Would you object if I arranged a meeting with Mr Forsythe to discuss the matter? Perhaps we can straighten things out?"

"Straighten all you want, Miss Perry, but I don't want that man in my office. As far as I am concerned, he's fired. And I am extremely annoyed with your company for recommending someone like him to us. I don't know if we can do any further business."

He was beginning to get emotional, but I was saved by Barbara bringing in a tray of coffee and biscuits. She gave me a look that I hoped meant "I've poisoned his coffee" then gave him a cheery smile and left.

I took the chance to reflect a bit on what he had said about his company possibly not doing any further business with us. Certainly, we didn't really need Parker Technology's money: they weren't our biggest client by a long way, and they were pretty bad about paying up on time, but Parker himself was a big noise in the industry, and knew a lot of influential people. Upsetting this man would not be a good idea.

So I sipped my coffee for a minute or so, then put it down and pursed my lips in a way that was supposed to say to him something like, "OK. Now, what I'm about to suggest might sound a little strange, but hear me out . . ."

What I actually said was, "What if you give us a week to either resolve this situation with Mr Forsythe –"

He interrupted me. "That will not be possible," he said, shaking his head.

"Please hear me out, Mr Parker. You must understand that you're putting me in a very delicate situation. Now, what if you give us a week to either resolve this situation, or to find you a replacement? Normally I'd insist that you as a client hold to your side of the contract, but I'm willing to leave that aside for the sake of good will if you'll just give us the time we need."

This was my double-whammy, my absolute masterstroke: First, it hammered home to Parker that he was in breach of contract, and second it gave me enough time for Vacationing Vicky to come home from her honeymoon and sort the mess out. Brilliantly done, Susan, I congratulated myself.

Parker considered this. "I'll agree on the condition that Mr Forsythe has no connection with my company during the week."

"I don't want to have to tell him that he's to be let go," I said. "Not until I'm certain that there's no other solution."

"That is *not* my problem," Parker said, getting to his feet. "You can tell him anything you like." He glanced at his expensive watch to see what time it was for rich people, and added, "I won't be returning to the office until two. I strongly suggest that you contact Forsythe and get him out of the office before then. And I expect that you resolve this situation by next Friday at the latest."

Oh *shit!* I'd been hoping that the boss would be able to take over this problem and let me off the hook, but she wouldn't be back until the following Monday. Now I really *was* in trouble.

I walked him to the lift, said a pleasant good-bye that I really didn't mean, then returned to the boss's office and collapsed into the chair. Barbara stuck her head in and asked how it went.

"Terrible. Look, I'll be out in a few minutes. I've got to talk to Neil Forsythe and tell him he doesn't have a job any more."

I phoned Parker Technology only to be told that Neil was on a call and he'd phone me back in about ten minutes.

So I sat and waited. I mooched around in the boss's desk drawers, and found an unopened packet of cigarettes and a lighter. I slammed the drawer closed. I hadn't smoked in years, and there was no way I was going to start again now, no matter how tempting it was.

Chapter Twenty-three

Neil Forsythe phoned me back at about ten-thirty. He was naturally a little surprised to hear from me. "Susan . . . What can I do for you?"

While I'd been waiting, I'd tried to come up with a delicate way to tell Mr Forsythe that his services were no longer required. Normally, if one of our clients wanted to let someone go, they'd come to us, Vicky would work out what was to be done, and she'd get Barbara to do it. But this time the decision was all mine. There was no way I could leave everything hanging until Vicky got back from foreign climes.

So I asked Neil if he could meet me as soon as possible, that I had something important to discuss with him.

He paused, then said, "I see. I was sort of expecting something like this. I suppose that bastard Parker has been talking to you?"

I nodded, and then I realised that it was a wasted nod because I was on the phone. "He has. Maybe you can fill me in on what's going on, because he won't tell me anything."

"I'll meet you, but not here. Or at your office."

Parker Technology was based in Donnybrook, so I decided that Ranelagh would be a good half-way point. "What about the Four Provinces in Ranelagh?" I asked. "It'll take me about fifteen minutes to get there."

Another pause. "Ah. You want to meet as soon as that . . . Which means that I'm not coming back. Make it half an hour, I'll need time to clear my desk. That'll be about eleven, OK?"

"That's fine. I'll see you there."

I went out to Barbara and told her that she was in charge until I came back.

"How long will you be?"

"I don't know. Probably not more than a couple of hours. I'll ask Neil to give me a lift back."

"Assuming that he's allowed to take his company car with him," Barbara said.

"Then I'll get a taxi, or something." I noticed one of Kevin's friends fiddling around with the photocopier. "What did Kevin offer his mates to encourage them to come in and make the office look busy?"

She grinned. "Well, he promised them twenty-five quid each, but I said that you'd type up their CVs and they could use the copier all they wanted and play games over the network at lunchtime. I thought that would be a bit easier to explain to Vacuous Vicky than fifty quid suddenly going missing. Oh, and Sam phoned. He wants you to phone him back."

I groaned. "God, not now! Look, I've got to go. If he calls again, tell him that I was dragged away to an emergency meeting. It's even true."

"OK."

"And don't go chatting him up," I said as I grabbed my bag and jacket. Then I remembered the package I'd been planning to post to J. There wasn't going to be time to send it off now – Fridays in the Post Office is always complete madness. "Shit. Barbara, can you post this for me? I won't get a chance."

She took the package from me. "A box number? Oooh! What's this?"

"A long story. I'll tell you later. Assuming that I live through the day. Oh, and if you get the chance, dig out the Parker file and see if we still have all the details about the other people we interviewed for their Sales Director. No, on second thoughts I'll get it now. I want to get the copy of Neil's contract." I ran into the boss's office, and found the file. A quick flick through the contract told me that it was straightforward enough, and I certainly didn't remember anything unusual about it, but I decided to bring it along just in case. Then I charged out, shouting goodbyes and telling the others that Barbara was in charge.

"Just make sure that you're back before two," Kevin called after me.

I nodded and waved as I ran. I knew exactly what he meant. I had to have everything settled before Bernard Parker got back to his office. Ideally, Parker would discover that Neil Forsythe had cleared all of his stuff out of the office and left nothing but the door swinging closed and a trail of dust heading over the horizon.

If I'd realised then that there was no way Kevin could have known what Mr Parker had said about him wanting Forsythe gone before he got back to his office, I would have saved myself a lot of trouble later on.

As I walked I went over the whole mess as well as I could considering that I didn't have a clue what was really going on. I began to wonder if Neil had slept with Parker's wife, or something like that, but then I remembered Parker's wife and I knew that there was little chance of that: she was a real man-eater, and Neil Forsythe was just not her type. She liked her men tall and lean, with strong, dark features and impressive silver hair. I knew this because I'd met her at one of Parker Technology's functions and she'd spent ages chatting up a visiting foreign client. Meanwhile, her darling hubby had been chatting up *my* boss. The Parkers were a well-matched couple – it was a marriage of inconvenience.

I was beginning to get an idea of what my boss had to go through on a daily basis. Maybe, I said to myself, those sudden spur-of-the-moment meetings she always has to go to are actually real meetings, and not just shopping expeditions with her friends.

This seemed to be a very real possibility for a few minutes, until I remembered that she always comes in wearing something new and expensive the day after such meetings.

An ambulance charged through the lights in Ranelagh, and snapped me out of my daydreaming. I blessed myself as it passed, and wondered what Sam the Atheist would think about that. I decided that it was something I'd mention that night when he called for me.

Neil Forsythe was waiting in the Four Provinces when I arrived. He had a half-drunk pint of Guinness in front of him, and he looked like he might be settling in for the day. His jacket was off and his tie and top button had been loosened. It was really weird seeing him like that: every time I'd met him – at the two interviews he'd done with us, at the launch of one of Parker Technology's products, and at the impromptu visit he'd paid us to present me with a box of choccies to thank me for getting him the job – he'd always been immaculately dressed. Now, he looked like a broken man. He sat slumped forward, resting his elbows on his knees, just staring at his drink.

There was a small, open cardboard box on the seat beside him, containing a mug, a *Dilbert* desk calendar, a couple of notebooks and a ruler. Probably the only personal items he had accumulated in the office for the few weeks he was employed.

He smiled when he saw me, though. "Susan . . ." He gestured towards his drink. "What will you have?"

"I'll get them," I said. "Guinness?"

He nodded. "Thanks."

When I returned with his pint of Guinness and a Club Orange for myself – there was no way I was going to risk getting drunk at a time like this, no matter how much I wanted to – he had regained a little of his composure.

"So," I said. "Do you have any idea what's going on?"

He took a deep breath, let it out slowly, and shrugged. "Not really. Everything was going fine until about a week ago. Then Parker just started getting really nasty. It was like every time he saw me he just saw red."

"Has anyone else noticed it?"

"Damn right they have. The others in the office just can't believe what's going on. They were saying that they've never seen him like that before. And then when I got your call this morning, I knew that that was it. Bang! Just like that, fired." He rubbed his hands up over his face and through his thinning hair. "I *really* don't need this. I had a mild heart attack a few years ago, and I'm not supposed to get stressed."

"Well, I have to be honest with you, Neil, we can't get him for unfair dismissal. You're still in your probationary period, and he can decide at any time that you're not suited to the company. And that's clearly what he's done."

He nodded. "Yeah, but that's bollocks. I've *never* been more suited to a job. I could have made them millions. I have all the contacts, I know the software, everything was perfect. Only last week he was telling me how well we were doing, and how pleased he was that I was on board."

"Our contract with Parker Technology says that he has to provide us with a good reason if he wants to let you go. He's refused to do that, but to be honest I don't think that we'll be able to force the issue. He also refused to even give me a *hint* as to what his problem is. Though he did say that he'd tell Vicky, but not me."

Neil gave a cold, harsh laugh as that. "Such an arrogant bastard. What else did he say?"

"Not much. He demanded that you be let go, and that we find a replacement as soon as possible. I managed to get him to agree to give us a week to either solve the problem with you – which he said wasn't going to happen – or find someone to replace you. But he insisted that you don't show your face in their office again."

"Well, thanks for trying anyway," Neil said.

"It does mean that he'll have to pay you up until the end of next week," I said, "and you'll have your car until then. I know it's not much of a consolation."

He cheered up a bit at that. "That was good thinking. Thanks for that. Money is pretty tight these days."

"Well, we have a contract with you to find you a job, so we'll honour that," I said. "There's always people out there looking for good salesmen."

"Yeah, but my reputation will be shit when Parker starts to bad-mouth me."

I thought about this, then said, "I'll try and get him to agree that in return for not providing us with a report on why you're being let go, he has to keep quiet about it."

"Now, *that* is good thinking," he said, cheering up a bit more.

I sat back and relaxed, happy to have made at least some progress. "We still have to find out what his problem is," I said. "There's no point us providing him with someone new if he's just going to crap all over them too."

"True . . ." he said, thoughtfully. "Now that you mention it, I've been assuming that he's treating me like shit because of something I've done. What if that wasn't it?"

"You mean, what if he was pissed off at the company?"

He nodded. "Anything strange happen between Wednesday and Friday of last week?"

"Nothing that I can think of."

Neil took a long drink on his pint, and smacked his lips. "I can't think of anything myself. Except that you're in charge, of course."

"Only temporarily," I said. "She Who Sits Above in Shadow has gone on her holidays."

"Anywhere nice?"

"The good ol' US of A," I said. "She . . ." I stopped. The pieces were beginning to fall into place. "Hang on, hold on a minute."

Neil sat patiently and watched me as I frowned in concentration. After a couple of seconds of frenzied concept manipulation, I had an answer for him. "She's on her honeymoon. I'll bet you anything you like that our noble Mr Parker had an affair with my boss – either that or he's been after her for years – and when he found out that she's just got married again, he was pissed off and took it out on you. No one is supposed to know she got married."

"And somehow he found out and decided to make things difficult for her, by sacking me and giving you grief while she's away." He smiled. "That's remarkable, Holmes. How do you do it?"

"Years of meditation and self-denial," I replied. I was all keyed-up now, and I desperately wanted to get back to the office so I could tell Barbara what had happened – even though I'd been sworn to secrecy about the boss's marriage. But Neil was still raging about the way Parker had been treating him, and I really didn't want to leave him like that.

We stayed there for hours, with Neil gradually getting more and more drunk, and me desperately wishing I was. Of course, I got his whole life story . . . He got married when he was twenty-two, and it really didn't work out – they'd had "irreconcilable differences" and he and his wife slowly drifted apart, until she finally moved out. Then his career: He had been an English teacher in a boys' secondary school for seventeen years, until, he said, he got sick to death of correcting essays about "The Day I Played for United" and teaching them how to use apostrophes.

Neil got hungry about one o'clock, and insisted that I join him for something to eat, so we went into the carvery and had our pick of the menu – my company was paying, so I made sure I had the most expensive stuff I could find. While we ate, Neil wanted to know all about me, and that led to a few more drinks. I had to continually remind myself that I was supposed to be working.

Considering how badly the *rest* of my day went, I should have out-insisted him.

Chapter Twenty-four

I finally got back to the office just before three. Kevin and his two friends were playing *Quake* over the network, and apparently having a wonderful time. I could tell by all the gleeful cackling and the shouts of "You bastard! You shot me in the back!"

Barbara seemed relieved to see me, but I knew from the look on her face that all was not well.

"What's happened?" I asked cheerfully. I decide that whatever it was, it couldn't be as bad as what I'd just gone through.

She answered with a simple question that completely shattered my illusions: "Did you remember to do the wages?"

I responded in the appropriate fashion: "*Shit!*" It was the last Friday of the month, and everyone was due to be paid. Before she left, Vicky had pre-signed all the cheques, and told me that I was to courier them over to the accountant, so he could give them the necessary second signature and send them back. All of this had to happen before three, because the cheques for the freelancers had to go out by courier, to arrive in time to catch the banks.

The sudden development of light-speed travel notwithstanding, this was almost certainly *not* going to happen.

It turned out to be barely-controlled chaos for the rest of the day. Panicky phone calls to couriers, taxis, the accountant, our freelancers, the banks . . . Faxes to most of the same. I found the cheques and sent them off to the accountant anyway, after making sure that he'd be there. I promised the courier a twenty-quid tip if he waited for the accountant to sign the cheques and got them out to the freelancers in time.

Naturally, because I was panicking and not thinking straight – not that I ever do think straight anyway, but this time I was heading for the world championship of wonky thinking – I forgot to tell the courier to come back to the office first, so that I could give Danny, Barbara and Kevin *their* cheques.

This led to a brief but incredibly angry meeting with Kevin and Danny demanding their money. Actually, Kevin was doing most of the arguing: Danny just sat there calmly and alternatively agreed with both of us, which only made matters worse.

It didn't look like the courier would make it back to us in time for the banks, so I had to write more cheques for my colleagues – this time by forging the boss's signature – get another courier to drop them in to the accountant, ask him very nicely to sign them, and get them couriered back to us. They made it to the bank with about five minutes to spare.

During all this, I had to ignore personal calls from Sam, Sharon, my landperson Mary-Anne, Sharon again, and Anthony. I also had to contend with the boss of the office downstairs who wanted to use our fax machine because his was broken: he was in a fine Friday afternoon mood and wanted to stay for a nice long chat. Then the girl who came to do the cleaning every second morning arrived. She was also supposed to be paid on the last Friday, but I'd completely forgotten about her and had to pay her out of petty cash.

At one stage things got so bad I even considered giving my mother a call, to ask her what I could do, but then common sense snapped into action and told me not to be so stupid: If I ever mentioned anything like this to her, she'd keep bringing it up for the rest of my life.

As it was, the only thing that was keeping me going was the thought of meeting Sam that evening, but every time I went to phone him back, all hell broke loose again.

At about half-past four I told Danny and Kevin that they could go home early, to make up for all the trouble. The real reason was that it meant Kevin would no longer be able to bug the shit out of me the way he had been doing all afternoon.

Of course, it wasn't fair to Barbara that the others got to leave early, but I explained to her that I needed her there, and not just to answer the phones and protect me from salesmen. I needed a bit of moral support too. Besides, I'd given her a half-day the previous Monday.

She didn't mind staying. At least, she *said* that she didn't. I promised that I'd make it up to her.

So there were only the two of us left when Bernard Parker phoned to see how I'd resolved the situation with Neil Forsythe . . .

"I met with Mr Forsythe this morning," I explained, desperately trying to decide whether I should let the vindictive bastard know that we'd figured out what he was up to. "We discussed the situation, and I have to say he was as surprised by your dissatisfaction as I was." OK, not bad, I said to myself. That was fairly neutral.

"I hope you made it clear to him that he's no longer welcome in the company."

"I did. Mr Forsythe mentioned that up to about a week ago you seemed very pleased with him."

"Things change, Miss Perry."

Damn right they do, I said to myself. "Now, as I explained to you this morning, we have a contract with Mr Forsythe to provide him with a satisfactory position. He has become concerned that these recent events might lead to a tarnishing of his reputation. I was wondering whether you were planning to mention this situation to anyone else. To be frank, we'd rather you didn't."

"Well, *to be frank*, I really don't give a damn about Forsythe's reputation."

All right, I said to myself. Back down, be polite, and worry about it on Monday morning. "OK," I said. "Perhaps I can meet with you early next week to see if we can sort anything out."

There was a pause. "Listen, Miss Perry, I've told you over and over what it will take to sort things out. Get rid of Forsythe, get me someone else. I mean, for Christ's sake, what does it take to get *through* to you?"

"It takes reason, Mr Parker. And you are *not* being reasonable. I will speak to you next week."

"All right. We'll play it that way if you want to. I'll go over your head. Give me a number where I can reach Victoria in the States."

"I can't do that," I said. By this stage I was shaking, but I did my best to stay calm. "I've been given full authority to act on any decision as I see fit. And I've decided that I will speak to you next week."

He jumped in just as I was about to slam the phone down. "Wait a minute. Wait just one minute. Who do you think you are talking to?"

"You're a client, Mr Parker. That is one of the reasons I haven't hung up on you."

"And do you realise how much my company is worth to you?"

As it happened, I had the figures right in front of me. "Well, last year you paid us just over seventy-two thousand pounds for a variety of services."

"Which is a damn sight more than *you* are worth, so if you value your job you'll just shut up and do what I say."

Well, that was it. He'd gone too far. I figured that if my job wasn't already heading for the rocks then nothing else was going to make things worse. "As I *said*, Mr Parker, last year you paid us just over seventy-two thousand pounds. But less than a quarter of that was actually paid on time. You'll also notice that – for some reason that's not specified here, but I'm sure I'll find it if I look hard enough – we have never charged you any late fees. Which would have amounted to . . ." I tapped away on the calculator. "Four thousand, eight hundred and nine pounds. Approximately. I can work out the exact figure and have it on your desk first thing on Monday morning, if you like."

He calmed down quite dramatically. "I believe . . . That I shall have to seriously consider whether my company should consider working with *your* company in the future."

And then I knew I'd won, because he'd used the word "consider" twice in the one sentence, which meant that I'd caught him off-balance. To try and make things a little smoother, I said, "Look, we're getting nowhere with this. Why don't we just agree to meet on Monday? There's not much we can do before then anyway."

He agreed, and all of a sudden I felt like a complete gobshite, because what I'd meant to say was, "Why don't we agree to *speak* on Monday?" So now I'd committed myself to another face-to-face meeting with the insufferable prick.

As soon as I hung up, Barbara came into the office. "So? What happened? You were close to screaming at one point."

"He pissed me off, the fucking bastard!"

"I could tell."

I checked the time. "Look, Sam's going to be here any minute. The three of us will go out and get absolutely plastered and I'll tell you everything."

She took a deep breath. "OK. Don't kill me for this, it's not my fault."

"Aw, what *now*?"

"Sam phoned again a few minutes ago. He's been phoning all day, remember? He says he can't make it. Some family emergency or something. He says he'll phone you tomorrow."

"Shit."

"And Sharon phoned a couple of times. She said that she's heading off to some party tonight and you can come if you call her back before she leaves work, because she's going straight there." Barbara looked at her watch. "Which was about ten minutes ago. *And* . . . your friend Anthony phoned to say that if you were going to the party, phone him because he could give you a lift, and he wants to talk to you about something."

I sighed. "And I don't suppose that any of them said *where* this party was? Or who was having it?"

Barbara grinned. "Now, what sort of a Personal Assistant would I be if I didn't check things like that? See? I knew how busy you were, I knew you wouldn't get a chance to phone them back, so I got all the details. It's Sharon's cousin Jenny, the one who had the flat before you did. They're having a house-warming, and you're specifically invited. If you ask me, that was Sharon's idea, so that she could get a chance to check Sam out."

"Well . . . Sam can't come, but what are *you* doing tonight?"

She shook her head. "Sorry, got plans cast in stone."

"I don't like going to parties on my own, but I might get bored sitting at home watching videos and crying. Give me the address anyway."

"What do you mean 'give you the address'? Don't you know?"

"I have absolutely no idea," I said, rather abruptly. "It doesn't matter anyway," I added, trying to sound not quite so pissed-off. "I'm knackered after today."

Barbara went home a few minutes later, so I took the time to make a few notes on what I had to do the next week. I didn't have anywhere else to go anyway. As I searched through Vicky's desk drawers looking for an empty folder I found the packet of cigarettes and lighter.

I said to myself, well, I'm the boss for the next week, and by God I need something to calm me down. So I opened the pack and took out a cigarette.

I lit the cigarette, and inhaled gently. It may not be politically correct to say this, but it felt absolutely great.

Chapter Twenty-five

Eventually, I went back to the flat and settled in for a long evening's mope. It occurred to me that I could phone Sharon's mother and ask her where Jenny's new house was, but I decided that I really wasn't in the mood for company anyway. Besides, I didn't think I could face everyone asking me where Sam was.

I admit I was a bit disappointed that Sam couldn't make it, because I really was in the mood for a little romance. I was feeling so sorry for myself that I decided that I just had to write the events of the day in my diary. It was something I always seemed to do when I was stressed out, and that had certainly been the most stressful day I could remember. However, it was taking far too long and it wasn't nearly as interesting as moaning to a real person, so after a while I just put the kettle on and sat back and read through some of my older diaries.

I got my very first diary on my tenth birthday. The diary started, as they do, on the first of January, but my birthday is in March, so, being something of a precocious child, I'd decided to save paper by simply crossing out the dates and days and writing in my own.

A couple of months later I'd obviously come to the conclusion that this was a stupid plan, so I just skipped a lot of pages and continued on the real date. I'd drawn a little right-pointing arrow on the last entry, and an arrow on each subsequent page, right up until the entries started again. Clearly, I must have done this with the idea that the older me might not be able to understand what had happened. The older me was not too impressed with the younger me's attitude, but the older me knew that there wasn't much she could do about it.

The first entry goes something like this:

Monday, March 21st

I am ten years old today. That's a whole tenth of a century. Sally and Brona are upset with me because today I'm older than they are. They're both only nine, but Sally will be ten in a few weeks and Brona won't be ten until next August. Then we will all be the same age again until next year, when I am eleven. Two years after that I will officially be a teenager and no one will be able to tell me what to do.

Fintan was really, really mean all day yesterday. He knew that today was my birthday, so he kept pushing me and calling me names. I hate him.

I will write down all the things he does to me and when he is older I will show him this and make him very sorry.

Love,

Susan

OK, so it was corny, but it wasn't bad for a ten-year-old. The rest of the entries were pretty much the same, until I got to about twelve, which is when I really started getting interested in boys. George Michael was my first true love. Once I discovered him, even Harrison Ford faded into the background.

This was the time of leg-warmers and *Flashdance*, of great songs like "Big in Japan", "Church of the Poisoned Mind" and "Wouldn't it be Good?" Bands like Kajagoogoo, Bow Wow Wow and the Rock Steady Crew were very important to me, but I thought that Frankie Goes to Hollywood and The Stranglers were absolutely terrifying.

It was a time when I fell in love every second day, and had my heart broken every other day. The most ordinary, average boy could look like an Adonis to me: it didn't matter if he was skinny, spotty, greasy, obnoxious or stupid – or all of the above – if I decided I liked a boy, there wasn't much that could change my mind about him for at least a week. They didn't even have to pay any attention to me for me to begin to suspect that they were secretly in love with me.

I had crushes on boys for the weirdest reasons: because I liked the way he laughed, or because he let me go ahead of him in the queue at the library. As I read through my pre-teen years, I found pages and pages written about a boy who I sometimes used to see when I was on the way to school: he used to pass me out on his bike, and I can't recall for certain that I ever saw his face.

It was a time when I couldn't grow up quick enough,

and I couldn't wait to be old enough to live on my own.

I looked around my untidy flat. Well, I'm certainly old enough now, and I'm *definitely* grown up.

I flicked through my diaries until I found the first mention that I realised I was going to be of above-average height:

One of the girls in first year keeps calling me Lanky. That's just because they're all tiny. They're like toys or something. I'm up to Dad's shoulder now, but I suppose I won't grow much more. Fintan is still a lot shorter than me, but Dad says that boys take longer to grow. In Fintan's case, that's probably because he has to keep stopping to ask for directions.

He's also getting really spotty. Much spottier than me. But he doesn't wash every day, so I suppose that could be it. And his hair is really greasy.

I don't know what's wrong with him, but he keeps barging into my room, usually with Anthony close behind. It's always "Can we borrow this record?" or "Have you got the scissors?" or something stupid like that. I suppose he'll grow out of it. At least he has Anthony to keep him under control. All of Fintan's other friend are real creeps. They're always annoying me. Anthony's the only one who's nice to me.

He speaks really softly, and he's very gentle, and he's always clean. Maybe he's a ~~homasexaul homosexual~~ *gay.*

I laughed when I read that. Anthony was certainly *not* gay. He probably just had a crush on me or something.

I was still reading at about twenty past eight when there was a knock on the door. It was my landlady, Mary-Anne, and as soon as I saw her I remembered that she'd phoned for me in work.

"Mary-Anne! God, I completely forgot to call you back!"

She didn't look happy, and I desperately tried to figure out whether I'd done something wrong. Or worse, forgotten something. Like the rent . . . No, that wasn't it. I'd paid her a month's rent in advance, and that was only a few weeks ago.

"Susan, can I come in for a minute?"

I nodded, and gestured to the good chair. "Sure. Sit down. Would you like a cup of tea?" The flat was in a complete mess, so I tried to pitch my voice in a manner that suggested I'd just been in the process of tidying up.

She paused to consider the offer of tea, then sat down. "Yes. Yes, I would, thanks."

"What can I do for you?" I asked as I set about filling the kettle.

"I've a bit of bad news, I'm afraid. Mrs Brannigan died last night. It seems that she fell out of bed and hit her head on the edge of the press."

I almost dropped the kettle into the sink. "Oh God . . Did she . . . I mean, how long was it before someone found her?"

"One of her friends called to the door at about a quarter to eleven. When she didn't get an answer, she rang my bell. Mrs Brannigan's – I mean she *was* – always very punctual, always there when she knew someone was calling. I went up to the flat and found her and called an ambulance. They said that it had probably happened some time during the night."

I suddenly felt very, very cold. I sat down on the edge

of the bed. "I heard something, a crash, last night." My voice was very weak. "I thought that it was just those two next door making their usual noise. If I'd known . . ."

She was silent for a few seconds, then she said, "Susan, she probably died instantly. She was very old. There wasn't anything anyone could have done."

Tears began to spill down my cheeks. "I only really spoke to her once," I said. "She sort of invited herself in."

Mary-Anne smiled warmly. "And she probably examined everything you had and told you all about herself."

I nodded.

"She always said that you could tell a lot about people from the things they owned. She liked you, though. She called in to me a few days ago, and said that she thought you were very intelligent, very polite." Mary-Anne smiled again. "She said that you reminded her of what she was like when she was young."

I really couldn't think of anything to say. Mary-Anne had shared a house with Mrs Brannigan for years; it should have been *me* comforting *her*. "What was her name?" I blurted out. "I don't even know her first name!"

"Florence. She was eighty-two."

"Does she have any relatives?"

"Just a sister that I know of. She was married, of course, but her husband died about ten years ago, just before she came here. Their daughter died when she was about thirty. It was some sort of aneurysm."

"She liked Sandra and Brendan," I said, for no reason

213

other than it was the only thing that came to mind. "She said that they told her they were married, and they'd had to elope."

"I don't know if she really believed that," Mary-Anne said, "but that's what she was like. Until she knew better, she judged people at their word."

"So, what are the funeral arrangements and everything?" I asked. "I should go."

"She would have liked that. One of her friends is arranging everything. She phoned me earlier to say that the burial is on Monday in Deansgrange – the family has a plot there – but I'm not sure which church she'll be taken to, or what time. I'll let you know. I've spoken to the others, but none of them can make it. Andrea would just fall apart, and Brendan and Sandra said that they're busy. Roger just isn't interested. He said that she wouldn't have wanted him there."

"Yeah. Well, I haven't really met the others, but Brendan and Sandra are full of shit," I said, then realised who I was talking to. "Sorry."

"I wouldn't have put it that way myself, but in principle I agree."

I remembered that I was supposed to be making tea, and got back up. "I forgot about the tea."

She shrugged. "It's OK. I don't really feel like it now. But thanks." She got to her feet. "I'll let you get back to what you were doing."

I really didn't want her to go. Despite the situation, it was nice to be able to talk to someone. "I wasn't doing anything important," I said. "Just wallowing in self-pity.

It was a pretty bad day. Though this has thrown everything into perspective."

I suddenly remembered that I was in charge at work . I didn't know how much time I'd be able to take off to go to the funeral. But then I decided that work could go to hell for all I cared. Besides, they'd managed to get along well enough without me while I spent the morning with Neil Forsythe. They could just do the same on Monday. And if Mr Parker wasn't too happy about it, then tough shit to him.

Mary-Anne must have seen that I didn't want to be alone, and I guess she didn't want to be on her own either, because she invited me down to her flat, where we spent the rest of the night talking, sharing three bottles of red wine, and playing with her cat and four kittens.

At about two in the morning I staggered back up to my flat, collapsed on the bed and had the first good night's sleep in what felt like weeks.

Chapter Twenty-six

I woke next morning with the worst hangover I'd ever had. I don't normally drink wine, because I'd discovered long ago that it gives me a really bad hangover. But for some reason I hadn't bothered to think about that the night before.

The best hangover cure I knew was a good eighteen hours' sleep, but the flat was still in a total mess and I really couldn't afford the luxury of a lie-in. Besides, I wanted to phone Sam at work and see what family crisis had forced him to cancel our date.

The second-best hangover cure that I knew of was to kneel in front of the toilet and shiver, while muttering the sacred words, "Oh God, Oh Jesus! I'm never drinking again!" This little chant is optionally followed by serious retching and the copious use of toilet paper to remove strings of saliva from the chin. It worked every time.

With this performance completed, and my body once more beginning to resemble a human form – during the process I always looked and felt like a random pile of cold, uncooked pieces of chicken – I had a lovely warm shower, until someone else in the house flushed their toilet. At that point, I did that screeching and grabbing of taps that you do in such a situation, and a few minutes later I actually began to feel roughly human again.

The next thing I did was decide that I couldn't face breakfast. With that difficult decision made, I started to tidy things up. At the beginning, I could only tidy the shelves and sort out my clothes that were already in the wardrobe, because I wasn't really able to bend down, but after an hour or so I was back to my true self, kicking stuff under the bed and ignoring the dusting like there was no tomorrow.

I tried phoning Sam's video shop, but there was no answer, even though it was after twelve. Then I phoned his flat, but there was no one there either. So I went back into the flat and for a few minutes just stood there, looking around, wondering what I was going to do. Obviously, there were lots of things I *should* have done, like the washing up, and the laundry, and actually giving the place a real tidying-up, but it was Saturday, I'd had a very tough week in work – well, a fairly easy week topped with a complete bitch of a Friday – and I just wasn't in the mood.

It occurred to me that I could go and visit my parents, but they were probably away for the weekend as usual. So I phoned Sharon, who – thank God – was actually in, and quite agreeable to my plans to squander the afternoon with me in the town, looking at clothes we wouldn't buy in a million years.

Shopping is the most interesting time waster of which two friends can partake on a Saturday afternoon. Especially in Dublin, which has more shops per square mile than any other city in the world (this figure comes from my own imagination, and is based on the fact that it seems like it might be true).

The city centre has one great advantage over the big suburban shopping centres like The Square in Tallaght or The Blanchardstown Centre: there are actually different types of shop. In the average Mega Mall – or Bloody Huge Shopping Centre – you get eighteen clothes shops (two types: those you can't afford to shop in, and those you wouldn't be caught dead in), three book shops (selling stationary and huge remaindered books along the lines of *Five Thousand Great Cooking Techniques for the Over Fifties*, or *The World's Shiniest Sports Cars*, or three hundred copies of last year's *Mandy* annual), twelve shoe shops in which they have great shoes in every size except the one you want, seven separate but strangely identical "sport shops" that only sell runners and tracksuits, two rival hairdressers' (where they have a variety of options: for just seventeen pounds fifty, they'll comb your hair for you), four different cafés that only sell ham and cheese croissants and yesterday's custard slices, seven brightly-lit fast food joints (at least one of which is masquerading as a "family restaurant"), one place that will print a T-shirt with humorous slogans containing the words "sex" and / or "beer", at least two enormous department stores, several versions of the "flavour of the month" shop (computers, mobile phones, Christmas stuff, etc.), and finally something really off the wall, like a shop that sells only lime marmalade or ankle chains.

At least in the city centre there is a lot more from which to choose . . . That is, all of the above multiplied by four, plus pubs. And in town you can get your bag nicked for free.

Despite what their adverts might have you believe, it's a lot more expensive to shop in one of the Mega Mauls. In the city centre there are cool places like Henry Street where you can buy lighters at three for a pound, or socks for the same rate. In fact, a few years ago you couldn't move on Henry Street for all the people selling socks. I remember Anthony referring to it as the Sock Market. He thought this was hilarious, but the rest of us didn't get it, until he ploughed on: "Trading was brisk today on the Sock Exchange . . . The 'Footsie' was up three points." We responded with, "Oh, very clever. Like the *Stock* Exchange. That's a good one." Around the corner on Moore Street you can buy an assortment of quality fruit for next to nothing, which is a lot better than buying it at my local newsagents where they happily charge forty-five pence each for oranges the size of grapes.

Sharon and I met at our usual place: the main entrance to the St. Stephen's Green shopping centre. We didn't go in, though, because we'd been in there before, and it was a pretty scary place because there were more escalators going up than going down. It seemed to me that before long the upper floors would reach critical mass, the glass roof would crack and people would come squirting out like lava in tracksuits.

So we wandered down Grafton Street and spent a few minutes looking in the windows of Laura Ashley at all the stuff we wouldn't wear in a fit. Then we dropped into HMV to see which videos and CDs were going cheap in this week's monster sale: it was the usual stuff: *Demolition Man, Groundhog Day, Chris de Burgh's Very Best Hits Ever (This Time We Really Mean It),* and a double CD called *Fifty Great 70s TV Theme Tunes,* which I bought and which Sharon laughed at me for buying. We squeezed our way past a group of people standing around doing very good impressions of "people just about to give money to the buskers" and found ourselves outside Bewley's.

"Coffee?" Sharon asked.

"Certainly," I replied. "I'm absolutely exhausted. We must have walked nearly five hundred yards."

The coffee in Bewley's isn't always the best, but it's hot and wet, so that must stand for something. And they have those machines that spray boiling-hot fizzy milk in the general direction of your cup while making a really cool noise.

As luck and a good deal of elbow work would have it, we managed to get a table all to ourselves. We squeezed into our chairs and barricaded ourselves with bags, then set about the awkward task of trying to unload everything from the tray onto a table that wasn't much more than two feet square.

When I was taking off my jacket I found that I still had Chief Vicky's cigarettes and lighter in my pocket. I took a cigarette out and lit it.

"Since when did you start smoking again?" Sharon asked.

"Yesterday," I said. "I had such a bastard of a day yesterday. Anyway, I haven't officially started smoking again because first of all, this is only my second one, and second of all I didn't buy these, the boss left them in the office."

Sharon used to smoke too – we all did, when we were teenagers – and she had that look in her eyes: the look that said give me a cigarette right now or I'll kill you.

"Want one?" I asked.

"Yes," she said. "But I won't. I don't think I can afford it."

"So, what about this party last night?" I asked, manoeuvring various cup, saucers and plates around to get the best possible fit.

"It wasn't bad. We sort of kept expecting you to turn up, though."

"There are many and varied reasons why I didn't. The short version is that Sam couldn't make it. Some sort of family crisis, apparently. I tried to phone him this morning, but there was no answer. So, did you meet anyone *nice*?" I said, with a devious grin and much eyebrow-waggling.

Sharon hesitated. She seemed to be on the verge of saying, "yes" but in the end she went for, "maybe."

"*Maybe?* What sort of answer is that?"

She grinned back. "Well, I didn't really meet anyone *there*, but someone gave me a lift home and it took longer than expected."

"You didn't drive, then?" I asked this because I knew that it wasn't what she was expecting me to ask . . . I wanted her to be eager to tell me, so that I could pretend it wasn't such a big deal.

"Nope. I was planning on getting plastered. And you know what it's like when you try to get drunk . . ."

"Yeah," I said. "You get completely pissed, but you *think* that you're sober."

"Well, I didn't get drunk, because there was some creep all over me all night. He seemed to think that he was on to something, even though I kept ignoring him. So the other guy I sort of met was heading home about eleven, and he offered me a lift."

"And you got home at . . . ?"

"Just after five," Sharon said. Then she quickly added, "but *before* you jump to any conclusions, we didn't get up to anything much. We just talked and snogged a bit. Well, a lot."

For some really strange reason, I felt a little jealous. I had the sudden urge to start talking about Sam, but I could see that Sharon really wanted to carry on, so I said nothing and let her tell me about this wonderful man she'd met.

She told me what they'd been talking about, how

much fun they'd had, and how they're going to meet up again on Sunday afternoon. What she never mentioned was his name . . . It didn't take me long to figure out that it had to be someone I knew.

I made a few probing but seemingly-innocent questions like, "what sort of car does he have?" and "what's his favourite movie?" but I just couldn't think who it might be. I was just on the verge of grabbing her by the throat and screaming, "What's his bloody name!?" when she mentioned that he had his own business.

"It's Mark, isn't it?" I said suddenly. "Mark thingy, from the video shop. I can't remember his second name. Jesus, Sharon, he's about ten years older than you!"

She gave me a look that I swear she'd spent all morning practicing in the mirror. "So? What's that got to do with it?"

"Nothing," I said. "I was just a bit surprised. I didn't know you even fancied him."

"Neither did I, but we just got talking on the way home, and you know what it's like when you can't stop chatting with someone. Both of us were trying to get the last word in all the time." She sipped at her coffee, grimaced, and opened another sachet of sugar. "He was wondering whatever happened to you."

"I hope you told him that I ran away from home to join the circus."

"He probably would have believed me if I had," she said. "He thinks you're bloody crazy. In a nice way. No, I told him that you'd moved out and were happily living on the southside."

"Great, condemn me forever. So what *is* his second name?"

"Shanahan. And his first name is really John, not Mark. He comes from one of those huge families from the country where for some reason everyone is called by their middle names."

"Then it's a good thing his middle name isn't Mary," I said. I was still a bit stunned by the news. "Wow. An older man! And you're meeting him again . . ."

"I went out with an older man before, remember? Brian MacLaherty was eighteen and I was fourteen. That's more or less the same proportion."

"Yeah, but Brian MacLaherty had the mental age of twelve, so he was really a toy-boy," I said. "I wonder what he's doing now?"

"He's a barman over at Readings in Drumcondra, my mother said. He's studying to be an engineer, apparently."

"I wonder if his dandruff ever cleared up," I said.

Sharon grinned. "Mam said that he's almost completely bald. He has a little tuft of hair in front that he keeps long and swept back. And he's got really fat as well. With round John Lennon glasses that dig into the sides of his nose."

"Mmm . . . Sounds lovely."

"What's Sam really like, then? Are we ever going to get to meet him in person, or are we just going to see him next time we go to Frodo's?"

"Frodo's was only a nixer. It was probably fate that we met that night . . . I hope you *do* get to meet him," I said. "We went out on Thursday night, and had a brilliant time. He was supposed to call in to see me last night after work, but like I said, he couldn't make it. Actually, it's probably just as well we were so busy yesterday, because otherwise I would've been shitting bricks all day. Barbara's been dying to meet him. And *now* she's wondering about my Mystery Man."

That made Sharon sit up and take notice. "Your Mystery Man?"

So I started to tell her about J, and his ad in the paper, and the letters we'd sent each other.

When I got to the end, she looked me up and down. "You're telling me that you actually gave your *name* and *address* to a complete stranger who put an ad in the paper looking for someone he could *hate*? Jesus Christ, Susan! That is the stupidest fucking thing I have ever heard of!"

My immediate reaction was to protest, but then I realised she was right. My God! How could I have been so dumb? I mean, the news is full of stories about psychos stalking young women, and I'd certainly seen enough slasher movies, the sort that have trailers with the impossibly deep American voice-over: "It started as a game . . . She thought it was just a bit of fun. She had no idea how serious it was about to become."

"He's not like that," I said to Sharon. "No way. I mean, he doesn't strike me as the psychopathic type."

"And you can tell this from his letters? What, you've analysed his handwriting and you can tell he's not a killer?"

J *was* OK, I was sure of that, but I couldn't think of an easy way to explain it to Sharon. I ended up telling her everything we'd written to each other, and by the time I brought her up to date she was a bit more relaxed about it.

"Still," she said, "You're really, really strange sometimes. How can you start off a correspondence with a total stranger?" She thought for a few seconds, then said, "Hey! You said that he was middle-aged! And you have the nerve to slag me about Mark!"

"You mean John, of course," I said, in a feeble attempt to change the subject.

"I mean, talk about the kettle calling the pot black!"

"Snooker references don't apply," I said. "And anyway, I'm not going out with him, I'm just writing to him. It's actually good fun being able to be incredibly nasty to someone you don't even know. Everyone should try it."

"Yeah, my therapist suggested that when I came back from 'Nam. So what does Sam make of all this?"

I sniffed haughtily. "Actually, Sam and I enjoy a mature relationship based on mutual trust and respect. So I told him it was none of his damn business. No, I told him about it, but he thinks I'm weird anyway, so I don't think it changed anything. Actually, you'll never guess what he said the other night . . . He said that one of the reasons he liked me was because I was smarter than him."

Sharon was impressed. "Marry this man."

"You'd never know," I said. "Do you want to be my bridesmaid?"

"Sorry, I'm washing my hair that day," she said.

"Really? I'll be sure to put a notice in the papers."

"Oh, ha ha. You could ask your special friend to do that, he's *very* good at putting notices in the papers."

"So what about *your* special friend? Does he charge himself fifty pence if he forgets to rewind his own videos?"

"Yes, and he still wouldn't do it so he barred himself from his own shop. But then he gave in. That's nepotism for you."

"Maybe we should swap," I said. "I've always wanted to go out with someone who works in a video shop. Oh! Wait a minute! I already am!"

Sharon suddenly looked serious. "My God, if the four of us ever get together, I'm going to be so pissed off! It'll be bloody videos this, videos that all night long. You'll be worse than a bunch of football fans during the World Cup."

"That's why wives get all dressed up when they go to the pub, you know. To try and distract their hubbies from talking about football and cars."

"It never works, though. I mean, Mark nearly started talking about football last night. I almost had to thump him to get him to shut up. So he talked about football movies instead. What's the one with Sylvester Stallone and Michael Caine?"

"*Escape to Victory*," I said. "I can picture Sam in the exact same situation. Though he's only mentioned football once or twice. He says his dream is to play for Crystal Palace in the FA Cup final."

"Oh God!" Sharon groaned. "Not Crystal Palace!"

"Don't tell me . . . Mark's favourite team?"

She nodded.

We looked at each other, and at the same time we raised our eyes and tutted. "Men!"

Chapter Twenty-seven

Sam, it turned out, did *not* actually have a very good reason for cancelling our date. It turned out that a cousin of his had arrived from Germany, so they went to the pub and got pissed for the night. Well, his cousin got pissed: Sam just stayed with him because, he said, he had to "make sure Gerry was all right."

He phoned me on Saturday evening, just after I got back from town, and apologised. I was not pleased about his cancellation – especially since he could have just left word with Barbara about where they were heading – and I said as much.

"Yeah, well we waited in for ages and when you didn't phone back, we just went out for one. And you know how it is."

I did know how it was, but he wasn't getting off lightly, especially not after the sneaky little "when you didn't phone back" phrase, which was clearly designed to make me think it was all *my* fault. "Well, I had the worst day of my life yesterday," I said, adding a heaped tablespoonful of extra guilt onto his conscience, "and I wouldn't have minded some company last night."

"I know. Look, I said I was sorry. I'll make it up to you. What about tonight?"

"Do you want to come over?"

"Yeah, sure. What time?"

"About eight?" Then it occurred to me that his cousin might still be around. "Will you be alone?"

"Not if you're there," he quipped.

I wondered if it was time to forgive him yet, and say something a bit on the lovey-dovey side, but then I decided to wait until he arrived and see whether he actually turned up on time, and – more importantly – whether he'd bring me something nice made out of chocolate.

"OK, I'll see you then," I said.

The good-byes were a little awkward, but done in a fairly positive mood, so I decided that he'd probably be forgiven by the time he arrived.

I went back into the flat and went through the usual dilemma of whether I should dress up or dress down. I had the vague feeling that tonight might be the night when we finally got down to some serious sexual business: after all, the last time we met we'd professed our love for each other, so now that the relationship was officially "not based on sex" we could put the lights on low, have a nice romantic meal, play some smoochy music and have a damn good shag.

In the end I decided to go all-out and dress like he'd never seen me before. This didn't mean I was going to wear a Winnie the Pooh costume with a pillowcase on my head and a pair of wellies with the toes cut out . . .

I had a couple of hours to kill before he arrived, so I had a quick shower then did my hair, which involved turning on every light in the place and sitting in front of the mirror while I carefully eliminated every single one of those damned individual silver highlights that come with age. When that was done, I put my hair up, didn't like it up, let it down again, and decided it looked better up, but for some reason I couldn't get it to look the same, so I gave up and left it down.

I rifled through my vast collection of mostly inappropriate clothes, found some things that were absolutely perfect, discovered that they needed to be ironed, put them back, and resumed searching.

I decided that this was the chance to wear the really over-the-top and bursting-at-the-seams lingerie that Sharon, Laura, Wendy and Jackie had bought me for my twenty-first. The basque was the sort of thing that, if it was displayed in a shop window, would cause the male passers-by some serious car crashes and more than a few whiplash injuries. It was low-cut, strapless, hooked up the back, and made of purest cheap simulated red satin and black lace.

I'd only worn it once before, and that was a few years ago, when I was a lot slimmer. It took absolutely bloody ages to hook the bastard up, but I decided that the effect was worth it: it took inches off my waist and spread them to my hips and chest. Not that I needed the inches in either of those places.

Next came the obligatory stockings. I mean, you can't wear a basque like that and then just go around with thick white knee socks or Damart thermal underwear, not unless you're really weird. I was lucky enough to find a pair of stockings without a single run in them.

I wore my short black velvet fitted skirt, with a reasonably matching black silk blouse, fairly dangly gold earrings, my choker with the little fake jewel, and a gold chain bracelet.

I had about half an hour to go, so I buffed, shaped and polished my nails, then painted them a deep, seductive red. As usual when I've just done my nails, my head got all itchy and I had to resist the urge to scratch like mad. Strangely, television commercials never show those unconvincing coathanger supermodels trying to scratch their head with the end of a spoon while waiting for their nails to dry.

Once they'd dried, I headed for my little dressing table and sorted through my make-up. I wasn't sure what look to go for at first, but then I remembered a make-over article I'd seen in one of Barbara's copies of *Woman's Way*. I must have forgotten one of the steps, though, because the "smokey eyes" technique had the undesired effect of making me look less like a seductress and more like a panda.

Once I'd finished with my Q-tips and copious amounts of eye-make-up remover, and made another, more subtle, attempt, I had a quick search under the bed and found my black stilettos, slipped them on, and examined myself in the mirror.

It took me less than .001 of a second to realise I was way over the top, but there wasn't much time left before Sam arrived, so I removed my jewellery and toned down the make-up. There was no way in hell I was going to removed the basque after all the trouble I'd gone to.

I was half-way through another quick tidy-up when the doorbell rang. I tottered out on my high heels, opened the front door, and there stood my darling Sam, dressed in an old grey anorak.

He was *supposed* to have been seduced off his feet, but for the first few minutes Sam sat in the flat looking incredibly awkward. He muttered a vague, embarrassed apology about the way he was dressed – he'd removed his anorak to reveal a very tattered pair of jeans and an Iron Maiden T-shirt – and generally couldn't bring himself to look me in the eye.

I tried to be cheerful, as though nothing was wrong – as though he wasn't supposed to have brought me the box of chocolates that he didn't bring, but which I would have been overjoyed and surprised to receive – but it wasn't easy with him sitting there like a scolded puppy. A badly-dressed scolded puppy at that.

"So," he said eventually. "You look nice."

Nice! *Nice!* Oh, thanks a bunch! But I didn't let my disappointment show. I just smiled and said, "Thanks."

"Do you want to go out somewhere?" He asked.

I shrugged. "It's up to you."

"I don't mind."

"Whatever you like," I said. I wasn't going to give in and make the decision *this* time.

"We could go out for dinner, but I suppose I'm not really dressed for it."

For McDonald's you are, I thought. "I am kind of hungry," I said. "We could order a Chinese. Or a pizza." OK, so I *did* give in. It was either that or starve to death.

Sam nodded. "Sure." He paused for a long time. "Look, I'm really sorry about last night. But I haven't seen Gerry in about five years, and he just turned up out of the blue."

"What's he like?" I'd decided to give him a chance to get over his embarrassment, guilt and plain old anxiety. If he doesn't loosen up after this, I said to myself, I'll have to start talking about movies.

Luckily, he did begin to relax. He told me everything there was to know about Gerry, his family, and their various scandals. I knew he was starting to feel more comfortable when at one stage he hopped up out of the chair and made tea all by himself, without being asked or anything.

Then he was kneeling on the floor, flicking through my CD collection and commenting on the various groups, which told me that he wasn't really that comfortable after all, but he was trying very hard.

He cheerfully told me that I should get one of those special yellow markers which you use to draw around the rim of your CDs to make them sound better. I was on the verge of telling him that no such thing exists when he turned around and grinned at me. "That was one of the first urban legends I ever heard," he said. "I believed it for years."

I smiled back. "Me too. I even went looking for one. Have you heard the one about putting a CD in the microwave? Apparently you get this tremendous light show."

"Yeah, it's called 'your house is on fire.' Gerry was telling me that in Berlin a couple of years ago all the cafés and restaurants took the vinegar off their tables, because all the junkies were coming in and sterilising their needles in it."

"I haven't heard that one before. It sounds the sort of thing that isn't true, but hearing about it would probably make the café owners take the vinegar off anyway, just in case any junkies *did* try it. Besides, vinegar isn't sterile, is it?"

"I have no idea. Gerry said that since he heard that he hasn't touched the stuff." Sam sat down and crossed his legs. "Apparently, there's a chipper in town and if you go in and ask for 'chips and fish' they'll ask you if you want vinegar and salt on them. And if you say 'please, yes,' they'll give you your chips and fish for nothing."

"I haven't heard that either," I said. "But no one asks for 'chips and fish,' or even 'fish and chips.' They ask for a large single and a fresh cod."

"A-ha!" Sam said, waggling his index finger at me. "That's true, *unless* they want a batter burger. There. I've run rings round you logically."

"All right, now I really am starving. Pizza?"

Sam took a deep breath and made a big show about

coming to a decision. "Let's order a Chinese instead. Are there any good places around here?"

I nodded. "There's the China Cottage in Ranelagh. Sometimes if we have to work late we order something from them."

He stood up. "Great. It's on me."

And with that, he went out to the phone, carefully looked up the number, called the China Cottage, said "Yes, I'd like to order a delivery, please," then dashed back in to me because he'd forgotten to ask me what I wanted.

"Chips and fish," I said. "No, make it Satay Chicken Kebabs, with boiled rice."

The food arrived about twenty minutes later. Sam even warmed a couple of plates in the oven. "Chinese food goes cold too quick," he said, almost apologetically. We didn't have anything to drink, so Sam filled two glasses at the tap.

We put on a CD, turned off the main light, and sat on the floor as we ate. We ended up sitting side by side, more or less leaning against each other. It was very cosy.

I reached over to my jacket and took out my cigarettes.

"I didn't know you smoked," Sam said, almost shocked.

"Only occasionally," I said. "Does it bother you?"

He shrugged. "Not really. I don't much like it, but I have to admit that it can be sexy watching a beautiful woman smoking."

Well, that clinches it, I decided. I did my best to smoke as sexily as I could: by pursing my lips and closing my eyes when I inhaled, and letting my chest swell out. I was extra careful not to blow the smoke out my nostrils, which I always thought was about as sexy as cleaning an aquarium.

Pretty soon we were lying on the floor having a good snuggle. Sam put his arm around my waist, and said, "you're very tense."

"I'm not tense," I replied. "It's just that I don't really fit into this basque." I propped myself up on one elbow and slowly undid my blouse. "What do you think?"

"I think I've died and gone to Heaven," he said. He reached his hand out gingerly, and felt the basque at my waist.

I leaned forward and kissed him deeply, then his hand was on my breast, squeezing gently.

After a few minutes, the basque was getting more and more restrictive. I lay back on the floor, and said, "Would you like to give me a hand undoing this?"

He didn't need to be asked twice.

Chapter Twenty-eight

I was back in work first thing on Monday morning. Mary-Anne was picking me up at ten to go to Mrs Brannigan's funeral, so I'd dressed for the occasion.

When he came in, Kevin started to go through the usual "are you going for an interview?" ritual, but I wasn't in the mood, so I abruptly explained that a friend had died, and I was going to her funeral.

While he lacks a lot in social skills, Kevin can occasionally tell when to shut up and go away. He slunk off to the kitchen to make coffee, and left me alone in the boss's office, sitting behind her big, important desk and feeling like a fraud.

I prayed that the day wasn't going to be anything like the previous Friday, especially not since I was going to be gone for a few hours in the morning. I extended the prayer to cover the rest of the week, and added a few PSs along the lines of "Don't let Vicky find out how badly I've managed to screw up with the Parker Technology account," "God, if you let nothing else bad happen for the rest of the week I'll start going to Mass again," and "Please don't let me be pregnant."

That last one kind of caught me out. It hadn't occurred to me before, and just ambushed me from one of the dark corners of my mind, sort of jumping out, waving a red flag and shouting "Pregnant! Pregnant! Felt a little sick this morning, didn't we? I wonder if it's too early to start looking at colleges?"

OK, I wasn't on the pill, but Sam *had* used a condom every time over the weekend that we'd had full, penetrative sex. The little leaflet with the packet of Mates had said that they were the most effective deterrent against unplanned pregnancy (I presumed that they meant to imply "not including celibacy.") I'd read the leaflet several times on Sunday morning when Sam was asleep more or less on top of me and I wasn't able to reach a book.

I *had* actually felt a little sick that morning, but the reasons for that were many and varied – and didn't necessarily point to pregnancy – and I listed them to myself. For a start, I explained to myself, Sam and I didn't get out of bed except to go to the toilet until late yesterday Sunday night, and then it was only because he had to catch his bus. *And* I'm going to a funeral today – that can't be good for me, especially since I actually heard Mrs Brannigan falling out of bed. And there's this damn place as well, and having to face Bernard Parker at some stage today.

No way, I decided. I couldn't be pregnant. It just wouldn't be fair.

But the zygote fairy pays visits without considering the fairness of the situation, and where the tooth fairy donates money for the little present that you leave it, its counterpart leaves a little present and takes all of your money and the next eighteen years of your life.

I sat there at the boss's impressive power desk with nothing else to do but worry until something else arrived to take my mind off things.

That something else arrived in the shape of Barbara, who sauntered into the office without a care in the world – or at least, that's how it looked to my bitter and depressed eyes – and greeted me by waving cheerfully through the glass in the boss's office door.

I got up and went out to her. Before she could comment on my attire, I said, "the old woman who lives in the flat upstairs died on Thursday night. I have to go to her funeral today."

"Jesus. Did you know her well?"

"Not really," I said, "but apparently she was very fond of me. I just think, you know, that I should pay my respects. Will you take over while I'm gone?"

She nodded. "Sure. What time will you be back?"

"I'm not sure. It probably won't be until after three. I'll be leaving around ten."

"OK." Barbara looked at me for a few seconds, then said, "did Sam ever show up?"

I was relieved that she'd changed the subject: I hadn't wanted to do it because it seemed disrespectful to the memory of the late Mrs Brannigan. I felt a little guilty about not going into great lengths about what a wonderful old woman Mrs Brannigan had been, but the truth was that I hadn't really known her. So then I also felt guilty about not getting to know her better.

I pulled the emergency brake on this particular train of thought, and answered Barbara's question. "Yeah. He phoned me on Saturday evening, and came around."

"Do anything?"

"We just stayed in," I said, not yet feeling guilt-free enough to describe what we'd been up to.

She sensed that I wasn't about to go into detail, and she had more tact than to press me on the subject. "Well, you can tell me about it some other time. What are you going to do about Parker?"

I was even more relieved that we were talking about something that didn't involve feelings – apart from absolute loathing – and explained that I'd given the matter a lot of thought, and that the best thing to do was put him off for as long as possible, and try and phone Vacationing Vicky at her hotel in the States later that afternoon.

Barbara didn't react as I'd expected. She didn't say, "Yes, that's the right thing to do." She didn't even come close to it. What she said was, "I wouldn't do that. Sort the bastard out yourself. She left you in charge, with full authority, so use it. If we have to lose Parker as a client, then good riddance to bad karma, that's what I think."

"Maybe you're right," I said, suddenly wishing that the roles were reversed and she'd been the one left in charge. I didn't want to face Parker today – especially since I really *didn't* have the time – so I decided to phone him and arrange a meeting for the following morning.

Bernard Parker was not a happy man. That much always seemed to be true, but when I phoned him it was clear he was "not happy" multiplied by twelve. He got up on his high horse and galloped around the room. Metaphorically.

"I thought we'd agreed to meet today!" he almost shouted into the phone.

"We had," I said, "but a matter of a personal nature has arisen, and I won't be able to meet you until tomorrow morning."

"That's not good enough, Miss Perry. I'm very, very disappointed. In fact, I'm insulted. Do you really think my schedule is fluid enough to change at your whim?"

"I said I was sorry, Mr Parker. Much as I would love to meet with you today, and get this matter sorted out, I'm afraid it's not possible."

"I see," he said, and I could picture him saying that with his expensive teeth tightly clenched. "If you were any kind of professional, you wouldn't let your personal life get in the way of business."

The man really knew how to annoy me: I snapped. "And if *you* were any kind of professional, you'd have the decency not to say something like that." I hung up on him.

Barbara came into the office and grinned, raising her fist in triumph. "Well done!"

"Don't tell me you were listening in?"

"Damn right. You did the right thing. I mean, what a *prick*!" She marched around the office, as proud as if she'd been the one who'd made the call. "Listen, here's what I'll do now. I'll phone Parker's secretary and tell her that you're very upset, and ask her if she knows what the problem is. Then I'll tell her that you have to go to a friend's funeral, and the last thing you need is Parker giving you trouble."

"Woah! Hold on! I'm not sure that's fair."

"It's true, isn't it? I'll phone his secretary and give her a real bollocking. With any luck, she'll take it out on him."

"But what if she says something and he starts to take it out on *her*?"

Barbara considered this, and shrugged. "Well, he'll probably take it out on her anyway. And at least this way she'll know why."

We were saved from this rather nasty course of action by the phone. Barbara answered it, said "please hold," and covered the mouthpiece. "It's Parker. Do you want me to tell him to go and bugger himself backwards with a wire brush?"

"No. I'd better take it."

"Miss Perry, Bernard Parker here." He sounded a bit calmer this time. He'd obviously had a little think, and come to the conclusion that he couldn't bully me *too* much. After all, his company needed mine more than we needed his.

I wondered whether I should apologise for hanging up on him. Then I wondered why I was even wondering that. "Mr Parker."

"All right, we both said some things we didn't mean.

Let's just arrange a time to meet and get this matter sorted, agreed?"

"Agreed," I said.

"What about tomorrow, at eleven, in my office?"

"Fine."

"Well then, I'll see you tomorrow."

He hung up, and then I was kicking myself because if I'd been thinking clearly I would have been the one to call back and make peace. Now he had the upper hand *again*. Assuming that he was thinking along those lines. Which he probably was, because I knew that his shouting and stubbornness weren't directed at me, it was just the political game he was playing to get back at my boss.

I went back out to Barbara. "You hear that?"

"Yeah. Your best bet tomorrow is to go along and be incredibly nice. Promise him that you'll sort everything out with as little fuss as possible. That'll stop him in his tracks."

"Maybe," I said. "But I was also thinking of telling him that Neil Forsythe is considering suing us, and if he does that we'll have no choice but to sue Parker."

"I'd save that for a last resort if I was you,' Barbara said. "But it's not a bad one all the same."

Chapter Twenty-nine

Mary-Anne called just before ten, and whisked me away to the funeral. I think she was glad of the company, because she'd only met a few of Mrs Brannigan's friends before, and didn't know any of them that well. She did know Mrs Brannigan's sister, and introduced me to her. I was amazed at how similar the old woman was to her late, departed relative. It was like a TV series where the producers kill off a character, realise that she was one of the most popular on the show, and then try to recoup their losses by employing the same actress as a close relative.

The church was packed with old people. It took absolutely ages for Communion to end, because none of the church-goers could move too fast. Their zimmerframes kept crashing off each other. And every one of them spent hours with Mrs Brannigan's sister, telling her how much they missed Florence, and saying that if there was anything they could do . . .

I didn't like funerals. When my grandmother died I really didn't want to go. It wasn't the ceremony itself that bothered me, it was the finality of it all. There you are, trotting through life, with assorted kids and grandkids coming to visit every couple of weeks. You've had a good life, generally lost all the bitterness of youth, and everyone loves you. On top of that, you don't have to go to work any more. Then all of a sudden, bang, you're dead.

Maybe there is a Heaven, maybe there isn't. Sometimes I thought it'd be less sad if there was no Heaven, and when you died it was all over. But because people believe in an afterlife, when you die it's all "she's with the angels now," and "she's at rest, finally, Lord have mercy on her." It's like they're dismissing all the things you've achieved in your three-score and twenty or however many it's supposed to be.

I only realised that I was crying when Mary-Anne nudged me and handed me her handkerchief.

After the burial – and the tea and sandwiches Mrs Brannigan's friends had organised – Mary-Anne drove me back to Ranelagh, and on the way I found myself telling her everything that had happened in work. It was only much later that I realised that what I had actually been doing was using her as a kind of surrogate boss: an older authority figure who would tell me the right things to do. Someone who would say, "do this, this and this, and the problem will go away," or, "yes, that's what I would have done," or – better still – "leave it with me. I'll sort it out."

She was very sympathetic, but in the detached way that acquaintances can only be. She nodded in the right places, told me that she was sure that if my boss had had enough faith to leave me in charge, then whatever I decided to do must be the right thing. At the very least, she said, if I really made a mess of things, the responsibility still lay with my boss.

Later that day, I thought about this a great deal. No matter what the situation is, responsibility should always filter to the top. If the lowest employee in the company screws up and costs the company millions, then surely his supervisor shouldn't have put him in a position where it was possible for that to happen. So the supervisor should take the blame. That automatically brings up the question of whether that supervisor should have been in charge of an employee who could cause so much damage, so therefore the super-supervisor should take responsibility, and so on. All the way up the corporate ladder.

But the more I thought about this, the more I realised that it was utter crap, because eventually you're going to get to the stage where you say, "well, if God hadn't created the universe to begin with, none of this would have happened."

So somewhere along the line someone has to stand up and say, "it was my fault."

In my case, that person was me. I'd assured Vicky that I was capable of doing the job. Well, I might not have specifically *said* that, but over the years I'd played enough mind games on her to make her think that I was the best thing since sliced toast-to-be. I was surely responsible for *that*.

It was a quiet afternoon in work. Moments of boredom punctuated with moments of even greater boredom. I didn't really know why I was continuing to dwell in Vicky's office, but I just couldn't bring myself to sit out with the others. I tried to tell myself that it was because I needed the solitude to work, but that was crap because I wasn't *doing* any real work.

What I did do was read through everything in our files about Parker Technology. I was hoping to find some dark, hidden secret that I could use to get Parker off my back. I was thinking along the lines of finding out something about his true alien origin, or a kidnapping gone wrong, or details of a time when he was indicted for smuggling drugs. The only thing I did find out was that reading through files was not very interesting.

I found myself daydreaming, and – for the first time in ages – the daydream came in the form of a movie trailer . . .

A montage of scenes: Me (played as usual by a younger and taller Kathleen Turner) in a very dark basement, searching through a dusty filing cabinet. Then, half-hidden in the bushes surrounding my wonderful house, Bernard Parker (played by James Woods) watching me taking something we can't see out of a filing cabinet. Whatever it is, it's glowing like the contents of Marsellus Wallace's briefcase in *Pulp Fiction*.

A deep American voice: "What she found would change her life . . ." Meaningful pause. "Forever."

Another montage of scenes, this time a lot faster: An exploding car. Me wearing only a nightie at my dressing table, gasping at the reflection of someone standing behind me. Me, gagged and bound, tied to a wooden chair, then someone splashing a bucket of cold water over me. James Woods as Parker: "Where is it?" Me, panicky: "I don't know what you're talking about!" In the darkness, a sudden glint of light on a huge knife. Daytime, children getting off a yellow school bus. A bright-eyed young boy is approached by two black-suited men: "Your mother sent us to collect you, Todd."

Me screaming: "Give me back my son!" Parker: "Give us the package." A man falling from a window ledge. A big American car crashing through the glass revolving door of a large office block.

Credits: Kathleen Turner. James Woods.

Fade up quickly. Me, holding a gun against Parker's head, whispering menacingly: "Now. Give me back my son." Fade to black.

Credits: A Woman Scorned. Directed by Renny Harlin.

This trailer and a couple of variations – one based on *The Sound of Music*, for reasons that escaped me – ran through my head a couple of times, until a well-dressed and deeply annoying man appeared on my mental TV and said, "Whenever you buy or rent a video, you need to be sure that the film you choose is suitable for those at home."

Well that's just *great*, I said to myself. Now I'm fantasising about Simon Bates.

Chapter Thirty

I spent the evening alone, worrying. For the first time I was beginning to regret moving out of home. I missed my parents. I even missed my brother, despite his moodiness.

Of course, lately I'd been pretty moody myself. I put that down exclusively to work. It's one thing to spend your day getting paid for doing almost nothing, but it's quite another thing to be in charge of other people who are getting paid for doing almost nothing.

I decided that I wasn't cut out for management. I didn't want responsibility. I didn't want to be in charge. I certainly didn't want to be in a position where I could get fired if I did the wrong thing.

What I *did* want, I concluded, was a cigarette. I was rather astonished to discover that there was only about five left in the packet. I tried to remember when I'd smoked them, but it was too hard to think back over the past few days without going into "Total Panic" mode. Things have not been easy, I told myself. Damn right, I answered. And they're going to be absolutely shit tomorrow.

I told myself that I wasn't going to let things get to me any more, and that business was business. If Parker insulted me, I wouldn't take it personally.

I also told myself that I wasn't going to have another cigarette because I'd only get hooked again, but then I had one anyway.

As part of his plan to wreck my head, Bernard Parker was actually quite charming when I met him the next day. He began the meeting by profusely apologising for the way he'd been treating me, and tried to explain it away by telling me about the pressure he'd been under of late.

We were in his office, which was roughly the size of a dodgy politician's stud farm. Parker sat in a huge leather swivel chair with more controls than the space shuttle, in front of a leather-covered desk that looked at least a hundred years old. Pushed to one side of the desk was a top-of-the-range laptop computer. Gloriously coloured fish swam on its screen, and I'm pretty certain that displaying the screen saver was the only use to which he'd ever put the thing: he may have been the owner of a high-tech computer company, but that didn't mean he had to know anything about technology himself. In fact, I suspected that he had only recently mastered the up and down controls on his chair.

He'd been polite and charming to a degree that I'd previously thought impossible in any race other than humans. After giving me a little tour around those parts of the company where the work was actually done – I'd been cheered to notice that he didn't really know the names of most of his employees or have any idea what they did there – he'd brought me to his office, encouraged me to sit in the slightly lower-tech chair reserved for visitors, and buzzed his assistant for coffee.

Notice that I didn't say that he buzzed his *secretary* for coffee: the secretary was outside in her own little office, no doubt doing secretarial things with remarkable efficiency. Parker's assistant was a skinny young man who looked about twenty-one. He knocked once and opened the door with his elbow as he held a tray of coffee, expensive biscuits and – Food of the Gods! – After Eight mints.

I helped myself to the After Eights, but I wasn't fooled by any of it. "I know what you mean by pressure, Mr Parker," I said after the assistant had scurried away. "I've been under a bit of pressure myself." Most of it from you, you bastard.

He nodded. "I can imagine. I really should have been more considerate. I'd assumed that you were next in line to the position of command in Complete Office Solutions. It was only when I read through our files that I noticed that you were the one who put together most of our contracts. And I have to say you made a very good job of that." He tried to smile in a way that suggested he thought most managers were cretins, and that it's the good old salt-of-the-Earth people like the two of us that really keep these small companies running.

At least, I assumed that was what the smile was supposed to convey: a sort of "we're not like most managers, you and I. We know that the well-being of the individual worker is of paramount importance."

OK, maybe I was reading too much into one smile, but now that I was seeing him on his home turf, and seeing how his people reacted to him, I knew that he was doing his best to be devious and underhanded. And I knew that he thought I wouldn't see through it.

I also had a very strong feeling that he was going to spend most of the morning praising my work. He'd then get around to suggesting that what Parker Technology really needed was someone like me who could think on their feet, and get the work done. Someone who could see the truth behind the layers of bullshit.

That, more or less, was what he tried. In fact, he even used the phrase, "someone who can seek out the truth through the layers of – if you'll pardon the expression – bullshit" which was so close to my original that for a mad second I considered suing him for breach of copyright.

I saw quickly that that was how he was planning on getting back at my boss: He'd found out the hard way that I was a useful person to have around, so he'd decided to poach me from her. Firing Neil Forsythe was one thing, but he could really get to Vicky by taking me away from her.

We skirted around the Neil Forsythe problem for a few minutes, but I could see that Parker was anxious to put the next phase of his plan – offering me lots of money and prestige in return for working for his company – into action.

"We should decide what we're going to do about Mr Forsythe," I insisted. "If you really don't feel you can work with him, then fine, I've already got my team looking for an alternative for you, and there's no doubt I can place Mr Forsythe with another firm . . . I assume that you won't be making public your objections to him?"

I could see he didn't like that one bit, but I had him over a barrel – horrible thought – so he agreed as smarmily as he could. But he did add, "I'd rather not provide him with a reference."

I conceded that point. "That's not a problem. He wasn't working here long enough to require one, anyway. We can just say that he decided that he didn't want to continue working in the education circuit. All those years of being a teacher have put him off."

Parker nodded. "Very good. You see, Susan, *that's* the sort of thinking that I need around here."

Here it comes, I said to myself. Money and power.

"What would you say if I offered you a position with us?"

I didn't give any sort of answer. I knew what I wanted to say, and I was bloody well going to wait until the moment was right.

He continued, a little unnerved by my silence, "I don't know what you're currently earning, but I'm sure that we can at least double that. You'll also need a car, of course. Something to impress my clients. A Rover, maybe. But we can sort that out later."

I still remained silent.

"And of course there are other benefits. We have sister companies throughout the United States, for example, and if you wanted to combine your holidays with business trips, the company will pay for your entire stay."

This was the time to speak, I decided . . . "Naturally, if I were to accept a position with your company, I'd have to have authority. I work well in my present job because I know I'm trusted to make the right decisions. I understand the aims of the company, and I'm trusted to make decisions that will benefit Complete Office Solutions in the best possible manner."

He nodded, urging me to continue.

"For example, if you were to hire me, and if it was also within my brief to recruit the best possible people, one of the first people I'd hire would be Neil Forsythe."

Parker reacted as though I'd just slapped him. *"What?"*

"Hear me out, please," I said. "Whether I liked Mr Forsythe or not would not be an issue. Personal feelings should not get in the way of the company. I would expect to be given full authority to question – without reprimand – any decision made by any other person in the company, including the owner. If, again for example, someone in the company made a decision that I felt was based on personal feelings and was to the detriment of the company, I would expect to be able to reverse that decision."

He drummed his fingers on the edge of his expensive desk.

"I would expect to have the authority to review the running of the company at any level. If I concluded that one of the employees was being treated unfairly, I would be allowed to take whatever action was necessary to rectify the situation. If I concluded that the higher management were spending more than they were worth, I would be able to reprimand them and curb their spending. Another example: Your office furniture, Mr Parker . . . I would guess that it cost probably the equivalent of half a year's salary for one of your programmers. That is extravagant, and wasteful, and completely unjustified. You might feel obliged to explain that it's important to make a good impression on your clients, and that's fine if you don't mind working with clients stupid enough to judge the quality of your software by the cost of your desk, but if you had any integrity you would be concerned with creating the best possible products. You must remember that I'm in a position to know that your staff turnover is very high – even for the computer industry – and now that I've met your staff I can see why. They *hate* it here. They hate that you make a fortune and pay them far less than the industry average. They also resent you for getting rid of Mr Forsythe – who was well on target for making your company a huge profit – for a purely personal reason."

Before he could jump in and start raging at me again, I continued: "So. The truth is that I wouldn't work here in a flying fit. I think you're a self-centred, arrogant, stupid, petty man. But that's just my professional opinion. Personally, I think you're a class-A loser of the first order, a smug amateur who mistakenly thinks he can manipulate people for his own gain."

I stood up. "You are in breach of contract in the situation with Mr Forsythe, and my company will have nothing more to do with you."

And with that, I marched out of his office, down to the street, jumped into the first taxi and didn't know whether I should laugh or cry.

Chapter Thirty-one

"You should have seen me," I was saying to Sam. "I was bloody brilliant! I told him exactly what I thought of him, and he was too stunned even to react."

It was Wednesday morning, a mere twenty-four hours after The Great Conflict, and I was sitting in my boss's office with my feet up on the desk, on the phone to my beloved. I'd already gone through the story with Barbara and Mary-Anne, so I had it down to a fine art.

Sam was impressed, I could tell, but I wasn't sure whether he was more impressed with what I'd done or the fact that I was actually in a position to do it.

We talked for close to half an hour, until it finally dawned on me that I was not really giving a good example to the other staff members. I wrapped up the conversation fairly quickly, with a promise to meet Sam the following night for coffee and snuggles.

I wandered out to Barbara's desk, but she wasn't there. I could hear her at the far end of the office, talking to one of the others, so I ambled sprightly past the meeting room, down the little corridor, and into that part of the office where the real work was done. My own desk looked a little empty and strange. I hadn't actually used it in about a week. On the far side of the partition, Danny's head popped up when he heard me coming. He nodded a hello, and returned to his work. Ever the diligent worker, Danny didn't even take the opportunity of Vicky's absence to play a few games of *Tetris*.

Over at Kevin's desk, Barbara and Kevin also looked up.

"I'm going to get a coffee," I said. "Anyone interested?"

Kevin practically killed himself in his rush to get his mug into my hand. "Two sugars, no ice, hold the mayo."

I turned his mug over in my hands and peered at it as though I'd never seen anything like it before. "And you want your coffee . . . in this? What, I just pour it in through the big opening?"

He nodded. "Remember to keep the opening at the top when you're bringing it back, because I've a feeling that *somebody* –" he looked accusingly at Barbara "– left the gravity on when she went home last night."

"We should have After Eight mints," I said. "In Parker's office they served them with the coffee."

"After Eight mints?" Kevin said, making a face. "Barf-o-rama! I hate those things. We should have Christmas Pudding served on those little round crackers, as described in that famous song."

Barbara and I exchanged glances. This was clearly another of Kevin's legendary convoluted jokes. He made them up in his spare time and saved them until he could mangle a conversation enough to fit one of his jokes in.

"I give up," I said.

"What, haven't you ever heard it? 'Puddin' on the Ritz.' It's a classic."

"Very funny," I not-very-convincingly lied. "Danny? You want anything?"

He looked up again and shook his head. "I'm fine, thanks."

"Barbara?"

"I'll come with you," she said. "Anything to get away from his stupid jokes."

We went into the kitchen, and as I waited for the coffee to brew I remembered what Kevin had said about Barbara, about how he actually didn't like her that much.

"What were you and Kevin talking about?" I asked. "I thought you weren't too fond of him."

She hesitated. "I don't really know if I should tell you."

I was a bit taken aback by this. "Why not? Was it about me?"

Another little considered pause. "No, but it was the sort of thing that I wouldn't mention to Vicky, and since you're in charge now, I don't know whether I should tell you."

"Well, if I wasn't in charge, would you tell me?"

"Oh yeah. Definitely."

"Ah," I said, knowledgeably. "Gossip, is it?"

"Sort of. Look, Kevin was telling me that he overheard Danny on the phone this morning. Danny's been looking for another job, and he seems pretty serious about it."

"Shit," I said in my official capacity as replacement Vicky. "I'd rather not lose him. He's bloody good at his job. We'd be lost without him."

Barbara nodded. "I know."

"I'll talk to him," I said. "I'll see if he'll wait until the boss comes back before he makes any decisions."

She nodded again, and said nothing. I noticed that one of the things she didn't say was that there was a good chance Danny was leaving because of me. I hadn't exactly been very approachable in the past few days. She also didn't say that maybe the only reason Danny hadn't left *months* ago was because he thought that I might fall in love with him, and now that I had Sam . . .

Another of the things she didn't say was the opening paragraph of *Alice in Wonderland*, which has nothing to do with anything, except to show how easy it is to infer a meaning from someone else's silence. I realised that – regardless of Danny's own reasons for leaving – I was still thinking of him as a love-sick puppy who had no life other than waiting for me. Also, I was trying to look through his eyes with me as the centre of his universe, which I clearly wasn't if he was leaving, unless he was leaving because he was heart-broken.

That all occurred to me in a couple of seconds, and the conclusion I came to was that I didn't know what to do. Yes, I told myself, that is the true, correct conclusion. Momentarily pleased with myself at having been able to get a complete grasp of the situation, I realised that the truth was that I didn't know Danny as well as I'd thought, and that as his boss I should have been aware that he was thinking of moving on, but instead I'd been too wrapped up with sorting out Bernard Parker to notice that there were actually other people in the company, each with their own very individual problems.

I have to say, that actually made a lot more sense when it was running through my head at the time than it does now. But there you go, that's my thought process for you. Me thinking in a straight line is about as likely and as productive as an architect trying to design a house using crayons and a wonky ruler.

I don't know how much of that showed up on my face, but something must have slipped through, because Barbara suddenly said, "Look, whatever you're thinking, you're *not* doing a bad job. I don't know anyone else who could have dealt with Parker the way you did, there's only two and a half working days before the Vicky-Lady comes back, so just get a grip."

"You're right," I said. I had another little think, and this time I was able to come up with a more useful conclusion. And oddly enough, this conclusion was inspired by something else that Barbara *had* said.

When she'd mentioned Parker's name I remembered part of my diatribe to him. Specifically, it was the part about paying his staff less than the average wage.

I decided I would call a staff meeting for two-thirty in the afternoon, and do my best to rectify the situation.

Chapter Thirty-two

I made a few phone calls, then spent the rest of the morning going over the staff personal files. It felt really, really weird to read what the boss thought about each of my colleagues. It was also bloody surprising to see how badly they were being paid. I mean, I was earning enough to live on and buy videos. Every year I'd received an increment that was just above the inflation rate. I was always vaguely aware that if I hunted around I could make more money working for someone else, but I'd just never really been bothered. Looking for another job was just too much work. I was reasonably content to take what I had and leave it at that.

But that wasn't always true for the others . . .

Kevin was not very well-paid, and after reading through his file I could see why: he was actually crap at his job. On a day-to-day basis, he sort of ambled along, and he did have some brilliant ideas, but according to his file – and I checked this against the company records, so I knew it was true – he very rarely ever finished anything on time. In nine out of every ten cases, his work had been completed by me or Danny. And every time Vicky had taken him aside to try and sort him out, he'd cited a different personal problem that he was trying to overcome. He promised to try and do better, but somehow that never happened. I wondered why she still kept him on, but there was nothing that gave any reason.

Danny was earning the same as I was. Right down the line, his wages matched mine. He was hard–working, and always finished his work on time. The boss thought very highly of him, but she did make a personal comment to the effect that he was dull as shite and had no imagination. And *that* was when I discovered why Kevin hadn't been let go: without Kevin's ideas – the same great ideas that he could easily generate but never quite carry out – Danny would not be still with the company.

So, I said to myself after reading this, they're actually a very good team. They might not like each other personally, but together they do get the job done.

I also noticed – though it wasn't said anywhere, and I decided that was probably because Vicky didn't notice it herself – that neither of them realised how much they were dependent on each other. A few seconds after thinking this, I changed my mind: The boss *had* noticed it, but she knew that telling either of them would spoil the effect.

Not for the first time in the past couple of weeks, the boss had surprised me with her clear thinking.

I opened Barbara's file and had a damn good read . . . Barbara was paid more than any of us, and that really surprised me. Her official description was "Coordinator," and I'd always assumed that she was fairly low-paid and that she did those things she did because she couldn't really do anything else. But according to her file, she was – and I quote – "the most useful member of staff, after Susan."

"After Susan" . . . I was itching to read what Vicky had written about me, but I knew that I couldn't do that. Not because I had great integrity and self-control, but because my file wasn't there. The cow must have guessed I'd be peeking at the staff files and brought it home with her before she left on her honeymoon. I briefly considered breaking into her house, but I abandoned the plan when I realised that if I got caught it would probably reflect badly at my next Annual Performance Appraisal.

What I at first took to be the sound of a passing eighteen-wheeler turned out to be the "contents empty" warning from my stomach. I checked my watch . . . It was already five minutes into lunchtime, and the others hadn't had the decency to knock on my door and let me know. Or maybe it was courage they hadn't had: they knew I was going through their personal files. When the real boss is doing that I always give her a wide berth.

I peered out through the glass in the door. Barbara was at her desk munching through a sandwich and trying to do the Jumbo Crossword in one of the millions of magazines she stored under her desk. I decided that if the others were nervous about approaching me, then perhaps it was best that I didn't try to be pally with them over lunch, especially since they wouldn't then be able to huddle in a bunch and anxiously discuss their paranoid thoughts on the up-coming two-thirty meeting, like we used to do when the boss called a meeting.

I locked the personal files back in the filing cabinet, and went out to Barbara.

"I'm just heading home for lunch," I said. "I'll be back in about an hour. Mr Sulu, you have the con."

"Aye aye, Captain."

It was a nice, clear day, and the walk back to Ranelagh was without incident. I did have to tear myself away from the window of the video shop, but apart from that I arrived back at the house with few wounded and no fatalities.

Waiting patiently for me, propped up against my door, were two things: A small bunch of flowers with no card from the sender, and an envelope with very familiar handwriting.

I charged into my flat, put the kettle on, looked around for a vase for the flowers, gave up and used my only pint glass instead, lit one of the cigarettes I had given up only the day before, and sprawled out on the bed to read the letter . . .

Dear Susan,

I tore your fluffy cat to pieces as soon as I realised it was from you. Enclosed is one of its ears, as proof of my deed.

Your use of the word "shit" in your letter clearly demonstrates your neglected upbringing. I guess that you have a friend (or more likely a sympathetic social worker) to write the letters for you, and this friend is probably reading this letter out to you as well.

No doubt you have recently received a bunch of flowers, which were from me. I hope that they are dead, and that the weed-killer with which I sprinkled them has got into your system and is slowly killing you. The only thing that could make my life better would be deliberately not to attend your upcoming funeral.

May you have eternal torture in your new career as maggot food.

J.

The ear from the toy cat was glued to a piece of paper that had been cut into the shape of one of those boards that hunting people mount their animal heads on. I knew that I had no choice but to get a frame for the thing and hang it on the wall.

Chapter Thirty-three

At two-thirty we gathered in the meeting room. There were only the four of us, so it was a bit more intimate than I liked. Ideally, there would have been about twenty people, for several reasons.

The first reason is that some people really, really hate these sort of staff meetings. If there are enough people there they can hide behind someone.

The second reason is that in a bunch of ten or more, there'll always be a few people who really don't know each other. This gives the boss a bit of an advantage because she'll always look like she has a much better idea of what's going on.

The third reason is that there's always someone dumb enough to ask the questions that everyone else wants to ask but is too embarrassed to. For example, when I was in college we had this guy called Harvey Something, who wasn't ashamed to show his ignorance. Early on during the very first class, the lecturer muttered something along the lines of, "and we all know what Carl Jung thought about the concept of a single deity." The rest of us nodded to give the impression that, yes, actually we're all *quite* familiar with Jung's thoughts on the subject, thank you very much. Harvey Something was sitting only a few feet away from me. He looked blank, then raised his hand and asked the question we were all dying to know the answer to: Not "so, what *did* Carl Jung think about the concept of a single deity?" but "who the fuck is Carl Jung?"

The fourth reason is that it's much easier to give a total bollocking to a whole department than to one person. I mean, imagine if World War Two had taken place between just Hitler, Churchill, Roosevelt and Hirohito . . .

Roosevelt peered around the small, darkened room. Directly across from him was Adolf Hitler: He didn't look so tough. Roosevelt wasn't a big man himself, but Churchill was, so as long as Hitler wasn't stronger than he looked, Roosevelt and Churchill knew that they could gang up on him and beat the crap out of him in a couple of seconds.

Hirohito would not have been expecting this, Roosevelt knew, so he'd probably take a couple of seconds to react.

Churchill watched his American friend out of the corner of his eye. He saw Roosevelt give a slight nod.

"Now!" Roosevelt screamed as he vaulted over the table, landing a kick square on Hitler's jaw. He jumped on top of the Nazi's prone body, and within a split second had him in a headlock.

At the same time, Churchill moved with a speed surprising for someone his size. He charged towards Hirohito, but the Japanese Emperor was also faster than he looked: he jumped out of the way and picked up his chair.

Churchill slowed. "C'mon, Hiro . . . Put down the chair. You know you can't beat me."

"Is that what you think?" Hirohito sneered in a Japanese accent.

Churchill stared him down. "Go ahead. Make my day."

Hirohito said nothing. He was furiously going over the situation in his head. Things were looking bad. Maybe if he surrendered, he'd get a chance to fight another day . . . He took a deep breath and slowly lowered the chair. "All right, Winnie . . . I don't want to hurt you, and fighting never solved anything."

Churchill nodded, and relaxed his stance. As soon as Hirohito saw this, he raced forward, brandishing the chair like a club. But the British Bulldog was faster: he ducked under the arc of the chair and floored Hirohito with a roundhouse kick to the Emperors chest.

"So, what's the story?" Kevin said.

I was snapped out of my mental four-man production of "World War Two in Three Minutes." I was actually pretty annoyed at that, because I wanted to see how it turned out.

Time to stop daydreaming, I said to myself. "Right," I said. "We've only got a couple of days before the rightful heir to the throne returns from exile, so I was thinking that it's about time I got a better picture of what's going on. I want to know any problems you have, anything I can do to make things a little easier." I sat back, and waited for the deluge.

With one united voice, they said nothing. Kevin swung back and forth on his chair. Barbara twirled a pencil around her fingers. Danny just stared at the table.

"You're all fired," I said, in an attempt to break the tension.

Still nothing. Damn. This was harder than it looked.

"OK," I said. "Let's go around the table. Barbara?"

She shrugged. "Everything's fine. Except that I hate answering the phone. That's not in my job description."

"You've been doing it for ages," I reminded her.

"Yeah, and I've hated it for exactly the same number of ages. Every time Sicky-Vicky asks me what she can do to make things better, I tell her I don't want to answer the phone any more. It never makes any difference."

"OK," I said, making a note of that. "Anything else?"

She had a little think. "Yes. I don't like sitting outside the boss's office. I want to sit with everyone else. I hate having her peeking out to see if I'm still at my desk. She can't see any of you lot without leaving her office. It's not fair."

"I can understand that," I said. "But if someone's on the phone all day you can't have them too near the rest of the staff."

"Right. So it wouldn't be a problem if someone else was answering the phones."

"Good point," I said. "But you spend a lot of time on the phone anyway, organising stuff."

"A-ha!" She said triumphantly. "But it's the *ringing* of the phones that disturbs people, not the talking on the phone."

"Another good point." I noted that down too. "OK. I'll get back to you on that later. Kevin?"

He didn't hesitate to answer. "I want more money."

I'd been expecting that. "Fine. We can discuss that privately."

"Yeah, sure. But when? That's what I want to know. I've been promised a review every week for the past four months. So when are we going to do it?"

"When this meeting is over," I said. "I can't do it any sooner than that."

That took the wind out of his sails. "OK . . . Fine. That's good."

I made another little note. "Danny?"

"Everything's OK," he said.

"No problems?" I probed. "Nothing that I can change?"

The way he looked at me told me that I was indeed very likely to be the source of his unspoken problems. "I don't think so," he said.

I waited a few seconds in case he was going to add anything, and then I said, "OK. Well, you probably all know this but the situation is that we've almost certainly lost the Parker Technology business."

"Thank God," Kevin said. "Bunch of fucking morons."

I ignored the comment. "What I'd like to do is drum up some more business before Monday. To that end, I've asked Neil Forsythe to work for us on a commission basis. He's pretty certain that he'll be able to get a few leads before the end of the week. That seems a bit quick to me, but you never know. Anyway, one thing he's suggested is that we put together a promotional pack advertising our services. His idea is that we can just go through the phone book and send one out to any company we can think of. And if that doesn't work, we set up a deal to send it out as a flyer in one of the industry magazines. He's checking on prices for stuff like that."

"We could find ourselves with *way* too much work to do," Kevin said. "We should jack up our prices and just target the really rich companies."

"Maybe," Barbara said, "but the really rich companies don't need us. I think we should do our best to find out which companies are having trouble, and just target them."

I nodded. "Good thinking. Anyway, ideally, we'll have the text and layout ready before Monday. I know that's not going to be easy, and it might mean late hours or coming in at the weekend." Before anyone could jump in with their objections, I added, "And I'll make sure it's worth the effort for each of you."

My little speech was followed by a hearty and occasionally vicious discussion as to what "worth the effort" actually meant in real monetary terms, but I was able to get their cooperation by promising them that they could all have Monday off if we got the promotional pack ready on time.

"Even if we don't have to work late or at the weekend?" Kevin asked.

"Of course," I said. "It's not the time you put in that counts. I'm more interested in results."

We finished up at about three, with a plan to meet back at four for an ideas session. Kevin stayed behind, and once he didn't have support from the others he was actually quite meek.

I decided to get things over with as soon as possible. "You've probably guessed that I've looked at your file."

He nodded.

"Well, the boss is bloody good at keeping things quiet, because I had no idea what was in there. I'm not going to go into details, but basically she thinks that you're only barely worth the trouble."

Naturally, he was immediately defensive. "Yeah, but . . ."

I interrupted him. "Let me finish. I happen to think she's wrong, and that's understandable because she hasn't worked with you like I have. OK, so you're not great at getting your assignments finished, but you *are* a good thinker. In fact, I'm relying on you to come up with the goods on this promotional pack. So, I can't promise anything definite, but as soon as she comes back I'm going to recommend that she gives you a raise, starting immediately." I wrote a figure down on a blank page on my notebook. It was about three and a half thousand pounds more than he was currently earning. "How does this look?"

"Jesus!"

"Like I said, I can't promise anything. But I think there's a very good chance you'll get that. Or most of it anyway. I'll need some evidence to back this up, though, so the more brilliant ideas you can come up with in the next few days the better your chances."

He stared at the amount on the page, and nodding slowly. "OK. OK."

"Just don't go around grinning like an idiot for the rest of the day. This is between us for the moment. Don't go telling *anyone*. And don't mention it to Vicky if you get to see her before I do."

"Sure. Listen, Susan, that's great. I was starting to think that I wasn't going to last much longer here."

"You can start your brilliant ideas by coming up with some way I can keep Danny here."

He suddenly looked suspicious. "Shit, I told Barbara not to tell anyone!"

It was my turn to look suspicious. "You mean you *knew* Danny was planning to leave? And Barbara knows as well? And *you* told her?"

For once, he was stuck for words. "Well . . . I just said that I *thought* he was planning to go."

I let him off the hook. "Whatever. It doesn't matter now. The problem is that we can't afford to lose him any more than we can afford to lose you."

So Kevin said he'd go away and think of something brilliant to keep Danny with the company. I returned to my own office – and I have to admit I wondered briefly just when it was that I'd started to think of it as *my* office – and checked through our huge pile of CVs until I found one from a local eighteen year-old girl who was looking for work experience as a receptionist. I phoned her house, and left a message with her mother that she was to phone me back as soon as possible. She called back within the hour. I introduced myself, and asked her if she was currently employed.

"Not at the moment, Mrs Perry," she replied. I let the *faux pas* go.

"How much experience have you had with phones, faxes, computers and photocopiers?"

There was a pause. "Not really all that much." I could picture her biting her lip and thinking, "Shit, I shouldn't have admitted that."

I was in a generous mood. "It doesn't matter. If you're not busy this evening, can you call to the office around five-thirty? I'd like to talk to you."

"What, like for an interview?"

I smiled to myself. "If you like . . . Have you had many interviews?"

This time she caught on a bit more quickly. "Only a few," she replied. I was pleased with that, if she'd said that she hadn't had any, that would make it seem like she wasn't worth employing, and if she'd said that she'd had hundreds, then it would have seemed even worse.

"Well, come around at half five, and we'll talk, OK?"

"Great, thanks!"

We said goodbye and she hung up, and I could picture her rushing in to her parents shouting, "I got an interview!" This would be followed by panicky washing and ironing of good skirt and blouse, and quite a bit of the old "What are you going to say if they ask . . ?"

I was actually enjoying myself. Maybe I'd been

wrong about not liking being in charge. I could get used to this, I told myself. Of course, power corrupts, and absolute power corrupts absolutely – and Austin Powers corrupts Austinly – so I knew I'd better not get *too* comfortable.

I swung back in the big, comfy, expensive boss's chair, and lit a cigarette in the office that has a strict no-smoking policy, except for bosses.

Chapter Thirty-four

We started the idea session at four, and by five twenty we were all knackered. Kevin and Barbara had come up with some brilliant ideas, we'd argued them out, figured out our next plan of action, and then I told everyone to go home and get a good night's sleep because the rest of the week was going to be murder. On the way out, I asked Barbara to come in as early as she could the next morning, because the two of us were going to swap desks.

My interviewee arrived at exactly five-thirty. She was young, reasonably presentable, and – to my eyes – incredibly thin. I buzzed her in and brought her into my office.

I was actually quite amused by the whole situation. I remembered what my first interviews had been like: absolutely terrifying, as though the interviewer was doing a nixer as a cannibal.

"So, Jennifer," I said. "Now, your CV is a bit out of date. I don't suppose you have a more recent copy?"

She blushed. "No. Sorry."

"That's OK. I mean, I didn't give you much notice." I pretended to read through her CV as I desperately tried to think of something to ask her. "I see that you don't have any experience as a receptionist. Do you think that'll be a problem?"

"I'm a quick learner, Mrs Perry."

"OK," I said. "First, it's not Mrs Perry. I'm not even a Mrs. Just call me Susan. Second, imagine I'm the person on the other end of the phone." I tapped the phone with my pencil. "Answer it."

She put the phone up to her ear. "Hello?"

"Let's start again," I said. "Always say 'good morning, Complete Office Solutions,' or 'good afternoon, Complete Office Solutions.' Some places will want you to say 'Jennifer speaking' as well, but I don't think that's important."

We went through the opening ritual again.

"Good evening, Complete Office Solutions. Can I help you?" Jennifer asked.

"I'm looking for Susan Perry," I said.

She *almost* did the right thing. "Can you hold for a moment please?" She looked up at me. "Are you in?"

"I don't know. It depends on who it is."

So we started again, and this time she got it right. I decided right there and then that she might be naïve, but I'd definitely hire her on a trial basis. Unless she screwed up monumentally. Which of course would be my own fault.

I brought her through the office and gave her a brief run-through on how most of the equipment worked.

She caught me out by asking me how to do a conference call. I had no idea, so I just told her that it was the same as on most phone systems. I also made a mental note to ask Barbara to tell her.

Once that was done, we went back into my office. I explained the few rules we had, went through the working hours and holidays and told her the salary. It seemed pathetic to me, but it was slightly more than she'd be earning on the dole. Then I asked her when she could start.

"What, you mean I got the job?"

"If you want it."

"Is Monday too soon?"

"How about tomorrow morning at nine?" I asked. "We normally get paid on the last Friday of the month, so you just missed it, but if you start tomorrow I'll pay you for the first two days on Friday afternoon."

"I'll need time to go and sign off."

"That's not a problem," I said. "Just let me know."

I went home in a good mood. I was pretty pleased with myself. I'd solved Kevin's and Barbara's problems, got Neil Forsythe at least a couple of days' work, hired a total stranger and received a bunch of flowers and a letter from J. Not bad going at all, Mrs Perry.

Chapter Thirty-five

Thursday was murder in work, but not in the "My God, I'm going to screw up spectacularly and be fired and I don't know how to do anything and everyone hates me" way that I was used to. It was just work, work, work, from the time I got in to the time Sam phoned me to say that he was in Ranelagh in a phone box and where the hell was I?

It was a stupid question – I mean, he phoned the office, I answered, where else would I be? – but I didn't say that because I was very definitely the one at fault.

"Shit, I'm sorry," I said. "We're working a bit late. Look, I'll wrap up here. Do you want to make your way over?"

He agreed, and I had to give him directions. I'd given him directions before – for when he was supposed to turn up the previous Friday – but Sam's memory was like that. He could remember the name of every movie he'd ever seen, and who stared in it, and who directed it, but he'd have trouble remembering what – if anything – he'd had for lunch.

I went out to the others. I'd sent Jennifer home at

five: it was only her first day, after all, and she'd been clearly knackered from about three in the afternoon, and the phones didn't ring much after five. Not counting irate boyfriends who'd spent ages knocking on their girlfriends' doors.

Kevin, Danny and Barbara were still hard at it. We'd covered a lot of ground during the day, and already the product was beginning to take shape. I guessed that the only major thing we really needed to do now was to phone all of our clients – well, the friendly ones anyway – and ask them for quotes about how brilliant we are. In return, they'd receive a bit of free advertising. Neil Forsythe was planning on dropping in to the office the next day to report on his progress.

"It's a quarter past seven," I said. "There's no point in killing ourselves. You might as well all go home."

"Suits me," Kevin said. "I'm starving."

"Me too," said Barbara. "Hey, weren't you supposed to be meeting Sam?"

"Yeah, I forgot what time it was. That was him on the phone a minute ago. He's coming over."

She smiled. "Well, I'm not in any rush. Why don't we all go for something to eat and then go to the pub?"

Well, there it was. She'd said it out loud. I had wanted to keep him away from everyone for at least a few more weeks, but I'd been playing the part of the magnanimous boss for the past couple of days so I couldn't turn down the idea. "All right," I said, "but everybody's buying their own. I think I've spent enough of the boss's money already."

Kevin was agreeable – his only worry was that he might miss *Friends* if he wasn't home by nine – but Danny was harder to persuade.

"I think I'll just head home," he said, without looking at me.

I walked over to his desk, and sat on the edge. We hadn't really talked in ages. Not that we'd ever talked about anything much anyway, but occasionally we'd spend half an hour discussing topics that were only vaguely work-related. Danny didn't have much of a life at all, and I really felt sorry for him.

"Come on," I said, speaking quietly enough so that the others wouldn't hear me. "It's been ages since we all went out together."

"You know I'm not very comfortable with strangers," he said, rather pointedly. "I wouldn't be much fun."

"Maybe not," I said, "but you definitely won't be any fun if you *don't* come."

He considered it for a few seconds, then shook his head. I could see that his resolve was weakening.

"Look," I suggested, "I'll phone Jennifer and see if she wants to come along. At least then there'll be *two* strangers. And you won't be the only one feeling awkward."

"OK. If she says yes, I'll go."

I phoned Jennifer, who sounded even more nervous than she had the day before. Maybe she thought I was going to fire her or something. When I mentioned that we were all going out and she was invited, she relaxed, and said that she'd call around to the office in about ten minutes.

While I'd been on the phone to her, Sam had arrived, and was sitting in the lobby chatting to Barbara.

Eddie Rocket's was full. Flannagan's was full. The local Chinese restaurant said that they wouldn't be able to seat six for about an hour. It looked increasingly likely that we would be dining heartily on Big Macs until Jennifer told us about a pub that served great food and was always empty on Thursday evenings. Sometimes it pays to have a native on board.

We sat around the table in the traditional boy-girl-boy-girl format: me, Sam, Barbara, Kevin, Jennifer and Danny. This meant that Danny was also next to me, which I wasn't too happy about. It also meant that Barbara was next to Sam, which I wasn't very happy about either. Barbara wasn't happy at being stuck next to Kevin, but as she was also next to Sam that made up for it. Kevin didn't much like being next to Barbara, but I think he quite fancied Jennifer, so that evened out as well. For Jennifer, this was her first time out with a bunch of people who for the most part knew each other quite well and were all at least four years older, so I think she was too nervous to be happy.

It was ironic that the only person among us who was truly happy with the seating arrangement was Danny. The table around which we sat was on the small side – about the size of one of those little tables that people put their TVs on – so that meant Danny's leg was pressed against mine most of the time. Well, I'm not sure if it was deliberate on his part, but that's what I was thinking about during the opening half hour, when there was much doffing of jackets, ordering of drinks and comments to the effect of "I don't think I've even seen this place before."

The conversation was stilted at first, limited more or less to each of us asking Jennifer what she'd thought about her first day, and Jennifer replying that it had been harder than she'd expected. Once the emaciated chicken wings and day-old "fries" had arrived, the tension relaxed a bit and Kevin started to tell some fairly harmless jokes. They went down well, and pretty shortly he was well into his repertoire of extremely dirty jokes.

That was kind of awkward for me, partly because I was theoretically still in charge and if any of the other patrons of the pub took offence it would be me who took the blame. I was also kind of concerned about Jennifer. She was only eighteen, after all, and she probably wasn't used to sitting in a pub at all, let alone with a bunch of adults who were fairly free with their bad language.

And then poor little Jennifer – in whose mouth butter wouldn't even *think* of melting – started to tell some of the mankiest jokes I'd ever heard. She was interrupted at one point by the arrival of the lounge boy, who gathered up the glasses, took an order for more drinks and more food, and made a comment to Jennifer along the lines of, "I haven't seen you in here in a couple of years."

There was a minor scuffle at about twenty to nine when Kevin realised he'd have to run like mad to get home in time to see *Friends*, but he settled down when

Jennifer told him that she was taping it and she'd bring in the tape in the morning. I think he fell in love with her at that point, and I think she was warming to him: for the rest of the night it was all "Remember when Chandler's mother kissed Ross?" and "Remember when Joey moved out and Eddie was staying in the flat?" and "No, no, what about the time when Rachel's friends came to Central Perk?" This last was followed by the two of them raising their hands and screeching "we've got elbows!"

Barbara and Sam got into a deep conversation about me. They deliberately pretended I wasn't there, and gave me a real slagging. "Susan's probably the most intelligent person I've ever met," Barbara said at one point. "She was born with the Knows Everything gene." Sam laughed at this, and replied with, "She's very generous. I've never known her not to offer to let me pay when we go out." I made several attempts to join in, but it was clear that I was spoiling their fun. Sam kept turning to me and winking, as if to say, "We're only messing, I do still love you."

I wasn't annoyed at them for that – I mean, I could take a slagging – but it meant that I was left with no one to talk to but Danny, and he wasn't saying very much.

The others were all too involved in their own conversations to notice us, so I decided that it was probably a good time to try and sort things out with Danny. After all, we'd both had a couple of drinks, he was relaxing a little . . .

"So, Danny . . . You've been very quiet the past few weeks."

He nodded.

"Is everything OK?"

He took a deep breath. "That depends on what you mean by OK."

"What about the job?" I asked. "Yesterday you said everything was fine, but somehow I don't believe that." In my mind, an irate lawyer was pushing himself to his feet and shouting, "Objection, your Honour! Prosecution is leading the witness!"

"Well, what do you want me to say?" he asked, a little irritably.

I considered my words carefully before answering. "We've been friends for a few years," – objection, your Honour! Prosecution is a lying cow! – "and you've never really said much about yourself. For all I know, you're a mass murderer in your spare time."

He shrugged.

"So, what *do* you do with your spare time?"

"Not much. I read a bit. And I do a bit of swimming and cycling."

"Yeah, sure," I said. "That's what people put on their CVs when they don't want to admit that the only hobbies they have are drinking and smoking."

"And I make sculptures out of the frost that gathers on the inside of the icebox in the fridge."

I was impressed. "Really?"

He grinned. "No, not really. What do *you* do?" He nodded towards Sam. "When you're not with him."

Ouch! "Well, I read a bit . . . And watch a whole rake of videos."

"What's your all-time favourite movie, then?"

I started to tell him that I didn't have a single all-time favourite, but that given time I could probably narrow my list down to twenty or so, maybe thirty, and then I realised what he was up to. "That's my trick, changing the subject."

"Really? I've never noticed." Sarcasm dripped from his voice like the grease from the chicken wings we'd consumed.

I changed the subject back. "Really, what do you do?"

He shrugged. "You'd laugh."

"No I wouldn't," I replied, praying that I was right. "Tell me."

"I draw. Portraits, mainly."

I was impressed again, but at least this time I did have something to be impressed by. "Are you any good at it?"

"Yes. I am." No hesitation, no false modesty.

I hadn't been expecting that, so I asked, "Are you sure?"

He laughed. "As you might say, damn right I'm sure!"

"So, like, do you ever go out on a Saturday and bring a chair and sit on Grafton Street and draw the passers-by for money?"

"No, but I do a bit of freelance work for the police. You know, working with the victims, drawing the faces of their attackers."

Maybe it was the few drinks I'd had, but I was leaning towards believing this one. I almost said

"Really?" again, but caught myself in time. "Ever draw any famous criminals?"

"You mean 'infamous criminals'? Not yet, but I'm always hoping that someone will be attacked by one of the Spice Girls. Or the Nolan Sisters. Or The Corrs." He began to pat his pockets. "In fact, I have a list here of some of the famous people I'm hoping will go absolutely mental before I run out of paper."

"Hmm . . . And I suppose *all* of them are gorgeous women?"

Danny looked shocked that I'd even suggest such a thing. "Of course not! The brother from The Corrs is a man. If he was one of the attackers, I'd only give the drawing to the police on the condition that I could meet his sisters. Or Enya, if he knew her, which he probably does, because I imagine they all go to the same parties."

I was silent for a while, thinking about him, then suddenly blurted out a question that was on my mind: "Do you have *any* friends?" As soon as I'd asked, I wished I hadn't. It's not the sort of thing you ask someone like him.

He surprised me again, though, by answering quite honestly. "No, not really. I suppose that you and Kevin and Barbara are probably the closest friends I have." I noticed that his expression darkened when he looked at Barbara. "Well, that's not entirely true," he hastily continued. "I still meet up every couple of months with some of the people I was with in college, but they're not so much friends as acquaintances. And to be frank, I don't think that most of them would be interested in seeing me if it was just the two of us."

That was probably the most I'd ever heard him say in one go. I wanted to tell him that he'd make more friends if he just lightened up, but even more than that I wanted to get back to the subject of Barbara . . . "Right. I want to ask you something personal, and you don't have to answer if you don't want to. And I don't want you to think that she's spreading stories about you . . ."

"Ah," he said, clearly understanding what I was getting at. But he still waited for me to ask the question.

"So," I continued, keeping my voice low, "is it true that you slept with Barbara?"

He took another one of his deep breaths, glanced at Barbara, and said nothing.

I really felt like shit. I shouldn't have asked that. He wasn't as lightened-up as he seemed. "I'm sorry," I said. "Just forget I ever said that."

He looked at me. "It's not that I mind you asking. I don't. But I do mind answering. It's not the sort of thing you drop into casual conversation. Well, *I* don't anyway."

It was my turn to be silent, as I tried to figure out whether the answer was yes or no. Outwardly, I tried to give the impression that I was ashamed of intruding on his private life.

"A gentleman," Danny said, "does not make public the details of his sexual conquests. Especially not to someone he . . ." he hesitated. "Someone who does not actually *need* to know. No offence."

I could barely believe it: *he* was apologising to *me*. That was definitely the wrong way around.

Sam suddenly nudged me. "It's your shout. Pet."

I sneered at him. "What, you spend the whole night chatting up some other bird and now you want me to buy drink for you?"

"Yes. A rock shandy. And peanuts. And a cuttlefish for the bird."

Barbara thumped his arm. "Who are you calling a bird?"

"Do you want this damn cuttlefish or not?" Sam asked.

We were interrupted by Kevin getting to his feet and showing Jennifer his impression of Ross from *Friends*. It was not a good impression. Jennifer did her impression of Phoebe, and that was a lot better. Barbara caught my eye, nodded at the smitten Kevin, and grinned.

Beside me, in a tiny blank space on a beermat, Danny was drawing a very good likeness of Courtney Cox.

By the time we left the pub, it was way too late for Sam to get the last bus home. He made feeble attempts of pretending he'd walk me home first then go back to Ranelagh and get a taxi, but I wasn't fooled.

It was a cold night, and I hugged him close as we walked. "So, what did you think of my colleagues?"

"They're OK. Your man Kevin is gas. I didn't hear much out of Danny, though. But I thought that Barbara would never shut up."

"Really? I could see how awkward you found it when she was flirting with you."

"Is *that* what that was?" He shivered, and buttoned up his denim jacket. "Kevin seemed to be getting on all right with the new girl."

"Yeah, she has the same first name as his one true love, Jennifer Aniston. It'll be interesting to see what he's like tomorrow in the office. I'll bet you anything you like he'll keep finding reasons to walk past her desk."

Sam grinned. "Well, I would. She's a bit of a babe."

"Which bit?"

"Just her body. And her mind."

I made a big deal about being put out. "So, you prefer short women with no curves, then?"

"Not at all. I only love big fat birds. I promise."

I suppose that was meant to be endearing, or charming, or funny. He certainly *couldn't* have meant it to be tactful. I pretended that it *was* endearing, charming and funny. But it hurt. He could have dumped me there and then, he could have spent the evening shagging Barbara on the pub floor, he could have done or said almost anything else, and it wouldn't have hurt so much.

When we got into the flat, we undressed each other and spent the next half hour making love on the floor. It was not particularly pleasant for me, but for the sake of his stupid male ego I made all the right moves and all the right noises at all the right times.

Afterwards, we climbed into bed, and lay there, all wrapped up in each other's arms. Much later, when I was sure he was asleep, I cried.

And while I cried I was extremely careful not to sob too hard, in case I woke him.

Chapter Thirty-six

"Of course, we're going to have to run all this by your boss when she gets back," Neil Forsythe told me. "And she's going to have the final say. What are the chances that she'll want the whole thing dropped because it wasn't her idea?"

It was just after nine o'clock on Friday morning. Neil had bustled into the office all full of life. He'd poured over everything we'd prepared and he'd declared it to be "fucking great stuff" and "just what we need."

And now he was talking to me, and my mind kept wandering back to Sam. But it wasn't wandering back to give him a little hug . . . It was wandering back to hide behind a wall and see what he was up to.

"I don't know," I said finally. I shook my head briskly, as though my negative feelings could be thrown off by centrifugal force. "Sorry, I'm a bit preoccupied today." I flicked through the various pages that had been sitting lifelessly in my hands. They were advertising flyers of the sort that we were trying to do, and had been covered with notes in Neil's meticulous handwriting. It didn't take long to see that most of the flyers were just gimmicks with no substance. At least ours wasn't trying to be anything other than what it was: a way of telling companies what we could do for them.

"I was asking what the chances are that she'll drop the project because it wasn't her idea," Neil said, a little more forcefully this time.

I glanced up at him, and saw that he was practically staring at me. "I wouldn't worry about that," I said. "She's able to tell a good thing when she sees it."

"Yes, but *is* it a good thing? That's the question we're supposed to be addressing."

"I think so, yes. We've never really advertised before because we always had enough work coming in. Without Parker Technology, we're going to be down a few grand every month." I quickly read through the mock-up of our brochure again. It basically said that we were not a recruitment agency *per se*. What we offered were complete office solutions – hence the name. We could and did recruit personnel, of course, but we were also part image consultant, part management trainers, part emergency secretarial service – though it had been quite a while since any of us had had to fulfil that part of the duty, thank God – and part just-bloody-handy-people-to-know . . .

Out in the main office, Kevin, Danny and Barbara were on the phone to our clients, asking them for a few brief words to tell the world how brilliant we were.

Earlier, I'd overheard Kevin chatting to one of his mates who was a mid-level manager for one of our clients: "Repeat the following: Complete Office Solutions are without doubt the best-kept secret in the industry today." A pause. "No, go on. I'll buy you a pint." Another pause. "Well, it's not as if it's a lie or something. You'll get your name and the company name under the quote." Yet another pause. "Yeah, we could, but you have to *say* it, otherwise it would be libelous." Again a pause, longer than the others. "If you do, we'll invite you to the next office do. Look, just *say* the fucking thing!" And finally: "That's great. Thanks, Padraig. I'll see you at the weekend."

"We need to get some colour mock-ups done as soon as it's ready," Neil said. "Have we got a colour printer?"

"No, but they have one in the office downstairs, and they owe us for all the times they've used our photocopier and fax."

"All right," he said. "All right. We're going to make it." He was clearly chuffed with himself. "This'll be one up the arse for Bernard Parker."

We got through the rest of the day without any real trouble, and made our self-imposed deadline of five in the afternoon with about an hour to spare. I regretted promising the others the day off on Monday as a reward. We'd only worked a couple of hours extra the previous night. Then I corrected myself. We'd only worked a couple of hours over the seven and a half per day for which we were contracted, but since we generally dossed around for most of the working day, the fact that I'd managed to squeeze more than two full days out of them was nothing short of a miracle.

Anyway, a promise is a promise. I supposed that they deserved it.

Vicky's plane was due to arrive in Dublin Airport at about eight on Monday morning. I knew without the slightest doubt that she wouldn't be putting in a full day's work – I mean, who would? – but I also knew that she'd have to pass close to the office on her way home, so she'd certainly drop in for a while. Even if it was only to make sure that I hadn't bankrupted us or burned the building down.

It wouldn't look good when she arrived and saw that things had changed a little. Kevin, Barbara and Danny wouldn't be in. There would be an actual receptionist doing actual receptioning. I'd be ensconced at the boss's desk. And there was a good chance that Neil Forsythe would be floating around the office somewhere. I was going to have a lot of explaining to do . . . I was not looking forward to it.

But in some ways I couldn't wait for the weekend to be over. Sam was working until Sunday afternoon, so I'd promised Sharon I'd meet her for a drink or twelve in town. Naturally, she'd want to know everything – she thought I had a much more exciting life than she did – and I wasn't sure what I was going to say when she asked how things were with Sam.

I mean, what *could* I tell her? That on the outside everything was fine, but that last night he'd said something that really, really hurt me? No, there was no way I was about to tell her that. Sam definitely hadn't realised what he'd done, and maybe he'd never say anything like that again. So everything might be great between us forever. Maybes and mights are all very well, I told myself, but it was the fact that he hadn't even *realised* that he'd said the wrong thing that really bothered me: he wasn't able to see a comment like that from my point of view. He hadn't even noticed how upset I'd been, but I didn't really blame him for that: after all, I'd done my best to cover up how I felt.

And as if that wasn't bad enough, my father phoned during the afternoon . . . "Susan, I was talking to your mother – remember her? Tall, good-looking, gave birth to you? – well, she and I had the crazy idea that you might drop home some time and visit us."

"Well, if you're not off sunning yourself in Blackwater, we might be able to arrange something for this weekend. What do you say, Dad? Shall I have my people call your people?"

"As it happens, we're not planning on going to Wexford this weekend," Dad said. "Your mother's dragging me out to look at some houses."

"So that's really going to happen, then? It wasn't just a mad plan to force me to move out?"

He gave a short, humourless laugh. "It was a mad plan to force your brother to move out, but it hasn't worked yet."

"How is he?"

He began to get angry. "How the fu . . . How would

I know? He never talks to me. Your mother says he's fine."

Somehow, I could sense that Dad and Fintan hadn't sorted things out between them. Call me clairvoyant if you like, but I had the feeling that all was not well. "I'll try and talk to him if I see him, Dad. Will you be there tomorrow afternoon?"

"God knows. That's up to your mother." he said. "Ring before you come, just to make sure."

Well, great. So now I had to make appointments to see my own parents.

My parents would want to know everything that had happened in the few weeks since I'd last seen them. They'd ask about the flat, and I didn't want to tell them that the old woman who'd lived upstairs had died a week ago. My mother would berate me for not telling them earlier, then she'd be all over the place trying to get a Mass card and everything. And they'd want to know about work: the last time I spoke to them I'd mentioned that I was going to be in charge while the boss was on holidays. The odds of them *not* asking about that were about the same as the odds that Sam would one day get to play for Crystal Palace during the FA Cup final.

I'd told Sam that I'd meet him on Sunday afternoon. I tried to convince myself that the couple of days apart would be good for us, but I didn't really believe it.

Give him another chance, a little voice inside told me. He'll probably never do anything like that again.

Another little voice inside me disagreed, and said that I'd be better off without him.

The first voice told me to ignore the second voice. Everything would be fine.

The second voice insisted, rather loudly, that Sam was a waste of time and I'd be better off with almost anyone else.

The first voice told the second voice to shut up, because it didn't know what it was talking about.

The second voice took great exception to this, and went around to the first voice's house and set fire to its car.

Chapter Thirty-seven

I met Sharon in what had once been our old haunt, the Parnell Mooney. The place had not changed one bit since we'd last been there. It seemed to me that even the patrons were the same. Maybe all the pubs in the city centre buy their customers in the same place they get their furniture.

"So, how's everything going with Sam?" she asked as we stood squashed into one corner of the bar.

"Great," I lied. "How's Mark?"

She grinned. "Brilliant. I don't know why I never noticed it before but he's dead sexy."

"Oh, really? So it's not just a platonic relationship, then?"

"So far it is. Apart from a few snogs. I don't know what I'm going to say to my mother. She's always going on about how disgraceful it is when someone my age goes out with a man who's ten years older."

I nodded, understanding exactly what she meant: One of Sharon's neighbours was fourteen when she started going out with a man who was twenty-five. These days, that seems to be all the rage, but back then it was quite a scandal. "You could always lie and say that he's only twenty-eight, and that he just *looks* like he's thirty-five," I suggested.

"It wouldn't work. She knows him, remember? She's known him since he was a teenager."

"Then you could pretend that you're just friends and nothing is going on."

"Yeah, right. She'd really believe that. Sooner or later one of the neighbours would see us, and come charging around to the house. You know that lot, always thrilled to be the first with bad news."

"Well, at least it's not like he's your teacher, or something," I said, referring to the classic by Nobokov.

"I know what you mean," she replied, probably thinking that I was referring to the classic by The Police. "I might tell my Dad first. He's always been a bit more open-minded."

"Yeah," I said, "but that's because he's a man, and no middle-aged man can see anything wrong with going out with a much younger woman."

Thinking about it much later, after all that had happened, thirty-five didn't seem middle-aged at all, but as I was talking to Sharon I found myself thinking things like, "When Mark was sixteen and legally allowed to have sex, Sharon was only six."

I was jostled from behind by someone failing to attract the barman's attention. "Look, it's way too packed in here. Drink up and we'll go somewhere else."

Somehow, we ended up going back to Cabra, and into our local, where people I don't think I'd ever even seen before told me that they all thought I'd emigrated or something. I even got a free "welcome back" drink from the barman.

Sharon phoned Wendy and Jackie, and they arrived shortly afterwards. It felt like months since that night when we'd gone out to celebrate Laura's twenty-second birthday. I wondered aloud where Laura was now, but no one answered, so I assumed that she'd done something on them and no one was talking to her. That didn't bother me much, because I'd never really liked her anyway.

So the four of us sat, and drank, and laughed, and drank a bit more, and a bit more after that.

We were well on our way to getting pissed when it occurred to me that I'd never returned Anthony's call on the previous Friday. I decided to invite him around. It took me about ten minutes to find the right change among all the crap in my bag – well, actually it took me so long because I was too drunk to remember his number – but he seemed pleased to have been asked, and said that he wasn't doing anything more important than watching telly and he'd be around in a few minutes.

I hadn't realised how late it was getting. Just before Anthony arrived the barman did the old flickering lights trick, signalling that closing time was bearing down upon us. I saw Anthony at the door and rushed over to grab his hand. "Come on! We'll just make it for last orders!"

I did my best to drag him over to the bar, but somehow I couldn't manage it. It occurred to me that either I was drunker than I thought, or that he'd somehow put on eight stone in the past few weeks.

It turned out to be neither. Anthony just stood there, with his arm outstretched and me tugging feebly at the end of it. "It doesn't matter," he said. "I didn't come here for a drink. I just came to see you."

I thought that this was the most lovely thing anyone had ever said to me. Which just goes to show you that I really *was* pissed. I jumped into his arms – nearly knocking him over in the process – and gave him a big hug. "I haven't seen you in ages!"

He prised me loose. "I know. You were supposed to keep in touch, remember? And you were supposed to invite me out to your flat."

"Of course you can," I replied, in that unconnected way that only drunk people can manage. "You don't have to ask. You're my best friend. You don't have to ask." I started to poke him in the chest. "You can come and see me any time you feel like it." I turned towards the bar again. "Come on, we'll get a drink."

He shook his head. "Not for me. Look, are you staying with your folks tonight? Because if you're not, I'll give you a lift home."

"Anthony," I said, suddenly exasperated. "We only just *got* here!"

Despite his attempts to be serious, he laughed. "When you're ready," he said.

We went back to join the others. As soon as Jackie

saw him, she shoved Wendy out of the way and said, "There's a seat here, Anthony."

"Thanks." He squeezed himself in between them. "How are you, Jackie?"

She'd had quite a few as well, so she giggled like a schoolgirl. "I'm fine. I like your jeans. Are they new?" She gave Anthony's jeans the famous moving-the-palm-around-on-the-knee quality test. "Were they expensive?"

He might have claimed not to fancy her, but he didn't resist much. "Not really. They're Dunnes best."

Jackie let out a heavy sigh. "I know what you mean. Too many people think that labels are important. It's not what you wear that counts, it's who's wearing them." This from Jackie, who was such a major fashion victim that she had her own support group.

We staggered out of the pub at about midnight, with the suggestion from me that we all go to a club on Leeson Street. "You can all stay in my place tonight," I said. "There's loads of room." Which was not entirely true.

Luckily – even though I was disappointed at the time – no one else wanted to go clubbing. Sharon had to work in the morning, Wendy said that she was too tired, and Jackie wanted to slip away somewhere quiet with Anthony.

Anthony took my arm and steered me away from the others. "Bye," he called over his shoulder. "Susan wants to go home."

"No I don't," I said.

"Yes you do. Come on." He kept walking, and I had no choice but to go with him.

I glanced over my shoulder and saw that Jackie was

most likely putting one of her spells on me. "Sorry! It's not my fault!"

After a couple of minutes, I began to get annoyed with him. "Look, I don't want to go home yet."

"Yes you do," he repeated. "And you'd better stay awake in the car because I don't know the way."

By the time we reached the flat I was a little more sober, and I was no longer annoyed at him for dragging me away from the others.

He helped me up the steps – I wasn't really that drunk, but he helped me anyway – and I fumbled around with my keys. "I know it's one of these," I said loudly. "No, that's the one for the office." I held up one of the office keys. "Look, doesn't the marks on that key look like they spell out 'Mum'?"

"Yes, they does," Anthony said, gently taking the bundle from me. Even though he'd never unlocked my hall door before, he managed to find the right key in the first go. "In you go."

I leaned against the wall while Anthony found the key for the flat. He practically carried me in, then lowered me on the bed.

"I'm knackered!" I said, very loudly this time.

"You're drunk," he replied.

Anthony stood there for a few moments, wondering what to do. I imagine that his first instinct was to undress me and put me to bed, but he was too much of a gentleman to risk that, so he compromised by taking off my shoes and my jacket.

"Right, I'll let myself out," he said.

I reached out and grabbed his hand. "Don't go yet," I said. "I have to talk to *someone*."

He considered this. "OK. I'll stay for a while. Do you want me to make coffee?"

"Yeah. But there's no milk."

"I don't mind."

"Well, I do. Go out and get some, will you?"

He just smiled, and filled the kettle. "What was it you wanted to talk about?"

I watched his back as he worked, and I thought that it wasn't fair to dump all my troubles on him, especially since I hadn't seen him in ages. But I soon found myself telling him everything. I didn't tell it all in the right order, and I'm sure that I mixed up people's names from time to time – I definitely kept saying Sam instead of Danny – and I know I repeated a few parts, but on the whole he seemed to understand.

Anthony got really angry when I mentioned what Sam had said the night before. I tried to explain that Sam hadn't meant anything by it, but Anthony told me that wasn't the point. He shouldn't have said it in the first place.

In fact, he wasn't too happy about most of what I told him, with the exception of a few bits and pieces like the flowers and letters I'd received from J, and me telling Bernard Parker where to get off, and the fact that I'd managed to get Neil Forsythe at least a couple of days' work.

"I'd forgotten that you met Neil," I said. "You seemed to get on really well."

He nodded. "Yeah. I liked him a lot. I met him a few times after that, but I haven't seen him in a couple of weeks. I'm glad that things are working out OK for him."

Sitting cross-legged on the bed, I sipped my third mug of coffee and watched Anthony for a few minutes. The thought occurred to me that maybe he *was* gay after all. I mean, he could have had Jackie there and then in the pub, and she was really good-looking.

And maybe Neil Forsythe was gay as well, I thought. After all, he did say that himself and his wife hadn't been getting on for years before they split up . . .

"Anthony . . ."

"Yeah?"

"Can I ask you something?"

"You just did."

I smiled. "Can I ask you two things?"

He smiled back. "You just did."

"OK . . ." I had a little think. "Can I ask you *four* things?"

"Certainly."

"Are you gay?"

"No." He looked like he was about to add something, so I waited, but he said nothing else.

"What, just 'No'? Just like that?"

"What did you expect me to say? To break down and admit that I'm secretly a tortured heterosexual? The answer is no. I'm not gay. Or bisexual, or anything like that."

"Well, I have to say I'm a little disappointed."

He laughed. "So here I am with a gorgeous, half-undressed woman, in the middle of the night, just the two of us in her flat, and she tells me she's disappointed that I'm *not* gay? Thanks a bunch! That really does a lot for the old ego!"

"I didn't mean it to sound like that," I said. "I was just hoping that you'd have some dark, hidden secret that you wanted to share."

He shook his head. "I'm afraid not. I could make one up, if you want me to."

I did. And by the time we'd finished making up outrageous lies about ourselves it was almost morning. They generally began along the lines of, "When I was in Tierra del Fuego . . ." or, "I remember one time I was working late in the lab . . ."

I told Anthony that if he was too tired to drive home, he could stay, just as long as he didn't try anything. He told me that he was flattered that I didn't want my sexuality given a good seeing-to by his experienced loins, but if it was all the same to me, he'd go home.

Then I told him that if he stayed for a few more hours he could give me a lift, because I was planning on visiting my folks.

"OK," he said. "You've persuaded me." He kicked off his shoes and climbed onto the bed. "You promise you won't take advantage of me?"

I promised him that I'd do my best. Within a few minutes we were both sound asleep.

Chapter Thirty-eight

Once you move out of home time stands still there. I'd been gone for about a month, and nothing had changed. There was a pile of old bank statements, phone bills and ads that had come through the door sitting in an untidy pile next to the phone in the hall: When I let myself in the first thing I noticed was that the pile was exactly the same as it had been when I was saying my goodbyes. OK, maybe there were a few more ads from people trying to sell us garden gates and blinds, or from the local Centra telling us that we could get three litres of Coke for the price of two, or from estate agents wondering if we wanted to sell our house because now was a very good time – one of *them* was going to strike it lucky fairly soon – but on the whole no one had given the pile a good purging.

"It's me!" I called out as I pulled my key from the lock. "I'm home!"

There was no reply. I assumed, quite naturally, that there was no one in, even though the car was in the driveway. If I'd been a bit more paranoid, I would have assumed that they were all hiding. Silly idea. I went through the house and had a look, just in case.

There was a different issue of the RTE Guide open on the sofa, but apart from that everything in the sitting room was where it had been, with the exception of the eight or nine books I was usually reading at the same time. When I thought about this, I realised that those books, along with all my others, had been packed away into a couple of boxes and were now in my flat, still in the boxes, in the exact same place where I'd left them the day I moved in.

Maybe it's genetic, I decided, we're all missing the tidy gene.

As I pushed open the door to my parents' room it suddenly occurred to me that I might find them entwined on the bed. Maybe that was why my Dad had suggested that I should phone ahead before I showed up . . . To my relief the room was empty. That would have been *way* too weird for me to cope with, even though I was pretty certain that – judging by the number of offspring they've produced – my parents had had sex at least twice in their lives.

I went into my old room, half expecting to find that Fintan had finally moved his stuff in and covered up as much as possible of the pink wallpaper with Liverpool posters, but it hadn't changed at all. On the floor there were a couple of boxes of clothes and stuff that I'd forgotten to come back for: if I was lucky, I could persuade my Dad to drop them out to the flat for me some time.

They arrived back after about half an hour. My mother was delighted to see me: she gave me a big hug and I could see that she was close to tears . . . That was a bit much: I mean, it wasn't as if I'd been locked away in prison for years. And she phoned me practically every day in work, anyway. Then came, tea, sandwiches and questions: "How's everything going? Are you eating properly? What's your landlady like? Tell me everything!" Gradually, the questions became more specific: "Do you pay an electricity bill or is there a coinbox? Have you got your own bathroom? Do you have noisy neighbours?"

This last question I didn't really answer. I couldn't very well say, "Well, the couple in the room next to mine are tone deaf, and the old woman upstairs from me has a tendency to fall out of bed and die."

I turned the situation around and started asking my mother about the various houses they'd seen, but that didn't last for long, because Dad said that it was bad enough to have to visit the bloody places, he didn't want to have to be there for the postmortem as well.

My brother Fintan got home around five. He didn't seem to have noticed that I'd been gone, but then that was exactly like him. I tried to talk to him for a while, but he didn't have anything intelligent to say. After he made himself a quick crisp sandwich, leaving a trail of destruction from the press to the fridge to the table and back to the press again – with a quick detour to the kettle for what would have been a cup of tea if there had been any hot water, there hadn't, and he wasn't about to fill the kettle and wait for it to boil all by himself – he took himself off into the sitting-room.

My Dad had gone out to the back for an unspecified reason as soon as Fintan arrived home, and my mother had started making the dinner – but first a quick damage control session following Fintan's path – so I followed my socially challenged sibling into the sitting-room.

"So," I said, sitting down in what I'd once thought of as "my" chair, "how's life?"

He shrugged with only one shoulder – to use both shoulders would have been too much work – and stared at the television. Which was switched off. "OK."

"Seeing anyone at the moment?"

"Nah." He took a huge bite out of his sandwich and ruminated carefully. "Nah," he added, probably in case I'd suddenly developed the memory-span of a goldfish.

"Busy these days?"

He took another enormous bite. "The usual," he said, crumbs and bits of crisps spilling down his tracksuit top.

"Ever get that rash seen to?"

He stopped chewing and looked at me. "What?"

"It's called a conversation, Fintan. Normal people do it from time to time."

He raised his eyes. "What are *you* on? I answered you, didn't I?"

"I stole a car last night and ran over someone," I said, for no better reason than to see what he said.

"No you didn't. You were in the pub with Sharon and Anthony and your other mates."

"How do *you* know?"

He tutted, as though the answer should have been obvious. "I was *there*, wasn't I?"

That surprised me. Surely I couldn't have been so drunk that I didn't remember talking to my own brother? "Tell me the truth, then. Anthony said I was really pissed last night. Was I?"

He gave me the old economy shrug again. "I don't know, do I? I wasn't talking to you."

"Oh for Christ's sake! You knew I was there and you didn't even come over and talk to me! Jesus, Fintan, you're some piece of work, you know that?"

"What do you mean?" At least I had his attention, if not his comprehension.

"It doesn't matter," I said quickly. "If you don't understand what I mean, then there's probably no point in me ever talking to you again."

"You're a moody bitch," he said. "You go swanning off to live in your own bloody place and when you come back you think that we should all go around treating you like you're Lady Goliva. Or whoever she was."

"Lady Godiva," I corrected. "Everyone thinks she was vain, but she wasn't: She rode naked and bareback through Coventry to try and persuade her husband to lift some of the taxes he'd put on the townspeople." I wondered why I'd even bothered explaining that. "Anyway, I'm nothing like that. I'm not vain."

"Yes you are. That's why no one likes you."

"Hah! *Who* doesn't like me?"

"Fintan O'Shaughnessy, for one."

"Good," I said. "I wouldn't want him to like me. He's a total prick."

"And Sarah. She thinks you're a stuck-up bitch."

I nodded. Sarah was Fintan O'Shaughnessy' boring girlfriend. "Even better. Being liked by her would be worse than a death sentence. Not that she'd know what any sort of sentence was."

Fintan was practically jumping out of his seat, waving his finger at me. "See? *See?* That's what I mean about you being a bitch! Sarah would never say anything like that."

I sighed. "Fintan, Sarah *couldn't* say anything like that. For a start, she wouldn't be able to think of it, and for a finish she wouldn't know what it meant. She has the IQ of an empty beehive, without the honey."

"You really can't stand people who aren't as clever as you, can you?"

"No, I can't stand people who don't at least try and do something with their lives. I mean, look at you. If you wanted to, if you were able to *force* yourself to try, you could be anything you wanted. You're at least as intelligent as I am."

"Yeah, well, we couldn't *all* go to college, you know. We couldn't all go to Daddy and ask him for the money. Some of us had to go out and get a fucking job."

Now I really was pissed off at him. "Listen to me, you little prick!" I was close to screaming at him. "*Yes*, I went to college, and *yes*, Dad paid. But I worked every *bloody* morning cleaning shit and puke out of pub carpets and every weekend serving drinks to the same morons who puked on the carpets, and I paid Dad back *every* penny he gave me! OK, I've made something of my life, but I did it the hard way. And *you* . . ." I forced myself to calm down. When I spoke again, I was a bit quieter. "You, you just take and take, and when you're finished taking you complain. You had all the same chances I had, you just didn't bother. Because you were too scared. And you still are."

He shook his head. "I'm not scared of anything."

"You're too scared that you won't be as good as I am. So if you never try you'll never fail, so that gives you the excuse you think you need to sit on your arse all day and moan about how you never got anything."

"Fuck you," he said. "I work too, you know. I've got a job."

I laughed. "Yeah. You do. I'll give you that. But answer me this: where do we keep the iron? Or the Hoover? What temperature should you put the washing machine on for whites? How much does a large sliced pan cost?"

"What are you talking about?"

"Oh, I know! Silly me, that's all *women's* work, isn't it? OK, here's a question about *men's* work: when you're wiring a plug, on which side does the blue wire go?"

"Look, I know how to wire a fucking plug!"

"Maybe you do, but when was the last time you did it?"

He didn't answer. He was probably trying to count back to the last time he wired a plug, and it wasn't easy because he only has – let's see, what was it again? Oh yeah – ten fingers and ten toes, making a total of, um, twenty.

"Fintan," I said in my calmest voice, "when I was in college I worked four hours every morning. Then I had classes for another five hours. I studied at least two hours every day," – I didn't mention that I did most of my studying on the bus, where there wasn't anything else to do – "and when I came home I had to help with the washing, the ironing, getting the dinner ready, Hoovering, cutting the grass, shopping . . . All those sorts of things. What did *you* ever do?"

He pushed himself out of his chair. "Susan, fuck off. I don't have to listen to this." He marched towards the door, readying himself to either storm upstairs and slam the bedroom door, or storm outside and slam the front door. A good door-slamming sure makes up for all those years of lazing around the house.

"Before you go," I said, grabbing his arm. I pointed to his chair, where his crumb-covered plate still rested on the arm. "Pick that up and bring it into the kitchen and wash it. That won't kill you. And it's not someone else's job."

"Go fuck yourself," he replied wittily, and did his storming-out routine. Seconds later the front door slammed *really* hard: I didn't expect much else though, because he'd had lots of practice.

I sighed, got up, picked up his plate and carried it into the kitchen.

My parents were sitting at the kitchen table, staring at me.

"So," said my father. "How's Fintan?"

Chapter Thirty-nine

On Sunday afternoon I got the bus to Dun Laoghaire and called into the video shop to see Sam. He was due to get off at around four, and I arrived about ten minutes early.

He was serving a customer, but he looked up when I came in and smiled. "Be with you in a minute."

I stood awkwardly by the door, still not quite sure what I was going to say. Part of me wanted to tell him that it was all over, and that I never wanted to see him again. But that part had grown much smaller and weaker over the weekend, and now the majority of me wanted to forget the "unfortunate incident" and let sleeping dogs be bygones.

My *God* he's good-looking, I said to myself. It seemed to hit me every time we met: it was as though my brain wasn't able to retain just how good-looking he was. In a way, he reminded me of Ed Harris in *Knightriders*, only with more hair and fewer muscles.

I wasn't really into muscles anyway. Arnold Schwarzenegger never did anything for me – at least, not until I saw him in *Twins*, when he was dressed in a fairly normal shirt and jacket – and I still prefer Bruce Willis the way he was in *Moonlighting*, all suave and witty, before he became an action hero.

One movie star that he didn't look like, but I would have been happy if he had, was Billy Zane, the bad guy in *Titanic*. As it was, I suppose Sam was closer to Leonardo Di Caprio, which isn't a bad thing at all, but he's no Billy Zane. But then, I'm no Kate Winslet, so I suppose there's symmetry of a sort.

Sam had snuck up behind me and wrapped his arms around me. "What are you thinking about?"

"Movies," I said. "What else?"

Sam's boss arrived just then, so Sam was now officially hugging me on his own time. "You hungry?" Sam asked. "I haven't had anything to eat today."

We left the video store and wandered up to the centre of the town. "Where's good to eat around here?" I asked.

"Well, there's Burger King, McDonald's, Bits and Pizzas, De Selby's . . . Or there's the Miami, which is a sort of sit-down chipper. We can get chips and fish there."

"Only if they ask us if we want vinegar and salt."

"The vinegar and salt is already on the tables, despite the risk of junkies sterilising their needles," Sam said. "So I suppose that the order they come in doesn't matter much."

As we walked, I found myself talking about "great chip shops I have known," which was not what I *wanted* to talk about, but it was a lot easier than bringing up the real subject.

Sam didn't seem to notice that this wasn't just my usual prattle: This was prattle to take my mind off something important. "Do you put the salt or the vinegar on first?" he asked.

"I don't know. I'm never sure which is better. It's like the 'milk versus sugar' cornflakes dilemma."

"Sugar first," Sam said. "Definitely. Anyone who says otherwise is a degenerate. Putting the milk on first is a crime against nature."

"OK," I said. "So what about getting dressed? Do you put your jeans on first, or your socks?"

"Ah, that's easy. I toss a coin, and if it comes down heads I put my left leg into my jeans, then put on my right sock, then put my right leg into my jeans, and then my left sock. But if it comes down tails, I do it the other way around. Of course, if it lands on the edge, I just get back into bed because I know it's going to be one of *those* days."

"And what if the coin never comes down at all?"

"Then I get annoyed because I hate throwing my money away like that."

We soon found ourselves seated in the small café. I ordered fresh cod and chips, Sam ordered a chicken burger, also with the ubiquitous chips. We made minuscule talk until the food arrived, and then I asked Sam what he thought of me.

"What do you mean, what do I think of you?"

"Really," I said. "What do you think of me? Let's start with this: Am I a good person?"

"Yes," he nodded. "Definitely."

"And can I be trusted?"

"Yep. As far as I know. I mean, you've never given me any reason to doubt you."

"And do you care about me?"

He put down his fork and stared at me. "Yes. I love you."

"OK . . ." I fiddled about with my chips for a minute. "Sam, look, something's been bothering me, and I want to get it out in the open."

I didn't look up, but I could sense that he was watching me. "Go on . . ."

"I don't really know the best way to bring this up, but if we're going to have any sort of relationship, it'd be best if we were honest about our feelings, right."

"Right. I see what you're getting at." He sat back, and looked thoughtful for a moment. "OK. I'll be honest, then. On Thursday night when I called to the flat and you weren't there I was really, really pissed off with you. I was even more pissed off when you said that you'd forgotten because you were working late."

This wasn't what I'd been expecting . . .

He continued. "So, yes, I have to admit that I *was* flirting with Barbara, and I *did* do it to get back at you." He suddenly looked ashamed. "I'm sorry about that. It was childish and everything, but I couldn't help being annoyed."

All right, Susan, I said to myself, you've got an answer. It's not the one you were looking for, but it does kind of explain everything . . . "So I shouldn't take anything you said too seriously, then?"

He shook his head. "No. None of the bad things, anyway," he added with a smile. "I seem to remember saying some nice things when we were in your flat."

I had a little debate with myself whether or not I should mention the comment that had caused me so much worry. In the end, the "mention it!" team put forward a much stronger case and won by two falls to a knockout. "Remember when we were leaving the pub, and you were saying that you thought Jennifer was a babe?"

"Yeah, I was only kidding about that."

"And you were only kidding when I said 'So, you prefer short women with no curves, then?' and you said something like, 'No, I only love big fat birds'?"

I've never seen anyone go completely white so quickly – apart from Michael Jackson, that is. "Oh *fuck!* Jesus, did I *really* say that? I didn't mean anything by it!"

I could tell that he wasn't lying. I nodded. "I was hurt, that's all," I said. "I mean, I know I'm a bit overweight and overheight, but I just wasn't expecting you to say it. Especially not just straight out like that."

Sam reached out and held my hands. "Susan, I swear that I didn't mean to hurt you. And I swear that I'll never say anything like that again. I don't think that you're big *or* fat. I think you're perfect. I love you."

I wanted to say something along the lines of, "Well, you'd better *not* say anything like that again, because I've got enough things to worry about without you insulting me. If anything like that ever happens again, you can just forget all about me. I'm not the sort of woman who'll hang around for years taking abuse. I refuse to be anyone's doormat."

But I didn't say that. Instead, I said, "I love you too."

Chapter Forty

Monday morning finally arrived. It was Vicky's coming-home day, so I'd dressed extra-neat for the occasion, in the hope that seeing me all shined up and looking professional would take some of the edge off the chaos of the previous week.

I was in the office with Jennifer, showing her how to load paper into the fax machine, when the phone rang.

She answered. "Good morning, Complete Office Solutions. Jennifer speaking. How may I help you?"

She paused. "Jennifer Thompson."

Another pause. "Since Thursday . . . Who's speaking?" A few seconds later Jennifer cringed and handed me then phone. "It's someone called Victoria O'Toole," she whispered. "She wants to talk to you. She sounds mad."

I reached out and put the call on hold. "It's the boss. And she's always been mad," I said.

I went into my office – well, it would be my office for the next couple of hours, I hoped – and picked up the call. "Hi, Victoria! It's me."

"Susan? Who's that girl who answered?"

"I hired a receptionist," I said. "Don't worry, we're not paying her much."

"What on earth did you do that for?"

"Well, with you gone, and the way things have been around here, I couldn't just let Barbara sit around answering phones all day. Believe me, it was the best thing to do." Then I repeated, "the way things have been around here," just in case she hadn't caught it the first time.

"All right," she said, sighing heavily into the phone to let me know that she wasn't pleased and I'd have to work hard to convince her. "What happened?"

I took a deep breath. "The short version is that Bernard Parker decided to go absolutely mental and fire Neil Forsythe, for no reason. I had a major fight with him, which ended up with us losing the Parker Technology account. Which wasn't *my* fault. I tried everything I could think of to get him to change his mind. And then because of that I almost forgot about the wages and had a terrible time sorting that out. I did in the end, though. Anyway, because of losing the Parker account I decided that we needed to find more business. I was talking to Neil about this – I hired him on a temporary basis as a sort of marketing person – and he suggested that what we really need to do is advertise. So we spent all day Thursday and Friday putting together a sort of advertising package. It's just about ready. All it needs is your final approval."

Vicky was silent for so long I thought that she'd died. Eventually, she said, "My God . . . What else?"

"And Danny is thinking of leaving, and Barbara didn't want to sit on her own any more so I've moved her to my desk, and I gave Kevin a rise, and I gave them all the day off today because they put so much effort in last week." I tried to think of something else that had happened. "Oh yeah, and the guy from downstairs had to use our fax, so I let him. I hope you don't mind."

After another extremely long pause – it occurred to me that she was either writing this down or crying too hard to speak – she said, "OK. We're at the airport now. I'll drop into the office on the way home."

I knew that I had about an hour before Vicky arrived, so the first thing I did was send Jennifer home to change out of her jeans – I distinctly remembered telling her about the dress code, but maybe she'd managed to get confused between "optional" and "obligatory" – then I charged around the office like a maniac, tidying the place up, pushing the Hoover, straightening the magazines in the reception area, all that kind of thing.

When Jennifer got back, this time a little more presentable, I had her wash up all the cups and everything in our tiny kitchen, then I asked her to tidy up the bookshelves and wipe down every horizontal surface I could find. Apart from the ceiling.

I was pretty sure that Vicky wouldn't have brought her office keys on holidays with her, so I knew that we'd have a last minute warning before she arrived. I was right: before much more than an hour had elapsed, the buzzer rang, and Jennifer answered it. Luckily, she didn't do something stupid like tell Vicky that the office was on the second floor, first on the right. The boss knows such things.

I stood in reception practising an expression which was supposed to say, "Oh my God! You look *fabulous!*"

And then she rounded the corner, and marched in.

I said, "Oh my God! Victoria, you look *fabulous!*" in case my expression wasn't as easy to read as I'd hoped.

And she did indeed look fabulous . . . She was tanned, she'd got her hair bleached – or maybe it was the Florida sun – and she was dressed to kill. She was beaming from ear to ear, which gave me a strong hint that she wasn't about to skin me alive.

"Where's Nick?" I asked. Nick being her former fiancé now husband.

"He went on home. He wasn't able to sleep on the plane, so he just wants to get his head down for a few hours. Anyway," she said, "look at you!" She stepped forward, and for one horrifying moment I thought she was going to give me a hug. She stopped just in front of me, and looked me up and down. "You're all dressed up like you're working for a real company!"

I laughed to hear her say something like that. "Come on," I said, steering her towards her office. "I've kept your chair warm the past couple of weeks."

As soon as we entered her office, it was like old times again. She plonked herself down in her chair, waited for me to sit in the visitor's chair, and leaned forward. "What the hell have you done to my company?" Now that we weren't in front of Jennifer, she could put the nice act on hold.

"Victoria, I am really, *really* sorry about everything. Bernard Parker just went crazy all of a sudden. He threatened us with all sorts of trouble, and made my life absolute hell. He just got it into his head that Neil Forsythe wasn't working out – which wasn't true, because they stood to make a fortune from him – and came in here demanding that we get rid of Neil and get someone else to take his place."

"So what did you tell him?"

"I said that if he could give me some reason why Neil was a problem, I might be able to help him. But he refused to give me a reason." I hesitated. "To be honest, I know now that all he was doing was deliberately trying to make things difficult for me."

Vicky gave me the sort of look that most of us tend to reserve for those people who tell us that the some men working for the government are tapping their phone. "He just had it in for you for no reason?"

"No," I said. "I know the reason." Go for it, my ego suggested. The worst she can do is fire you. "He wanted to get back at you."

"Ah." She looked at me for a few seconds, then opened one of the desk drawers. "Funny," she muttered, mostly to herself. "I thought I'd left a packet of cigarettes in there."

"Oh, sorry," I said. "I took them."

"Things really got *that* bad, then?"

I nodded. "Worse. I came close to leaving a couple of

times." I pointed to a folder on her desk. "I've written up everything, it's all in there." I stood up. "I'll make some coffee while you read that."

I came back, *avec café* a few minutes later, to see that Vicky had taken off her jacket and was seriously studying the contents of the file. It looked as if this wasn't going to be just a flying visit after all.

I'd retrieved my cigarettes from my bag, and I offered her one. She took it and accepted a light without even really noticing, so I figured that it was OK for me to smoke as well.

It took her nearly half an hour to read through everything – I'd written it on Saturday and Sunday evening – and when she was finished her coffee was cold, so I buzzed Jennifer and asked her to make some more. I prayed that Jennifer knew more about coffee than she did about fax machines.

"All right," Vicky said. "Forgetting about the wages was bad. About as bad as it gets. That's *almost* the only serious thing you did wrong, but it worked out OK in the end. The only other serious thing you did wrong was give Kevin a raise."

I was relieved that she wasn't going to kill me for losing the Parker account, but I had the feeling that she was holding out on that one to hit me with it later. "Yeah, but I did make it clear to him that I'd have to discuss it with you first."

"So I see," she said, tapping the pages in front of her. "And you have all your arguments spelled out here . . . You really think that his input is that important?"

I nodded. "I know that he's crap at finishing things, but this company is supposed to provide ideas, and that's what he's good at. I mean, your own notes said the same thing, more or less."

"I hope you didn't show *him* my notes."

"Of course not. I only told him what I thought you'd tell him. And I've put his brain to good use on another problem," I added. "He knew that Danny was thinking about leaving, so I have him working on suggestions to encourage him to stay."

"So why *is* Danny leaving?" Vicky asked. "Because of you?"

I was a bit embarrassed to discover that she knew how he felt about me: I mean, until a couple of weeks ago *I* had absolutely no idea. "I don't know," I said. "I hope not. We all went out for a drink on Thursday night, and I got a chance to talk to him, but I wasn't able to get anything out of him. He was a bit quiet at first, probably because Sam was there."

She frowned and started to flick through the pages. "Sam? Who's he?"

"My boyfriend," I said. "He was supposed to meet me at the flat, but we were working so late I forgot. So he called here and we all went out."

"Good night, was it?"

"For the most part, yeah."

She slowly smiled. "Then you've managed something *I've* never been able to do . . . It's not easy to be friends with people and be their boss at the same time."

Jennifer knocked on the door, and came in with

coffee *and* biscuits. I was very proud of her. Of course, I hadn't tasted the coffee yet, but things were looking good.

When Jennifer left, Vicky asked me about her.

"She's very naïve in some ways," I said, "but she's not stupid. I think she'll work out."

"How much are we paying her?"

I told her.

She seemed impressed. "And that's for a five-day week?"

I nodded. "Nine to five. Though I think that if she really does work out, we should give her an increment after a few months. Otherwise she'll move on, and it'll be much easier for her to get a job after she's had some experience here."

Vicky agreed, and we spent a few minutes in more or less idle chat. She told me about the ceremony and the honeymoon, and what a great time she'd had. I asked her where Stephen, her son, had been while his mother and new father had been away.

She looked at me like I was mad. "He was at home. Where else would he be? He *is* nearly eighteen, after all. Stephen's well able to look after himself." She smiled. "I suppose romance must be contagious, because when I phoned him last night. He said he'd met a girl the other day. Isn't that sweet? His first real girlfriend."

I agreed that it was sweet, and I spectacularly failed to mention about the time Barbara had seduced Vicky's son during one of our office parties.

It was up to me to bring up the subject of Bernard

Parker again. "I don't know what he's going to tell *you*," I said, "so I'd better tell you the whole story." I explained in detail my various confrontations with the man, and I made it clear that in the end it was me who decided that we wouldn't be working with his company any more.

But Vicky didn't care. "You did the right thing. I only wish I'd been there when you gave the bastard such a bollocking." I watched her face carefully while she spoke, and to me she looked a little sad.

"He really hurt you, didn't he?"

She nodded. "It was all over years ago, but he was always phoning me and trying to get back together. He kept saying he'd leave his wife and come back to me. When he found out I was marrying Nick he went spare. I don't know . . . You'd think that he'd be pleased to not have to pay the alimony any more."

I nearly fell out of my chair. "You were *married* to him?"

She looked surprised. "Yes. Years ago. You didn't know?"

"No. I had no idea. I thought that you'd had an affair, or something."

Vicky laughed long and hard, but by the time she stopped, she was on the verge of tears. "Susan . . . I can't *believe* you didn't know. You've met my son. Don't tell me you never saw the resemblance? Bernard Parker is Stephen's father."

Chapter Forty-one

Vicky left the office shortly afterwards, telling me that she probably wouldn't be back in until Wednesday or Thursday. "You can phone me at home if there's any trouble," she said as I walked with her towards the lift, "but I suspect that you'll be able to handle everything yourself."

"Can I give myself a raise?" I asked.

She raised an eyebrow. "We'll talk about that next week. Maybe."

"So . . . I'm still in charge? I'm still the acting boss?"

"You can call yourself the office manager, or the Grand High Vizier, or Admiral Perry, or whatever you like. Yes, you're still in charge. Don't let them give you any shit."

The lift doors closed, and she was gone.

Jennifer came out and stood beside me. "So, can I go home and change back into my jeans now?"

"Sorry," I said. "I already told you about the dress code." I steered her back into the office. "Whenever someone comes in to the office, you'll be the first person they see. You have to look your best."

She sighed. "I *hate* wearing a skirt!"

"I know," I said. "You told me earlier. But you'd better get used to it. You're going to have to wear a skirt anywhere you work."

"Only if I'm a receptionist," she said. "I don't plan to make a career out of this."

"So what *do* you plan to do?"

She answered exactly as I expected: "I don't know."

I had to smile. "Well, while you're our receptionist, you'll wear what we say." I decided to show at least a little generosity. "And if you last three months without any serious disasters, we'll see what we can do about giving you a raise."

Jennifer considered this. "OK. It's a deal."

There really wasn't much to do for the rest of the day. Neil Forsythe came in shortly before lunch and we went over everything for the promotional pack. He declared it all to be "fucking great stuff" again, then invited me out to lunch to celebrate a job well done.

I declined, on the grounds that it wouldn't be fair to go without the others; they'd done as much work on it as I had. Besides, I added, it definitely wouldn't be fair to leave Jennifer on her own. Neil said that he quite understood, and perhaps we could reschedule it for another time. He then said that it was probably for the best, because he had to meet some potential clients at three, and it was best to be prepared.

He had seemed fairly keen on lunch, though, and I sort of got the feeling that he might be interested in me.

His feelings weren't reciprocated. I mean, I liked him a lot, but he was in his mid-forties. I wasn't interested in older men.

Neither was Sharon, I reminded myself, and now she's going out with Mark . . .

Well, I decided, there's not much work to do, there's no one around, I'm in charge, so I just might as well spend the rest of the day on the phone to my friends.

Jennifer, who also had nothing much to do, started talking immediately after Neil left. I was relieved to get a few minutes peace and quiet when she went out for lunch, but as soon as she got back the chatter started up again . . .

"What was I saying before? Oh yeah. So, like I said, we were planning to go to Blake's on Friday night," she said as she was taking off her jacket. "Well, we didn't. You'll never guess why. I'll tell you why," she continued, without giving me a chance to make a guess, "because Dave – that's Sandra's boyfriend, the one I was telling you about on Friday – he said that . . . No, it wasn't Friday, and I remember now because Sandra phoned just before you did so it must have been Thursday, and anyway she never phones on Fridays because that's when we go out. Where was I?"

"You were about to put the kettle on," I said.

"Oh yeah. Anyway, Dave said that there was this great place in Wexford, near Greystones, where . . ."

"Would this be *Wicklow*, by any chance?"

Jennifer paused in the act of heading into the small

kitchen. "Yeah, Wicklow. That's what I said. So we went there and they wouldn't let us in because Sandra doesn't look over twenty-three."

"But you said that she's *not* over twenty-three."

"I know, but even so, you'd think they'd let her in after all the trouble she went to getting ready."

I laughed. "Maybe next time she should get a note from her mother explaining that she's put a lot of effort into looking older, so please forgive her if she doesn't quite manage to succeed."

I was learning that when Jennifer had what she considered to be a hot story to tell, she couldn't be stopped. She went into the kitchen and shouted out the rest of her story. "So we went to this other place across the road. Of course, we couldn't just go straight in because the bouncer had seen us getting stopped outside the other place, so we drove around for a bit and came back. I swapped my long skirt for Sandra's mini, so that they wouldn't recognise us."

"Did it work?"

She bounced back into the office, grinning. "Yep. It was a brilliant idea. It wasn't too easy getting changed in the back of Dave's car, though, but it was worth it."

"Let me guess . . . It was Dave's brilliant idea, right?"

She sat down behind the reception desk. "I know what you're thinking! But we made certain that he was looking straight out the windscreen. So he couldn't have seen anything."

"Unless he looked in the mirror."

Jennifer's face dropped. "The bloody bastard!" She

reached for the phone. "I'm going to ring Sandra right now and tell her!"

I shook my head. "I wouldn't bother. There's no point making a fuss about it. Consider it a lesson. By the time you get to my age you'll be very familiar with these little tricks that men do."

She continued chatting while the kettle boiled. Well, "chatting" is not really the right word. Chatting implies that it was a conversation, but a conversation really has to be at least two-sided. I stood in the doorway of the kitchen listening to the ceaseless torrent of words – what Anthony would have called verbal diarrhoea – and wondered if I'd ever been that bad. OK, so I can be a little verbose from time to time, but at least I stop for air every couple of minutes.

I escaped once the coffee was made by telling her that I had a lot of work to catch up on. As soon as I mentioned the "w" word she shut up, just in case I found something for her to do. She disappeared back to reception, and I headed for the office that, it now seemed, I was time-sharing with Vicky.

The only thing I had to do – well, it was the only thing that I *wanted* to do at that moment – was write back to J. I'd brought his last letter in with me, and read it again. I could barely believe that it had only arrived four days earlier: so much had happened since then.

I made several false starts, but eventually managed to come up with a letter I thought was a worthy response . . .

Dear J,

That was the most pathetic bunch of flowers I have ever

seen. I mean, really! If you wanted to poison me, you should have sent a much more acceptable bouquet: as it was, I didn't even realise that the flowers were from you until I read your letter. The flowers went straight into the bin without me so much as touching them.

I am forced to wonder what a man like yourself did for a living before the operation. Were you perhaps a traffic warden, or a school headmaster, or the holder of some other odious profession? I ask because you are clearly more loathsome than your pathetic letters can convey, so it occurs to me that my hatred for you must stem from some other lack of quality. Or maybe it is a form of race memory . . . Perhaps your forebears were a long-believed-extinct race of sub-humanoids who were the natural enemies of my own ancestors. Perhaps I will never know. I certainly don't care.

But I should not be so vitriolic: I promise that I will take pity on you if I ever meet you and you offer to look after my car for a pound.

Disregards,
Susan.

Forty-two

I was pretty pleased with my letter to J, and I really wanted him to get the letter as soon as possible, so I squandered some of the company's money by phoning for a courier to drop my letter in to the paper's offices. It's this sort of thing that you can get away with very easily when you're the boss . . .

Naturally, it occurred to me that I was abusing my position of power. I justified it by telling myself that since I wasn't getting paid any more money but I did have a lot more responsibility, I might as well take whatever perks I can get.

Perks are a funny thing: there's the ordinary, harmless perks that everyone gets away with, like making the odd personal call in work, or using the computer, laser printer and photocopier for a reason that is not strictly connected with the job, like making copies of your CV. Or the old trick of bringing your battery charger into the office and only using it there. Then there are slightly more serious perks, like regularly taking home rolls of toilet paper, or staying late so that you can stuff a whole heap of office teabags into your pockets. Or sneaking into the stationary cupboard and taking all the biros, envelopes, rubber bands, Sellotape and Tipp-ex you can get your hands on. None of these are really considered to be stealing. More serious than that is something like getting petrol for the company car, and putting two packets of cigarettes and a Mars bar on the bill. Or ordering a supply of lightbulbs for the office, and coming in very early the day after they arrive and exchanging all your old, dead lightbulbs for newer ones.

Then there's downright deviousness, like deliberately sabotaging a swivel chair so that the company will get a new one, then offering to take the old one off their hands to save them the trouble of throwing it out. That's a pretty good one: if you're really technically minded, you might be able to do something similar with a computer.

I can see it now: a rather tatty shopfront with a hand-written sign outside reading, "Honest Susan's Genuine Secondhand Office Equipment and Toilet Rolls."

Office pilfering is one thing, but what if people in other professions started doing it? Imagine going into a zookeeper's house and finding a bunch of penguins in the bathroom: "Well, no one was *using* them . . ." Imagine discovering that your bus-driving friend has bus seats instead of living room furniture and a 45a in his garage, or your movie-director cousin has eighteen extras stashed away in the cupboard under the stairs . . .

One of the potentially great perks of my job – though no one else ever seemed to realise it, and I wasn't about to tell anyone – was that we were generally aware of any great jobs that were coming up before they were advertised. That was usually because it was up to *us* to advertise them . . . If I'd ever spotted a really cool job, and I'd been inclined to take it, it would have been very simple to just bin all the responses and apply for it myself.

Or, even better, I could have found out which of the applicants had the most money, then given them a call along the lines of, "What's it really worth to you to get this job?" I could have done this to two or three of them, started a little bidding war, and made myself a small fortune on the side.

I decided that I liked being in charge. Of course, I wasn't too happy about it when I was under pressure, but when things were quiet it was great. The others all had to look as if they were busy all the time: I didn't even have to pretend.

I phoned Sharon and spent a good hour chatting to her. She told me all about Mark – again – and I was playing the "Sam is great" card, so the conversation ended in stalemate. We speculated about the possibility of the four of us meeting up some night, and she seemed as keen on the idea as I was. After all, she still hadn't really met Sam, and I was dying to meet Mark again: he'd always been a good friend, and if it hadn't been for him coming up with the idea of phoning around all the video shops in Dun Laoghaire, I might never have got back with Sam.

And I *was* happy to be with Sam, even though I still

didn't entirely trust him not to say the wrong thing again. But that was me all over: I did my best to be strong and sophisticated, but when it came to matters of the heart I was as insecure as everyone else.

It was about a quarter past three in the afternoon when Sharon finally remembered that she was still in work and technically wasn't allowed to spend all day on the phone.

After she hung up, I looked down at my notebook and realised I'd been doing some pretty serious doodling. Normally, I end up drawing eyeballs and writing my name several dozen times, but this was worse than usual . . . I'd heard that writing your name over and over is a sign of insecurity – see? I *said* I was insecure, didn't I? – as is always having to be right about everything. Analysing everything you say and do and think isn't a very positive sign either.

I remembered the time a few weeks ago when it had seemed to me that Sam was far too eager to fall in love. Looking back, I could see that I was being paranoid again. Sam was in love with me, there wasn't any doubt about that. And I was in love with him. We were a couple. We did everything together – well, not everything because we didn't see each other that often – and we had more or less the same taste in movies and music. We were devoted to each other.

But then Little Miss Paranoid made a return appearance. She popped up out of nowhere, and said, "Well, if Sam's so devoted to you, how come he almost never phones?"

I scoffed at Little Miss Paranoid's pathetic attempts to put a damper on my relationship. But still, she had me worried.

After a few minutes, though, I concluded that there was nothing to worry about. Little Miss Paranoid was out to get me, that was all.

When five o'clock crawled around Jennifer disappeared so quickly I was tempted to have a good look around her desk in case she'd turned into a pumpkin.

OK, so Sam hadn't phoned. But why would he? I asked myself. We only saw each other yesterday. I considered calling him, but in the end I decided not to. He was probably busy.

Deep down in my heart of hearts, I knew what was *really* bothering me: As soon as I went home, there would be nothing to do for the evening.

It was one thing to be sitting around the office doing nothing – at least I was getting paid for *that* – but sitting around the flat on my own, metaphorically scratching my arse, wasn't much fun. I wondered if I could just stay late in the office and claim it as overtime.

Anyway, it was around then that I started thinking that life would be a lot more fun if Sam and I were living together . . . It was just an idle thought, I wasn't actually making any plans or anything, but it really seemed as if it would be fun. I'd never lived with anyone before – well, I *had* only just moved out of home – but I was interested in giving it a go.

I knew that Sam was working that night, and I

decided that as I didn't have anything else to do I might as well hop on the bus and pay him a visit.

He was very pleased to see me – that hadn't been a gun *or* a roll of quarters in his pocket – and we ended up in his place for the night, which meant that I had to get up at six the next morning and get a taxi back to the flat so that I could change back into my work clothes and arrive in the office before everyone else. And I wasn't just there to steal lightbulbs: I'd learned very early in my career that it's important to arrive before the boss and leave after her, that way she gets the impression that you're always there, so she's more likely to believe you when you call in sick. But now that I was the sub-boss I also had to make a good impression on my colleagues.

Anyway, Sam and I didn't sleep together that night, and that was the trouble. We stayed awake all night. If you know what I mean, wink wink, nudge nudge.

I was absolutely knackered for the rest of the week.

Chapter Forty-three

The following Friday evening, Sam arrived at the flat complete with a small rucksack that contained spare underwear, a clean shirt, and a toothbrush.

"I suppose you've come to stay for the weekend?" I asked as I led him in to the flat.

"Please, missus, if it's not too much trouble."

"Well, you'll have to sleep in the sink. I haven't got a bath."

"Ah," he said, "you know the old joke about the guy reading a ghost story in the bath? 'He felt a cold tap on his shoulder . . .' "

"I haven't heard that one," I said. "How does it go?"

Sam grinned and suddenly hugged me. "What time are we meeting the others at?"

"Approximately half-past seven-thirty o'clock precisely."

He examined his watch. "Which is about one hour and sixty minutes from now. And where will this rendezvous take place?"

"In Ranelagh, just up the road," I said. "Sharon's driving."

Sam put on a sulky face. "Well, that's just *great*! That means she won't be drinking so she won't be any fun. I hate her. Why do we *always* have to meet them on Fridays?"

"We need to stay on their good side just in case they win the Lotto, remember?"

"Yeah, but what are the odds against that? It's got be at least ten to one."

"No, it's only just gone half-past five."

There was a lot of inane conversation like this for a while, which slowly branched into a discussion about how busy each of us had been in work the past couple of days. At one stage I came close to mentioning that the weather had been particularly mild recently, but then my better judgement cut in and told me to get a grip.

Had there been anyone watching, they would have seen that we were both extremely nervous: this would be the first time we'd spent a whole weekend together. Sam had been able to get one of his friends to take his place for the weekend in the video shop, so he wouldn't have to keep rushing off to get the bus. We were going to be together for sixty-something hours without a break. We both knew that this would be a good test of the seriousness of our relationship.

Had there been anyone watching an hour later, they would have been rather startled to see the two of us stripped naked and rolling around the floor, doing a very good impression of two people having wild sex.

There is an unwritten law somewhere that says when two couples team up and go foraging for drinks, they pair off into smaller groups of matching genders: that is, Sam and Mark didn't pay any attention to their girlfriends, and I spent the night talking to Sharon, even though we'd known each other so long that there really shouldn't have been anything left to say.

This was the first time Sam and Mark had met, but rather than just awkwardly ask each other about their jobs or talk about women and cars, as most men would do when they first meet their girlfriend's best friend and her boyfriend (if that makes sense), these two spent hours reciting entire scenes from their favourite films.

Occasionally, Sharon and I stopped talking about our schooldays long enough to listen to our gentlemen friends. They went through a sort of "Best Bits of . . ." routine, covering movies like *Zulu, The Godfather* trilogy, all the *James Bond* and *Star Trek* movies, *Some Like it Hot* and assorted *Carry On* films.

They finished up the evening with a duet: a very accurate rendition of the opening scene from *Pulp Fiction.* Sam played John Travolta's character, Vincent Vega, and Mark played Jules, Samuel L. Jackson's character. They went through the scene almost word-perfect – they even got the accents right – and ended up with Vincent's classic line, "Let's get into character," which I thought was fitting and nicely done.

What none of us had realised was that most of the people in the pub had stopped drinking and started listening. As soon as Sam and Mark's scene was over, a lot of people started clapping, and next thing we knew they were shouting out requests: "Do the Blues Brothers! Do the Muppets again! *Casablanca!* Wallace and Gromit! The Marx Brothers!"

Sharon and I were practically under the table with embarrassment, but Sam and Mark lapped it up, though they declined all requests and fairly soon things were getting back to normal, until the barman came over to our little table and sort of loomed over us.

"Lads," he said, even though he was a lot younger than Mark, "I don't approve of that sort of language in my pub. You're both barred."

Looking back, I can see what he meant. Vincent and Jules were not exactly well-known for their politeness, and there were a lot of words used that I wouldn't repeat here.

But at the time, I was immensely pissed off. "Aw, come on! They were just having a bit of fun," I said. "It wasn't their fault that everyone stopped to listen!"

The barman shrugged. "Right. *You're* barred too."

Mark got to his feet and drew himself up to his full height, which was considerable. He stared down at the somewhat shorter barman, and said, very quietly, "Perhaps you'd like to reconsider?"

Sharon and I exchanged glances. Both of our expressions said "Oh *fuck!*" but we knew better than to say it aloud.

"I don't think so," said the barman, who was a lot braver than he looked. He stood with his arms folded and his legs apart in the classic Superman pose, which might have been impressive if he hadn't been wearing a red dickie-bow.

Mark seemed to mull this over. "OK," he said, in a friendly manner. "It's no loss to us. There are lots of other pubs around here. Is it OK if we just finish up our drinks first?"

The barman had to think about this one. If he said no, there was a chance that things would get dangerous, but if he said yes, then it might look as if he was soft . . . The whole pub had gone quiet again, as everyone prepared themselves in case they had to duck thrown glasses and chairs. "Sure," he said in the end. "You paid for them, after all."

"Good. Thank you," Mark said, sitting down. "And I'll remember what you said. I won't be using language like that again, no matter what pub I'm in."

The other patrons, seeing that there wasn't going to be any aggro after all, began to lose interest and turned back to their drinks. The barman relaxed. "All right," he relented. "If you promise that you're not going to do that again, you're not barred."

Mark smiled. "Great!" he said, very loudly. "After all, it *was* wrong of me to use language like that in a place where there are so many minors present."

It took a few seconds for this to sink in, then the barman exploded. "*Right!* The whole fucking lot of you are barred! Get the *fuck* out of my pub right fucking now!"

Mark stood up again, grinning like an idiot. "Dear oh dear. Language, please," he said. "The children will hear you."

As soon as we got outside, Sam almost fell about the place laughing. "Oh Jesus! That was *brilliant!* I can't wait to tell everyone that!"

Sharon was incredibly proud of Mark, and he looked pretty chuffed with himself.

It wasn't really chucking-out time yet, so we decided to go for something to eat before getting a few final drinks in. Sharon made a couple of hints along the lines of us getting something in the off-licence and bringing it back to my flat, but I didn't want that to happen, because four people in my tiny flat was a bit much. And besides, I wanted me and Sam to get around to finishing what we'd started earlier.

Being flatland, Ranelagh is packed with little fast-food places, most of which are pretty good, and the hardest part is always choosing just which one we wanted to visit. We ended up going to the Abrakebabra on the Triangle. The men insisted on paying, so myself and Sharon sat down while they were queueing at the counter. A minute later Sam came back to our table.

"We're just going over to the drinklink," Sam said. "Back in a few minutes, OK?"

When they were gone, I said to Sharon, "Well . . ."

"Well what?"

"They're getting on all right. I was half afraid that they'd just sit around gloomily for the night, waiting for us to shut up and pay attention to them."

She nodded. "I think Mark likes him. He doesn't really have that many friends."

"I know what you mean. Unsociable hours, and all that."

I opened my bag and took out my cigarettes. It was

my first of the day, not counting the two I'd had in the office, and the three at lunch, and the one after sex, and another two or three in the pub.

"So," Sharon said, "Sam's staying over for the weekend?"

"Yeah. It was a bit awkward when he arrived, but I think it's going to be OK."

She nodded. "I'm sure it will. A whole weekend of sex. That would be acceptable."

"What about you and Mark?" I'd tried to think of a subtle way to ask, but I'd had a few drinks and when I'm like that subtlety crashes through the window, shins down the drainpipe and charges away over the horizon with its arse on fire. Metaphorically.

Sharon made an almost embarrassed face. *"Nearly . . ."*

"How nearly?" I leaned forward eagerly. This sounded interesting. "What happened?"

"Well, he hadn't been with anyone for a while, so I think things got a bit too exciting for him." I saw that she really *was* embarrassed about it.

"Ah," I said with a knowing nod. "Immature ejaculation." I was deliberately being frivolous, hoping to break the tension.

She sneered at me. "Yeah. So? Want to make something of it?"

"Who are you calling a bastard?" I said, scowling back at her. "Did you spill my pint? Are you lookin' at my boyfriend?"

Mark and Sam returned at that moment, and Sharon and I had to put the amateur overdramatics on hold.

Eventually, after what seemed like years, Sharon and Mark got the hint and decided that it was time to go. Sam and I picked up a few things for breakfast in the twenty-four-hour Spar, and returned to the flat for coffee and sex.

Chapter Forty-four

On Sunday afternoon I managed to persuade Sam to come with me to visit my parents.

This was a big step for me, because my folks had never met any of my boyfriends, apart from Adam, my first, and they weren't too pushed about him.

I really wanted them to like Sam, though, and I wanted him to like them. I didn't care whether or not he liked Fintan, but my parents were important to me. I broached the subject with Sam by talking about them for a while as we lay in bed on Sunday morning. It went along the lines of, "My mother would really like you," and "You'd get on great with my Dad," until I felt that I'd softened him up enough.

I'd mentally prepared all my arguments in advance, things like, "I'm going to visit them anyway, so you might as well come along, unless you want to sit around here on your own for the next six hours," but Sam agreed almost instantly. I don't know, maybe he had this thing about riding on the bus.

Anyway, we arrived at about two, just as Sunday dinner was over. The Sunday meal was one of the rituals I'd completely forgotten about when I moved out, and I was kicking myself, because if I'd been thinking I would have spurred Sam into action earlier and we would have had a free meal out of it.

My mother hadn't gone to too much trouble over the dinner, and there really wasn't much point anyway, because there was only herself and my father.

They did seem surprised to see me though, and they were gobsmacked to find I'd brought a friend home . . . And a *male* friend, at that.

Maybe I'd watched too many movies, but I half-expected my Dad to say something along the lines of, "well, I see my little girl's all grown up now," or "so *you're* the young man who's been having sexual relations with my daughter," or to take Sam out for a walk around the garden and tell him things like "Susan is very precious to her mother and me, and I'd be very upset if she was hurt in any way. *Very* upset, if you take my meaning." He didn't do any of that, thankfully. Instead he just nodded a greeting and returned his attention to his newspaper. Actually, I think he was kind of embarrassed about it.

My mother was over the moon, of course. She fussed about Sam like he was her own long-lost son who had turned out to be royalty. She offered to cook another dinner for us, and when we declined she insisted on at least making sandwiches. She even cut them into triangular quarters and put them on a plate with crisps on the side. Thank God we didn't have any watercress in the house.

Sam was just as happy to be pampered, and he charmed her by telling her that the house was lovely and the garden was really nice. He answered her questions with, "Yes, Mrs Perry," and, "No, Mrs Perry," and, "Thanks very much, Mrs Perry," until she playfully slapped his arm and told him to not to be so formal and she should call her Joan.

"Joan?" I said. "I always thought your name was Mammy!"

She smiled at me. "Now you're just showing off, Susan." She turned back to Sam, and – the prisoner having been given a hearty meal – she officially began the interrogation: What's your surname? And your middle name? Where do you live? What do you do? Where did you go to school? What do your parents do? Where do *they* live? Where are they from originally? Really? That's quite close to where I'm from. What was your mother's maiden name? I might know her from school or something. Any brothers or sisters? Younger or older? And what do they do? And what size shoes do you wear, Sam? Do you prefer Honey Nut Loops or Frosties? And can you give me a breakdown of your DNA structure? Now sign this, and this. Press *hard* with the pen, because it has to make five copies. Now roll up your sleeve. Now take the Bible in your right hand and repeat after me . . .

And so on. It was almost as if she was compiling a biography. The Life and Times of Sam O'Neill. Soon to be a major motion picture. With John Travolta as Sam and Samuel L Jackson as Mark. With a younger and taller version of Kathleen Turner as Susan.

I already knew most of the information she squeezed out of Sam, except for his mother's maiden name . . . For some reason, I'd never thought to ask such an important question. I made a mental note not to forget next time. Anyway, my mother deliberated for ages before she was finally forced to admit that she had no idea who Sam's mother was.

All this was Mam's way of sounding him out, checking to see whether her only daughter had fallen in with a bad sort. Though now that I think about it, maybe mothers ask those sort of questions of their daughter's boyfriends just to make sure that they're not related.

My father had a much simpler approach: "What do you reckon about United's chances on Wednesday, then, Sam?"

"I reckon they'll do it," Sam said.

Dad nodded. He didn't smile or frown or do anything else other than continue reading, but I could tell he was satisfied.

We dropped into Mark's video shop on the way to the bus stop. The place was packed, but he was happy to see us.

At one point, a customer came up to the desk and asked when some movie or other was coming out. Both Mark and Sam answered simultaneously, "The first Friday of next month." The customer looked from one to the other, clearly unnerved at meeting *two* holders of the same arcane knowledge.

While we were talking to Mark, my darling brother happened to call in. It was the first time I'd seen him since our big argument, so I didn't know whether to even acknowledge him. But he took the initiative by speaking to me.

"Susan," he said with a nod. "Didn't think I'd see you around here today."

I almost answered with "Why shouldn't I be here? It's a free country!" Instead, I simply said that we'd been visiting the folks.

As soon as I said "we" Fintan realised that the man standing next to me with his arm around my waist was not, after all, merely an overly-familiar customer. "Fintan, this is Sam. Sam, my brother Fintan."

They nodded at each other in that way that men do when they really don't want to show any interest, but I could tell that each of them was sizing the other up, just in case they had to fight. You almost never get two men meeting each other and going, "Oh my God! I just *love* what you've done with your hair!" or "Where on *earth* did you get that tracksuit? I've been looking for one just like it for ages!" Men just can't do that sort of thing, for fear of being branded homosexual. But two women can discuss a third and say things like "She's very good-looking, isn't she?" and no one assumes that they're lesbians.

That reminds me of something else I've noticed . . . Because I'm of above average height, people I barely know will come up to me and say "You're very tall. What's it like being that tall? Do you have a lot of trouble getting clothes to fit?" They don't do it to short people, though. And they *never* go up to really fat people and say "You're very fat. What's it like being so fat? Do you have a lot of trouble getting clothes to fit?" But they'll do it to people who are incredibly thin. It's as if it's OK to keep hammering it home that you're really tall or really thin, but God forbid anyone should even mention the words "fat" or "small" around people who suffer from those problems.

I make it especially awkward for people because not only am I tall, which is considered OK to mention in public, but I'm a bit overweight as well, which they wouldn't dream of pointing out. Some people can't even mention low-fat milk in my presence without thinking that they've really put their foot in it this time.

Maybe that was one of the reasons I liked writing to J . . . In one of his first letters he mentioned straight out that he guessed I was overweight and ugly. I found his honesty very refreshing, on the theory that if I ever met him he wouldn't be disappointed.

Meanwhile, back at Mark's video store . . .

"What can I do for you, Fintan?" Mark asked.

My brother suddenly looked shifty. "I'm just browsing," he answered.

I could sense that Sam was itching to say something like, "The pornography is on that shelf over there," but he held himself back.

At the same time, I could tell that Fintan was dying

to know who Sam was, and why on earth he was going out with me. And he was jealous too, I could tell, because I had someone and he hadn't. Fintan could have had someone if he'd really wanted to. He wasn't bad-looking, and he could be quite charming and witty at times – at least, I seemed to remember a few occasions when he wasn't a complete moody bastard – but it had been years since I'd seen him with a girl. No girl with any self respect would have gone near him, anyway, but that wasn't the point: he didn't even make the effort. It occurred to me then that maybe he approached his love-life in the same way he approached everything else . . . If he didn't try, he wouldn't fail.

Then I did something that afterwards seemed incredibly stupid, but at the time felt like the right thing to do: I said to Fintan, "You'll have to come out to the flat some time." Before my common sense could step in – I think my common sense was hiding around the back having a quick smoke – I continued: "What about during the week? I'll give you a call and we'll arrange it."

He nodded. "Yeah. OK."

At that moment, my common sense came barrelling around the corner – out of breath – shouting "What did I miss? What did I miss?"

Sam and I said our goodbyes to Mark and Fintan, and headed for home. Naturally, this entailed waiting for an hour at the bus stop. But it was OK, because we put the time to good use.

That certainly gave the neighbours something to talk about.

Chapter Forty-five

For once, the post arrived before I left for work. This wasn't really because the postman was early as much as it was because I forgot to set the alarm clock and we didn't wake up until I heard the letterbox rattling.

I never got ready for work so quickly. I thought how great it would be if towelling came into fashion for work clothes, so I wouldn't have to bother drying myself when I got out of the shower. I was lucky enough to find a clean blouse and reasonably clean skirt. Sam, who didn't bother with a shower, lay in bed for ages, grinning as he watched me charging around like a maniac. Then he eased himself out of bed and was dressed and ready before I was, the bastard.

Sam didn't have to start work until noon, so he offered to walk with me to the office. On the way out, I checked through the mail and discovered a letter from J. Sam was immediately jealous – though he pretended to be merely "interested" – and wanted me to open the letter as we walked, but I decided not to grant his request. I wanted to savour the letter.

I forced Sam to leave me before we got too near the office, because I didn't want any of the others to see us together and get the right impression. So we kissed goodbye, and promised to phone each other, and all the things you do even though you know you're meeting the person again in a couple of days.

As I walked the rest of the way to the office, I went through a list of possible excuses, such as "You mean this *isn't* the day the clocks went back? They must have been having me on," or "I was sick all weekend, but I've just dropped into the doctor and he gave me the all-clear." My favourite excuse, though one I've never had the courage to use, went along the lines of, "Quick, turn on the radio! I might be on the news! No, really! There was a bank robbery and I saw the whole thing! I had to give a statement to the police and everything!"

I'd just about decided on "I was putting some clothes out on the line and I accidentally knocked the landlady's washing into the mud, so I had to wash it all again" when I got to the office, but there was no need for me to worry, because Jennifer told me that Vicky hadn't shown up yet, so I was able to fob her off with "I *hate* early-morning meetings with clients! They go on for *hours*," then I escaped into my office, and emerged a few minutes later trying to walk in a manner that suggested I'd been sitting at my desk for the whole morning.

Kevin and Danny were making coffee in the kitchen. Kevin poured a cup for me, and asked me how the weekend had gone. I wasn't sure whether he was just being friendly or if he was sucking up to me now that

I was higher up on the corporate ladder than he was.

Coffee in hand, I returned to my office and opened J's letter.

Dear Susan,

This is just a quick note to let you know that I really don't care about you.

However, in an attempt to improve your moronic vocabulary and thereby make your letters somewhat easier for normal humans to understand, I have decided that I will give you some basic instruction in the English language. You should consult a dictionary and learn the correct meanings of the words I give you.

The word for today is: Up

yours,

J.

I must have been tired, because it took me a couple of minutes to catch on to the insult at the end.

Time passed. The way it does.

Vicky started to come in to the office less and less often, trusting me to keep things running, which wasn't too easy, because gradually business began to pick up: Neil Forsythe's great plan to advertise the company was working . . . In fact, it was working *too* well.

Poor Jennifer was rushed off her feet all day. Between answering the phone, organising couriers, sorting out the incoming mail – and there was a lot of it – and generally trying to keep the office running smoothly, she barely had any time to relax. Most days, she wasn't even able to take a lunch break. One of us would have to man the phones long enough for Jennifer to run out and grab a sandwich, and then she'd eat it at her desk.

When she was at her busiest, Jennifer made noises along the lines of, "I really could do with an assistant." However, there were days when she had absolutely nothing to do, and she never seemed to catch on to the idea of using those slack times to catch up on all those long-term, low priority things that had a tendency to suddenly become short-term high-priority things. I was very tempted to tell Jennifer to work smarter, not harder, but I knew that she would not have taken such glib advice too well. I know *I* wouldn't have.

We did give her the raise after three months, and I think she got used to wearing a skirt and blouse, because she eventually stopped moaning about how much she missed her jeans.

As for me, I was organising meetings, talking to clients, sorting out problems, all that sort of stuff. I was permanently ensconced in Vicky's office now, and using her big desk. We'd moved a smaller desk in that Vicky used when we were both in the office.

I was usually in the office from eight until about seven, every day, and if Sam was working at the weekend I often dropped into the office for a few hours. It's amazing how much work you can get done when you're not interrupted by the phone every couple of minutes. On the plus side, I did get a raise – though it wasn't as much as I'd hoped – and Vicky got me a company car, because I was spending a lot of time visiting clients and going out to hotels and places to organise talks, and things like that. Of course, I had to learn how to drive properly first, but the company paid for the lessons.

Although they still didn't like each other, Kevin and Barbara turned out to be a very good team. Whether she'd meant to or not, she taught him to concentrate on his work, and not just sit around wishing that the day was over. In turn, she learnt how to think laterally, which was absolutely necessary in this job . . . For example, Jennifer was replying to a letter and got stuck on a word just as Barbara was passing through reception. Jennifer called out, "Barbara, is the word 'uncomplex' or 'incomplex' or what?" Barbara laughed. "The word you're looking for is 'simple.'"

Kevin, I could tell, was head over heels in love with Jennifer. She was a good few years younger than him, and though she was flattered by his attention, she was not quite flattered enough to say "yes" to any of his suggestions. So their relationship consisted of him showing off whenever he could, and laughing like an idiot whenever she told a joke.

We were so busy that we had to hire another couple of freelancers; Neil organised the whole thing, and even did all the necessary interviews, so that saved me a lot of work.

For the first few weeks, Neil himself worked with us more or less full-time, selling our services, organising seminars, pushing the publicity machine to the maximum. We considered killing him. But once everything got going, he found himself a job he was happier with, and soon he only dropped in about once a week.

Despite all of our efforts, Danny resigned.

Chapter Forty-six

Sam stayed with me every weekend, even when he had to work, and it wasn't long before we were like an old married couple. People started referring to us as though we were a single entity. If I ever went anywhere on my own, my friends would say things like, "There's something different about you today . . . Is that a new top? No, your hair is different . . . No, wait, I know what it is: there's a big Sam-shaped gap in the universe on your right."

My family, including Fintan, accepted Sam very quickly. They began to expect him to be with me every time I visited, and if he wasn't, my mother would take me aside "for a little chat" and ask me if everything was all right between us.

Fintan even came out to the flat to see me a couple of times, though he never said much when he got there, apart from things like, "Don't you have any *nice* biscuits?" He got on quite well with Sam, particularly when the subject of football came up, which it did with remarkable regularity.

On the night of my dad's birthday, Sam and I went out to visit them, and I got way too drunk to drive home, so my mother asked us if we wanted to stay . . . And here comes the really, really weird bit: She said, "You can sleep in Susan's old room. I'll just make up the bed." But she said it to *both* of us. So we did, and we had a tough time trying to make love as quietly as possible with me giggling like an idiot.

For some mad reason, every time she was out with the two of us Barbara started singing, "Susan and Sam, Susan and Sam . . ." to the tune of *Rosie and Jim.* That drove me absolutely batshit until I pointed out the fact that – amusing as her little song might be – I'd strangle her with her lower intestine if I ever heard it again. Naturally, she redoubled her efforts, and soon she was making up songs about me and Sam to the themes of every damn kids' TV show ever invented. My extremely vulgar version of "Barbie Girl" didn't bother her in the slightest, so I challenged her to write a song about me and Sam to the tune of "Blue Peter," but it was way too hard, so in the end she lost interest. She did, however, come to a brilliant conclusion: "Invent a new word that rhymes with 'love' and the world's songwriters will beat a path to your door."

Is there a word for half-anniversary? If there is, I can't think of it. Maybe it's bianniversary, or something. I'm pretty sure it's not sixmonthiversary, as Sam called it. Whatever. On the night of the half-iversary of the first time we'd met, we went out to dinner, and that was special in itself because lately we'd been staying in more often than not.

I drove us out to a very quiet restaurant somewhere on the west side of the city. We'd pre-booked and everything, and we'd even dressed up for the occasion. We were a bit early, so we went to the bar to wait for our table to be ready.

I found a table, and Sam went to get drinks, and just after he left someone very familiar walked past our table.

My mouth dropped open in surprise. "Danny? Danny Maloney!"

Danny jumped when he saw me, and almost spilled his drinks. He shook his head and said, "I don't believe it!"

I hadn't seen him since he'd left the company about three months before. I hopped to my feet and was about to give him a huge hug, but his terrified expression reminded me that Danny wasn't the sort of person who'd be comfortable receiving a hug in public. Besides, his hands were full. "My God! How are you? What are you doing here?"

Once he got over the shock, he seemed pleased to see me. "Susan . . . How are you?" His shocked expression was replaced with a huge grin.

"Ah no, I asked you first."

He nodded. "I'm fine. Great. And you? How's the company?"

"It's mad," I said. "It's so busy you wouldn't know the place. What about you? What are you doing these days?"

"Not much. I'm hoping to get a job teaching or something before the next term."

Danny had left Complete Office Solutions without

another job to go to. He'd finally decided that he wasn't happy there, and once he'd made his decision, that was that. Officially he was supposed to give a month's notice, but Vicky knew how unhappy he was, and told him that if he wanted to, he could leave there and then. So he did: he came back from his meeting with her, announced to the office that he was leaving, then he cleared out his desk and went. No goodbye party, no cakes, no collection made around the office for a farewell present, nothing like that. It took us weeks to get used to the idea that he was gone, but gradually we got used to life without him. The sad truth of office life is that no one is indispensable.

But now, seeing him there, I was so happy I was on the verge of tears. I wanted to ask him about everything that had happened to him since he'd left, I wanted to tell him all the news about the office, I just wanted – I suddenly realised – to be able to go back to the time when we worked side-by-side and I'd had no idea that he was interested in me. Despite everything I'd thought I'd gained since then, I wanted it all back the way it was.

And then I noticed that he was carrying *two* drinks. "Are you with someone?" I asked.

He nodded. "Yeah." He gestured with his drink towards a girl sitting in the corner, anxiously looking over at us. "Ariana. Do you want to join us?"

Bloody right, I said to myself. "Hang on, I'll tell Sam." I grabbed our coats, ran over to Sam, told him everything, and followed Danny back to his table.

Ariana was about twenty-three, fairly tall and thin,

and extremely good-looking. I mean, she was one of those girls you never see outside of ads for L'Oréal products. I was struck with an irrational, but thankfully fleeting, jealousy.

She was also German, and barely spoke any English. Danny had to do a lot of translating for us. I was a bit annoyed about that, because I'd worked next to him for years and I'd had no idea he could speak German.

When Sam arrived with our drinks, he practically fell over himself with shock when he saw Ariana. He had that rabbit-caught-in-the-headlights look all the time we were talking to them, and I could see him thinking "Wow!" over and over. He was only one step away from licking his lips.

It seemed very clear to me that Danny and Ariana were devoted to each other. They chatted away in German, and stared at each other all the time. He was half-looking at her most of the time he was talking to us.

"We met a few weeks ago when I was looking around for a job," Danny said. "I was thinking of going to Germany to teach English, and in one of the agencies I visited I met Ariana. She was looking for someone to teach her English. And it had to be someone with a reasonable amount of patience." He shrugged. "We just hit it off, I suppose."

After a while, Sam announced that he had to pay a visit to the little boys' room, and I instructed him to get more drinks and find out what had happened to our table. As soon as he left, Danny turned to face me.

"You know, I wanted to say something to you before

I left the company, but, well, I got scared. Anyway, all the time when we were working together . . ."

I nodded. "I know. I didn't know for ages, though."

He swirled the last drops of his drink around in his glass. "If I'd had the courage to tell you how I felt about you, would that have made a difference?"

I looked from him, to Ariana, who was still staring at him. "Yes. It probably would," I said. What else could I say? I didn't want to lie to him and tell him that, no, I'd never fancied him. Now that it was all over, and nothing I'd say would change things, there was no point in hurting his feelings just to cover up the fact that I never had the guts to treat him as anything other than a colleague. Especially now that he had someone else.

I shrugged. "But that's in the past. I'm sorry I didn't know. Sorry for me then, not for me now, if you know what I mean."

He smiled. "Susan. I *always* know what you mean. And I agree. I think I was very lucky." He glanced at his girlfriend. "I mean, if I hadn't left Complete Office Solutions, I'd never have met Ariana. And if you and I had . . . Well, I'm just saying that I don't think I made the wrong choice. In the end."

I returned his smile. "I know. I think that you and I were meant to be friends, not anything else. And if we'd ever got together, we might have spoiled that."

Danny sat back, and took Ariana's hand. He said something to her in German, and she smiled at me. *"Die Schrift im Spiegel,"* she said.

"What was that?" I asked.

"I told Ariana all about you, just after we met, and I described you as someone who spend a lot of time analysing herself . . . No offence."

"None taken," I said, because I knew it was true.

"Ariana told me that she had a friend like that, someone who examined herself so closely in the mirror that she didn't realise that the directions for her life were written on the mirror itself. *'Die Schrift im Spiegel'* means 'the writing on the mirror.'"

That was a good analogy, I thought. I didn't think it would stop me from analysing myself, but at least it was another way of looking at things. As if I needed that.

But something had been bothering me about Ariana, and it took me a few seconds to figure it out. I raised my glass to my lips, and just before I drank I said, "Ariana's deaf, isn't she?"

"Yes," Danny said quickly.

We didn't mention it again, and soon Sam was back with a tray of drinks and the news that our table was ready. We said good-bye to the others, and as we left I squeezed Danny's shoulder – I think that was the first time I'd ever deliberately touched him – and said, "Phone me. I mean it. And if you can't get a job, let me know. You can always come back to us."

I didn't look back as I walked away, but all the time I was thinking to myself, "There's the one that got away. And it was my own fault. But I made the right choice, in the end."

Chapter Forty-seven

I'd been writing to J a lot, and his letters grew more and more nasty. If they hadn't still had his trademark sense of humour, I would have stopped writing back to him. But every letter he sent was both vicious and funny – often hilarious – and I did my best to make mine the same.

A few weeks after we'd met Danny and Ariana in the restaurant, I received another letter from J. It was one of my few days off, and Sam had stayed over. As soon as I heard the letterbox rattle, I charged out into the hall.

"Yes!" I said, running back into the flat. "It's from J!"

I ripped open the envelope and read it aloud . . .

Dear Susan,

Though on second thoughts, "dear" is the wrong word. "Cheap" would be more appropriate.

I hope this letter finds you unwell. Many thanks for the bag of out-of-date crisps you send with your last demented scribblings. I am far too worthy to receive such a gift, so I put them into an old sock and buried them in the back garden in an attempt to confound future archaeologists.

I had a nightmare the other night that I met you, and I woke up in such a panic that I seriously considered reconciling with my erstwhile spouse. I would rather you did not write again, because my heart specialist believes that any further shocks might prove fatal.

Yours falsely,

J.

"I don't know why you write to that fucking psycho," Sam said, more than a little annoyed. "I mean, all he does is insult you."

"That's the whole point," I said. "That's why we do it. It's fun. And it's harmless. Haven't you ever had a penpal?"

Sam didn't answer. He sat on the edge of the bed and sulked for a while, then said, "you really like that guy, don't you?"

"I like the fact that he's not worried about hurting my feelings," I replied. "More than that, I can't say."

"Really? You wouldn't let *me* get away with saying what he says. What makes him so special?"

I really didn't know how to answer that. What was I supposed to say . . .? It's OK, Sam, you can insult me all you like . . . No, really. I won't take offence.

"Well?"

"Well what?"

"What makes *him* so special? How come he can say anything he likes to you, but if the rest of us say the wrong thing you jump down our throats?"

I wanted to ask him what he meant by "the rest of us," and what he meant when he said I jumped down their throats, but I'd lived in the same house as my brother for twenty-five years, so I was all too aware how easily a fight could start.

I sighed. "Look, Sam, I'm not going to have an argument with you over this. Let's just leave it, OK? I've known J a lot longer than I've known you." Which wasn't actually true, but Sam didn't have to know that.

The big fight came about a month after that.

Chapter Forty-eight

It was a Friday morning. I drove to work because I knew I had to visit a client in the afternoon. I couldn't find anywhere to park near the office, so I ended up miles away. And it was raining. And I hadn't brought my umbrella because there was no point, was there? I was going in the car so I wouldn't *need* an umbrella.

I was completely soaked by the time I got to the office. Barbara swooped up right behind me as I reached the door. She was shaking her umbrella dry.

"You're drenched," she said.

"Thanks for telling me. I hadn't noticed," I replied with pointed sarcasm.

Barbara was in too good a mood to allow me to spoil things. "Guess what happened last night?" she asked as we trudged up the stairs.

"No."

"Go on."

"Em . . . No."

"I'll tell you. I met your friend Anthony in town."

"Really?" I said, suddenly trying to pretend that I wasn't in a bad mood after all. "Whereabouts?"

"La Pizza on O'Connell Street. He didn't remember who I was for ages, though."

"Please don't tell me you made him guess." I unlocked the door to the office and darted in to turn off the alarm.

"No, but I strung him along for a while. And then he remembered that time when you brought him along to the do when Parker Technology was launching their software. He remembered seeing me there."

"Oh yeah, I'd forgotten all about that. I haven't seen him in ages."

"Yeah, he said that. He was asking how Neil was getting on here, so I had to tell him he wasn't working with us much any more. He also told me to tell you . . ."

I looked at her patiently. She didn't answer. "If you tell me to guess, I'll kill you."

"Jesus, you *really* need a cup of coffee," Barbara said.

"Anthony told you that? My *God*, he's good!"

She laughed. "Come on." She went into the kitchen and did coffee-making things.

I followed her in and hung my coat on the radiator, then made a feeble attempt to dry my hair with one of the cleaner tea-towels. "So what did he tell you?"

"Your brother and Anthony are mates again. Whatever it was, they sorted it out."

"That's brilliant!" I said. "Last time Fintan came to the flat he was saying that he'd met Anthony and they'd talked about going out for a drink some time."

"Well, they did." She looked at me expectantly. "So what else did Fintan tell you?"

I opened the fridge and examined the open milk carton. It didn't look too bad. I poured a drop into the sink and peered at it. "Does that look as if it's gone off to you?"

"No. It's fine. So?"

I shrugged. "So? What, you mean about Fintan? He didn't say much. He never does. He comes to the flat and I give him tea and biscuits, and he repays me by listening to all the lies I tell him about you."

"Yeah, sure." She hesitated, and then just smiled. "Well, I suppose you're glad that they sorted themselves out."

"I am. They were friends since before they learned how to walk. Maybe Fintan's finally growing up."

Fintan was still living at home. My parents' plan to move hadn't come to fruition yet – mainly because it was so hard for them to agree about the houses they visited – so I decided I'd phone my mother later and ask her if Fintan was getting on any better with Dad.

A few minutes later there was a buzz at the door. "If that's Jennifer after forgetting her keys again I'll murder her," Barbara said, going out to answer it.

I sipped my coffee, wondering if I'd get away with having a cigarette in the kitchen. I was almost back to being a full-time smoker now, but I knew that as long as I didn't get so bad that I was sneaking off to the toilet to have a smoke, or setting the alarm clock to wake me up in the middle of the night for one, I'd be able to quit any time I wanted to.

The one advantage with taking up smoking again was that I'd lost a bit of weight. That wasn't enough to outweigh the disadvantages, though. I'd been considering giving them up again, but I could still remember how much torture it had been the last time I'd given up . . . I should have just gone cold turkey, and quit immediately. But no, I'd decided that it would be best to cut down gradually. My plan was that every day I'd have one less than the day before: I soon found myself gripping the arms of my chair and staring at the clock, waiting for midnight to crawl around. In the end I only managed it because I went on holidays with the rest of the family and there weren't any opportunities to smoke.

"Hey, Susan!" Barbara called back to me. "It's for you! Delivery!"

I went out to reception. Waiting for me was the biggest, most spectacular bunch of flowers I'd ever seen in my entire life.

"Flowers?" Sam sounded a little puzzled.

"Ah, stop messing around," I said into the phone. "I know they were from you."

"What, there was no card with them or anything?"

"So, you *did* send them! Ah, thanks love!"

Sam paused. I assumed that he was going to string me along until he had no choice but to admit that the flowers were from him. Then, somewhere in the back of my mind, I found myself imagining that he *hadn't* sent them, but he was wondering whether to lie and pretend that he had.

When the pause went on long enough, I knew that my original assumption had been wrong. "Jesus. If it wasn't *you* who sent them, I can't guess who it was."

Sam gave a short, harsh laugh. It was not a happy sound.

By now I wished, desperately, that I hadn't phoned him. There wasn't anyone else in my life. Danny might once have been interested, but that had all ended long ago. If I had a secret admirer, that was hardly *my* fault. "I swear to God, Sam, I have no idea."

"Really? *I* have."

"Don't be stupid, Sam. J doesn't know where I work. And even if he did, he wouldn't send flowers like these. He might send a cactus or a Venus Fly Trap, but not these."

I shouldn't have called him stupid. "Look," he said abruptly. "I'm a bit busy. I've got to go."

"No, wait. Listen, they're probably from a client who was pleased with my work, or something. Around Christmas a lot of them send us sweets and bottles of wine and stuff."

"It's a bit early for Christmas presents," Sam said. "Oh . . . for fuck's sake. You really think I'm an absolute gobshite, don't you? You think I'll believe whatever you tell me. 'Oh, there's no one else, Sam. I promise. Now be a good boy and do what you're told.' Well, fuck you, Susan, if that's what you think."

"That's *not* what I think. Look, if there was someone else, and he sent me flowers, do you think I'd be stupid enough to tell you?"

He paused again. "You would, if you had your reasons. You're like that, always saying and doing exactly what you think it'll take to get people to do what you want. You're a manipulator."

"That's bollocks," I said. "And even if it was true – if *any* of it was true – what reason would I have to tell you that someone else sent me flowers?"

"Lots of reasons. You could be trying to force me to get you something, because you think that I'll think that I've got competition. Well, it won't work. I'm not that thick."

My head was thumping at this stage. "All right, look, this isn't getting us anywhere. We'll talk about it tonight."

"No, I'm going to stay in my place tonight."

That really hurt me. This would be the first Friday night in ages that we hadn't been together. "OK, if that's what you want. What if I meet you for a drink in Dun Laoghaire after work?"

"You don't get it," he said. "I don't want to see you tonight."

"All right. When?"

"I don't know. Look, I'm busy."

And just like that, he hung up. I was reaching out to hit the redial button when Barbara suddenly grabbed my hand and pulled it away. I hadn't even been aware that she was there.

"Think about this before you call him back," she said, almost glaring at me. She let go of my hand.

I bit my lip. "Barbara, I'm not going to let it all

fall apart just because he's got the wrong end of the stick."

Barbara reached out and took me by the arm. Even though she's a lot smaller than me, she's strong, and she hauled me out of my chair. "Come on. You're invited to a meeting in my private office."

Chapter forty-nine

We went out to the Ladies. Thankfully, there was no one else there. I sat on the window ledge and felt miserable.

"Let's be logical about this, not emotional," Barbara said. "I've broken up with a lot more people than you, so I know what I'm talking about."

"Barbara, we're *not* breaking up."

"Shut up and listen for a minute. Susan, imagine that you were in a relationship where you weren't really happy, but you didn't have the guts to end it. If something like this happened, you'd jump at the chance to be all 'hurt' and 'emotional' and 'need time to yourself.' That's just hypothetical, of course. I'm not saying that Sam is like that."

"What *are* you saying?"

"I'm saying that *you* are the sort of person who's able to see around problems and come at them from a different angle. Well, what happens if you look at this from Sam's point of view?" She tore a couple of dozen sheets of toilet paper off the roll and handed them to me.

"I can imagine what he feels like. Betrayed. Hurt. He feels that he's not the only one in my life. And he's afraid that he'll lose me." I sniffed and blew my nose.

Barbara nodded. "Right . . . That's what happens when you look at it from his point of view. Now what about *your* point of view?"

"What?"

"Get a grip, Susan. You're brilliant at lateral thinking when it comes to someone else's problems. What about your own problems? Do you think he overreacted?"

"Not really. He . . ."

"Bullshit. Most men would be a bit pissed off, a bit jealous, but that's about it. After all, you *told* him that someone had sent you flowers. If you were having an affair you wouldn't have mentioned it. And even if you did mention it, you wouldn't have pretended that you thought the flowers were from him. He knows you're not stupid." She took a deep breath, and shook her head. "If he doesn't have some other reason for acting the way he did, I'll be very surprised."

I sat there silently for a few minutes, occasionally wiping my mascara and eye-shadow all over my face.

"Occam's Razor," I said suddenly. "The principle of economy . . . There's no need to make needless assumptions about something. The simplest explanation is most likely to be the correct one."

Barbara nodded. "Yeah, but the hard part is figuring out *which* explanation is the simplest. That Sam reacted that way because he wanted to?"

"The simplest explanation is that he's just jealous," I said.

"I think this goes beyond jealousy."

"Maybe you're right," I said. "But *why* would he want to overreact?"

She shrugged. "How would I know? You know him better than me. You've practically been living in each other's pockets for ages. You should be able to figure it out for yourself. You've also got to wonder whether you're better off without him."

"No," I said immediately. "No, I'm not. I love him."

"All right," Barbara said. "Let's talk about that. I'll be back in a minute." She went out, and came back shortly with my cigarettes. "I thought you might need these."

I smiled as well as I could. "Thanks."

Barbara pushed open the door of one of the cubicles, put down the seat, and sat down. "*Why* do you love Sam?"

I lit a cigarette and exhaled a great plume of smoke. I was beginning to feel a little better. "I don't know. Because I do."

"Ah, *now* I see what you mean," she said sarcastically. "Really, though. What is it?"

"Look, you know that you can't put things like that into words."

"What did you like about him at first?"

"He's funny," I said. "He has a great sense of humour. And he's intelligent. And he's goodlooking. And we have a lot of common interests."

"Generous?"

"Well, if he had any money, he would be."

"That sounds like one of those needless assumptions . . . Has he ever bought you anything?"

"Sure. Lots of things."

"Such as?"

I shrugged. "Well, nothing expensive. Like I said, he doesn't have much money. You don't get paid much working in a video shop. But he usually pays when we go out."

"And how often is that? You said yourself that you hardly go out any more. I'll bet you anything you like that the only time he eats properly is when he's staying over in your place."

I was starting to get annoyed. "Look, Sam's not stingy. He pays his way."

"OK, OK. The point I'm trying to make is that you're assuming that he's generous, and all the evidence suggests that he's not. What if you're wrong about something else, as well? What if he *doesn't* love you?"

"He does," I said. "I know he does. He doesn't say it all the time, but who does? I've never heard my parents say they love each other, and they've been married for twenty-seven years. I never heard any of my aunts or uncles say it, and they're all still married."

"Answer me these few questions . . ." Barbara said. "Does Sam ever say he loves you when you're not just after having sex? Does he act all attentive and everything to you even if there's a really gorgeous woman in the room? Does he ever ring you out of the blue and say that he's not phoning for any reason, but he

383

was just thinking about you? Does he go out of his way to make you happy? Does he ever offer to pick up the shopping on the way to the flat? Does he ever do the washing? Does he ever make you coffee in the morning, and dinner in the evening? Does he even make the bed? Has he ever Hoovered the flat? Does he tell his friends that he can't meet them because he's meeting you instead, or does he just bring you along?"

"Jesus Christ, Barbara! No man does all that!"

She shrugged. "Well, here's one that should really mean something to you: Would Sam sit through a real weepy video just because *you* wanted to, or do you always end up watching what he wants?"

I burst into tears. "You can be a real fucking bitch!"

Barbara got up from the toilet seat, walked to the door, and turned back to me. "I know. But I'm not like that because I think it's fun. Sometimes I *have* to be a bitch. You'll see," she said as she walked away. "You'll see."

Chapter Fifty

I barely spoke to anyone for the rest of the day, and as soon as five o'clock arrived, I grabbed my stuff and ran out the door.

That turned out to be wrong thing to do. Without Sam, the flat seemed cold and empty.

It was the longest night of my life.

I kept going out into the hall, reaching for the phone, then changing my mind. There wasn't much chance that Sam would be pleased to hear from me. He wanted time on his own. He'd made that very clear.

Well, *I* didn't want time on my own. I wanted to be with him.

But maybe he was sorry now and he was just too embarrassed to phone me . . .

No, I told myself repeatedly. Don't give him the chance to get out of this the easy way. If he wants to phone me, he knows the number. He didn't want to see me tonight, so it's up to him to change his mind. I'm not going to go crawling to him, asking for his forgiveness, because I haven't done anything wrong.

I made endless cups of tea and left them all to grow cold. I kept turning on the TV, and then turning it back off again, because somehow it made me feel even more lonely.

I kept thinking about everything that Barbara had said. I still couldn't get over the way she'd been, as if she was deliberately trying to turn me against Sam. At one stage I started thinking that perhaps Barbara was the one who'd sent the flowers, just to cause the fight so that Sam would be free and she could go after him.

I had to force myself to stop thinking like that.

When it came to people, Barbara was very intelligent. And when it came to her friends, she was very loyal. I told myself several times that she'd been nasty because she'd felt it was the right thing to do.

As the night wore on, I began to realise that she might be right. A bit right. Maybe Sam was getting a lot more out of the relationship than I was. All I was really getting was someone who told me they loved me. I looked around the flat and took note of everything Sam had bought me. A few CDs, a lot of videos, some books . . . That was it, pretty much. But the value of a present doesn't count, it's the intention. So what if he worked in a place where he could get videos at a good discount? That didn't mean that the presents were any less important. And so what if there was a bookshop across the road and he was able to get discounts there too? The point was that he bought me those presents because he knew that they'd make me happy.

And then that annoying little voice inside me started saying things like, yeah, but most of the stuff he bought you were things you asked for. And, Sam can get CDs cheap from his DJ friend, who buys them by the bucketload.

I was starting to scare myself.

I opened the fridge, and the cupboards. Most of the food was stuff that Sam liked. I'd bought almost all of it.

I opened my wardrobe. All the clothes at the front were things I thought he liked me wearing. My old comfortable jeans and jumpers were tucked away at the back.

I went through the chest of drawers. Sam's was the top drawer. In it I found three pairs of socks with cartoon characters on them. I'd bought them for him, and he'd never worn them. A tie with the USS Enterprise on it, never worn. A Ben Sherman shirt – which cost a fortune – still in the bag.

The second drawer, mine: my jewellery box, unopened for ages because Sam didn't like the idea of me wearing jewellery that someone else had bought me, even if that someone was one of my parents. My big floppy hat, which I loved. Sam hated it. It hadn't seen daylight in months.

"Oh Jesus," I said out loud. "Barbara was right."

For the past few months, I'd been basking in the glow of that golden feeling, a glow that had long since faded, but I'd been too pleased with myself to notice.

I was everything Sam had wanted me to be. He said frog, and I was trained well enough to bypass the intermediate stage of jumping, and went straight to asking "how high?"

I was a puppet.

Chapter Fifty-one

Dear J,

I'm sorry to have to inform you that you're not the only hate in my life. My boyfriend Sam left me last week, and I hate him far more than I hate you.

He came around yesterday evening and took back everything he owned and everything he'd ever given me. He left this tie. I hope it chokes you.

Susan.

Dear Susan,

It takes too long for the paper to forward your stupid letters, so – as you'll see from the top of the page – I'm enclosing my address.

Your boyfriend Sam is clearly a man of great vision, though perhaps he should have left you long ago. I know I would have. Enclosed is a bottle of sleeping pills. I suggest you take them all at once, washing them down with a bottle of whiskey.

If you never write to me again, I'll assume that you've acquired some sense and are soiling the ground of an innocent cemetery. I'll keep an eye out for your name in the obituary columns, to make sure my day is sufficiently brightened.

James Talbot.

Dear James,
I would like to thank you for finally supplying me with your name – It will make the lawsuit go so much smoother. And as for your address . . . Woodlawn Crescent is a rather high-class area. I'm surprised the locals allow you to keep your cardboard box anywhere near their estate.

Your plastic bottle of sleeping pills made a real mess of the fireplace, when I burned them along with your letters, which endears me to you even less.

It's been nearly three weeks since Sam and I broke up, and with each letter I receive from you he looks so much better. He may have been a selfish bastard at times, but at least he washed his hands now and then.

If you must write back, try not to compose your letter while in a drunken stupor.

Susan.

Dear Susan,
By employing a very sophisticated decryption algorithm, I have finally begun to decode the secret message within your letters, which reads, in part, "Salvation today ascension romeo susan is a stupid cow breath-taking Japan utopia." As yet, I have no idea what this might mean.

*Nevertheless, I have withdrawn the standing order from
my account to Friends of the Earth in case they attempt to
bring your sort back from the brink of extinction.*

*Instead, I have invested in a whaling gun. I am keeping the
harpoons in the back garden in the hope that they will rust.*

*And as for how I write back . . . You are correct, I do tend
to need a drink or two before I can gather the courage to even
write your name.*

Yours insincerely,
James.

For a long time, I didn't even know I was supposed to
be working it out, but I had been writing to J for about
seven months, and as soon as I read his line about
decrypting my letters, I finally put the pieces together.

When he supplied me with his address, I did a little
checking, made a lot of phone calls, lied my heart out,
and pretty soon it all became clear. I wasn't sure at first,
but I had my suspicions, and now I was certain: I knew
who James Talbot was.

But what I didn't know was exactly *how* he had done
it, and whether or not it was all a big joke, so I continued
to write to him, and he continued to write back.

"James Talbot," in his letters, was a nasty, cruel,
devious, and sarcastic man. And at the same time I
found him strangely charming and fascinating. Very
different from the real man behind the letters.

What could drive a man to go to such lengths to try
and woo a woman? What would make him create such

a bizarre personality, when the chances of anything arising from his efforts were next to nil?

And – more to the point – how could anyone have known me so well that he always knew exactly the wrong thing to say, and to say it in such a way that it turned out to be exactly what I needed to hear?

Chapter Fifty-two

The Saturday after Sam cleared his things from the flat, I drove out to my parents. Before my mother could ask "Where's Sam?" I blurted everything out.

They'd been very fond of Sam – everyone had – and it took some convincing before they realised that I was never, ever going to go back with him. My Dad tried to tell me that maybe in time I'd see things differently, but I simply told him that when I was with Sam I hadn't been seeing things at all.

They plied me with cups of tea and words of comfort, and pretty soon I felt a bit better: in fact, I started to feel guilty about dumping my emotional baggage on them, so I must have been recovering.

When Fintan arrived home he was also full of sympathy, and there was no doubt that he already knew. I'd been on the phone crying to Anthony, so I guessed that Anthony had told him.

It was awkward for Fintan to show emotion, especially in front of my parents, but he sat down beside me and put his arm around me. "Do you want to go for a walk?" he asked.

I nodded. We promised my parents that we wouldn't be gone long, and as we left I saw my father watching Fintan, wearing an expression I'd never seen on him before. I couldn't tell whether the expression was pity, or sadness, or anger, but as soon as I saw it I realised that Fintan didn't just want to go for a walk for *my* benefit.

We were heading in the general direction of Lower Cabra. "It's been a long time since we did anything like this," I said, wondering what was on Fintan's mind. "Probably ten years."

"Could be."

"I suppose Anthony told you about Sam," I said.

"Yeah. I went out the other night with him and Lorna."

I looked at him. "Who's Lorna?"

"He didn't tell you? Jesus, that's just like him. He met her in some pub somewhere a couple of weeks ago. They're getting on great. I suppose he didn't tell you because he thought it wouldn't be fair, since you were so upset."

"Do you know what hurts me the *most*?" I asked suddenly, angrily. "It's not that Sam used me and then dumped me as soon as he saw a chance, it's that I didn't see it coming. I always thought I knew what was going on."

"None of us saw it, Sue." Fintan was one of the few people who still called me Sue.

"Aren't you going to offer to beat the shit out of him for me?"

He laughed. "I will, if you like."

I considered it. "Nah. I just want it over."

"Anthony was ready to kill him, you know. He's very fond of you."

"He should be," I said. "I'm great."

"Oh yeah."

"It's funny, though . . . For years I thought Anthony fancied me, but he never did anything about it."

"Neither did you."

"Well, no, but I didn't fancy him. But you men are different from us, you can't have a friend of the opposite sex without thinking about getting her in bed."

Fintan shrugged. "That depends on the man, though I suppose that in general you're right."

"And then I started thinking that maybe Anthony was gay. I even asked him, a few months ago."

"Well, that was a bit conceited. He doesn't fancy you so therefore he must be gay . . . Now *there's* twisted logic for you."

"Twisted logic is my specialty. Anyway, he said he wasn't, and I suppose that if he's going out with a girl now then he's probably *not* gay."

"No, he's not," Fintan said. "But I am."

Chapter Fifty-three

It took a lot of work to reconcile Fintan and my father. Dad wasn't so much upset that Fintan was gay – he was shocked, surprised and stunned, with a good dose of gobsmacked in there for good measure – but mainly he was annoyed that Fintan hadn't thought he could talk to him about it.

But, as Fintan put it, how do you say something like that to your father? He couldn't just sit him down and say, "Dad, it took me a long time to figure it out, but the truth is that I fancy men. Oh, and unless you and Mam have another boy, or Susan marries someone whose surname is Perry, the family name stops here."

As you can imagine, my parents went through the whole range of emotions, ranging from "where did we go wrong?" right through "how could he do this to us?" until, finally, "as long as he's happy, as long as he's not getting hurt or hurting anyone else, that's all that counts."

My Dad told me that he'd suspected that Fintan was gay, but since they never spoke, there was no way he could broach the subject. Dad was not the sort of person to have prejudices . . . He never made racist or sexist jokes, he generally believed in equality for all, but when he realised what had been bothering Fintan, Dad learned that his world was a lot smaller than he'd previously imagined, and that in the real world people could and did have vastly different approaches to life than his own.

Anthony had known for years. I have to point out that nothing ever happened between them: Fintan wasn't desperately in love with Anthony or anything like that, but it had caused enough friction between them that for a long time their friendship was put on hold. In fact, I think that Anthony suspected long before Fintan himself did.

Fintan told me that he'd had one brief relationship with a man, and he'd felt so guilty about it – most of Fintan's friends were the sort of "real men" who sit around getting drunk and telling jokes about "fags," "queers" and "homos" – that he'd started to try and force himself to be "normal." He went out with a few girls, tried to be interested in them, but he wasn't.

And Sharon knew. My best friend knew, and she hadn't said anything to me. I guess in part it explains why there had been so much animosity between them . . . Sharon had seen Fintan with his former lover – Fintan still won't say who it was, and Sharon didn't know him, but I guess that's not important – and she'd asked Fintan about it. He'd been hurt, ashamed of himself, and they'd had a pretty vicious argument.

"What *could* I say?" Sharon asked when I'd confronted

her. "What could I do? I couldn't just tell you that I'd seen your brother snogging another man, could I? You'd never have believed me."

"Yes I would," I responded, though I wasn't certain about that.

"No you wouldn't. Look, I tried to talk to Fintan a couple of times about it, but he wouldn't say anything. He just kept telling me it was none of my business. And you know what sort of temper he has; the more I tried to get through to him, the more annoyed he got."

So I asked Fintan why he hadn't mentioned it to me before.

"Because I was scared," he said.

"*You've* never been scared of anything in your life," I said.

"I was scared of this. Look, Sue, it's not like being gay is acceptable. You know what my friends are like. Once they find out they'll never speak to me again."

"Fintan Dunbar's okay. He wouldn't have been bothered one way or the other. Fintan O'Shaughnessy, though . . . Yeah, he's not likely to be happy."

Fintan nodded. "He'll start thinking about the time we went camping when we were twelve, and all the times we went swimming."

I wanted to say that he'd be better off without Fintan O'Shaughnessy as a friend, but I knew that wasn't what my brother wanted to hear.

"What about Sharon?" I asked. "She says she tried to talk to you about it. You probably lost that chance years ago, though."

"Yeah, well if I'd said anything she would have blurted it out to Laura and all your other mates. And then *you'd* have found out. Then where would I be?"

"Right where you are now," I said. "Only you'd be a lot younger. Look, what are you going to do?"

"You mean, am I going to come fully out of the closet?" He shook his head. "No. It's too soon. I want to get away from here, get a flat or something. Start again."

Of course, Fintan didn't change overnight from being an angry, repressed and generally moody little bastard into a kinder, gentler, loving brother. He never actually made that particular transition all the way, but I think that knowing that I accepted him helped. And I did accept it, despite the fights we'd had over the years, I still loved my brother, and suddenly finding a reason for his moods made it a lot easier. Besides, I thought it was kind of cool, even if it was weird to imagine that I'd never have any nieces or nephews.

It was Friday night, four weeks since I'd broken up with Sam. I was over him, there was no doubt about that. But I'd reinforced my previous rule about not going out with men I met in nightclubs, because they were always the sort of people who like going to nightclubs. That rule didn't exactly apply to the situation with Sam, but I decided that it would have to do until I found another motto.

Sharon had got off early from work, and called to the flat. We'd seen each other more over the past four weeks than we had over the previous six months. When she arrived, I went through the usual "Do you want a cup of coffee?" ritual, where I asked the question aloud but silently said a little prayer that she'd say no, because it would mean washing a cup.

Sharon was wise to this trick. "Yes," she said. "But the question is, do you have any milk?"

"There might be some in the fridge," I said from the comfort of the good chair. "But I can't be too sure."

"You need a fridge with a glass door."

"I need someone else to make the coffee."

"Look, *I'm* the guest. Make coffee."

I sighed and pushed myself to my feet. "If I *have* to."

"So, what are we going to do tonight?" Sharon asked, taking possession of the good chair. "Where do you want to go?"

I made a half-hearted attempt to fill the kettle so that I'd have hot water to do the washing up, but it was too hard because the sink was full, so I gave up. "Let's have our coffee continental-style," I suggested. "In glasses."

I didn't have to boil the kettle to make coffee, because I'd splashed out and bought a real percolator. It was one of the many things I'd bought recently in an attempt to cheer myself up.

"Fintan said he's going to call around," I said, carefully watching her reaction.

Sharon made an unpleasant face. "You didn't tell me *that* when you suggested going out tonight."

"I forgot," I lied. "Look, it's about time you spoke to him. He doesn't have anything against you, and believe me he could do with a friend."

"I told Mark about him," Sharon said. "I wasn't sure whether I should, but I did anyway. He said he already knew. Fintan had been renting gay videos. He'd threatened Mark with all sorts of harm if he said anything to anyone. That didn't bother Mark. He said you wouldn't believe how well those videos go down."

"As it were," I said smuttily.

"So what's Fintan coming here for, then?"

I shrugged. "No real reason. Most of his friends have dropped him. Particularly that prick Fintan O'Shaughnessy. At least Fintan Dunbar is still friends with him."

"You don't suppose that *he's* gay as well?"

"I don't know. Does it matter?"

"Not really. Still, it makes you think, though."

"And *you* knew all along and didn't tell me, you bloody cow. I'm supposed to be your best friend."

"True," she said. "But it wasn't for me to tell. I mean, I know *lots* of things that I don't tell you. Lots and lots of juicy secrets. But I'm not going to tell you. Not a chance. You can beg all you want, but my lips are sealed."

I didn't know it at the time – I thought that she was just messing around – but Sharon knew who James Talbot was.

My God, sometimes I could *kill* that girl!

By then, I'd more or less figured out about James myself. But I still didn't know how it was done, but if I'd known that Sharon knew, then I would have known how. If you see what I mean.

When Fintan arrived a few minutes later, he was a bit put out to see Sharon there, but he didn't say anything. He accepted a glass of coffee and sat in the less-good chair.

"Does anybody want Jaffa cakes?" I inquired.

Both of my guests agreed that Jaffa cakes would be acceptable to their discerning palates at that hour of the day.

"Good," I said, and grabbed my jacket from the back of the door. "I'll just go out and get some. While I'm gone, why don't you both just sit and stare at the floor and not talk to each other?"

I don't know how long it took them, but by the time I got back they were on speaking terms. I guessed that Fintan had been telling Sharon everything, because his chair had been pulled closer to hers, much in the way someone would when they don't want to talk too loud in case the neighbours have a glass to the wall, ceiling or floor.

They seemed to be in a fairly good mood, but I got the distinct impression that I'd arrived back too early. I decided to have a shower.

Sharon and Fintan were still in discussion when I emerged towel-wrapped, squeaky-clean and with dripping hair. "Look," I said, "there's only so many showers and trips to the shops I can make. What are you talking about?"

Sharon looked up. "Get dressed. We're all going out."

"Where?"

"There's a pub in town that Fintan wants to go to."

"No, wait!" Fintan said. "I didn't mean *now!*"

But his protests fell on deaf ears.

I'd never been in a gay pub before, and believe me it was quite a revelation. At a quick glance, it looked just like any other pub – I mean, the walls weren't all pink and frilly, or anything, not that I'd expected them to be – but after a few minutes it was clear that the couples for the most part were of the same gender.

We sat next to a group of men who were chatty enough. It was a bit awkward for me. Because of my great height and size, they initially assumed that I was a transvestite or transsexual. I didn't know whether I should be insulted, but Fintan assured me later that they hadn't meant anything by it. Once I corrected their mistake, they then assumed that Sharon and I were a couple, so we had to sort that one out too.

Fintan didn't meet anyone there that night, but he was happy to have been accepted.

On the way home, Sharon said, "It's weird, but if a lesbian goes into a lesbian pub when it's singles night, in theory she can get off with *anyone* in the place. A straight person in a singles pub only has half the options."

"So, would you go back?" Fintan asked.

"Would *you?*" Sharon said.

"Yes. Sue?"

"I don't know," I said. "But if I do, I'm going to dress down for the occasion. I'm not going to face that again, all those disappointed men finding out that my cleavage is real, and disappointed women discovering that I'm not remotely interested in what they look like naked."

"You never know until you try," Sharon said.

"Oh, believe me, I know. Besides, I'm thinking of taking a sabbatical from the dating scene for a while. I want to get myself sorted out before I end up getting stuck with another Sam."

I definitely didn't want to meet another Sam. I wanted to meet someone completely different . . .

I thought about it for a very long time, and I finally decided that, one way or the other, it was time to sort things out between myself and J.

Dear James,

I have now completely gotten over my hate for Sam, and you have been moved back to the top of my list.

I will be at home on Thursday next, and in case you bother coming around I will have newspapers spread across the carpet to try and cut down on what will undoubtedly be a huge cleaning bill.

I must go now, as I am off to the hardware store to pick up some rat poison for your tea.

Still not yours and never will be,

Susan.

Chapter Fifty-four

James Talbot was, as his letters had said, a middle-aged man. He was of average height, slightly shorter than me, with thinning hair and a rotund figure. He was wearing a trenchcoat and a trilby, and looked sort of like a detective in a BBC series.

I stood at the door and looked him up and down, then sniffed and coughed theatrically. "You must be James Talbot."

He doffed his hat, bowed, and said, "And you must be Susan Perry's ugly brother."

"Come in," I said, trying not to smile. "Wipe the shit off your feet."

Talbot arched an eyebrow. "*That* I shall do when I leave."

James peered around the flat, and stood examining the single boring reproduction painting that had been in the flat long before I moved in.

"Anything I can help you with?" I asked.

He shrugged. "I'm just browsing. Do you have any Picasso?"

"I'm not sure. I do have some Nescafe."

"Hmm . . . What about Da Vinci?"

I shook my head. "No, he only has Maxwell House."

"Monet?"

"No thanks, there's plenty in my penny jar."

"What about Van Gogh?"

I thought about this. "Would you mean Seamus Van Gogh, the famous local landscape gardener?"

"I imagine I might mean his even more famous brother, Vincent."

I filled the kettle and got out two clean cups: I'd forgotten to steal some coffee from work, so I decided that we'd have instant. "I'm not sure what we have. I'm only minding the house for my mammy."

He grinned at me. "And what time will your mammy be back?"

"That depends on who's pregnant, who's sleeping with whom, and who is rumoured to be selling their house."

"I see. Let us just pray to God that no one around here has bought new curtains. We could be here for the rest of our lives."

"In that case, I don't think there's enough Nescafe for the two of us. We'll have to fight for it."

We talked for hours, and all that time I never said anything that indicated we already knew each other. I decided that, never mind his real name, this man *was* James Talbot, letter-writer extraordinaire. He too had decided to play that game, and didn't once slip up.

"Can I have some more of that disgusting coffee to wash down the taste of the cooked dish-cloth you mistakenly call cake?" he asked.

"Certainly. You can have as much coffee as you like. The more you drink the less time you'll have to talk."

"It's not the talking that I'm having trouble with, but the listening."

"I can tell you haven't had much practice with the latter."

"Unfortunately, this is not my normal voice. I have a bit of a cold at present." As if to demonstrate his cold, Talbot took Sam's *Star Trek* tie from his pocket and blew his nose on it.

I almost choked laughing. As I recovered, with tears streaming down my face, Talbot said, "I would have pounded you on the back to aid your coughing fit, but for want of a nail-endowed two-by-four."

Through my tears and laughter, I said "And but for the undoubted pleasure it would have given you, I would have let myself choke to death."

James Talbot shrugged into his coat as he stood at the door. "It is with no small relief that I now take my leave of you. It has been a most unpleasant evening."

"If you must stand in the garden, Mr Talbot, please walk around so that the grass dies evenly. And furthermore, please do me the favour of begging at a few doors as you pass down the street. I'd hate the neighbours to think that I was socialising with you."

He glanced at his watch. "How about dinner

tomorrow night? There's a charming little Scottish restaurant in Ranelagh. It goes by the name of . . ."

I interrupted him. "McDonald's?"

"I suddenly fear that you are too clever for me. I'm off to the joke shop to get my money back." He backed away from the door, still watching me. "Tomorrow night, then? Assuming that your mother does make a return appearance by that time?"

I peered past him, into the road. "I don't see your team of wild horses. I imagine that you will be bringing them tomorrow, because nothing less would encourage me to visit that particular Caledonian eaterie. I would much prefer a quiet beverage in the local public imbibing emporium. With someone else."

"Indeed. If you were to be in the Four Provinces tomorrow night at about eight, I would almost certainly not turn up."

"I do believe I'm washing my hair tomorrow night."

"Ah, that time of year, eh? I have a friend in the fire department. I shall send him and his crew around in the morning with their hoses to aid you in your task." Talbot doffed his hat once more, and turned towards the gate. "Tomorrow night?"

"Nothing would give me less pleasure," I said as I closed the door.

Chapter Fifty-five

"So, did you meet him?" Barbara asked the next morning in work. She was barely in the door, and I just "happened" to be hanging around reception, not at all waiting for her.

"Yes."

"And? Were you right?"

"Oh yeah. Definitely."

She laughed. "Jesus, I'll never look at him the same way again. So, what happened?"

"We just sat and talked. I think he really enjoys playing the part, and I have to admit I enjoyed it myself. He never *once* let on. If I didn't know better, I'd swear that they were completely separate people who just happened to look alike. He didn't say anything that might suggest he was anyone other than James Talbot. And I have to admit, he's like no one I've ever met. I mean, he's obnoxious and very funny at the same time."

"Who are we talking about?" Kevin said, as he came into the office.

Barbara and I looked at each other. "No one you know," we said at the same time.

Kevin shrugged, a bit pissed off at being left out, and slunk off to his desk.

"So are you meeting him again? As James, I mean?"

"Yes, definitely. Tonight, at eight, in the Four Provinces." I hadn't really decided until that moment. But, yes, I told myself. I did want to see him again.

Business had been so good that Complete Office Solutions had opened another branch, this one on the north side of the city. I wasn't officially working there, but on most days I had to make at least one trip out to sort out some problem or other.

We had installed Jennifer in the Phibsboro office, and a few new people, who were all under the tutelage of Danny Maloney. Danny had come crawling back begging for a job. Well, actually that's not true. We went crawling to him, offered him more money, a position of power, and all the Status Reports he could eat.

Vicky spent most of her time there, leaving me in charge of the Rathmines office, and business wasn't too bad. OK, so it was tough trying to keep two separate offices running, but it looked as if we were going to at least break even by the end of the financial year, which wasn't bad after such an investment.

I drove out to the Phibsboro office just before lunch. As usual, I couldn't find anywhere to park, so I ended up parking closer to my parents' old house in Cabra than I was to the office.

As I walked down to the office, I saw Danny and Ariana having lunch in Eddie Rocket's. I dropped in to say hello.

"Susan," Ariana said. "Did he turn up?" Her English was definitely improving.

I nodded. "Yes, right on time."

"I told you he would," Danny said. "You owe me a pound."

"Sure," I said. I fished around in my jacket pocket and took out a handful of pennies. "There's about a pound here. I got them from my change jar this morning."

Danny looked at Ariana. "Well, that solves the problem of the tip."

"Do you want to come to our party?" Ariana asked me. "It's on next Friday in the flat."

"Maybe," I said, after some consideration. "Can I bring a friend?"

"Would this be the same friend you met last night?"

"And whom I'm also meeting tonight," I said. "I don't know whether I'm being a complete fool or not. I mean, it's not like James Talbot is even real. So much happened between us before I knew that he was the one I was writing to, and that's pretty hard to deal with."

"It'll work out fine," Danny said. "Trust me."

"No, but I'm just concerned that he might have put me so high on a pedestal that he can't reach me. If you know what I mean."

Danny smiled. "Susan, I *always* know what you mean."

We left Eddie Rocket's a few minutes later, and walked down to the office. Danny kissed Ariana good-bye, promised to see her later, and followed me in.

"You're really mad about her, aren't you?" I asked.

"I am. Yeah. We're good for each other, I think."

"You certainly are. You've finally started to come out of your shell. It's about time, too. See? All it took was the love of a good woman."

"Or the friendship of a good woman," Danny said.

In reception, Jennifer had the usual huge pile of things for me to read through and decide whether to sign or bin. "Vicky wants a meeting at half-three," Jennifer said. "And Barbara phoned to say that you'd better get moving on the Boseman contract. She says they're *still* waiting for those revisions."

"Yeah, well, I've been busy recently. Phone Barbara back and tell her I said she should get started on it herself."

"Hah!" Jennifer said. "She *said* you'd say that, and she told me to tell you that you could cram the Boseman contract right up your . . ." She stopped, blushed and looked away. "Sorry."

I turned around. Neil Forsythe was standing behind me. He smiled at Jennifer, then nodded at me. "Afternoon, Ms Perry."

"Good afternoon, Mr Forsythe," I replied. "How can we help you today?"

"Oh, I'm just browsing."

"You're missing your hat today, I notice."

"I do not possess a hat."

"Of course not," I said. "Now, who on earth could I be thinking of?"

Chapter Fifty-six

The boss said that I could go home early, because she knew I'd been panicking all afternoon and wasn't able to work anyway.

Of course, since *I* was the boss now it wasn't too hard to persuade her.

I was just leaving the office when Kevin stopped me. "Susan, I need to know what you want me to do with this . . ." He was holding a preliminary meeting report from one of our clients. He held it gingerly by the corner, as though the work contained within might be contagious.

I was tempted to say, "Kevin, do what you always do: spend hours on the phone to your friends and end up doodling Batman logos all over the document. And don't forget to give it your special mark: the brown coffee ring of quality."

But the boss couldn't say things like that. The boss had to maintain a certain aloofness from her staff. She couldn't be seen to be too friendly or cheerful with them, because otherwise they'd walk all over her. So I said, "Kevin, what do *you* think you should do?"

He shrugged. "Give it to Barbara?"

"No . . . Guess again."

"You want me to work out a schedule of meetings and make a few suggestions?"

"That would be more like it."

"Yeah, but you see that's not *my* job. This is, like, a first contact sort of situation. I don't know anything about this sort of thing. I'm used to working with the client when all this is sorted out."

"You have to learn how to do it sometime. Besides, Barbara is busy. You get working on it, and if you get really stuck, go to her. Or, better still, have a look at what we did for some of the other clients in this situation. Use your imagination. That's what we pay you for."

"OK . . ." he said reluctantly. "OK."

He stayed for a couple of seconds, looking awkwardly at the meeting report, probably waiting for me to grab it from him and say, "Oh, for God's sake! I'll do it."

"Go on," I said. "You should have had it done hours ago. What were you doing all afternoon?"

"Aw, come on! I was swamped!"

"It's no good telling me *now* that you were swamped. You should have said that earlier, when there would have been time to give it to someone else. You have to have it finished by Monday morning."

He trudged away back to his desk. I watched him go, and wondered how much longer I could keep him on.

OK, so he was full of bright ideas, but most of those ideas seemed to be concerned with ways of avoiding work. He was just marginally more useful to have around than to let go, so he was safe for the moment, but pretty soon he'd have to learn a very valuable lesson: just because I saved his ass once didn't mean that I was going to do it again. There were only so many chances you could give someone.

OK, I said to myself. Forget him, it's half-past four on Friday, and work is over for the week. There are more important things to worry about.

I had a shower, got changed, did my hair, and there was still two hours to go before I was supposed to meet James.

I considered tidying the flat up a bit, but there really wasn't much to do: lately, I'd trained myself to be more tidy, to wash up things after I'd used them, and not just when there was nothing else clean, and to put my books and things back on the shelves when I'd taken them down.

I hadn't gone totally military about it, though. I mean, my books and videos weren't in alphabetical order or anything like that, and occasionally the laundry basket got so full I couldn't put the lid on it. I never got so obsessive that I did things like wash the curtains or defrost the fridge. I was still a slob, just a more organised one.

I decided to kill the two hours by doing something I hadn't done in a long time: I updated my diary.

That wasn't the best idea in the world, because when I re-read the entries about Sam I got really annoyed at myself. It was Sam, Sam, Sam all over the place. It seemed kind of weird to me that I'd ever loved him as much as I did.

As the weeks had passed and the wounds began to heal, I'd slowly realised that Sam hadn't been so bad. He was selfish, that was all. And maybe if J hadn't sent that bunch of flowers to the office, and me and Sam hadn't fought about it, we'd still be together: Sam was never so bad that he couldn't change.

I didn't know whether it was a mistake to break up with Sam. I'd never know that. But maybe it wasn't important. OK, so we might have had a wonderful life together, but then again, we might not. We could easily have been one of the many couples who have that sort of fight *all* the time, and seem to get along perfectly well otherwise. I could have ended up just like one of those middle-aged women you see who are deeply in love with someone who treats them like shit most of the time.

I flicked through my diary until I reached the page for that day, and I started to write:

Shortly after I write these words, I'll be meeting James Talbot for only the second time . . . But as Neil Forsythe, I've known him for a lot longer.

Are they even the same person? I can't tell. I think of them as two different people. When he called to the flat yesterday evening, I had to keep reminding myself that this was the man who was caught up in all the trouble with Parker Technology.

I spoke to Anthony this morning, and he told me everything:

Anthony met Neil when I'd invited him along to the launch of Parker's new software. They hit it off, and became closer friends than either of them let on to me. When Anthony realised how much Neil cared about me, they sat down and decided what they should do about it. They guessed — correctly, as it turned out — that I wouldn't be interested in a man who was so much older. So Neil put a personal ad in the paper, and Anthony "found" it and read it to me. And it worked.

And here I am now, not necessarily in love with the man, but definitely very interested. I can't guess what's going to happen next, but I don't care about that. I'm not looking for the ideal life-long partner any more. I'm looking for someone I can be happy with.

I know that, given the right circumstances, I could have been extremely happy with Sam. But I also know, now, that I will never compromise when it comes to love: happiness isn't worth a damn if it can break down at any moment.

Maybe it doesn't matter where my life takes me, maybe it's the journey that's important.

Chapter Fifty-seven

I bought a drink and sat down at the first available table, with my back to the door. I was a little early, but I didn't want James to arrive on time and have any reason to think he was going to be stood up.

I heard the door open behind me. I looked up as a shadow fell across the table. It was Sam.

"Your new receptionist said you'd be here tonight," he said. "I would have called to the flat, but I only just got here." He was looking good, I have to say. He'd managed to get himself all clean and shiny, new haircut, new clothes. "How are you?"

"Fine. You?"

"I miss you, Susan. I'm sorry. I want you back."

I stared up at him. *"What?"*

He looked uncomfortable. "I want you back."

I slammed my drink down. "You left me. You just decided that you wanted to get out. Didn't give a damn what *I* thought about it. Now you expect to just walk back into my life. Get lost."

Sam took a newspaper out of his pocket, brandishing it like a weapon in his clenched fist. "It's him, isn't it?"

"Who?"

"That guy you were writing to. That bastard from the Personals column." He threw the paper down in front of me. I guessed from the look in his eyes that he'd found out about James, realised that I wasn't waiting around for him, and was making a last attempt to win me over. He wasn't going about it the right way.

I picked up the paper. It was opened at the personal ads page. Sam had circled one of the ads.

I read the ad quietly, more to myself than to Sam: "'Middle-aged man, formerly tired of the same old love interests, has now found younger woman for tedium and hate.' There's no box number." I smiled, and glanced up at him. "I said get lost, Sam. It's over."

I looked back at the paper, re-reading the ad. Sam turned and marched away.

I heard the pub door open once more, then a slight scuffle and Sam saying, "Watch where you're going, you old fart."

Then I heard a very familiar voice say, "How good of you to leave and raise the average IQ of the customers by a couple of dozen points. May your voice one day break, preferably at the same time as your neck."

Then another shadow fell across the table. A balding,

large-framed, middle-aged man wearing a trenchcoat and a trilby sat down opposite me.

"Oh," said James Talbot, with a disappointed expression on his face. "It's *you*."

I studied him for a few seconds, and slowly smiled.

Here comes that golden feeling . . .

The End.